PENGUIN BOOKS

Falling For You

Emily Maple is a writer living in Berkshire with her partner and their occasional dog, Archie the boxer. Emily has worked in casting, marketing and education, but everything always ends up boiling down to her true love . . . writing! Emily is the international bestselling author of four novels under the name Olivia Beirne.

Falling For You

Emily Maple

PENGUIN BOOKS

PENGUIN BOOKS

UK | USA | Canada | Ireland | Australia
India | New Zealand | South Africa

Penguin Books is part of the Penguin Random House group of companies
whose addresses can be found at global.penguinrandomhouse.com

Penguin Random House UK,
One Embassy Gardens, 8 Viaduct Gardens, London SW11 7BW
penguin.co.uk

First published 2025
001

Copyright © Emily Maple, 2025

The moral right of the author has been asserted

Penguin Random House values and supports copyright. Copyright fuels creativity, encourages diverse voices, promotes freedom of expression and supports a vibrant culture. Thank you for purchasing an authorised edition of this book and for respecting intellectual property laws by not reproducing, scanning or distributing any part of it by any means without permission. You are supporting authors and enabling Penguin Random House to continue to publish books for everyone. No part of this book may be used or reproduced in any manner for the purpose of training artificial intelligence technologies or systems. In accordance with Article 4(3) of the DSM Directive 2019/790, Penguin Random House expressly reserves this work from the text and data mining exception.

Typeset in 10.4/15pt Palatino LT Pro by Jouve (UK), Milton Keynes
Printed and bound in Great Britain by Clays Ltd, Elcograf S.p.A.

The authorised representative in the EEA is Penguin Random House Ireland,
Morrison Chambers, 32 Nassau Street, Dublin D02 YH68

A CIP catalogue record for this book is available from the British Library

ISBN: 978-1-804-95310-5

Penguin Random House is committed to a sustainable future
for our business, our readers and our planet. This book is
made from Forest Stewardship Council® certified paper.

To Chris,
I love you

Prologue

Annie

Okay, I need to get you up to speed.

I squint as the strobe lighting shines directly in my eyes, bouncing off the sequined cape from my bat costume and creating a little disco ball around me and . . . well . . . whoever this half-naked guy is who I'm inexplicably attached to. I don't mean attached in the way of *how will my heart beat without him*, I mean, literally attached. As in, my bat wing has stabbed him in the chest and ripped open his shirt and now we're inches apart, pressed together in the middle of a dance floor. I don't even know his name.

Oh, and I can't get free.

'Sorry . . .' I shout for the millionth time, trying my best to bend the plastic boning of the wing out of his shirt buttonhole whilst not touching his bare chest. I can't bring myself to look at his face; this whole thing is embarrassing enough as it is.

A group of dancers bump behind me, pushing me closer towards him, and my hand accidentally brushes his torso.

'Sorry!' I shout again and I can't help it this time, I steal a glance at his face, just to make sure steam isn't coming out of his ears. Not that I'd blame him. But he doesn't look mad – he looks alarmed (sure), but not mad – and as he catches my eye I see a flash of kindness. It makes my heart feel a bit fuzzy, until someone bumps me from behind again and something cold splashes down my back.

'Argh!' I squeal, instinctively leaping forward.

'Here,' he shouts back, making his voice loud enough over the music. 'I'm sure we can untangle it . . .'

Tanya is hovering nearby, helpless with laughter. 'Annie, just stay still,' she says. 'The more you move, the worse it'll get.' But I hardly register her, transfixed by the man staring down at me.

He takes my hand and together we start bending the plastic to try and free it from the loop of his buttonhole. His hands are firm, and they fold around mine with no awkwardness at all. Like they've held my hand a thousand times before. My eyes flick up to his face – he's so focused on the task in hand that he doesn't notice – and I smile. He has a beard that skims across his strong jawline and behind his mask I can make out his dark eyes.

I gasp as with one final *crack* of my wing, we burst free. We both spring backwards and I laugh awkwardly as we look at each other.

'I'm so sorry, did I break your costume?' he asks.

I look down and wince at my bent wing. 'No, it's my fault – I should have checked before opening them. Are you okay?'

For a moment, he just stands there with his shirt still

Falling For You

undone, until he realises his chest is bare and quickly turns away, swearing to himself.

As the music fades into another song, I catch his accent.

'Are you American?' I ask.

He turns back towards me, his shirt now fully buttoned up. He takes in my outfit, his eyebrows raising.

'Yeah . . . and are you a . . . bat?'

I push out my chest with pride. 'Let me buy you a drink,' I say, reaching forward and putting my hand on his arm, 'it's the least I can do.'

He glances around and for a horrible moment I think he's about to say he's here with someone else, but then he turns back to me and smiles.

'Sure,' he steps back and holds out his arm, 'after you, Bat Girl.'

I laugh. 'Right this way, American Boy.'

I lean back on the sofa and swirl my drink, taking a second to look into this man's eyes. A smile creeps onto my face, pretty much in the position it's been since we sat down together. There is something about him I can't quite put my finger on. It's like this weird electricity, an addictive energy. Something inside me has just clicked, and I feel like I've known him forever. Which is mad, considering I've only known him for about ten minutes.

It must be the alcohol.

He looks into my eyes and leans towards me. We've been gradually getting closer as our conversation has taken off, popping and fizzing between us, bouncing back and forth like a game of tennis. My heart rate quickens as I feel his breath on my face, smell his woody aftershave.

I think he's about to kiss me.

I really want him to kiss me.

I tilt my head towards him, feeling like I may burst, when suddenly he jumps, pulling his phone out of his blazer pocket. When he looks at the caller ID, all the joy and spark that was alive in his face seconds before vanishes.

'I'm so sorry,' he says, getting to his feet, 'I've got to go.'

I open my mouth to say something, but he slips back through the crowd before I can even react.

Just like that, he's gone.

I didn't even get his name.

Chapter One

SEVEN DAYS EARLIER

Annie

My name is Annie Glover and I have a confession.

I am addicted to autumn.

I can't help it. I love absolutely everything about it. If there was an autumn addicts group, I'd be first in line preparing to swear on a pumpkin-spiced latte not to buy any more oversized scarves or chunky-knit sweaters. I'm the person who stuffs my sweaty body into a crocheted jumper on 1 September, even when summer is still roaring in the sky. I give a little cheer when I see the new Starbucks menu come out, and I once felt my eyes well up when I crunched on the first autumn leaves that had fallen on the pavement.

(I need to point out here that I was very hormonal at the time, and later that day also cried at my flatmate Penny making me a cup of tea without asking when I got out of the bath. But still, no ordinary person cries over a leaf. Except, perhaps, Alan Titchmarsh.)

I love the way the leaves change to golden yellow and

rich, plum red. I love the moment you step outside and it feels as if you're breathing in toothpaste and your cheeks are being lightly pinched. I love the feeling of going 'back to school', seeing children in fresh uniforms and stocking up on shiny new stationery at WHSmith. It brings a little glow right below my heart, every year, without fail.

I know a lot of people claim to love autumn, but really the reason that they love it is because it's leading up to Christmas. That is not true love. For me, Christmas is like the after party. I'm still wearing my cosy jumper and ridiculous scarf, but I've reluctantly swapped my witch's hat for a Santa one.

Which brings me to what I love about autumn the most: Halloween.

I love the costumes. I love the Halloween films. I love all the themed foods and the way everyone dresses up on TV. It's the only time of year where everybody celebrates being a bit weird and wonderful on the same day by letting out their inner spook.

I look at myself in the mirror and feel a swell of pride.

If Halloween costumes were an Olympic sport, I'm not saying I'd win gold but I'd certainly be a medallist.

Actually, screw it. I'd win gold. I look great.

I had the idea for my costume the day after the annual Halloween party that Penny, Tanya and I threw in our flat just outside Clapham last year. I was face down on the sofa, trying to nurse my double hangover (one induced by the vodka, and the other induced by the fact that my favourite night of the year was over). To cheer me up, Tanya started telling me how great everyone said my costume was. I had dressed up as Wednesday Addams and my costume had included a secret compartment, meaning I could scare the life out of everyone by using one of my hands as Thing and simultaneously trick them into thinking I had three hands. I mean, yes, Liam almost fell off the balcony mid-cigarette when I used the third hand to offer him a lighter. But still, it was fantastic.

Anyway! It was then that I started brainstorming my next 'unassuming' costume and the idea came to me: I was going to be . . . a bat.

Now, I'm not one of those people who take Halloween as an excuse to dress up as a sexy witch or prowl around in a mask. I mean, sure, I can totally see the appeal. Who wouldn't want to stomp around in a nightclub feeling like the fifth member of Little Mix for an evening? But for me, I can't resist the chance to completely transform myself into something grotesque, and I'm not the only one. I (almost) make a living out of it.

I turn to the side and narrow my eyes in the reflection.

Mum taught me how to sew when I was a teenager. I found hovering behind her in Topshop excruciating, looking at the clothes that other girls my age wore. None of them felt quite right on my awkward teenage body. Honestly, I don't know how the other girls had the confidence. So, I asked Mum if we could make my clothes ourselves. I did textiles at school, and it turned into a regular activity that Mum and I spent most of our Sundays doing. It's even become a little business for us: the Stitching Witches. It doesn't make enough for us to do it full-time, but it's still fun.

It turns out I'm pretty damn good at it. People come to me

year after year requesting their costumes, and I have quite a following on social media now. It's not just Halloween; I'll make costumes throughout the year ... as long as they're looking for something slightly bizarre and over the top. If you're looking for a sexy, Victoria's Secret-style costume, I'm not your girl. If you want to convince people that you've dislocated your shoulder, which jerks out every time they touch you, hit me up.

In an ideal world, I'd spend my life making these costumes, and maybe one day it'll happen. I mean, it could happen now, if I was content living in a shoebox for the rest of my life and stealing breadcrumbs off the birds in the park.

My costume this year is black, and ever-so-slightly furry. Not in a chic, Sarah Jessica Parker way, more how otters look when they slip out of the water. Sleek until you touch it.

At first, it looks like a giant cape. It scrunches around my neck with an elaborate black collar, covering my whole body. But when you pull a lever, the wings pop out and reveal what is *underneath* the cape, and you see the catsuit I've made. The bones of the bat's body are embedded using thick plastic straws, and grotesque patches of fur sprout out randomly.

On the night, I'll slick back my dark hair and wear red contact lenses, and then when everyone has had a few drinks and they're least expecting it, I'll pull the lever and BAM, my costume will be fully unveiled.

I pick up my phone and take a picture to send to my mum, my biggest fan. She replies almost immediately.

WOW! LOVE IT!

I smile.

Halloween is this weekend, and finally all my hard work will have paid off.

Mum is one of the only people who fully understands why I love Halloween so much. It's the one time of year where you're celebrated for being a bit weird and quirky, and I feel confident behind the mask of my costume. For once, I want people to look at me.

Even though I'm dressed like a bat or a witch, or even a rotting carcass . . . on Halloween I feel more like myself than any other night of the year.

And I don't care if I'm thirty-two or ninety-two, I am never letting that sense of freedom go.

'Excuse me, sorry . . . excuse me . . .'

Being five foot tall, carrying two laptops and a coffee in rush hour on the tube should be illegal. Actually, it should be a bush tucker trial. It's an absolute bloody endurance test.

I pop myself into a free space, right in the corner of the carriage. The doors of the Northern line squeeze shut, forcing everyone to suck themselves in slightly, praying that the train actually moves and nobody will have to gracefully offer to step off and wait for the next train (spoiler: nobody ever offers; it's more of an awkward stand-off where everyone avoids eye contact until the person closest to the door is gently shoved back onto the platform and nobody mentions it).

I am surrounded by a sea of navy blue and grey. Business folk galore. I first arrived in London with Penny and Tanya ready to take on the world, aged twenty-two, and freshly equipped with my shiny new art degree. I'd had three years of being top of my class and everyone begging me to make their costumes for them for every themed night of our social calendars. I also had that impenetrable bravado that comes from three years of bobbing around in the university bubble, completely unaware that you're about to be spat into the real world where not only are you not at the top of your class any more but nobody really cares that you were in the first place.

By this point in my life, I had an entire wardrobe filled with clothes that I'd made myself, with the odd piece that Mum had created. I don't know where I thought I'd work, as none of my clothes were 'fashionable', but I knew it would be something to do with designing and making clothes. I knew it in my bones! I was so confident!

Until the three of us found a flat and I realised that, in order to live there, I'd need to fork out nine hundred pounds a month, before bills. Every month. My 'successful' business was making about five hundred pounds each month, which felt like an enormous success to us all as broke, desperate students. But as graduates trying to make it in London, it was laughable.

So, I tucked my elaborate tail between my legs and started trying to flog my soul to the corporate grind. But guess what? Nobody wanted me there, either. Once Penny had been snapped up at a university to do her PhD and work as a scientific researcher, and Tanya had taken a junior position in fashion PR, I desperately grabbed with both hands the first job I was offered and refused to let it go. I was so terrified that I'd lose it and have to give up my life in London and move back to my hometown in the Cotswolds that I put my heart and soul into it, and it turned out, I'm actually good at it.

You're looking at Annie Glover, Relocation Consultant. I know, right? Put that on a business card and smoke it.

I found the advert pinned up on the noticeboard at my local newsagent and, honestly, it felt like a sign from the universe. By this point, I'd been madly sending my CV into the abyss only to be ghosted with such force that it made me wonder whether I even existed. When I saw the ad, I literally ripped it off the noticeboard and ran away with it, in a mad panic that someone else might steal the only job I felt that I could *actually do*.

It said this:

Looking for PA/receptionist for my consultancy. Call Pam.

That was it. No list of fancy benefits, no promise of a communal fruit bowl or dress-down Fridays (why do employers think this is what everyone wants? Who is spending their free time desperately searching for a place where they can finally wear their wacky tie out in public?).

I rang Pam immediately and found out that she lived in Battersea, where she was running her Relocation Consultancy. Which basically means that we help find homes, schools and whatever else a client might need when they are being relocated for work. For three years, it was just me and Pam, sharing a desk in her back room and mindlessly racing from one client meeting to the next to try and get the business off the ground.

But seven years later, we're in a swanky Moorgate office with a team of six and our own desks. Along with a pay rise and fancy new job title, but the desks were the biggest deal for everyone. Nobody wants to share a desk with I'll-eat-an-orange-on-the-phone-and-leave-the-peel-all-over-the-keyboard Kevin.

I now have my own list of clients and spend a lot of my time going out for lunches, showing them potential houses and schools and trying not to visibly wince when they inevitably turn their nose up at the *gargantuan* home I've shown them because it's too close to a bin on the street or something equally absurd.

I'm essentially rubbing shoulders with the rich and travelled and helping them to set up their shiny new lives in shiny new London.

I take a deep breath and puff out my chest as we sail past Bank.

Okay, the next stop is mine.

I eye up the people around me, trying to make it clear that I'm going to need to part these bitches like the Red Sea in approximately ninety seconds.

The train growls to a halt and I start to shuffle forwards, the flock of padded shoulders shifting from one foot to the other like claustrophobic pigeons.

'EXCUSE ME!' I bellow, in my loudest voice. 'This is MY STOP!'

Everyone clucks and totters around a bit more, reluctant to get off the train even for a moment in case they aren't let back on.

But I have to get off, I cannot stay trapped on this train until High Barnet. Pam won't believe me if I say it's happened for the third time this year.

'Excuse me!' I yell, and bury my face forwards, pushing my way out. I spot people glancing down in alarm as I barrel past their waists towards the light of the open door.

'Sorry,' I mutter, heat rolling up my body as a variety of odours hit me in the face. 'I just need to... Sorry... I...'

I gasp as I pop out onto the platform, as if the carriage has just birthed me, and push myself up to my full height.

'Right,' I mutter to myself. 'Well done me.'

'Good morning, everyone!' I sing as I burst into the office. We have part of the third floor of an enormous corporate building. It sounds fancy but really means we have one room, a toilet and a kitchen, and we have to share a lift with lots of serious people in suits.

We were given free rein with the office when we first got in, so Pam handed us all some paintbrushes and told us that she couldn't afford an interior designer. My controlling behaviour took over immediately, and I found myself fighting flashing images of all my colleagues going rogue and painting self-portraits or something equally horrendous and 'fun'. So, I shepherded them all off to the bathroom as quickly as I could and told them to paint it white. An hour later they were so bored that they all went to the pub – it worked like a charm.

Pam gave me her credit card and told me to 'Annie-fy' it, so I did. I painted the walls a gorgeous mossy green and used a shimmering silver paint to draw a huge tree that curled over the ceiling. It was the most fun I'd had in years – holding that paintbrush felt a bit like I was reconnecting back to my energy source.

'Good morning, Annie.'

I look round at Pam's voice and, as expected, I see her hunched over her laptop. Pam has wild blonde hair which grows out instead of down in tight, springy curls. She's wearing a loose, oversized shirt which reaches her knees and big, jangly necklaces around her tanned neck. She built this business from nothing and spends so long craning over her laptop that her back has developed a slight hump and the skin around her eyes is creased from the hours of squinting at the computer screen. She always has an unlit cigarette in her mouth, ready to smoke. I've spent *hours* telling her off for smoking inside, though she rarely even smokes them these days. She's too busy.

'Morning, Pam,' I smile, putting my bag down on my desk. 'How are you?'

'I need to ask you a favour.'

I used to take offence at Pam's utter disregard for small talk. When it was just the two of us, I'd bumble in every Monday, excited to talk about our weekends and see if she's watching the new series of *I'm a Celeb* . . . and I'd be met with silence. Or, worse, a look of complete bafflement.

I lean on the desk opposite hers. 'Sure, what's up?'

Pam scowls at her computer, clicking her mouse vigorously.

'This turned up today.' She kicks a box by her foot and I

glance down, my heart turning over. 'I have no idea where it's come from, or what it even is.'

I know what it is. I also know where it's come from, because I ordered it after a particularly jolly night in the pub with Pam where I thought she was so full of spirit and joy that *of course* she'd want an entire box of Halloween decorations delivered to the office to spruce the place up a bit. All I'd have to do is ask her, just out of manners really, because she'd definitely say yes.

Except, I went home and ordered it on the company credit card, went to sleep and swiftly forgot all about it. Which also meant, forgetting to ask Pam.

'Oh,' I say, trying my best to sound curious as I kneel down to look at the box, 'it looks like Halloween decorations.'

Oh my God, these are *fantastic*! I'd forgotten how brilliant this company were.

I start leafing through the decorations excitedly. There's cauldron bunting, ghosts that sway off the ceiling and –

'A talking pumpkin!' I cry, pulling it out of the box in amazement. 'Pam! Look at this!'

Pam doesn't break her eye contact with her laptop.

'Right,' I say, taking a deep breath and forcing myself to remain professional and not start laying out all the decorations in height order so I can send them to my mum and we can both fangirl over how great they are. 'I've got you, Pam. I will put this all up around the office for you.'

Pam points her pen at me and I jump. 'Not that singing pumpkin shit,' she says. 'That can go in the bin.'

'It can't go in the bin!' I squeal, holding the pumpkin to

my chest like it's my first-born child. 'There are two of them! They belong together.'

Pam looks up at me, and I see a smile quiver on her thin lips. 'Fine. Take them home with you.'

I beam. 'Really?'

'Yes, seeing as you ordered it all anyway.'

I feel my face fall and I'm about to gush an apology when I notice Pam smirking at me.

'You're the boss,' I say, doing a fake curtsy. I'm about to turn and walk into the kitchen when I spot Pam's computer screen, filled with pictures of India.

'Oh!' I say. 'What are you looking at?'

She snaps her browser shut and goes back to her emails. 'Don't be nosy.'

'Was it India? Are you thinking of travelling?'

'*Rodney* is,' she says pointedly. 'He's got this mad idea about us taking a year off and travelling around the world together. He thinks we both work too hard.'

'You do work too hard.' I raise my eyebrows at her but she clicks her tongue at me, laughing.

'Do you want a coffee?' I call over my shoulder as I walk into the kitchen.

There are six of us who work here now, but for the first hour of the morning it's usually just me and Pam, and to be honest, that's when I like it best. I mean, sure, she doesn't want to engage in any small talk whatsoever and some days she doesn't even look at me from over her computer, but I quite like it. It's always the same, and there is something quite calming about that.

'Go on, then,' Pam says. 'But a normal one, none of your pumpkin shit.'

I laugh, rolling my eyes as I pull our two mugs down from the cupboard.

Like I'd waste my pumpkin spice syrup on Pam. She doesn't even know who Morticia Addams is.

Chapter Two

Nate

London seduced me. There, I said it. And like any great seduction, it did it so slowly that I didn't even notice until I was slap bang in love with it.

It's my brother, Stevie's, fault. He moved here from our childhood home in New York when he was nineteen, right when I'd finished college. I was supposed to be the exciting, adventurous one. But there I was, moving back in with our parents while he hopped across the pond to attend the Royal Ballet School. At first Stevie stayed with our Aunt Tell, but now he's in Camden in a small, two-bed flat above a record shop. I never really understood why he moved out, but he always brushes it off when I ask him. We got pictures of all the landmarks at first, the novelty of the first subway (or 'tube' as he called it), the first pillar-box-red bus, the first selfie with the guards standing to attention at Buckingham Palace – but then it evolved as Stevie did. As he sank comfortably into London life, we started getting pictures of nights out in Soho, his 'dinner' in Chinatown at 3 a.m., the sparkling River Thames as he walked to dance rehearsals every morning. It always looked so exciting and, well, inviting.

Then there was the second layer of seduction: all the British TV shows. *Made in Chelsea*, where it's always bright blue skies and crisp sunlight, *Sherlock* with the clipped, precise accents and *Line of Duty* with the camaraderie of an English country pub. Mom and I even got into the British Christmas films, and spent each year watching *The Holiday*, *Love Actually* and *Nativity*. Everything about it was so picturesque, so rosy-cheeked, and just so . . . perfect.

But the thing is, although I had this secret love affair with London, I never actually wanted to go. It felt like the exciting, eclectic cousin of New York. Over the years, friends of mine would flit off, hopping over the pond under the guise of a 'gap year', but then they'd fall in love with the city, or another person, and never come back. If I'm honest, I couldn't fully trust in myself that I wouldn't do the same thing. I mean, Stevie had as good as moved over permanently, and if I did then Mom would be left in New York without either of us. I couldn't do that to her.

But then things changed. Mom started to get a bit . . . Well, worse. Everything got a bit worse, actually. Dad lost the sparkle behind his eyes. I felt if one more person added even the smallest feather to my cart, I'd kick it all over like a flailing buckaroo and pelt off into the distance, never to be seen again. Stevie didn't understand, really. I'd tried speaking to Dad, but he shrugged it off, saying he was fine. Though he never tried to claim Mom was fine. I didn't know how I could help her, and there was no point speaking to Mom about it. You don't want to tell a sick person how scared you are of them being sick. So I just sat back, doing whatever I could but ultimately feeling pretty helpless. Until one day she dropped a name into conversation like a little piece of gold dust, and I realised how I could help.

Her sister. My Aunt Thelma. Or Tell, as Mom calls her.

I hadn't heard Mom mention my Aunt Tell for years. They spoke on the phone at Christmas and on birthdays, and we'd occasionally get some form of ridiculous newsletter through the post, stuffed full of updates about her fabulous single life in London and what she'd been up to. But that was it, and I thought Mom was fine with it. Until a few weeks ago, when she was having a particularly bad couple of days, and said five words that flicked a switch inside me:

I wish Tell was here.

And there it was. My catalyst, propelling me into London. I tried to call Aunt Tell, I messaged her, I even wrote her a letter since she seemed to enjoy the post so much. I told her about Mom, how she'd been asking for her, how she wasn't well, how great it would be if she came back to New York to visit. But she didn't answer.

Some people might take this as a sign to shelve Aunt Tell, to tell Mom that she wasn't around and then just move on with life. I, however, saw this as a challenge. Go to London, find Aunt Tell, bring her back to New York. Make Mom happy, make everything that little bit better.

And the thing is, once Mom mentioned Aunt Tell, she didn't stop. She started regaling me with stories about their childhood together, the fights they had as teenagers and the trouble they got up to behind my grandmother's back. She described Aunt Tell's appearances on the stage and how proud she was, how talented Tell had always been and how she always performed for her in their shared bedroom. Every time she spoke of her it made the need to bring Aunt Tell back to New York burn a little stronger in my chest. If Mom looked this happy when speaking about her, if she *remembered* so much about her and their lives together, then imagine what could happen if she saw her in person and they spent some time together. Or even just spoke on the phone? Or received a letter from her? At this point, I would have settled for anything. Weeks went by and my calls, letters, emails – you name it – were all ignored. Aunt Tell didn't want to be found, she made that pretty clear.

I never told Mom that I'd been writing to ask Aunt Tell to come to New York. I couldn't tell her that her own sister was ignoring her, and I had no idea why. But I could go to London and find out myself. So that's what I did, and that's what led me to this moment. Sat in a coffee shop off Oxford Circus, sheltering from the rain in the middle of October in London. Pillar-box-red buses swishing by, people ping-ponging clipped voices back and forth, strangers at the counter ordering coffee. I arrived four days ago.

I lean back in my seat. I'm nestled in a corner, right by the window. It's a small café, the walls painted a lemon yellow with rusted orange shutters and wonky, teal metal tables. The café is buzzing with people, nipping in and out, clasping their coffees and paper bags filled with glistening treats. Condensation swells at the window, with teardrops of water running down at the corners and pooling in the deep-green window frames. I prod my phone and it looks back up at me lifelessly.

I'm currently working as a writer for a New York magazine, *Take the Time*, reviewing lifestyle events and activities. It's a decent job, and I spend most of my week nipping into new bars and restaurants, the odd art gallery and – if I'm very lucky – a Broadway show. Then I write about the experience. They have offices all over the world, and my editor Stefan barely batted an eye when I suggested I transfer to the London office for six months. That was my first sign from the universe that going to London to track down Aunt Tell wasn't a bad idea. The second was the reaction of Stevie, who immediately kicked out his housemate (who, to be fair, he did often refer to as 'Awful Albert') and started sending me an itinerary of what we could do together. He failed to mention that, as a performer, he works six days a week and so is never around to do all these fun things. Hence my sitting alone in a café all morning.

I sip my bitter, black coffee as my plan circles around my mind.

But I'm not here for fun. I just need to find Aunt Tell and bring her back to New York. She will make Mom happy and that will make everything a little bit better.

After eking out my coffee for as long as possible and avoiding eye contact from other customers who are desperate for a seat, I finally step outside into the crisp afternoon when Mom calls. It's our usual upbeat conversation. She's always brighter in the mornings, and laps up the details of the café, the hubbub of Oxford Street and the descriptions of the Londoners swarming like a pack of ants.

After we say goodbye, I plan to go back to the flat, but the jeers and commotion of football-mad Londoners all crammed inside various pubs is too fascinating to ignore. Also, I know that Stevie won't be home from work until way after midnight, and there's only so long that I can sit staring at the four walls, waiting for him to come through the door.

So, I walk into the first pub that looks as if it may have a seat for me, pull out my notebook and start operation Bring Back Tell.

Also, it aids one of my resolutions about making the most of my new life in London: getting into football. We've all seen *Ted Lasso*: surely I can be the new loveable Yank? Just without the moustache and the optimism? I catch sight of myself in the pub window. I wouldn't call myself unattractive, but let's say in all these British films I've watched, I wouldn't be cast as the Jude Law character. My hair is dark and curly, and my beard is unruly. In my defence, my hair would be better if it wasn't constantly damp from all the British rain.

I look down at my notebook. I have Tell's number, I know I could just call her and ask if I could come round. But I've already done that, haven't I? She made it pretty clear to me in New York that she didn't want to hear from me, for some unknown reason, even though she was happy to have Stevie stay with her when he was at dance school. Not that Stevie relays it in the same way on the rare occasion that you can get him to talk about it using more words than 'She's a dick.' So I need a new plan of attack.

'Excuse me?' I catch the eye of the bartender. 'Can I have another one?'

He is a portly man, wearing the same blue football shirt as the rest of the crowd, with large, bushy eyebrows which he raises at me, expertly.

'Sure,' he says, picking up my glass. 'Same again?'

I narrow my eyes at the range of ales, each named more whimsically than the last. So far I've tried the Hoptimus Prime (surprisingly average), Fursty Ferret (quite nice) and Golden Champion (not for me). Each pump has an eccentric character on the front, and I fixate on a cartoon rabbit wearing boxing gloves, eyeballing me. This needs to be my last pint; my head is feeling a little fuzzy.

'Hopping Hare, please,' I say, and the bartender nods and plucks a clean glass from under the sink.

I look around as a wave of 'go on's starts up around me, and each person lurches out of their seat like pieces of popcorn. One of the players is racing down the pitch with the ball, and despite myself I suck in a breath. The bartender is frozen mid-pour. The player is flanked by two men from the opposite team as he gets closer to the goal, jabbing their feet around him to try and get the ball. Effortlessly, the player spins the ball away from them and before I can blink, he curves his foot round the ball and launches it into the air.

My heart is racing as I watch, and I suddenly feel as sucked into the TV screen as the rest of the pub. His teammate sees the ball, jumps into the air and knocks his head against the ball. It bounces off his hand and smacks the back of the net, flying past the goalkeeper's outstretched hands and scoring into the goal.

Before I can stop myself, I throw myself off my chair and

cheer, punching the air. My ears are ringing and I feel so alive that it takes me a moment to notice that nobody else is cheering. Actually, everyone else looks pretty furious.

'It's a handball, mate. It doesn't count.'

I turn around to see an older man next to me. He's probably in his late fifties, wearing a flat cap, and is smiling at me kindly.

I quickly sit back down and take my pint off the bartender, trying to control the embarrassment rippling up my body.

'Ah, right,' I say, laughing, 'because he hit it with his hand, I guess?'

The man nods. 'That's right.'

I take a sip of my new beer. This one is biscuity and slightly foamy. It's the nicest one so far.

'Well, that makes sense,' I mumble into my pint. 'It is called football, after all.'

'That it is.'

I glance around to check the rest of the pub aren't pointing and cruelly laughing at me, like my imagination would have them, but they're back to being fully absorbed in the game. Thank God.

'You're new to football, then?' the man asks.

I look back at him and nod. 'Guilty as charged.'

'Sounds like you might know more about American football?'

I shrug. 'I don't know much about that either, to be honest.'

'Baseball?'

'No.'

'Basketball?'

'Nope.'

'Ice hockey?'

I shake my head and the man tries and fails to hide a smile. 'I'm not really that into sports,' I admit. 'I thought I'd try and get into football. Be a good way to really experience British culture.'

He cocks his head. 'It is a big part of us,' he agrees.

I take another sip of my pint. At least that's one thing I've gotten right.

'I'm Remy,' he holds out his hand. It's wide and wrinkled. Stevie would have a field day reading his palm.

'Nate,' I say, shaking his hand. 'Good to meet you, Remy.'

An hour later and I'm still in the pub, my notebook open in front of me, my neat lists filled with the little nuggets of information I managed to collect from Mom before I left New York. What Tell was like, what food she enjoyed, what they used to do together. Why she hasn't answered the phone to me or replied to any of my messages for the past few weeks.

Well, not that one. Obviously.

'Another one?'

I look up at Remy as he slaps my back, nodding towards the bartender. I smile. We're three pints deep now and my eyes have gained a blissful, blurred layer which makes everything look a little bit fuzzy. I close my notebook and thank Remy as he taps his card on the machine.

'How long have you been coming here, then?' I ask. 'Do you live around here?'

Remy looks over his shoulder as a gaggle of young men swarm into the pub, loosening their ties after a day in the office. He raises a hand to a few of them and then moves back round on his bar stool.

'I'm just by Primrose Hill,' he says. 'Do you know it?'

I shake my head. 'I don't know much about London, to be honest.'

'When did you get here?'

'Four days ago. I'm still getting over the jet lag.'

The bartender places two frothy pints in front of us and we chink them together.

'What are your big plans, then?' Remy asks.

I take a sip of my pint. 'I don't really have any. Explore London, do some family shit, go back home.'

Remy pulls a face and I realise I've given the most boring answer known to man.

'What do you do?' I ask, bending forwards to make room for a girl squeezing past me.

Remy almost looks surprised at this question. 'I'm a cabbie.'

Before I can stop myself, I lean over and thwack him on the arm. 'Remy! You're a cabbie! That's awesome!'

Remy laughs awkwardly and I immediately feel the need to explain myself.

'Sorry,' I say quickly. 'You're just a bit famous in the US. Like, do you drive one of those black cabs with the lights?'

He presses his lips together and nods. 'That I do.'

'And do you know all of the back alleys and secret ways to get around the city?'

He drinks his pint, looking at me out of the corner of his eye like I might be winding him up. I hold my hands up in defence.

'I'm just a crazy American. First time in London and all that.'

'Are you about to ask if I know the King?'

I chuckle into my pint. 'No. Why, do you?'

He laughs, shaking his head and giving me a shove. 'I do know where he lives, though.'

'That's awesome!' I cry, before catching his eye and feeling the penny drop.

Damn, I need to stop drinking.

'Right,' I say. 'Another pint?'

Chapter Three

Annie

Our door rattles open, warped from the constant autumn rain that has been lashing the streets of London all day for the past six weeks. Outside, the leaves are starting to change from the cooling shades of olive, moss and fern we have throughout the summer to a rainbow of juniper, cherry red and fiery orange, and although the rain has been lightly splattering my shoulders since I ducked out of Clapham Junction station, it's still slightly warm outside. Too warm for me to comfortably be wearing my cable-knit jumper and oversized scarf, not that that's going to stop me. I've shoved my reluctant summer wardrobe under my bed – I am not pulling it back out.

Tanya, Penny and I live in a maisonette, and by that I mean, we live in half a house. It's a tall townhouse which has been sliced down the middle and given to two landlords who barter it off to people who are desperate to live in London.

The obsession with London that seems to burn through the veins of so many people makes complete sense to me. The constant buzz, the fizz of languages you collect when walking down the streets, the feeling that every bar, café or shop you walk into could be filled with people from the other side of the world, from a completely different walk of life. It's exciting.

And yes, the majority of these eclectic, exciting people don't talk to each other and barely make eye contact. But ten years later and I'm still here. All of us are: Penny, Tanya and I. Sworn into a secret pact.

Tanya is easily the most beautiful person that I know. She has smooth, dark skin, high cheekbones and bright, warm brown eyes. Her Afro hair springs out of her head in tight curls and reaches her chin. She also has legs up to my armpits and, to top it all off, she has a lovely personality too.

Penny and I look more similar, which makes sense as we often act like squabbling sisters. With her blonde hair, pink cheeks and bright green eyes, she's obviously beautiful too, but not like Tanya is, more like me. We both cried about this when we were hungover at university, looking back at pictures from the night before where Tanya looked like a supermodel and we looked like we'd just won a competition to meet her.

I met Penny and Tanya when we were all slotted together in identical rooms next door to each other in our university halls. The three of us were a bit different. Tanya, tall and beautiful. Penny, painfully brainy and technical, and, well, me. The kooky one who loved making costumes and still made all her own clothes. But we just fitted together. Tanya made us cool, got us into all the parties and was fiercely defensive of us if we ever had a guy not treat us well. Penny was dependable; she could drink us under the table but also make a fantastic stew with eight of your five-a-day and a strong cup of tea. She's also a total wind-up and is possibly the most annoying person I've ever met. And I made their Halloween costumes every year, and any other fancy dress that a uni night out demanded. We were the best-dressed, best-fed, most empowered threesome on campus. So, when we all graduated, we moved into our own flat in Clapham and haven't moved out since.

There have been boyfriends over the years. Tanya has moved out a few times, and Penny's long-term boyfriend Mike semi lives with us, but we've all clung to each other like sleeping otters. I know our days are numbered, though, as at thirty-two, we're officially creeping towards the decade filled with marriages, babies and mortgages, and I don't think the three of us could all find partners who'd be happy living in a commune.

But for now, it's still the three of us.

I kick the door shut and immediately begin to charge up the stairs.

'Hello!' I shout. I can hear the TV pattering in the background and I look up and see a horrified Tanya, and an amused Penny.

'Oh my God, what happened?' Tanya says, uncurling herself off the sofa and rushing to help me. 'Did you get made redundant or something?'

I drop the bags with a thud. 'What? No – much better than that, I got us all these amazing Halloween decorations.'

Penny grins, her eyebrows raised. 'How come?'

'Work didn't want them – isn't that mad?' I say, slumping down onto the sofa in our living room and ripping my jumper off before I combust.

'Oh my God,' Penny scoffs, pulling out my string of inflatable cauldrons. 'What is this?'

'Annie,' Tanya says, her mothering tone taking over. 'What's going on? We don't need all of this. We still have the decorations from last year.'

'We don't have one of these,' Penny points out, holding up a paper skeleton mask to her face.

'Well, I thought you can never have too many decorations,' I say.

'I'll make us a tea,' Penny says, getting to her feet.

Tanya tucks her feet under her on the small armchair and I busy myself looking through the decorations.

Crikey, I did buy a lot . . . but it's my weak spot. Everyone is addicted to something. Tanya is obsessed with anything miniature (which I find odd as she's taller than everyone) and Penny is obsessed with recipes. Pam is obsessed with . . . well, work. I'm obsessed with Halloween decorations. So, when a shop window drapes itself in light-up pumpkins or flashing bats, I can't help myself. And really, I don't think anyone can blame me for that.

'Here we are,' Penny says, handing me a steaming mug and plonking herself down next to me.

'Also, this means that our Halloween party this year will be *epic*. I mean, our house will look ridiculous. We might even end up on the news!'

Penny and Tanya exchange glances and I suddenly feel as though they're communicating telepathically.

'What?'

'I don't think I can come to the Halloween party this year,' Tanya blurts, half hiding behind her mug of tea.

My mouth drops open. We've been hosting our Halloween parties every year since our first term at university. We spend the entire week leading up to it decorating the house, making it as creepy as possible. Last year, Penny did this incredible trick with a mirror in the bathroom that made it look like there was someone standing behind you while you were washing your hands. We had to take it down until the night of the party, as we kept falling for it in the middle of the night and waking each other up screaming.

'You can't come?' I repeat. 'What do you mean? What else are you doing?'

It's the one night of the year which is etched into our diaries in blood. The Saturday of Halloween is our party. I mean, friends of ours start talking about it in August.

'I have a work event,' Tanya mumbles.

'On a Saturday?' I cry incredulously.

'It's a PR event for a new perfume,' she says. 'They're holding a masquerade ball. It's one of my clients, I kind of have to go. But I can bring you guys along with me.'

I force myself to pause. *Stop being a brat, Annie.*

'Oh wow,' I say. 'That's really cool . . . sorry, I just really love our party. It's like our thing, isn't it?'

I look at Penny who shrugs back at me. 'Yeah, it's a lot of work though, isn't it?'

'Don't you like it?' I cry. Penny reads my expression and quickly corrects herself.

'No, of course I do. It's like, the best night of the year.'

'The best,' Tanya agrees firmly.

'But, like, work is insane at the moment,' Penny says, pushing her fingers through her hair. 'I could do with not having to spend so much time organising it all. I have to work late every night this week.'

'Ew.' I grimace.

'And this way we can just go to a cool party instead. Like, it's still fancy dress, right?' She looks to Tanya who nods happily.

'Oh yeah,' Tanya says. 'People will go nuts for it. It's a really high-key event too,' she adds. 'I've seen the budget for it. It's huge. They have performers there and everything. You could get snapped up!' She points at me. 'There will be so many people from the fashion world there, you should take some business cards. I bet you'd sell loads of costumes.'

I smile. Tanya is always offering to introduce me to fashion colleagues to get me in the door as a seamstress or designer of some sort. But what I make isn't fashionable. It's cartoonist and grotesque and a bit weird, and not in a cool way. Nobody is going to go to Zara and buy a jacket with manoeuvrable bat wings.

Tanya and Penny are both smiling, and I can feel how desperate they are for me to agree, which suddenly makes me feel like a spoiled child. Have they been planning this conversation?

'Yeah, of course,' I say, forcing a smile on my face. 'That sounds great.'

Tanya claps her hands. 'Oh yay! I'm so happy! But we'll do the party as normal next year.'

Penny nods. 'Definitely.'

Chapter Four

Nate

'Nate?'

I look up as Stevie pops his bleached head round the doorframe, a red spatula swinging from his hand.

'I'm making a stir fry, do you want some?'

'Sure, man,' I say. 'Thanks.'

Stevie nods and turns back into the kitchen before I can offer any help. It would be an empty offer, as the galley kitchen barely has room for one of us Simpson brothers, both towering over six foot three with our gangly, clumsy limbs. Stevie has a short fuse when we're together and I'd probably end up with a lump in the shape of a frying pan square on my forehead.

Stevie has lived in this Camden flat for almost six years, since graduating and moving out of Aunt Tell's place. I've tried asking him whether he still sees her, but he always bats the question away. I haven't even told him my real reason for being in London: I'm worried he won't be happy about it.

'Here you are,' Stevie says in a sing-song voice, passing me a bowl of steaming noodles.

'Thank you, smells great.'

He nods and starts working at the noodles with a pair of chopsticks. I'm the big brother, three years older than Stevie. (Although he's been twenty-four for the past six years, so who knows how large our age gap will really stretch.)

We've always been quite different. He's got more talent in his big toe than the majority of the human population have in their entire body, and he's one of those rare people who have made their dreams a reality. He got a scholarship to train with the Royal Ballet when he was nineteen, and that's where his obsession with London began. Everyone is in awe of him back home.

He's also a giant pain in the ass.

'Very nice,' I say, noticing that Stevie is eyeballing me as he waits for me to compliment his cooking. 'The next Betty Crocker.'

He rolls his eyes at me. 'She made cakes, you moron.'

I pull a face at him and he smiles, shaking his head. When he's with his mates, his accent slips into this weird, cockney drawl, like a chameleon effortlessly changing its colours. But it's no use when he's with me; I draw our home accent straight back out of him.

I glance out of the window as blue lights flash through the flat. A light sprinkle of rain has been washing through the sky for the past hour. Little beads of water sit on the fiery leaves of the maple trees lining the street, entirely out of place in this grey, built-up part of Camden. But they're still there, proudly waving at each passer-by, ready to show off the twists and turns of their bark, carrying the stories of the thousands of people who have walked past barely noticing their existence.

At some point soon, the leaves will let go and helicopter through the sky. But right now, it's the stage of autumn where they are just about clinging on. It's not their time yet. It'll come.

'So,' Stevie says, swallowing his last mouthful and putting his bowl on the rickety coffee table. 'What did you do with your last day of freedom?'

I chew my mouthful. I moved to London just under a week before my new placement started in order to give myself time to explore the city. Find my favourite coffee shops, pop by some museums, soak in the culture and stumble across historic sites.

'I went up to Oxford Street and watched soccer in a bar.'

Stevie almost chokes on his drink. 'Soccer? You mean football.'

I shoot him a look – the cockney accent is back. 'Yeah, that.'

'Get you,' he says, plucking up the television remote. 'Shall we watch *Made in Chelsea*?'

'Sure.'

'Are you totally in love with London yet?' Stevie asks. 'Will you be staying here forever?'

I sigh. 'That depends.'

'On what?'

'On whether it rains this much all the time.'

'Ah yes.' Stevie cocks his head whimsically. 'All part of the charm.'

Falling For You

He puts the remote down as three picture-perfect women pop onto the screen, all holding coffee cups and raising their eyebrows in disgust at each other.

'And did you hear from Mom?'

'Yup,' I say, turning my phone in my hands. It's only 3 p.m. in New York at the moment. 'I said you'd call her.'

'Why?'

'Because you're her son?'

'I'm too busy,' he says. 'This is my only evening off. I'm in shows the rest of this week. I won't have the time.'

'Well then, text her,' I shrug. 'Send her a selfie, whatever.'

Stevie scoffs and I smirk. Even with his shaved, bleached head, silver earring and tattooed arms, when he strops, he may as well be six years old again.

'Oh, come on,' I grin. 'You have time to chat to every man in London,' I point to his phone on the coffee table as, right on cue, it lights up. 'I'm sure you can spare five minutes for our dear old mom.'

He shoots me a look, but he's grinning now. 'It's not every man,' he says, picking up his phone. 'Screw you. Oh! It's Facebook Marketplace.'

I sit up. 'Oh great, are you getting a new sofa? I'll chip in.'

'What? No,' Stevie narrows his eyes at his phone screen. 'I've found this amazing talking pumpkin for Halloween.'

I groan, sitting back down. 'I hate Halloween.'

'Yes . . .' Stevie says, using his fingers to zoom in on the picture and turning his phone to show me. 'But this should do the trick to annoy the cat upstairs – it's due some bad karma.'

'Why?'

'It pissed on my rug.'

I take a final look at myself in the elevator mirror. My dark hair is pushed back, finally seeming to adjust to the sogginess of London, and (after a thorough talking to from Stevie) my beard is trimmed, and therefore slightly less unruly than yesterday.

It's my first day in the London office of *Take the Time*, the 'best events magazine' if you believe everything our marketing team is feeding you. I've spent the past eight years (and what was left of my twenties) working as their feature writer, covering events all over New York City and Manhattan. It's a pretty cool gig. Or it was, until all of my mates who took turns to be my plus one would rather sit in with their other halves, and I realised that yeah, that actually sounded quite nice and I'd like to do the same. Except I didn't have an other half. Sure, it's pretty impressive to take a woman on a first date to a Broadway show or the launch of a new menu at a restaurant, but the novelty wears off. Usually about the time the 'let's sit in together instead' conversation comes around and I reveal my true, introverted self and realise that they were far more interested in the fancy meals and elaborate dates than they ever were in me.

The elevator pulls up to the eighth floor and pings open. I step out dubiously.

'Nathaniel?'

I look up as I hear my name bounce towards me in a clipped British accent. For a moment I'm half expecting to see

Hugh Grant bumble over and offer me a cigarette. Instead, it's a lanky guy with big teeth and even bigger hair, all quaffed above his head like the fifth member of ABBA.

'Hi,' I say, holding out my hand. 'It's Nate.'

'Brian!' the man says back happily, giving my hand a firm shake. 'Welcome to London! Fancy a tea?'

'Do you have coffee?'

Brian pulls a face. 'The machine is broken. I make a good tea, though.'

I'm about to decline when I clock every other person in the office, holding a mug.

I feel like it's an unwritten British rule: never turn down a cup of tea in a first meeting. It would be a sign of the utmost disrespect.

'Sure,' I say. 'Thanks.'

I've managed to avoid cups of tea since being in London. It's not that I don't like it, it's just that . . . fuck it. I hate it. It tastes like dishwater and I have absolutely no idea why anyone drinks it.

I follow him as he wanders through the office, presumably towards the kitchen.

'That's Kat,' Brian says, flicking his wrist towards a girl sitting behind a computer who nods at me, 'accounts; Fernanda,' another woman nods, 'IT. Paul, Simon, Gary, Greg, socials,' a set of men raise their eyebrows at me one by one, like meerkats popping up over the parapet.

'Helen is HR but she's not in yet aaaaaaaaaaand . . .' he spins on his heel to face me and I stop walking to avoid crashing into him, 'the lazy writers usually work from home,' he gives me a knowing look and then laughs, 'but you'll meet them soon. Kayleigh, Scott and Jen.'

I nod, realising I've had the same grin pinned on my face since I stepped out of the elevator. I relax.

'Right,' I say. 'Great to meet you all.' I offer my hand in a wave around the office. They all lift their heads in recognition and bob them back down, hiding behind their monitors. And plants.

'How's the jet lag?' Brian asks, flicking the kettle on.

'Yeah, all good . . . I've been here five days, so I think I've gotten over the worst of it.'

Brian laughs. 'I hear you. I visited the Singapore office at the start of the year, it fucked me for days. But how is New York? I don't know if we have quite the nightlife to compare, especially the events we get invited to.' He leans back on the counter as the kettle sputters behind him. 'But we still have some good ones. Do you like Cirque du Soleil?'

I tuck my hands in my pockets. 'Sure. I could cover that.'

Brian pushes his lips together and shakes his head. 'No, you can't. Unless you want to fight Scott for it. He gets those tickets every year.'

He gives me a look like he's speaking in a language that only he and I understand.

'Right.'

'But there are some other great things you can go to,' he says. 'We have some fantastic pantomimes if you're still here at Christmas. Have you been to a panto before?'

'No, I haven't.'

'Oh no he hasn't!'

I stare at him, bewildered. 'Sorry?'

He throws his head back and laughs, dropping a teabag into each mug. 'I'm joking with you. Are you a sports guy? Sorry, can I just . . .' He goes to open the fridge and I move out of the way awkwardly.

'Ah yes,' I say, finally feeling myself relax a little. 'I'm actually getting into football.'

Brian raises his eyebrows at me, clearly impressed. 'Oh yeah? What team?'

Finally. Something I can talk about. I lift my chin proudly. 'Chelsea.'

Brian's face drops. 'Seriously?'

I stare at him, waiting for him to burst out laughing as part of another weird joke I don't understand. But he keeps staring at me as though I've admitted to stabbing my grandmother over breakfast.

'Yeah?' I say.

To my alarm, Brian rolls his eyes, sloshing milk into both mugs.

'Ah. We're all Tottenham,' he says, shaking his head and giving a chuckle. 'That really is bad luck. Don't let the team hear you say that. They won't let you live it down.'

I blink at him.

'Right,' I say eventually. 'Well, I'm sure I could be a Tottenham fan too . . .'

'Definitely don't let the team hear you say *that*.' He laughs, jostling my shoulder, and I try to laugh along.

'There's your tea,' he says, picking up his mug and

handing me mine. I take it and automatically take a giant sip, forgetting for a moment that it isn't coffee, and feel my face contort.

Oh God, that is absolutely –

'What?' Brian says, his eyes narrowing. 'What's wrong with it?'

'Nothing!' I say quickly, noticing Greg and Gary from socials popping their heads up. 'Nothing. It's delicious. Thank you.'

He peers at me, taking a step forward. 'Why did you pull that face, then?'

'What face?'

'Like it tastes horrible? The milk isn't off, is it?'

Oh God, I cannot let him realise on my first day here that I hate tea. I will be ostracised.

'Nope,' I say, forcing a huge smile, 'it's perfect. I always pull a weird face when I drink a . . . hot drink.'

He looks at me for a minute before accepting my answer.

'Okay,' he shrugs, 'well, make yourself at home. Pick whichever desk you want and just . . . start writing!'

A cold wash of dread sweeps over me.

Just start writing?

'I usually review events and things . . .' I say, following him out of the kitchen, 'is there anything you want me to cover?'

'Nope!' He smiles. 'We don't have much on at the moment. So just write whatever you like, see where inspiration takes you.'

He catches the look of panic on my face and shakes my shoulder. 'You're a writer, you must be full of ideas!'

I laugh weakly as Brian walks off, leaving me at an empty desk.

Well, if I wanted to know if Brian was a writer himself, I know now for sure.

Every writer knows that, actually, we never have any ideas.

Ever.

Chapter Five

Annie

I grip the pin between my teeth as I reposition the material against my sewing machine. It's a thick fabric, almost too thick for my machine, but the brief was a ghost costume that could survive an outdoor Halloween party set in the grounds of a castle.

In my eyes, anyone who is cool enough to go to that level of commitment for Halloween deserves a good costume, so I'm going all out. All the bells and whistles, pockets and thermal linings. I'm nothing if not practical.

I reposition the fabric so it's perfectly aligned, adding another pin so it stays firmly in place. Once I have received the brief from the client along with their measurements, I design the costume. This usually involves hours of sketching and scribbling, stitching my favourite parts from each design together until I come up with the perfect outfit. Then, using the measurements the client sent through, I adjust the pattern to make sure it'll fit correctly and set about sourcing the fabrics. I go to a fantastic shop in Camden. There are a million fabric shops in London, half of which are far closer to me. But they don't have Jade, the shop owner.

Jade is around thirty, with electric-pink hair and big, glittery earrings. Her shop is like an Aladdin's cave: streams upon streams of glistening, beautiful fabrics, every colour under the rainbow. I could spend hours in there, admiring each roll and imagining what I could make with them.

'Are you all right, love?'

I narrow my eyes before sticking the final pin into the fabric to tack up the hem. I nod at Mum, who is balanced against my copy of *Pride and Prejudice*, on FaceTime. She's in her kitchen, half bent over a bubbling stove as she peers into the camera. My mum is a wiry woman with thin, wild hair and an extensive collection of pashminas. You can find them coiled round her neck like fabulous snakes all year round. She gets away with it, as whenever someone notices how enormous her collection is, she proudly tells them that she made them all herself. Then, instead of being slightly deranged for being so obsessed with cashmere scarves, she's suddenly very impressive.

It makes me want to learn how to make wine.

'Yes,' I say. 'That hem was just a bit tricky. The fabric is so thick.'

'Let's see it?'

I hold an offcut up to the camera and Mum nods knowingly. 'Gone are the days that you'd wear a simple bedsheet.'

'Gone are the days where you're expected to freeze to death in order to look good,' I say, grinning at Mum as she laughs.

'Aren't you supposed to be the young one living it up in London?' she says. 'You shouldn't be worried about being cold.'

I glance around my bedroom, my blanket firmly draped over my legs.

The first year we moved in, the three of us were still a bit naïve after spending three years living in 'bills included' accommodation at university. We went wild with the thermostat. I remember walking around the flat in December in a *T-shirt*. We were all, 'we deserve a warm home' and 'we work hard for our money, we've earnt this', and blah blah idiotic blah.

Well, we had the shock of our lives when our bill came through in the spring. We made a solemn oath to each other that we'd keep ourselves accountable and not turn the heating on until the twentieth of November at the very earliest, unless it snows.

We have thin, rattly windows and an attic that puffs all our heat away like a cheerful steam train. We haven't had snow, but I'm pretty sure there are icicles forming in my nostrils.

'I'm always worried about being cold.'

Mum still lives in our family home, an old farmhouse in the Cotswolds. It has wooden beams and sage cabinets, and an enormous reclaimed-wood dining table that stretches across the conservatory and sits our entire extended family every Christmas. All fifteen of us.

Growing up it was just us three, but our house was always full of friends from school, relatives and pals of my parents popping round for a cup of tea or a steaming Sunday roast.

On the odd occasion that I take Tanya and Penny back

home to 'escape to the country' (as Penny likes to call it), they cannot understand why I ever wanted to leave. Once, I caught Tanya 'joking' with my mum about lodging in my old bedroom (she swore it was a joke when I questioned her, but I saw her face when she bit into Mum's apple crumble. The intention was real). Don't get me wrong, I loved living there. But I love living in London too. Even if it does mean that the only person making me an apple crumble on a Sunday for under £11.50 is Mr Kipling.

'What are you making?' I ask Mum, as she picks up a wooden spoon and starts stirring an enormous pot.

She frowns, her glasses momentarily steaming up. 'I'm batch-cooking some bolognese,' she says thoughtfully. 'It's the best way to live these days.'

I go back to my sewing machine. This order came through on our site on Friday, with a desperate note that they need it by Wednesday at the latest to give them enough time to find an alternative in case it isn't right.

Some people might see this as an insult, but I see it as a personal challenge to make this girl a costume so incredible that she'd feel silly for even *thinking* that she'd need another option. She came to the Stitching Witches, and we are the best.

This month so far, I've made two Little 'dead' Riding Hoods, four evil cats, one pixie, and now one thermal ghost. I could have made double that if I didn't work full-time.

Halloween is this weekend, and we're bound to get more desperate orders as the week goes on. Mum always tells me that after the twenty-first of the month, I should say that the deadline has passed and I can't make any more. But I can't resist – all I have to do is look at the weird and wonderful requests and I'm hooked. I get a bit possessive over it, as if it's already *my* project. Nobody can make this outfit as good as I can, even if it means I stay up all night for an entire week cooped up in my bedroom and develop a hump in my back like Igor from *Despicable Me*.

Actually, he'd be quite a good Halloween costume.

It's all worth it when I receive a photo of the person in my costume, looking confident and excited. I know they'll spend the night batting off compliments about how great they look. They'll have a cloak of power draped over their body for the night, and I'll have been the one to give it to them. How can I say no to that?

'What are you dressing up as for Halloween, then?' I ask, taking the fabric out of the machine as I get ready to sew the hem.

Halloween was always a huge deal in our house. In fact, we were 'the' house in the area. You know the one. People would travel there to trick or treat and have their photos taken outside. My parents would go nuts for it. Dad would spend hours decorating the outside of the house, sticking severed hands into the soil that stretched up, ready to snatch the ankles of any passing children. He'd drape fake cobwebs over the front of the house and drop a giant spider from my bedroom window that would glisten when the light of a passing car hit its back.

Even though I haven't lived at home for over ten years, they still go full throttle. Everyone in the village loves it – so much so that in my dad's home office there are twenty-five framed pages from the *Cotswolds Herald* of Mum and Dad, grinning proudly in front of their terrifying house. I'm featured in almost all the pictures too, up until I moved out to go to university.

'Well,' Mum's eyes light up, 'I think I'll go as a witch. I found this amazing YouTube video on how to reconstruct your face with make-up, so I'm going to give myself these huge eyes and I got this fabulous wig online.'

By fabulous, she means grotesque.

'And I think Dad wants to go as a clown.' She picks up a pepper grinder and twists it into the pot. 'He's been quite inspired by Stephen King's *It*. I said I'd help him out, I think we have some bits and pieces lying around. Did you finish your costume?'

I press my foot on the pedal and hold the fabric tight as the sewing machine whizzes over the hem of the dress.

'Yes,' I say. 'Although I'm not sure if I can wear it.'

'Why?' Mum asks. 'Does it not fit right?'

I try not to scoff. As if I'd make a costume for myself that didn't fit properly.

'No,' I say. 'Tanya and Penny want to go to a ball on Halloween.'

Mum's mouth drops open. '*A ball?* On *Halloween?*'

I smile to myself. Mum is the only person who would share my reaction. One of utter disgust. Really, I should have called her and put her on loudspeaker as soon as Tanya suggested the ball, just so I had some reinforcement.

'Yeah,' I sigh. 'For Tanya's work.'

'A Halloween ball?' Mum says wonderingly, and I can tell that she's trying to find the silver lining to spin. 'That could be fun?'

I push my fingers through my hair. 'Well, it's more of a masquerade ball. Like, it is a Halloween theme, but I think people are more likely to be wearing fancy dresses and suits.'

'Well, that's not Halloween at all!'

'I know.'

'It would be such a shame if you didn't get to wear your costume,' Mum says, putting her bolognese to the side and looking straight down the camera earnestly.

I shrug, feeling like a teenager.

'Why don't you come home and spend Halloween with us?' she says, her eyes lighting up. 'Dad's talking about doing something creative with popping candy and balloons or something.'

I smile. 'No, it's okay. I'm sure it'll be fun.'

I can't run home to my parents just so I can dress up in the outfit I want. A ball is far more sophisticated and 'cool' than a house party. Penny and Tanya are really excited.

I'm thirty-two. I guess it's just time for me to grow up a bit.

Or, you know, find a way to wear the bat costume anyway.

'Argh! I hate this stupid, bloody oven!'

I peer up from my notebook at Penny, who is bent

over double and peering into the little glass square door of the oven, her face gradually turning a deeper shade of red.

The kitchen is the oldest room in the house. It's still that weird shade of brown that was fashionable in the sixties, and has an oven so white and prominent that it looks like a toy one you'd buy in Aldi. It has four gas rings, three of which don't work, and a temperamental oven which only has two options: scalding hot or ice-cold.

Which – as a woman who wrestles with an aggressive period every thirty days – I can relate to.

When we first moved in, we wrote a strongly worded email to the landlord. Or Tanya did. Penny and I stomped around the house cursing wildly as Tanya tapped out a neat, well-composed message that wasn't going to get us kicked onto the streets the moment she hit 'send'. The landlord sent us a brief, non-committal reply and we soon realised that – from his skyline penthouse in Dubai – he really couldn't care less. He's actually like the bad boyfriend that we've all just grown to accept. We expect so little of him that when he does show any kindness or humanity, we practically build a shrine to him in the hallway and praise him like Jesus Christ.

Last Christmas he sent us a little plastic Christmas tree that sang carols and danced, and we all lost our minds. One night we got so drunk on mulled wine that I caught myself almost crying with gratitude over it. I had a strong word with myself the next morning.

Thou shall not get drunk and cry over terrible landlords with tacky, dancing Christmas trees.

'What's it doing?' I ask, looking up from my notebook.

I've been making a list of all my finances for the month. I know. I'm super organised. With the business being busy this month, I'm constantly running to the Camden fabric shop to stock up on supplies, paying for postage and thread and whatever else I need. So, every now and then I need to make sure I am actually *making* money from it all. If I was a baroness with lots of money, then I'd spend my life making these costumes and give them out for free, but unfortunately, I'm not quite there yet. I don't think E.ON Energy would appreciate a custom-made witch costume instead of the £58 I owe each month for our electricity bill.

'It's what it's *not* doing,' Penny mutters, still glaring at the oven door. 'It's ruining my bread.'

I look back down at my notebook. It was only a matter of time until Penny, the scientist, decided to tackle sourdough.

'Something smells good!' Tanya says happily, bouncing into the kitchen. I swallow a smile as Penny snaps up to standing, a look of anguish painted on her face.

'The oven is screwed!' she wails. 'It's ruining my bread! I've spent *weeks* working on that dough.'

Tanya's face falls. 'Oh no, are you okay? I'm sure it'll still taste great.'

I smile to myself. I quite enjoy sitting back and watching Tanya fall into her role of mother around Penny. Penny and I act more like sisters – we bicker about what to watch on TV and laugh at stupid jokes that make absolutely no sense – but

Tanya is the one we go to when we need help. She seems to always know how to fix everything.

Penny slumps onto the plastic dining table opposite me as Tanya flicks the kettle on.

'I was coming in to say I have some good news,' she grins. 'I've had some more information about the ball.' She plucks three mugs out of the cupboard, correctly assuming that we all want a cup of tea.

'I think it's going to be pretty spectacular,' she says. 'It's a proper PR event.'

'What does that mean?' Penny shuffles her seat round so she's facing Tanya.

'Basically, it means that we'll get loads of free stuff!' She beams. 'There will be free drinks and food and they *always* have little goodie bags to give out.'

I lean my head on my hand. 'Are you sure we're allowed to go? We're nothing to do with fashion.'

'Your costume will beg to differ,' Penny quips and I puff my chest out in pride.

'It's fine,' Tanya flaps her hand. 'You might just have to pretend to be influencers or something.'

Penny scoffs. 'Oh God, what does that mean?'

'Just take the odd selfie,' Tanya shrugs, and I laugh at Penny's horrified expression as Tanya sets the mugs down on our polka-dot tablecloth and sits on the third chair.

'People will be taking pictures of you anyway,' Penny says, nodding to me.

'Well, I don't know if I'm allowed to wear my costume yet.'

Tanya's head snaps round to face me. 'What? Of course you're allowed to wear it! You must wear it!'

'It's not a ball gown. Isn't it a masquerade ball?'

Tanya bats me away. 'Just add a mask and you'll be fine. We're on the guest list, baby, we're golden.'

Chapter Six

Nate

I zoom in on my laptop screen, the patches of green stretching apart to reveal road names and buildings. Aunt Tell lives in Epping, which is about an hour on the train from here. We could go by this weekend, just pop in and see her. All I have to do is persuade Stevie to come with me, without telling him my reason. If I tell Stevie it's because I want to persuade Aunt Tell to come back to New York with me, he'll get all weird and closed off like he always does when I bring up Mom. You don't have to be a psychologist to work out why – you can see the guilt painted across his face at being on the other side of the world while I'll have to deal with Mom being sick. But you *would* have to be a psychologist to get him to talk about it, or even acknowledge a single feeling exists inside his eccentric, defensive mind. I've given up trying. He'll come to me eventually, and if he doesn't, I'll just buy him a pint.

'All right?'

I look up and double-take Stevie as he walks into the living room. He's wearing a tank top, which is tight against his lean body, baggy joggers and a single hoop earring. None of this is out of the ordinary; it's his full face of make-up that nearly makes me fall off my seat.

'Is this your new act?' I ask, trying not to laugh at his exaggerated lips, fan-like eyelashes and painted-on eyebrows which arch up the side of his face.

Stevie clicks his tongue at me, opening his bag and throwing his water bottle inside.

'I'm getting a cab and I hate the dressing room at this place,' he snaps. 'It's easier if I do my make-up here and then get changed once I'm there.'

I nod, taking a sip from my cold bottle of Corona.

Stevie created Stevie Trixx, his drag persona, a few years after he finished dance school. It made total sense, Stevie's a fantastic dancer . . . but he's also a performer. He loves making people laugh and gasp on stage and he's always been so creative.

'What time is your cab?' I ask, moving my bag so he can slump onto the sofa next to me. He closes his eyes, pushing a thumb and forefinger against his temple, the long, glittery nail catching the light and sparkling.

'In about ten minutes,' he says.

'Hey!' I say, sitting up as the thought drops into my mind. 'You might have my new mate, Remy, as your driver. He's a cabbie!'

'Is he a homophobe?'

I pause. I'm not stupid enough to believe that just because someone is nice to me means that they wouldn't act vile towards someone from another walk of life. But I do like to think I'm a good judge of character.

'No,' I say eventually. 'I don't think so. He's a nice guy.'

Stevie begins to heave himself off the sofa and I sit up straight. I need to grab him and lock down this weekend before he goes out. God knows what time he'll get back from his gig tonight.

'Stevie, are you around on Sunday?'

He clambers to his feet, walking over to the mirror and peering at his cheek. 'Don't know. Maybe. Why?'

'I thought we could go and visit Aunt Tell.'

I try to say it lightly, like I'd suggested catching a movie or going to watch a game, but Stevie knows me too well. He turns to face me, his inexplicable eyebrows raised.

'Aunt Tell? Why?'

'Because it would be nice to catch up with family,' I say, inwardly cringing as the forced words come out of my mouth. It sounds so fake. 'I haven't seen her for years, and as I'm in London it would be rude not to.'

Stevie peers at me for a second, then whips back round to the mirror.

'Cool, well, have fun. But I'm not going.' He snatches up his bag and blows me a kiss.

'Stevie!' I gabble, getting to my feet. 'Why not? It'll be nice! I really think—'

'Byeeeeeeee!'

And with that, the door swings shut.

Great.

'Right, I'll take this one slow, mate.'

'Thanks, man, I just . . .'

All the words leave my body as the ball smacks against the wall and shoots past my left ear before I'd even taken an intake of breath.

I stare at Remy open-mouthed as he chortles to himself.

'God, you're worse than I thought you'd be.'

It's Saturday, and after a week of going into the office every day and trying to befriend my new colleagues, I was ready to spend the day locked in my bedroom with the lights off, scraping any remnants of social energy off the floor and putting them back in my body, ready to do it all again on Monday. Stevie was gigging all day, and apart from a call with Mom I was fairly content at the idea of hibernating. And then I got a message from Remy.

What are your plans tomorrow, lad?

We'd exchanged numbers after spending the majority of the evening chatting at the pub, but I wasn't expecting to actually hear from him.

I certainly wasn't expecting him to ask me to play squash with him. A sport which, up until about forty minutes ago, I'd never even heard of.

'I told you, I'm not a sports guy!' I say, leaning my back against the wall as Remy retrieves the ball. He's wearing loose shorts and a white T-shirt, with matching sweatband across his forehead. His eyes glint every time he picks up the ball and it's making me wonder whether he only invited me along for an ego boost.

'Right,' Remy bounces the ball a few times on the floor. 'Ready?'

We're at a leisure centre in Primrose Hill. It's a characterless building with a strong smell of chlorine and several retired people milling around with towels round their necks.

Although I shouldn't underestimate them. Remy's in his late fifties and is absolutely caning me.

I bend my knees, my fingers clasped around my racket as I lock eyes onto the ball.

Right, I can hit one. It's not that hard.

Remy flicks the ball into the air and taps it with his racket. A surge of adrenaline rushes through me as I lurch forward, thwacking the ball with all my might. It ricochets off the wall and I turn towards Remy to celebrate, while he immediately hits it back and it sails past me. I may as well not even be there.

'I was about to say that was pretty good,' Remy grins at me, flicking open the top of his Lucozade Sport and tipping the orange liquid down his throat.

'I'll take that,' I laugh, rolling my eyes.

'So,' he says, bouncing the ball against his racket. 'How's all that family stuff going then?'

I snort. 'Still pretty shit!' I say.

He gives me a questioning look but doesn't say any more. Usually at this point I'd change the subject, but there is something about Remy that feels so far removed from my ordinary life that it feels all right to talk to him.

'My mom isn't well,' I say, dropping onto the bench as Remy starts tapping the ball to himself against the floor (much lighter than he was hammering it to me).

'Oh?'

I bend down and lean my elbows on my knees. 'Early onset dementia.'

God, I hate saying that. Every time I say those words they fly out of my mouth like they don't belong there. I want to wrestle that horrible phrase down and launch it out the window.

Remy catches the ball and turns to me. 'I'm sorry, lad. That's fucking horrible.'

I shrug. 'My brother lives over here but he hardly ever comes home, and she has a sister who lives in London.'

'Oh yeah? Whereabouts?'

'Epping,' I say, and Remy nods. 'Mom has started talking about her, and I tried calling and writing to my aunt to see if she'd come home for a while and see Mom, but she ignored me.'

'Right.' Remy starts tapping the ball up and down on the floor.

'So I thought I'd come here to persuade her myself.'

It's the first time I've said my plan out loud, and as I say it, I suddenly feel like an overly optimistic Dickens character, arriving in London with only the clothes on my back and a heart full of dreams.

Remy turns to me. 'That's very optimistic.'

I shrug. 'I am American.'

'Well, that can't be all you do here,' he says. 'What are your other plans?'

'I'm not sure yet. Work, explore London. See the sights and all that.'

He bounces the ball in my direction. 'I host a speed-dating night once a month, you could come along to that.'

'Speed dating?' I say, dodging out of the way as the ball rockets towards the wall behind my face. 'You old dog, Remy.'

He gives a sheepish smile. 'No, no, I just help run it. It helps raise money for the pub. I'll sign you up.'

'Like you signed me up for squash?' I say, getting to my feet and picking up my racket.

Remy chuckles. 'Well, with any luck you'll be better at dating than you are at sport.'

I'm about to say something cutting back, when Remy hits the ball against the wall and it immediately flies past my poised racket.

Remy raises his eyebrows at me, grinning. 'Even if that's quite a low bar.'

'Hello?'

I step out of the shower and tuck a towel around my hips as Stevie's voice booms through the flat.

After a few more games of squash with Remy (if you can call it that), we went to a pub round the corner for a beer and a sandwich before parting ways.

I decided to stroll back through Primrose Hill park, as the crisp autumn air was refreshing against my warm, post-exercise face. But then the clouds gathered and it started to rain, and of course I had no umbrella or coat with me. My legs would not have complied if I'd tried to break into a run after the hour or so of forced fun Remy had tricked me into. So I strolled through the rain, letting the beads of water hit my face and drip down my neck. There is something quite freeing about turning your face to the sky and letting the rain come down on you, ignoring the natural instinct to race under the nearest shelter or duck your head under your arms. By the time I got back to our flat, my skin was pale and prunish and my hair was dripping wet. Two small puddles surrounded my shoes when I took them off by the front door.

'Hi, buddy,' I say, pushing the bathroom door open, which nearly takes Stevie out as he tries to slip into the kitchen whilst walking down our impressively narrow hallway.

He dodges the door expertly. 'All right?'

I grab another towel and give my hair a rough rub.

Stevie picked up this odd expression almost as soon as he moved to London. I tried to ignore it at first, but when he started answering almost every phone call with an 'all right?' I had to stand my ground. Was he asking me a question? Or telling me he was okay? Commanding the conversation? I couldn't tell and it was driving me mad.

Anyway, I told him how ridiculous it was, but he was having none of it. Now I think he says it more on purpose just to annoy me. A rookie error on my part. Never tell Stevie that something he's doing annoys you unless you're willing for him to start doing it tenfold.

'Yeah,' I say, choosing to believe that on this occasion, it is meant as a question about my wellbeing. 'Good, you?'

Stevie nods and I hear the kettle start to bubble. Stevie also adopted the addiction to tea when he landed in the UK ten years ago. I head into my boxroom and pull a sweatshirt and pants on, then follow him into the kitchen.

'All good,' he says, peering inside the cupboards. 'Although we have no food in.'

'I can get us take-out,' I say, pulling out my phone. 'Oh, while you're here, shall we call Mom?'

Stevie keeps his eyes fixed on the cupboard. 'What, now?'

'Yeah. We keep missing each other all day and I know she'd like to hear from us both.'

Stevie closes the cupboard door and turns his back to me, now facing the sink. 'I can't, I've got some stuff I need to do.'

I pull a face at the back of his head. 'Like what?'

'Also,' he turns to me and walks out of the kitchen, 'I've done you a favour.'

I look up from the reams of delivery options on my phone. Burger, Chinese, Indian . . . it's just like New York.

'I've got us invited to a party.'

'No thanks,' I say, looking back at my phone as I follow him into the living room. 'I'm good.'

'It's tonight,' Stevie is saying, as if I hadn't spoken. 'A masquerade ball.'

'Sounds horrible.'

God, that looks like a good burger. Twenty pounds, though, including delivery – that feels like a lot.

I really need to get to grips with how much things are supposed to cost here. I feel like I'm walking around with 'Hey buddy, I'm a friendly American, scam me!' stapled to my forehead.

'It's basically like black tie and dresses and then we wear a mask. Or, like, fancy dress.'

'Right.'

'It's a PR event for a huge perfume or something. They've hired performers and everything.'

I look up at Stevie, leaning against the doorframe. 'Are you performing?'

He shakes his head. 'No, not my kind of performing. But I know one of the girls who has been booked and she was given a load of tickets to, like, fill up the event.'

Okay, I think I'm going to have to get this burger. I don't care if it's twenty pounds and I'm being ripped off; I'm starving and it looks great.

'Well, have fun,' I say, plucking my bank card from the coffee table.

Stevie raises his eyebrows at me. 'You're coming, Nathaniel. This wasn't a question.'

I smirk. I know Stevie is serious when he full-names me.

'Why?' I say. 'You know I'll hate it. Just leave me here, I'll be fine. I'll watch sport or something.'

'You hate sport.'

'I also hate going to fancy parties in fancy dress,' I quip, pointing my bank card at him.

'I can't leave you by yourself on a Saturday night.'

'I'm a big boy,' I say, giving a fist pump as my order goes through. 'Oh shit!' I look up at Stevie desperately. 'It's not going to be here for an hour. Are you kidding me?'

Stevie rolls his eyes. 'Look, I'll sort your outfit. It'll be fun. You're not spending your second Saturday night in London sitting in this flat by yourself.'

'Fine,' I mutter, all defiant energy having left my body the moment my burger slipped out of my fingers and into standstill traffic.

'Great.' Stevie punches my arm. 'I'll be back later with your outfit. Enjoy your burger. We need to leave here at nine.'

I go to reply when Mom's name flashes on my screen.

'Wait, Stevie, Mom is calling now!' I call after him. 'Can't you just . . .'

But my words are lost as I hear the door slam and I sigh, pushing my fingers through my damp hair and answering the call.

'Hi Mom, how's it going?'

Chapter Seven

Annie

I look at myself in the mirror and feel my shoulders push out with pride.

After weeks of sketching, cutting, gluing and sewing . . . My costume is complete, and it fits me like a glove. Something I pride myself on is to never make a costume that you can't sit down in. We all know the type. It looks amazing when you're stood up and strapped in so tightly that even a rogue cough could pop your left breast out. Heaven forbid you try sitting *down*. Well, say goodbye to your internal organs as they spill out of your mouth in protest at having nowhere else to go. Or, worse, pop out of your bumhole in an angry prolapse.

Hmmm . . . which would be the worst to happen at a party?

That's a pretty good 'would you rather' question. Maybe I'll save that for the next time I'm on a date.

Anyway, wearing one of my costumes will not have you flirting with a trip to hospital or sacrificing something important like a kidney. They're all made from thick, stretchy fabric. It doesn't stick to your skin and highlight every dip and curve; it skims over your body like a comfy yet fabulous hug. I mean, this all started because I was making clothes for myself, and who wouldn't want that?

My bat costume has a black, slightly furry bodysuit that dips into a sweetheart neckline around my chest. Over the bodysuit I'll be wearing flared trousers made from lace with gems and diamantés glistening through the fabric. The best part is the cape, which billows behind me in a heavy velvet fabric and then when I pull the little lever . . . out pops an incredible set of wings.

My hair will be loose and my mouth (although painted red with lipstick) will trail small specks of blood down my chin. I did toy with the idea of getting grotesque fangs to complete the look, but I decided against it. I didn't want to not be able to talk to anyone. Or, worse, sing a bit too intensely and accidentally spit them out and lose them in the myriad of legs on the dance floor.

Although that would be pretty terrifying. Imagine a pair of teeth landing in your drink?

My outfit is almost the exact same as the sketch I drew in the summer. I mean, I had longer legs and much better eyebrows in that sketch, but hey, you can't have it all.

'Okay!' I call, coming out of my room. 'What do you think?'

I jump into the living room, holding my arms stretched wide in a 'tah dah!' motion. Penny and Tanya are both sitting on the sofa, craning over Penny's phone. When they see me, they look up and gasp.

'Wow!' Tanya gushes. 'Annie, it's incredible. Did you really make all of that?'

I nod. 'Yup.'

'Give us a twirl,' Penny says, clambering to her feet. 'I want to see it all.'

I hold my arms in the air like a ballerina and twirl on the spot as Tanya claps her hands together.

'I think it's the best one you've made,' she says. 'Honestly, those trousers are *sublime*.'

I grin. 'Thanks.'

'Can you make me a pair after?' she adds, peering at the lace. 'I'm serious.'

I shrug, laughing. 'Sure.'

'Are you going to wear a mask? We have to, don't we?' Penny asks Tanya, who nods.

'Yeah,' I say. 'I just need to finish it off.'

'You'll look great,' Tanya says, picking up her water bottle. 'It makes me wish I was going in fancy dress.'

I pause, my smile faltering. 'What do you mean? Are you not?'

'Well, not really,' she says, shaking her head. 'I've got this amazing dress which is quite *Bridgerton*-esque and a mask, but it's not nearly as cool as your costume.'

I look at Penny, who is curled up on our armchair. 'What about you, Pen?'

She looks up from her phone. 'I've got a dress, too; it's not as fancy as Tanya's but it is pretty nice.' She turns her phone towards me to show me a picture. 'I managed to get it from a charity shop.'

I look at the photo. It's a gorgeous, pale pink, floor-length silk dress.

Penny catches my expression. 'What?'

'Nothing,' I say, suddenly feeling ridiculous standing up in front of them in my bat costume like a five-year-old. 'I just thought we'd all go in fancy dress together.'

'We are!'

'*Proper* fancy dress,' I say, flapping my arms stupidly. 'You know, scary Halloween costumes.'

'Oh, I'm sorry.' Guilt sweeps across Tanya's face. 'The theme is masquerade ball, so I just thought I'd wear a dress this year. There will be lots of other people in scary costumes, though!'

Penny frowns. 'Really?'

'Yeah! They've hired performers and I'm pretty sure the waiting staff are all dressing up as witches.'

I raise my eyebrows at her. 'So I'll look like I'm working there?'

Penny snorts and I kick her.

'You'll look like the best-dressed person there,' Tanya says, her eyes earnest. 'Honest.'

I shrug, flopping onto our lurid pink beanbag.

Penny puts her phone down. 'You are still going to wear it, aren't you?'

I look down at my fingernails, and for some ridiculous reason I suddenly feel like I might cry. 'Well, if I'm the only one I'll look a bit stupid.'

'No, you won't!' Tanya says at once, and I see the protective-older-sister side of her take over. 'It's so incredible that you can make these costumes. If you let me pass on your Instagram to some of my clients, you'd be working in Dior like that.' She snaps her fingers with such conviction I can't help but smile.

'You have to wear it, Annie,' Penny says. 'How long have you been working on it for?'

'About six weeks.'

'And you're seriously not going to wear it because we aren't wearing fancy dress?' She raises her eyebrows at me. 'That's ridiculous.'

'That's easy for you to say,' I say childishly. 'You're going to look like a princess.'

'I'm wearing Uggs underneath.'

'No, you're not.'

'Comfort is key.'

'Annie, if you don't wear your costume I'll be really upset,' Tanya says. 'And actually, we won't go to the ball.'

She folds her arms triumphantly and I resist the urge to point out that this would work in my favour, as I'd much rather stay in and throw our annual Halloween party like we normally do.

'Okay, fine,' I say, giving in to their intense stares. 'I'll wear it.'

'Yay!' Tanya claps her hands again. 'Now, who wants a biscuit?'

I nod and get to my feet, my costume suddenly feeling hot and a bit too tight around my body. The bodice feels itchy and the trousers, which a moment ago felt loose and freeing, now feel as though they're gripping my thighs and splitting at the seams.

I shut the door to my bedroom and carefully peel the

costume off and step into my normal clothes: baggy trousers and an oversized hoodie. To my annoyance, I can feel the tears burning behind my eyes again. I blink them away crossly.

'For goodness' sake, Annie,' I say to myself, turning to look at myself in the mirror. 'Just because they don't want to go in fancy dress it doesn't mean you have to have a meltdown. It's no big deal! It's just one night of the year! Get over yourself.'

But I somehow can't shake this cold feeling in my gut that this is about more than a Halloween costume. It's the first time they've both gone along with the grain and I've been left to be the odd one out. We're usually the odd ones out together.

It's not very fun being the odd one out when you're alone.

Chapter Eight

Nate

I take a swig of my beer, feeling a stab of annoyance as the mask itches my nose. Like it does every time I move my face in any way whatsoever. Stevie wrangled me into this mask in the cab ride over. It's a cheap thing, made of some form of fake silk. You know, the kind that crackles with electricity and will no doubt give me an electric shock or turn me into a superhero if I don't pick my feet up properly when walking on any carpet. I tried taking it off the moment we got here, but there was a guy on the door making sure everyone had their masks on.

I did wonder for a second if Stevie had booked me into some sort of sex party. I know I've told him I'd like to meet someone, but Jesus, that would be some level to go to just to help me out with some matchmaking.

We're now standing at the bar, both swigging beer. The ball is set up on the top floor of the hotel, which is sandwiched behind a load of clubs in Soho. All the walls are decorated with blood-red drapes and the tablecloths are sleek and pearly with mountains of decorations. Milling around the floor are the other guests, standing in groups and delicately sipping from champagne flutes. Unlike me and Stevie with our cheap, static masks, their masks are crafted to their faces, curling around their eyes and made from a sturdy, customised plastic. The room is pretty full, and each person looks more expensive and important than the last. I'm amazed we got in so easily. Sweeping across the floor are various wait staff, all dressed in smart trousers and waistcoats with fake knives sticking out the back of their necks. Their not-so-subtle nod to Halloween.

But it's the performers who are the most eye-catching. They're towering over the crowd of guests in stilts, some bent in two with a set on their arms and their legs, dressed in incredible jet-black catsuits. Their stilts are covered by huge streams of fabric, and their heads are entirely covered in masks. They look like some form of megaspecies that's the product of a bat mating with a giraffe.

'Do you reckon you could do that?' I ask Stevie.

'What?'

I nod to one of the performers who prowls past us both.

Stevie watches them. 'I can walk very well in heels.'

'I know.' I take another swig of my drink.

'We're going to have to dance soon, you know.' Stevie raises his eyebrows at me and I huff into my beer bottle.

'I hate dancing.'

'I know. Sadly I was the only one to be gifted in that department.'

I shoot him a look.

Stevie wanted to arrive at the ball early to make sure that we got in okay. His dancer friend, Emmy, was on the door and wanted to sneak us in before anyone pulled out a guest list. I did ask Stevie why we're here if we're not on the guest list, but he lightly told me that the dancers knew that the event hadn't sold out, so they all invited some mates to fill the place up a bit and enjoy the corporate life for once.

I can see what he means. Every waiter skimming past is carrying a tray topped with bubbling glasses of something expensive, or little canapés that seem to change with each circle of the room. We didn't even have to pay for our beers. Stevie just took them from the bartender and turned away, almost expertly, and nobody said anything. I tried not to scoff in Stevie's face and hand over my card, but he shot me a look which told me all I needed to know. It seems that everyone here is so rich that they don't need to spend any money at all. Hey, maybe that's how they all got so rich in the first place.

I give my mask a tug as a flock of women swan past us, all dressed in sleek gowns.

Earlier today, I looked up Aunt Tell's address on Google after Stevie left the flat to 'go out' and I worked out my route to get to her house in Epping tomorrow.

I've decided that if I'm going to turn up unannounced, I need to do it politely. So, I've planned my journey to arrive at eleven thirty in the morning, laden with flowers and cake and a big, 'hey, look at this, your nephew is in London!' smile.

Stevie used to say how she never did much when he was living with her, so I'm hoping that I'll be a welcome surprise (which feels a bit presumptuous considering she's spent the past few weeks ignoring me). We can spend the day together chatting and reminiscing. I've only met her around eight times in my entire life, so God knows what we'll reminisce about, but I'm hoping my visit will end with Aunt Tell being so full of nostalgia for her childhood that she'll be with me on the first flight back to New York to see Mom. And there we have it. I can go back home, Mom will be happy, and everything will go back to normal.

Well, not this current normal. A better normal. The normal we used to have.

Chapter Nine

Annie

So it turns out that there is a foolproof plan to find the confidence to wear your homemade bat costume to a fancy party when your mates are next to you looking like contestants for *America's Next Top Model*.

I don't think there will be many people who need to see this plan, but I'll share it anyway. Just in case.

Step one: have a temper tantrum. Now, it's quite important that you do this alone, especially when you are thirty-two years old. My temper tantrum involved taking the costume off, crying into my pillow whilst watching *Mean Girls* and repeatedly thinking *Why me?*

Honestly, I was one play of Evanescence away from being right back to my fourteen-year-old self.

Step two: call your mum. Okay, yes, I was still in child mode at this point. In my defence, my mum is the only person who loves Halloween and costumes as much as I do and fully understands the effort it takes to make an entire costume from scratch. She's also my biggest hype woman. If it were up to her, the costume would have bigger wings and some form of smoke machine.

Step three: play Beyoncé. I don't need to explain this one. It is tempting to play Adele and crawl back into bed but, and I must stress this is of the utmost importance, if you do that then there is no going back. You have been warned.

Step four: get drunk before leaving the house, have your friends take several photos of you and dance intensely to 'I'm Every Woman' by Whitney Houston.

Et voilà! You have me, in full bat costume, at the masquerade ball surrounded by glamorous, leggy, beautiful people, feeling like the most powerful person in the room.

Or, at least, that's how I feel right now. Once the vodka wears off, who knows how I'll feel. As long as they don't play Adele I should be fine.

If they play Lewis Capaldi, I'm screwed.

I catch sight of my reflection in one of the many mirrors dotted around the ballroom and feel myself glow with pride.

It's not very often I'll say this, but I look fantastic.

Not in the same way that Tanya or Penny look fantastic. Obviously. Tanya had been thinking about this masquerade ball for weeks so had plenty of time to plan her outfit. She's dressed like an extra in *Bridgerton*, with an incredible gown that pushes her boobs up to her chin and an elaborate, swirly mask that twists over her eyes. Her Afro hair is tinted with blonde flecks at the bottom, sitting perfectly. Honestly, she was made for this theme.

Penny is wearing her pale pink dress. It's less dramatic than Tanya's but more slimming. Her mask is gold and attached to a long stick that she holds up to her face, in a mysterious, very cool manner.

I take in my surroundings. Tanya wasn't joking when she said that this was a party that we couldn't miss. I'm still amazed that we were let in, to be honest, but Tanya strutted up to the bouncer with such confidence that he ticked our names off the guest list without even looking. It's in a huge, grand ballroom, with an embellished ceiling and an enormous, glistening chandelier. A DJ is propped up in the corner, bopping around, and swanning around the dance floor are waiters and waitresses dressed in impeccably neat uniforms and wearing elegant masks. They do all have knives sticking out of various parts of their bodies, though, which I quite enjoy.

In the corners of the room, you can see the branding for Midnight, the new fragrance, that we're all apparently here to celebrate. I'm still not sure how I feel about spending Halloween (my favourite night of the year) at a product launch for a beauty company, but I have to say, I don't think I'll ever get to go to an event as grand as this again. I wouldn't be let in.

Penny loops her arm in mine. 'Come on, let's go get some drinks.'

Almost everyone here is dressed like Tanya, elegant and stunning, but there are some people towering on stilts and bent double, with gory make-up and smiles that split their cheeks. I'm not totally alone, I just look like I've been hired to be here as a performer.

Well, there are a few people also in fancy dress, but not nearly to the same extent that I am. Although that's not new for me. Nobody is ever dressed as extravagantly as I am.

Penny plucks two flutes of champagne from a passing waiter and turns to spot Tanya, who has weaved through the crowds towards some colleagues. I shrug as Penny hands me a glass and we clink them together.

'You really do look amazing.' Penny grins at me. 'When are you going to do the wing reveal?'

I look around. At some point I need to pull the lever and have my bat wings pop out in all their glory. This was fine to execute when the night was going to be spent in our flat, filled with my friends who all know I'm a bit weird and love me anyway. Now I'm at a very fancy event and I'm slightly concerned that I'll display my wings and immediately be bundled away by security for fear of being some form of protester. What sort of protester would arrive in a full bat costume I'm not sure, unless there's something funky in those perfume bottles that's harmful to animals.

Hey, maybe I *should* be protesting.

I might just need some more vodka.

'I'm not sure,' I mumble into my glass, my cheeks warming as another clique of beautiful strangers waft past us. 'I have to do it, otherwise I'll be annoyed at myself for the rest of the year.'

Penny's eyes widen. 'You can't not do it – it's amazing! People need to see it!'

'Yeah, okay,' I say. 'Anyway, how's your week been?'

'Fine. Boring. Same old.' Penny shrugs and looks around the room and I know the conversation about her work is over. The funny thing is, Penny is an actual scientist. She was part of the team that developed the Covid vaccine, for

God's sake. She's by far the smartest person that I know, and I could spend hours listening to the thoughts stored up in her brilliant brain. But to Penny, her job is the most boring thing in the world. She cannot understand why anyone would want to talk about it, and when I slip it into conversation how brilliant she is, she gets annoyed and brushes it off.

So, I've learnt not to dig too deep and certainly not to bring it up in front of any of our friends, and heaven forbid any strangers. Even though it's the coolest thing about any of us. Unless I'm drunk, that is. Give me four tequilas and sign me up for *This Morning*. She'd be nominated for Pride of Britain before she'd finished her drink.

'You know, for a beauty event, everyone looks very . . .' Penny makes a face. I turn around so we're both looking at the same collection of poised, perfect strangers.

'Beautiful?' I suggest.

'Well . . . yeah,' Penny says. 'But like, where is the imagination? You'd think someone would be wanting to steal the show at an event like this.'

'What, like wearing a bat costume with real wings and hanging upside down in the ladies' loo?'

Penny laughs. 'Were you planning on doing that?'

I shrug. 'You'd have to give me a leg-up – the pipe I spotted earlier is pretty high.'

'What if it breaks?'

'Free special effects.'

'Of course.'

We drift into silence and I continue to sip my champagne.

Falling For You

Tanya swans over a moment later, her dark skin sparkling as it catches the light of the giant chandelier.

'Hey, guys,' she says, swiping a champagne flute as it sails past. 'What do you think? Are you having fun?'

Penny nods politely. 'Yeah, it's great.'

Tanya raises her eyebrows. 'Honestly? I didn't organise this event, remember, they're just my client. Real feedback is helpful.'

'It's really boring,' I say flatly. 'Nobody is dancing! Everyone is just standing around looking perfect.'

Tanya looks over her shoulder and nods, chewing her lip. 'That's just what the client was saying.'

'It's not your event though, right?' Penny says. 'So not your problem to fix?'

'No . . .' Tanya says slowly, still peering around at the grand ballroom. 'But if I do fix it then they'll love me forever and let's be honest, Christmas is round the corner and I'd love a bonus. Okay,' she turns back to face us, 'if I get them to play a good song, will you dance?'

'Only if it's a good Halloween song,' I say. 'I'm not getting my bat out for anyone.'

I pause. 'Not a euphemism,' I add into my champagne flute, concerned that Tanya may expect me to flash my vagina as soon as I hear the opening bars to 'Thriller'.

Tanya nods. 'Got it.'

'Oh!' Penny squeals, grabbing my arm. 'Annie should open her wings, too! That'll get people onto the floor!'

'Really?' I mumble.

'Great idea,' Tanya says, spotting the DJ. 'Okay, I'll be right back.'

'Meet you on the dance floor!' Penny calls after her. 'Come on,' she adds to me, plucking another two champagne flutes. 'Get this down you.'

Five minutes later, as I'm gurgling down the dregs of my champagne, 'Bump in the Night' by Allstars starts to pump through the speakers. I grin and Penny whacks my arm.

God, I'm amazed that the DJ even *had* this song.

'That's our cue!' she giggles. 'Let's go!'

She hurtles towards the dance floor and I scurry after her. This is our favourite Halloween song. I mean, yes, you have 'Ghostbusters' and 'Monster Mash', but really, everyone knows that this is the best one.

We start to dance, and as the chorus beats around the room, other people sashay around us. Penny's blonde hair swings around her as she shakes her head, singing along loudly. One by one, people throw their arms in the air and shake their hips, chanting along to the chorus. Penny takes my hand and spins me in a circle and I laugh, the warm champagne bubbles popping in the pit of my stomach.

'It's working!' Tanya cries, bouncing up next to us. 'Penny, this was a great idea, you genius.'

Penny flicks her hair and gives Tanya a wink as she joins us.

'Come on,' Penny nudges me. 'You need to do your wings!'

I glance around, suddenly feeling a bit nervous.

'Yes!' Tanya cries, spotting my expression. 'You need to do it, they're incredible, Annie!'

'Is it not a bit much, for here?' I say, looking at the girl next to me who is dressed as a dog (I mean, come on. What's scary about *that*?).

'No, it's perfect,' Tanya says defiantly. 'Go on, Annie. Do it!'

'Hang on,' Penny says, pulling out her phone. 'Let me film it! Okay, I'm ready.'

My fingers coil around the string on the inside of my cape.

'Ready?' Tanya grins at me. 'Three, two, one . . . go!'

'ARGH!'

Oh no.

Chapter Ten

Nate

I need to start by saying, yet again, that I never wanted to go to this party. Halloween is for children and college students, not adults. I mean, God. Stevie wanted us to go in matching fancy dress! We're not newborn twins. We're fully grown adults and yes, okay, Stevie loves fancy dress, but I'm much more comfortable wearing jeans and a jumper. Halloween for me is just an ordinary Saturday night.

Stupidly, I thought I'd won the battle as Stevie flitted out of the door. I was getting ready to slump in front of the TV and make myself comfortable for the evening, and then Stevie came home with two black masks and a bottle of vodka, and told me that a taxi was arriving to pick us up in thirty minutes.

And now I'm here, on the dance floor, wearing a suit and a static, slippery mask. Stevie is opposite me, bopping from side to side and flicking his head around to try and catch eyes with one of the (many) attractive people milling around. I don't fit in here – I'm far too gangly and not nearly chiselled enough. But I've got a champagne glass in my hand and I quite like this song, so I can't complain.

Or, that was until I got impaled by a wing, right through my suit jacket.

'Oh my God . . . I'm so . . . I'm so sorry!'

The girl attached to the wing tries to move, but this just forces the wing to ping round and pop open my shirt buttons. I yelp and try to spring backwards, but she's fully attached to me, and now we're facing each other. The tightness of her costume means that her body is almost pressed up against my – now exposed – chest and I instinctively hold my breath.

'Argh!' she squeals.

'It's fine,' I gasp. 'I'm sure we can untangle it . . .'

I look round for Stevie, but he's caught the eye of a man dressed as a cat and disappeared through the crowd. I may as well be dead to him.

'Annie, just stay still,' another girl is saying, not even trying to hide her laughter. 'The more you move, the worse it'll get.'

'Yes, please don't move,' I say gruffly, imagining what part of my clothing she will tear off next. I take the wing and try to bend it out of my jacket, but it's rammed so tightly within the buttonhole that it's stuck.

I move it as carefully as I can, desperate not to break it. 'Okay,' I say, 'I just need to . . .'

'Yeah, if you just . . .' the girl says, taking hold of the wing with me. 'I think we need to loop it like . . .'

She twists the wing around the buttonhole. I try not to jump as her warm hand touches mine, but she's fully focused on getting herself free. Of course, she probably hasn't even noticed that she's practically strapped to me and my half-naked chest. Assuming she can't feel my heart racing.

'Look,' she says, her face scrunching up as she successfully bends the wing. 'I've almost got it.'

Around us, everyone has carried on dancing. The busier the dance floor gets, the closer we're pushed together. I follow the guidance of her hands around the wing, and with a snap, she's free.

We spring apart.

'Oh, thank God!' she cries, and it's only then that I look at her properly. I'm amazed I hadn't noticed her before.

She's petite, around five foot, with dark hair and sparkling eyes that are glistening under her mask. Where everyone else is wearing some form of ball dress or some pathetic ears and tail pinned in place, she is wearing a full-on costume. She is head to toe in grotesque, gory brilliance and her wings jut out dramatically, like she's about to take flight. Although, one of the wings is now slightly lopsided.

'I'm so sorry, did I break your costume?' I ask.

She looks down at the wing and I notice her wince. 'No, it's my fault – I should have checked before opening them. Are you okay?'

'Yes, I'm fine. I . . .' I run my fingers through my hair, glancing down at my chest and remembering that my shirt is still open. 'Oh God,' I mumble, turning on the spot and quickly doing up the buttons, swearing quietly to myself.

'Are you American?' she says, when I finally turn back round to face her.

I nod. 'And are you a . . . bat?'

Falling For You

She beams, the pride shining from her face.

'Let me buy you a drink,' she says. 'It's the least I can do.'

I loop the final button through the hole. Well, Stevie is nowhere to be seen, so I may as well get drunk with a beautiful, bat stranger.

'Sure,' I say, gesturing for her to take the lead. 'After you, Bat Girl.'

She looks over her shoulder and grins at me. 'Right this way, American Boy.'

Chapter Eleven

Annie

One thing I did not take into consideration is how I would get the wings *back down* once I'd revealed them in all their glory. When I made the costume, I had every intention of popping them out in the comfort of my flat so I wouldn't need to try and push them back into place. But now I'm squashed up against a bustling bar, next to a (pretty hot!) man and attempting to not impale anyone else.

I mean, yes, vodka gives you the confidence to get the bat out, but it does not give you any form of thought or preparation for what to do when you *can't get it back in*.

'Sorry,' I mumble, glancing to a gaggle of girls who are looking at me like I'm carrying the plague as I try and push my wings down. 'I just . . .'

'Hey.' I glance up at the American guy, properly looking at his face for the first time, which is half hidden by his mask. I initially offered to buy him a drink because I felt bad for almost stabbing him and to have an excuse to flee the dance floor immediately. Turns out I was so distracted trying to flee that I didn't notice how hot he was.

He's wearing a suit, so gets zero points for Halloween

creativity. His mask is also too small for his face, but he has a defined jaw and deep, brown eyes. And there is something else I can't quite place. A feeling just below my heart. It's glowing.

'You go sit down,' he smiles at me. 'I'll get these.'

I'm about to argue, but as I open my mouth I'm shoved closer to the bar by a group of impatient drinkers and I feel my left wing prod into the side of the person next to me. If I don't get out of this crowd soon, I'm worried someone will rip the wings right off my back.

'Okay,' I say gratefully. 'Thank you.'

As carefully as I can, I manoeuvre my way out of the crowd and sit down on a plush, deep-red sofa to the side of the dance floor. The music has switched from Halloween-themed to general pop, but Tanya's plan has worked a trick. The dance floor is buzzing with people jumping around and throwing their arms in the air. I can just about spot Tanya's long arms flailing and see flashes of Penny's blonde hair, and I smile. Tanya catches sight of me and gives me a concerned look and I nod, giving her the 'okay' sign back with my hands.

The adrenaline the vodka was giving me has fully seeped out of my system, and now that I'm sitting alone with a bent wing, I suddenly feel incredibly exposed. Every time someone glances in my direction I get a sharp flash of paranoia that they're laughing, nudging their mates and pointing at me. It's making me feel a bit sick.

I get to my feet just as American Boy is coming back, holding a beer and a gin and tonic.

'Sorry,' I say. 'I think I need to leave.'

I'll get a taxi home and just pretend this whole evening never happened. I'll spend the rest of the night looking on Instagram at the pictures of people wearing the costumes I've made and live vicariously through their smiles.

'Leave?' He looks down at the drinks. 'Why? You can't leave.'

I look up at him. Of course, he's just bought me a drink.

'Sorry,' I say. 'I'll pay you for the drink– how much was it?'

He shakes his head. 'That's not what I meant. I just . . . Why would you leave? Have you ripped someone else's shirt open?'

Despite myself, I laugh. 'No. Just yours.'

'Then what is it?'

I glance back up at him. His eyes are kind. I'm about to tell him how it doesn't matter and that I just need to go and make a break for it. But seeing his worried face, I feel like I can tell him. I mean, it's not like I'm ever going to see him again.

'I just feel like a dick.' I sigh.

'A dick?'

'Like, a bit of an idiot.'

He smiles. 'I know what "dick" means.'

I laugh again. 'Look at me,' I gesture down to my costume. 'What was I thinking?'

'I think you look great,' he says, his face serious.

That warm feeling in my chest glows a bit brighter.

'Come on,' he says. 'Let's have this drink. If anyone is looking at you, it's only because they're jealous.'

I take the glass, feeling myself relax. We both sit back

down on the sofa. 'That's easy for you to say,' I reply, gesturing to his suit with my glass.

He looks down at himself. 'Me?'

'What's scary about your costume?' I continue. 'Who are you meant to be?'

He takes a better look at his suit. His shirt is a crisp white and unbuttoned at the top and his blazer is now draped over the back of the sofa. I can see the outline of his muscular arms under his shirt.

'Ah, well, I am dressed as "man who won't go to therapy and blames his issues on other people". If anything, I'm much scarier than you.'

I laugh into my drink. 'Okay, that's scary. Is it based on true experiences?'

He shakes his head, taking a swig of his beer. 'God, no.'

I smile and lean forward, my wings jutting out against the sofa.

'Are you all right?'

'Not really,' I huff. 'These wings are a pain in the arse. I didn't think about what would happen when I tried to sit down.'

'You should complain to the person who made them.'

'Well, I do love to complain about myself,' I say, pushing a wing under my arm and clamping it down the best I can. 'There, that will do for now.'

'Wait,' he says. 'Yourself? Did you make your costume?'

I smile, the pride that was fuelled by vodka returning. 'I did. I make my own costume every year. I made it before

I realised we were coming here,' I add, nodding towards a group of girls who glide past us in ballgowns.

'That's incredible.'

I smile. 'Thanks.'

'Is that your job, then? You're a costume maker?'

I take a sip of my drink. 'No,' I say. 'I just do costumes on the side. What do you do?'

I notice him fiddling with a ring that he's taken off his pinkie. It's a gold band with a small green stone on it.

'That's nice,' I say, glancing down at the ring.

He looks down at it, caught off guard. 'Ah. It's my mom's. I'm a writer.'

'Are you here on holiday?'

'Nope.' He pushes his lips together. 'I decided to throw it all in and spend a few months living in the bright lights of London.'

I raise my eyebrows at him. 'There aren't many bright lights here.'

'Tell me about it. It's rained non-stop since I've been here. You know, they don't tell anyone that? Every film about London is all sunshine, no rain at all.'

I give him a knowing look. 'It's our best-kept secret.'

He takes a sip of his beer. 'Well, are there any other secrets I should know?' His eyes glint at me and I'm surprised to feel my stomach swoop. 'You can tell me . . . this love of tea is all an act, right? You don't all actually love it that much?'

I gasp in mock horror. 'Blasphemy!'

'Oh no.'

'You can't say that in a room full of Brits, are you crazy?' I grin at him.

'You actually like it, then?'

'Love it.' I smile. He almost looks disappointed. 'Hook it to my veins. I have about six cups a day.'

'*Six?*'

'That's on a good day. If I'm in a bad mood it could be closer to eight.'

He runs his fingers through his hair. 'Just when I thought you might be perfect.'

I smile into my glass, my heart jumping about my body. We fall into a loaded silence as we both sip our drinks.

'Can I tell you something?' he asks.

'Sure.'

'This is the nicest conversation I've had since moving here.'

It's mad, but it catches me so off guard that it takes my breath away. He looks so serious, and he's looking right into my eyes, leaning towards me slightly.

'Really?' I manage.

He nods.

Excitement shoots up my body as he leans a bit closer. Oh my God, I think he's going to kiss me. I want him to kiss me.

'Until you met a bat?' I say.

He smiles. 'Until I met Bat Girl.'

He's so close to me now that I can feel his breath on my face. I could easily kiss him. But for the moment, we're just looking into each other's eyes. The music is blaring around us, but I can barely hear it. It's like we're the only two people in the room.

'I think I . . .'

I pause, waiting for him to finish his sentence, when he stops. He leans back, as if he's being pulled out of a trance, and reaches for his phone from his pocket. I watch him, my heart dropping as I feel the moment slip through my fingers. Suddenly, his face changes as he looks at the name flashing on the screen.

'I'm so sorry,' he says, 'I've got to go.'

'But . . .' I start to reply but he's already on his feet. He holds his phone to his ear and paces through the crowd towards the door.

I watch him go, my heart chasing after him, until he dips into the night with a phone pressed to his ear.

He's gone.

I didn't even get his name.

Chapter Twelve

Nate

It's impressive how quickly you can get a flight out of London if you're prepared to ignore any figure and blindly hand over your credit card. Miraculously, my passport was in my pocket as my form of ID for the party, not that I needed to use it to get in. We weren't even on the guest list.

I left the party as soon as I saw Dad's name flash up on the screen. I hailed a cab and asked to be taken to the nearest airport. Apparently, there was one right in the city.

I tried looking for Stevie as I left, but it was hopeless. It was so busy in the ballroom that all the phone signal had been sucked into the void – Dad's call must have snatched the final collective bar of signal. Although now I'm waiting at the airport for my flight, that's all I'm left with. Time.

I texted Stevie whilst I was in the taxi. I sent him the flight information once I'd booked in and offered to cover his ticket, but I just got a one-line response.

Let me know you land okay.

He didn't even ask how Mom is. Stevie and I are a unit. We're brothers, two sides of the same coin. But sometimes, he can be a real dick.

I lean back against the cold plastic chair, trying to ignore the dubious glances of passers-by as they clock me in my suit. I look like I've just run out of my own wedding.

Stevie will be right where I left him, just quite a bit drunker, on the dance floor with a stranger. He didn't give any of this a second thought. As always, it's me who has to pick up the pieces. Doesn't he think *I'd* rather still be at the party, chatting to a beautiful girl in the first normal, nice conversation I've had in months? Maybe even more than months?

I curse to myself under my breath as the conversation passes in front of my eyes. I've spoken to girls in bars before, loads of times. But this was different. She was different.

I run my fingers through my hair.

I didn't even get her name. I barely said goodbye, I just leapt up and ran away like I was about to transform into a werewolf after spotting a full moon. I mean, God, what must she think?

Feeling a rush of adrenaline, I pull out my phone again and send Stevie a voice note.

'Stevie, one more thing. Can you find the girl who is dressed as a bat and tell her I'm sorry? Will you see if she wants my number? We were chatting before I had to leave.'

As soon as it swoops onto my screen I feel a frisson of embarrassment. How pathetic, sending a desperate voice note about someone when you don't even know their name.

I jump as my phone buzzes. For a split second I expect to

see her. Maybe Stevie has miraculously found her and I can apologise and explain.

It's not Stevie. It's Dad.

I'll pick you up at the airport. Mom okay, just confused. Have a good flight.

I sigh as I finish reading the message and slip my phone into my pocket.

I'm not an expert on life or death, but I think that dementia is possibly the cruellest way to lose someone you love. It happens so slowly. You feel like you're watching them gradually fade away, day by day. Then some days, they remember everything about you and it's like nothing has happened at all and it was all a horrible dream. It fuels you with hope that the nightmare is finally over, and you have your person back. Sometimes it lasts a few days, a week even, usually just long enough to trick you that everything is going to be okay.

And then it sneaks back up on you again. Pulls a bit more of the person away. That lovely, familiar conversation you had the day before is only a memory for one of you.

I know we all think it, but I truly did think that my mom was invincible. She worked two jobs as we were growing up. She was on the school PTA and baked for every cake sale and fundraising event. She worked on the reception in a hospital, and cut and coloured people's hair in the evenings. Every night we'd have someone different round at our house, sitting in our kitchen with a cape wrapped round their neck. They'd chat away as Mom snipped and painted like they were best friends, no matter how well she really knew them. She had that knack with people. She made you feel like she'd known you forever. She made everyone feel safe in her company. She'd look after you.

It crept up on us all. The thing is, you don't think you have to look out for it. Why would you? Everyone forgets things. I've misplaced my keys. I've forgotten to take the bins out. Did I turn the oven off? I think I have those thoughts every day. Doesn't everyone? How was I supposed to know that they were warning signs? That something cruel and relentless had gotten its teeth into Mom and was slowly dragging her away?

She was diagnosed five years ago. By this point, Stevie had been in London for five years. I didn't expect him to move back to Manhattan, but I did expect him to visit more, which he didn't. We've never properly spoken about it.

She was having a good day when I got offered the position in the London office and was adamant that I must take it. I hadn't told her the real reason I was going. She didn't know that Aunt Tell had been ignoring me for weeks, and I didn't want to worry her, so I made it sound like this big, exciting idea that I'd go to London to stay with Stevie and explore the city.

She worried about Stevie, and I know she thought I'd go and look after him like the good big brother I was. She could never understand why I was hanging around so much anyway, and why I would even consider turning down the chance to go on a great adventure. You can't really tell someone that the reason you don't want to go is because of them.

Because you're scared of what will happen if you do leave. That if you turn your back for a second, they might really slip through the cracks and you won't be there to catch them.

Dad called this evening to say that she'd fallen down the stairs. Apparently, she'd been confused about where they started, and her legs didn't quite pick themselves up in the right way. She hit her head and every part of her body as she knocked each step on the way down. She was in hospital now. Dad was with her.

He wasn't telling me because he expected me to come home, but he didn't try and stop me either. Dad wanted me to be in London as much as Mom did, but I saw the fear in his eyes when I told him I'd decided to go. Like he'd have to deal with it all alone. Mom was always the carer of the family; Dad was the fixer. But he can't fix this, none of us can.

Chapter Thirteen

Annie

'You didn't even get his name?'

I take the steaming mug off Tanya as she slips into bed beside me. Penny is folded by our feet like a faithful cat, the only one to turn down a morning cup of coffee, which I'm quite glad about. Her face needs to lose its green hue before she eats or drinks anything in my bedroom.

'He literally answered his phone and ran out of the place. He didn't even look back at me.'

'Pig,' mutters Penny.

'All he left was this,' I say, picking up the ring on my bedside table.

It took me a moment to realise he'd left it, otherwise I would have tried harder to follow him. It's one thing to chase after a guy because you want his number (desperate, cringe, no thank you) but it's another to do it to return their prized possession and then *happen* to get their number at the same time (heroic, coincidental, yes please). But he was long gone before I noticed it glistening on the bench next to me.

'That's a woman's ring,' Tanya says, picking it up to examine it.

'Pig,' Penny says again. 'I bet it's his wife's.'

'Maybe that's who called him,' Tanya says. 'Although, why would you wear your wife's ring?'

'Maybe she's dead,' Penny says, barely audible as her face is pressed against a cushion.

'So, his wife was ringing him from beyond the grave?' Tanya asks sceptically.

'It was Halloween,' Penny says. 'And that would explain why he ran out so quickly.'

'He said it belonged to his mum,' I say, taking the ring off Tanya and putting it back beside my bed.

'Maybe she's dead.'

'Stop thinking everyone is dead!'

'I feel like I might be dead.'

Tanya laughs. 'Well, I did try and stop you from ordering sambuca.'

'You didn't try hard enough,' Penny groans, rolling onto her back. 'You should have locked me in a toilet or told the barman that I was underage.'

She spots my raised eyebrows and thwacks me with her arm. 'I was wearing a lot of make-up, I could have got away with being seventeen.'

'That's nearly half your age.'

'Fuck off! I'm thirty-two!'

'Guys!' Tanya squeals, as Penny and I start kicking and pushing each other from across the bed. 'Stop it! I'm going to spill my coffee!'

I put my arms in the air as a surrender and Penny drops back onto the bed.

'So, he just left?' Tanya says. 'You didn't get his phone number?'

I shake my head, my heart turning over. 'All I got was that he was an American writer.'

'Ah,' Penny says sarcastically. 'A real one of a kind, then.'

I shrug at Tanya. 'I guess it just wasn't meant to be.'

'Well,' she says, reorganising my pillows, 'it was a good night. I think everyone had a good time, there were loads of people dancing by the end.'

I nod. 'It was fun.'

'I'm sorry about your runaway guy, though,' she says, hooking her arm in mine.

'Ah, it's fine.' I lean my head against her shoulder. 'He was just a guy.'

But even as I say it I feel my heart thud, because I know that I'm not telling the truth.

'Have you eaten breakfast?'

I put a hand on my hip and look at Pam, who – like always – is hunched over her laptop, her thin lips pressed together in concentration. She is in the exact same position that I left her in on Friday.

'Huh?' she grunts at me, not breaking her stare with the screen.

'Breakfast,' I repeat, waving my hand in front of her eyes. 'Let me get you something. Shall I go down to Pret?'

I glance out of the window. Today the sun is high in the sky, but there's a light chill floating through London. As I walked to the tube earlier this morning, it had snatched my breath away and I'd nestled my chin into my oversized scarf. The amber leaves are curling at the end of their branches, moments away from snapping off and leaving the trees spiky and bare. It's my absolute favourite weather today. Not quite cold enough to wear a coat, with the sun still glistening, but cold enough to feel a shock in your lungs every time you take a breath.

God, I love autumn. I mean, someone pass me my pumpkin spice latte and put *Strictly* on for goodness' sake!

'I'm fine.'

'It's the most important meal of the day!' I sing and finally Pam looks up from her laptop.

'Well, someone is chipper this morning.'

I feel a pang in my chest. I always go into 'chipper' mode when I come into work, it's my role here. It fits into my and Pam's dynamic. We can't both be moody and distracted all the time. God, the place would be a nightmare.

'I'll make you a coffee,' I say. 'And then I'll go down to Pret.'

Pam gives me a thumbs-up and goes back to the laptop. I wander into the kitchen and fill up the water in the coffee machine, then lean against the counter as an Instagram post flits onto my screen. I immediately fill with pride as a young woman pops up, wearing one of my designs. She wanted a werewolf costume, which I absolutely loved making. It's actually quite disgusting. It has a gory snout that attaches to a headpiece, dripping congealed blood down the chin, and a huge, hairy chest bursting out of a floor-length, haunted-ghost-woman-style dress. She looks incredible, but not just because of the costume. She's growling in the photo, her hands in tight claws and a glint in her eye. She looks like she's having fun, and that's what Halloween is supposed to be about. It's my aim with every costume I make.

Well, apart from mine. Apparently that aim was to stab a stranger in the chest and rip his shirt open.

I slip my phone back into my pocket and put Pam's mug under the spout of the coffee machine, clicking the cappuccino option, even though I know what she really wants is a double espresso.

Let's face facts: I've lived in London for ten years, I'm on and off Tinder like a cat on a hot tin roof. I've chatted to guys in bars before, and many of them have left the conversation halfway through (rude). I usually wake up the next morning barely able to remember what they looked like, let alone feeling any type of way about them.

So, why is this different? Why does it feel a bit like I've been dumped and left with the melodramatic feeling that life is unfair? Why do I suddenly have the urge to look out of a rainy window and sing every song Adele has ever written?

I take Pam's mug out and put mine in its place, selecting the latte option.

It must be because it was Halloween and he said he liked my costume. I mean, at the heart of it I am, of course, self-obsessed. He complimented my most prized work – of course I want to see him again. Perhaps I am just so egotistical that I want to see him again simply so I can soak up his compliments like a deranged, narcissistic sponge.

But . . . it wasn't that, was it? I felt something before

he complimented me. I don't really know what, I just felt something.

And then he ran off into the night like bloody Cinderella.

I sigh, trying to squash my confused feelings down my body as I walk back into the office, handing Pam her coffee. She has the grace to look up at me as I come over. I perch on the desk next to her, holding my mug in my hands, making it clear that I'm here for a chat, whether she likes it or not.

'Go on, then,' she says, taking her mug and closing her laptop screen. 'Tell me all about your favourite night of the year. How was your party? How many costumes did you make?'

I smile, turning my phone towards her and showing her some of the photos my customers have sent over. 'Around fifteen this month.'

Pam raises her eyebrows in a 'get you' way.

'Look at these,' she says, pulling a cigarette out of her shirt pocket and propping it in her mouth. 'You really made all of them?'

'I did. My mum usually makes a few too, but this time it was mainly me.'

'And what about you? What did you wear?'

I take the phone back and find the photo of my costume. Tanya did a full-on photoshoot for me before we left. Mainly so I could send pictures to Mum and Dad and use it for our business Instagram to show off our latest costumes. But also because it's quite a fun part about living with your best friends. I could feel like a severed toenail and all it would take is Tanya and Penny ramping me up and telling me how to pose and I'd be feeling more like a severed toenail with glittery nail varnish on.

Pam lets out a slow whistle when she sees the picture. 'Blimey.'

'I'll take that as a compliment.'

'What happened when you opened the wings, then?' she asks, pinching her fingers so she can zoom in. 'I bet everyone was in bits.'

'Well,' I sigh, taking the phone off her. 'Yes and no.'

'Oh?'

'I stabbed a guy when they opened.'

Pam snorts.

'And ripped his shirt open.'

'Crikey.'

'And then got stuck to him for a good ninety seconds.' Hmmm. Now I look at it like that, it's no wonder he made a break for it.

Pam laughs a deep, gravelly laugh. 'That's one way to get them.'

'Well,' I say, feeling myself redden as I pick up my coffee. 'He actually left not so long after that and we didn't exchange numbers or anything, so . . .'

Pam looks at me expectantly. 'But it doesn't matter,' I babble. 'One of those things.'

'Your costume looks great, though,' she says and I smile.

'Thanks. How was your Halloween? Did you get any trick or treaters?'

She frowns, taking a swig of her coffee. 'Of course not. I closed the curtains and turned off all the lights.'

'Pam!' I laugh. 'What about Rodney?'

Where Pam is round and hunched, Rodney is tall and lean and I don't think I've heard him say more than eight words in the entire ten years I've worked here. But they always hold hands, and I occasionally catch them looking at each other in a way I've never seen Pam look at anyone else.

'Oh, he doesn't care,' she waves a hand at me. 'Now, how's your diary looking today?' She pulls her laptop lid back open. 'Can you get over to Richmond this afternoon to look at a house? We have a family of five moving in eight weeks, the dad is coming next week to look at properties. Can I put you on it?'

I feel a little thrill. I'm always the first one that Pam asks for new clients, not that either of us would ever admit that.

'Sure,' I say. 'Of course.'

'Super.'

'But Pam,' I add sternly, as she begins to hunch back over her keyboard. 'First, breakfast. I'm going to get you a bagel. And a chocolate muffin.'

Chapter Fourteen

Nate

I landed back in New York at around midnight. Well, actually, according to my crumbling body clock that had finally let go of the New York time zone and reluctantly adjusted to London time, it was about 4 a.m. So, when Dad got me back home and I crawled into bed in my childhood bedroom, I was wide awake. I stayed there for about an hour before I decided that being alone with my thoughts in the darkness was not the best way to spend the rest of my Saturday night. I went downstairs with the idea of making myself some hot milk, or whatever it is they do in films to help when the main character is wide awake in the middle of the night.

To my surprise, I found Dad sitting at the kitchen table in the dark, holding his head in his hands.

'Dad?'

He almost jumped out of his skin at my voice and immediately sat up straight.

'Christ, Nate,' he said, laughing a little. 'What are you doing awake at this time?'

Have you ever wondered with your parents about whether you're seeing the real them? They're always acting strong for you, looking after you, protecting you from everything that they can. When do you see the real them? When do they let their guard down?

Well, right then I felt as though I'd walked into a moment where Dad had taken his mask off for a tiny breather. And then as soon as I walked in, he shoved it back on so fast that it made him catch his breath. I didn't know whether to ask if he was okay or just run back upstairs immediately.

'Couldn't sleep,' I said, after a beat. 'It's almost morning in London.'

'Ah,' he said. 'Of course it is.'

'Why are you up?'

'Oh,' he said, gesturing down to his empty glass. I noticed that he'd been drinking. 'I'm not. I'm going up now.' He stood up and clapped me on the shoulder, hiding his eyes from me. 'Night, son.'

I felt paralysed as I watched him leave. A part of me wanted to grab his arm and make him talk to me, but a bigger part of me knew that he wouldn't want to do that. What would be the point? It's not like it can fix anything.

I ended up sitting at the table for a few hours, leafing through an old copy of *The Great Gatsby* that was lying around. Dad must have been reading it to Mom, it's her favourite book. She reads it every holiday, every year.

'Is she okay?'

I'm pulled back into the moment as Stevie's voice echoes down the phone. He rang me, croakily, as soon as he woke up and read my messages. It's about seven in the morning now for him. It's still just me sitting at the kitchen table.

'I don't know,' I say, leaning my head against my palm. 'I haven't seen her. She's been asleep since I arrived. Dad has seen her and says she's okay, though.'

'So she's in hospital?'

I sigh. 'Yeah. We're planning to go and see her later.'

I hear Stevie exhale and I feel a pang of guilt.

'I'm sorry I didn't come and get you. I did try to find you,' I say. 'But I texted you, so you could have met me at the airport.'

As soon as I say it I want to kick myself. Talk about sticking your finger in the wound, Nate.

'I was trolleyed, man.'

'Trolleyed?'

'It's an English word. It means drunk.' I can hear Stevie smiling. He's trying to wind me up. 'I thought it was quite fun.'

I roll my eyes. 'That's a weird one.'

'When are you coming back? *Are* you coming back?'

I take a deep breath.

'I've barely thought about it,' I say honestly. 'I mean, I've left my laptop at yours, but I could go back to work in the Manhattan office and ask you to ship it to me.'

'You're paying for that.'

'Yeah, yeah.'

'You've got to come back though, right? I thought you were making a new life for yourself in London – you can't give up after two weeks.'

God, he is such a pained artist. It's like he's about to burst into song.

'I don't know,' I say. 'It depends how Mom is.'

'Okay, sure,' Stevie sighs. 'Well, tell her I say hi and send her my love.'

Irritation prickles at my skin. This is our mom. Why is he talking like a greetings card?

'Tell her yourself.'

'What?'

'Well, you're going to call her later, right?'

I hear Stevie puff. 'Well, yeah, if I can! I've got a show tonight and with the time difference it isn't the easiest thing.'

'I managed to do it when I was in London,' I say before I can stop myself. Even though he's thousands of miles away, I can see the furious look he'll be giving me right now. But I don't care, he deserves it.

'Yeah, whatever,' he snaps. 'I've got to go. Bye.' Then he pauses. 'Look after yourself too, Nate.'

The line goes dead and it's back to sitting at the kitchen table, looking at the space where Mom normally sits. Just me and the silence of the night. Alone.

I'm not sure how much time passes with me sitting at the kitchen table staring into the distance. It's enough time for my eyes to glaze over, making everything shift slightly out of focus and allowing me to dip into a state of meditation.

Eventually, when it's starting to feel as if my head might fall off my shoulders from sheer exhaustion, Dad reappears. He's in his chequered shirt and jeans, a white T-shirt peeking out under the undone top button. He's tall and thin, with chestnut hair and olive skin, which has been carved with lines for as long as I can remember. Mom once said he had 'twinkly eyes', which I never understood, but I do now. He's a man of few words, but when he smiles his eyes have a little sparkle to them. A small twinkle.

Mom was always the one that took charge in our family. Organised the holidays and the birthdays, decided on the dinner and made sure our clothes were ready for school. She'd even organise her own Mother's Day if she had it her way. Dad is always right behind her, though, smiling. Twinkling.

'Hi, Dad,' I say, as he lifts a coffee pot in my direction. I go to shake my head, and then realise I desperately need something to keep me awake. 'Actually, yeah. Thanks.'

He nods and starts to make the coffee. His jeans are high-waisted and his shirt is neatly tucked in. The brown belt he wears every day is tightened carefully in place, always one notch too tight in my opinion. I don't know how it can be comfortable.

'Have you heard from Stevie?'

I look down at my phone. I haven't heard a peep from him since our call. He'll be getting ready for the show now. I don't even know where he's performing today.

'This morning,' I say, taking the coffee off Dad gratefully. 'He rang to check on Mom.'

Dad nods, sitting in the chair opposite. 'Good guy.'

I try to squash down my anger, resisting the urge to challenge how Stevie could be the good guy when I'm the one who's dropped everything to travel across the world to check on Mom. He can barely be bothered to pick up the phone to call her.

But that wouldn't be helpful, so I keep my mouth shut.

'Visiting hours start from eleven,' Dad says. 'So let's get something to eat before we go. We don't want to eat there,' he smiles into his coffee, 'the food is terrible.'

'Have you been there before?' I ask, surprised.

Dad glances up at me, and I can see him debating whether to lie to me or not.

'A couple of times.'

'For Mom?' My heart rate starts to pick up again. Even though I know that she is safe, tucked up in a hospital bed surrounded by the best people to take care of her, I suddenly feel an immense panic that something else is going on.

'Yeah,' Dad nods sheepishly. 'It's not the first time she's fallen, and she burnt herself just after you left.'

I gape at him. 'Burnt herself? How?'

He gestures towards our electric cooker. 'Stuck her hand on the hob ring. Didn't realise it would be hot.'

We've had that cooker for years – fifteen years, easily. Mom uses it every day, she loves cooking. How could she forget that the hob ring is hot? That's something you learn when you're four years old.

'Why didn't you call me?'

'I didn't want to worry you.'

'Well, I'm worried,' I say, running my fingers roughly through my hair.

We drift into silence, sipping our coffees. Well, Dad is sipping his coffee, his dark eyes gazing off into the distance. I'm picking at my nails angrily.

I take a deep breath. 'How's it been?'

He surfaces from his trance. 'What's that?'

'How's it all been? Here?' I move my arm to gesture around the kitchen. 'With Mom.'

'Oh, you know.' Dad gives me a lopsided smile. 'Never a dull day.'

'Dad . . .'

He sighs. 'It's hard, Nate. You know what it's like. You've been with her for the past five years.'

'I shouldn't have gone,' I say, my chest burning. 'I don't know what I was thinking, but I'm back now.'

Dad looks at me, eyebrows raised. 'You're staying, are you?'

'Yes.'

'Your mom won't have that.'

'It's not up to her,' I say, gripping my coffee cup tightly so it singes the palms of my hands.

Dad goes to speak, and then looks up at the clock.

'Come on then, son,' he says. 'Let's get a sandwich and go see your mom. We might need to stop for another coffee too, you look like you need it.'

He gets to his feet and I frown. 'Isn't there coffee there?'

He laughs gruffly. 'Yup. Terrible.'

We use up all our words on the way to the hospital – not that we shared many to begin with. But Dad doesn't need to say much, and to be honest I'm not sure how easily I could hold down a conversation either. My head is spinning. I can't believe this time yesterday I was getting ready to go to a *ball* without a care in the world, miles away from my life here. I was wrapped up in Stevie's world, the glitz and glamour of my new, exciting life in London. I danced with strangers and even met the most beautiful woman I've ever seen.

A jolt of anger shoots through me and I curse myself, not for the first time since I left the party last night.

Why didn't I get her phone number?

It would have taken me seconds to get it. I could have explained to her that I had to go but that I'd call her the next day. What was I thinking?

But that's the thing. I wasn't really thinking, was I?

I look out of the window as we skirt past a parade of shops.

She was from London, that much I know, and she said that she made costumes. I wonder what she's doing now. Maybe she's spending the day with a guy who didn't ditch her halfway through a conversation with no explanation.

I frown. No, it's not worth thinking about.

Why do I care so much? The conversation lasted less than ten minutes. She probably doesn't even remember me.

Is there a way I could find her when I get back to London? Just so I can explain and apologise for what happened? Or would she find that incredibly creepy?

I take a deep breath, trying to force myself to remain in the moment as we arrive at the hospital. Dad doesn't even need to think as he pulls into a parking space, knowing exactly where to leave his car and how the ticketing system works. It makes my heart hurt.

How many times has he actually been here with Mom since I've been gone? She'd hardly ever been to hospital when I was living here. I've only been gone for a couple of weeks – how have things gotten that bad so quickly? Is it because I've gone? Has she finally started letting go now that her two sons are on the other side of the world?

Does she think we don't care about her any more?

'Right,' Dad says, clapping his hands together, pulling me out of my spiralling thoughts. 'Ready?'

'Sure, Dad,' I mumble. 'Let's go.'

When we were children, Mom always had this incredible knack of knowing exactly what you were thinking. Whenever she used to read my or Stevie's mind, we'd look at her wide-eyed and gasp, 'How did you know that?' She'd give us a cheeky look back like it was the most obvious thing in the world and say, 'Because I'm your mom!'

Now, arriving at the hospital, it's like Mom is still as tuned in to my thoughts as she was back then. Like she knew I would be terrified of seeing her all curled up and vulnerable, slightly grey-looking and fragile. So, she did something about it.

As I walk into the room, she looks as full of life as she always does. If anything, she needs to tone it down a bit or the hospital will accuse her of faking the whole thing for attention.

'Nathaniel!' she cries as soon as she sees me, holding her arms wide, ready to envelop me in a huge hug. I try and ignore the tubes attached to her hand as I hug her. She smells like pine cones, like she always does. I like to think that she's worn the same perfume every day for so many years that it's just permanently part of her skin now.

'What are you doing here?' she says, as I sink down onto

one of the plastic chairs. Dad leans forward and gives her a kiss. 'Why aren't you in London?'

'I came back,' I say. 'I'm back for good, actually. It was just a holiday.'

Mom frowns at me, her face stern. 'No, it wasn't. You were going over to start a new life, a new adventure. Don't you talk to me like I can't remember.'

Despite myself, I laugh. God, dementia is weird. Mom couldn't remember how to walk down a flight of stairs two nights ago, but she perfectly recalls a conversation we had last month.

Much like mine, Mom's hair is dark and curly. It falls down to her shoulders, but only just. Her curls are so tight that if you pulled them straight, they'd almost reach her middle. Stevie and I used to like to do that when we were little and giggle as we let them go and they'd ping back up to her shoulder blades. She has half-moon glasses that she has always worn on a chain and fierce, dark eyebrows which have defined her face long before the supermodels made them fashionable.

'Well, I'm back now,' I say. 'Anyway, how are you? How are you feeling?'

I take her hand gently, wincing as I notice the red blisters from where she burnt herself.

'Oh,' she bats me off. 'I'm fine! This is all a bit of drama over nothing. Who hasn't fallen down the stairs once in their life? I just tripped.'

I push my lips together. This is where it gets you. She makes it all seem so ordinary and like we're crying over nothing. She's so stern about it that occasionally I fall for it and start second-guessing myself. Is it really dementia, or are we all just obsessing over something that's not there?

But then she'll try to run away from you in the middle of the night and look terrified if you try to touch her and suddenly you see it, the ugly beast with its claws firmly dug into her. You can't deny it after that.

'It's been quite nice here actually,' she continues, her tone light and conversational. 'The nurses are wonderful. There's one who looks just like Stevie. Have you heard from him?'

I meet her eyes. 'Yeah, I have. He's at work, but he sends his love.'

A line I must have used one hundred times before.

'How are you . . .' I look down at my hand entwined with hers and my heart lurches. My pinkie finger is bare. The ring has gone.

'What?' Mom says. 'What is it?'

'I . . .' I stare at my hands, mentally trying to remember the last time I saw it. Mom gave me that ring when I was about fourteen and Stevie had started wearing her jewellery. She didn't want me to feel left out so she gave me her emerald ring. Since she got sick, I've started wearing it on my little finger.

I was wearing it at the party, I'm sure of it. I showed it to that girl . . . and then . . .

Shit. Did I leave it there?

'Sorry,' I say, realising that Mom is staring at me, looking worried. 'Nothing. I just left something at a party I was at before I flew over here.'

Mom brightens, slapping me lightly on the arm. 'A party!' she swoons. 'With Stevie?'

I smile reluctantly. 'Yes. He dragged me there.'

'How is London?' she says, pulling her sheet further up her body. 'I want to know everything. Have you fallen in love with Keira Knightley yet?'

I try not to laugh. Guess who watches *Love Actually* every Christmas?

'Not quite.'

'Well, have you met any nice people?'

I sigh. It seems stupid to tell Mom about a girl I'll never see again, but she looks so happy to be chatting with me about my new life in London, and what else do I have to tell her about? That I figured out the best bus route to and from work and I enjoy sitting on the top deck because it feels a bit like a rollercoaster?

'There was someone at the party, actually,' I say, and notice Dad look up from his newspaper.

Mom squeals. 'And?'

'I think she's got my ring.'

Mom practically passes out. 'You gave her a ring! Oh, Paul!' She grabs Dad's hand excitedly.

'No,' I say quickly. 'Not like that. God, I don't go around proposing to girls I've just met! What do you take me for?'

'A romantic?' Mom smiles and I roll my eyes at her.

'We were at a Halloween party that Stevie dragged me to and she was dressed as a bat.'

She frowns. 'A bat?'

'Yeah. It was fancy dress. Or it sort of was. Her costume was the best. She made it herself.'

Mom gives me a look. 'Very impressive.'

'But it doesn't matter anyway, as I ran off without getting her name, let alone her phone number. So I'll never see her again.' I say it quickly to try and fight off the inevitable pang I get every time the memory replays in my mind.

'Why did you run off?' Mom says, outraged. 'That's very rude, Nathaniel.'

'Well, Dad was ringing.'

'So? You can speak to your dad anytime!'

Mom catches a look between me and Dad and I see realisation fall on her face. Silence stretches between us as we all stare at the horrible ominous elephant in the room.

'You know, me and your Aunt Tell went to a Halloween party once when we were teenagers. I don't know how Tell snuck me in, I was far too young.' She knits her hands together, smiling. 'She put a sheet over my head so nobody could see how young I was and told the bouncer I was a ghost. I was wearing huge heels, so I looked taller. Then as soon as we got in, I whipped it off.' She laughs to herself. 'It was so much fun. Your grandma was furious when she found out. Tell used to do things like that all the time. She was so *naughty*.'

I smile. If I hadn't had to fly back here then I would probably be at Aunt Tell's by now, chatting about Mom. I might even have managed to persuade her to come back to New York with me.

'When are you going back to London, then?' Mom asks again, breaking the silence.

'I'm not sure I am,' I say, trying to make my voice sound light. 'It was a nice trip, but I'm glad to be home.'

'Nathaniel.' She gives me a stern look. 'You are going back to London. I'm not having you stay here.'

'I want to stay here.'

'Well, I don't want you to. I want you to go back to London so you can tell me more stories about what being a Londoner is really like.'

'Stevie can do that.'

I want to kick myself as soon as I say it. Stevie could do that . . . if he ever called her.

'Nathaniel,' she starts again. 'You need to go back to London. I'm fine. *We're* fine.' She reaches out and takes Dad's hand.

His eyes have started to twinkle again.

Chapter Fifteen

Annie

I tap my foot and glance at my watch, trying my best to stay calm and not obsess over the amount of time Jade, the shop owner, is taking to find the fabric I've requested.

Twelve minutes. I have twelve minutes to do an eleven-minute walk to my next house viewing and meet a new client. And Jade isn't even back with my fabric yet.

I pull my eyes away from my wrist and look out of the window. London is particularly beautiful today. We're in the first few days of November, and as we slowly edge towards December, the Christmas spirit is lingering around the corner, but we're not quite there yet.

Instead, we're in the blissful in-between time where everything feels a little bit still. The trees are bare, finally free of the colourful coats they've boasted all autumn. Now they stand skinny and spiky, branching up into the sky in jagged, naked shapes. But you can still find the ambers and golds of their leaves scattered over the London parks and hidden patches of greenery.

The air has turned crisp and fresh, the sort that shocks

your lungs every time you take in a long breath, and Londoners now walk down the streets wrapped up in oversized scarves. It's like we're hibernating, saving our energy before reappearing in our full glory as soon as December arrives, when everyone is expected to roll their bodies in glitter and don a set of novelty earrings.

Shit. I've just wasted two minutes thinking about how beautiful London is. I've lived here for ten years; you'd think I'd have got over it by now.

I got a call late last night from Mum, saying that we've had an order come through for a gremlin costume for an eighteenth birthday party. Apparently it's a fancy-dress theme with everyone dressing in an outfit beginning with the letter G (for birthday boy, George). Even though I was half asleep when she called, as soon as Mum started talking I felt my mind spark awake with ideas. I could see the costume twisting together in front of my eyes and knew I had to get to the fabric shop as soon as I could or I wouldn't be able to concentrate at work.

I knew my favourite Camden fabric shop would have what I had painted in my mind. Sure enough, almost as soon as I walked in, I spotted a sample of a metal-grey, shimmery fabric with midnight-black and aubergine-purple scales glistening under the light. I snatched it up immediately and ran to the till.

Although Jade is lovely, she's unbelievably slow and always likes to have a chat. Usually I love this, but I have a meeting in . . . oh God, seven minutes.

'Here we are!' I hold my breath as Jade reappears.

'Thanks, Jade,' I say. 'Sorry, I'm in a bit of a hurry.'

'No bother,' she says happily, carefully folding the fabric and wrapping it in tissue paper.

I hold my card out, ready to jab it into the card reader, when I hear the bell ring behind me as someone else walks into the shop.

'Hello, Stevie,' Jade says. 'How are you?'

Oh God, please don't start talking to this person before I've paid. I cannot politely listen to small talk right now. I'll explode.

'Sorry,' I gabble. 'Jade, can I just . . .'

'Oh!' She laughs and taps a button on the till. 'Yes, of course. Thirty pounds, please, love.'

I tap my card and grab the bag of fabric. I turn to charge out of the shop, almost crashing straight into the tall blonde man behind me.

'Shit, sorry!' I call over my shoulder, as I leap out of the door and onto the pavement.

Six minutes to do an eleven-minute walk. Thank God I'm wearing trainers and a good bra.

Ten minutes later and I'm charging around the corner to Spitfield Street, my feet burning and the back of my neck damp as I place silent curses on every slow walker I've been trapped behind. In particular, the couple who refused to stop holding hands and took up the entire pavement, too distracted being all in love and unbearable.

I take a deep breath as I spot Katie, my favourite estate

agent. As we tend to deal with fairly affluent clients, they almost always come with a high price point for their new homes. This means that we generally use up-market estate agents, which is fun.

Katie is smiley and always just as giddy as I am about walking into these grand houses. Not that either of us ever let on. Also, she'd never bat an eyelid at me for being late.

'I'm so sorry,' I gush as I reach her. 'I had a nightmare getting here.'

Katie smiles. 'No worries. Your client isn't here yet.'

'Thank God.' I unwrap my scarf as quickly as possible, my face burning.

'So, do you want a quick debrief?'

'Yes, please.' I dig around in my bag for some perfume. 'I am listening, just making myself smell less gross.'

Katie flicks open her folder and starts going through the notes.

'Oh,' I say, 'before I forget, was there an interior designer on this one?'

Katie gives me a knowing look. 'Of course. Thomas Tyrrell.'

I pull a face. 'Fancy!'

She laughs. 'I'll leave you to it.' She hands me the keys. 'Just drop these back once you're done. Also, I love your jumper.'

I look down and realise I'm wearing a jumper I made last spring. It's tangerine orange, knitted in a thick wool with strands of hot pink woven through.

'Oh, thanks!'

'You're going to tell me you made it, aren't you?' She grins and I laugh.

'Yeah, I did, actually. But it's—'

'Don't try and tell me that it's rubbish or something ridiculous like that.' Katie holds a hand up at me. 'I like it, own the compliment. It's cool.'

I press my lips together. 'Thank you.'

She waves at someone behind me and I turn, noticing my client get out of a shimmering black Mercedes, slamming the door shut behind them. I haven't met this woman before, but you can spot one of my clients a mile off.

They're always immaculately dressed. The clothes are always plain and tailored, skimming across their bodies perfectly, but never with too much skin on show, and they always have glossy, expensive-looking hair. The men have shiny shoes and glistening cufflinks, and the women are tilted in delicate high heels.

Basically, they're the opposite to me, in my knitted jumper and Doc Martens. But I think that's why they like me. I'm an ironic Brit. They absolutely love Pam.

'Hi,' I say, giving my most winning smile and holding out my hand. 'Is it Michelle? I'm Annie.'

The woman shakes my hand and removes her sunglasses. 'Hi, Annie,' she says. 'Thanks so much for showing me around.'

I smile, gesturing for her to follow me up the stone steps. 'Not at all. Right this way.'

Michelle is head of HR at a global tech firm and is being

sent to London for twelve months to work in the Bank office. She has two children, both under four, a husband and her mother coming with her, and they move in five weeks. This means I have to find them the perfect house, nursery for the children, and any other amenities they might need.

I use the word 'need' loosely. Nobody *needs* a private sauna and steam room. But that's what I'm paid to do.

I click the front door open and can't help but let out a gasp of delight. The walls are a crisp white, with wooden panelling and glistening, champagne-coloured lights. The chestnut wooden floor sparkles under the light, and the staircase curves upwards, wrapped within a thick, black banister.

I check myself as Michelle walks in behind me. Right, focus, Annie. You're not moving into this house, and for good reason. One month's rent in this place is a third of your annual salary.

'I'll leave you to have a look around,' I say. 'I'll be waiting here if you have any questions. The place comes with all the furniture you see, but of course if you need anything that isn't here but you're interested in the house, let me know and we'll be able to arrange that for you.'

Michelle nods, her eyes scanning the hallway as she wanders through to the kitchen. I lean back on the banister and pull out my phone as it starts to vibrate in my pocket. I see Mum's name flash onto my screen.

'Hey, Mum,' I say, moving towards the window. 'I'm just with a client. And I picked up the most amazing fabric earlier.

I'll start making the costume tonight. I have an idea in my head, so I'll send you over a sketch to get your thoughts. Did they send over their measurements yet?'

'Oh!' Mum says, and I realise I've caught her off guard by my barrage of information. 'Not yet. I'll check.'

'Great. I'd like to get started tonight.'

'Sure. Listen, I was calling to see if you were still coming to Richie's christening on Sunday?'

I pause. Richie is thirty-eight.

I frown, fighting off an unpleasant image of a hairy, burly Richie in a princess christening gown. 'Richie's christening?'

'His daughter's,' Mum explains, reading my mind. 'Arabella. Her christening. I did tell you about this.'

I have no memory of this.

'Well, I've already RSVP'd on your behalf and said you'd come,' Mum says, reading my silence and taking an uppity tone I don't hear very often.

I roll my eyes, feeling like a teenager. 'Right. So, really, you're not ringing to ask me if I'm coming? You're telling me I'm coming.'

'Reminding you,' she says sweetly. 'Why don't you come home tonight after work and have dinner with us? Then we can go together in the morning. I have a dress you can wear. I finished making it this week. You'll love it.'

'What colour is it?'

'Purple.'

'No, thank you.'

'Dark purple! Like an aubergine colour.'

Hmmm. That does sound quite nice.

'Okay, fine. Thanks, Mum.'

'Message Dad with the time you'll get into the station and he'll pick you up.' I can hear her smile and my heart warms. 'We're making stew.'

Chapter Sixteen

Nate

I elbow my way through our flat door.

I only travelled with the suit I was in for the ball, which meant that during my stay in New York, I had to wear the clothes I had intentionally not taken with me to London. Think high school jerseys and jeans that skim the top of your ankles and are stained with various mystery patches from years ago. Why Mom never threw any of these clothes out, I have no idea.

In a way, it was a stroke of good luck, otherwise I would have been stuck in my suit, or wearing the plaid shirts and faded jeans that Dad has worn for the past twenty years. Although I'm pretty sure he only has one pair, so that would have left me in one of Mom's dresses. Stevie would be thrilled. Or, if I looked better than him, furious.

'Hello?' I call through the flat as I kick the door shut behind me. As soon as I stepped off the plane I was greeted with a steady torrent of rainwater, hitting me at all angles. It's what I heard one passenger describe as 'wet rain', which sounded insane to me, but her friend nodded seriously and they both carried on chatting like it was completely normal.

My flight didn't land until nine, and it's almost midnight now. From the silence that greets me as I walk through the flat, I gather that Stevie is out at another gig. Even if he hadn't said hello back, I would have heard his music. He's like a walking Spotify megamix. One day it's ABBA and Cher, the next it's Green Day and Sum 41. He's been that way ever since we were kids.

The London streets were bustling as I sailed through the city on the top floor of the 24 bus. I could see clusters of people huddled under canopies outside bars, sucking on cigarettes and hunching their shoulders, and restaurants humming with groups of friends and lovers, leaning over tables and laughing. Out of nowhere, I felt an odd pang of longing as I watched them, like I wanted to jump off the bus and join in. They all looked so happy. It's the first time I've experienced London the way I had imagined it would be in my mind.

Well, that and the night I met Bat Girl.

Stevie hadn't managed to find her after I'd left the ball. He didn't see my messages, which I'm kind of glad about. If she wasn't already royally freaked out about me running off without even saying goodbye, let alone apologising, my drunk brother ambushing her with a second-hand, desperate apology would probably have tipped her over the edge. And Stevie isn't exactly subtle in his plots to find me a girlfriend, so God knows what he would have said to her when he was fuelled by gallons upon gallons of espresso martini.

Yeah, it's a good thing, really. If I was meant to see her again, then Dad would have called thirty minutes later. By that time I could have asked for her number and her *name*, for God's sake. But he didn't, so this is just how it's meant to be. Although I really miss that ring.

I grab a beer from the fridge before stretching out onto the cold, lumpy sofa. Stevie has done his best, filling the place with plants and artwork, but it's missing the comforts of my New York pad. Well, a decent sofa is the least you would hope for.

In typical Mom fashion, she was fine for the entirety of my visit. She continued to downplay everything, remaining steadfast that she just tripped over her own feet and fell down the stairs, just as anyone could have done. There was no reason for me to have come back.

If I hadn't been with her the past five years, I would have believed her. She was so convincing, it's almost impossible to imagine that she isn't fine. But I know the truth, sadly.

She shooed me out of the house and back onto a flight to London at the first opportunity, insisting that I carry on living out our London dream, taking care of Stevie and finding Keira Knightley or Emma Watson. She shamelessly told me that she was living through me and made me promise to send her more postcards. (I didn't even realise that was a thing any more. I call her every day and send her pictures constantly – is that not good enough?)

I ended up only being in New York for three days, taking some last-minute time off work. Thankfully, working as a writer means I can pick the work back up again pretty quickly if I write in the evenings, so Brian wasn't concerned about the short notice when I called him up. However, this has put me back a week or so in my quest to find Aunt Tell. But on the plus side, Mom did chat about Aunt Tell a lot over the past three days, which made me feel more confident about my plan. If she loves her so much, then surely Aunt Tell must love Mom that much too? Maybe it'll be quite easy to persuade her to come home for a bit to visit Mom.

Dad didn't say much during my visit, just stayed by Mom's side and made himself busy around the house. But when my taxi arrived, he hugged me in that tight, strong way he always does and told me to take care of myself, and we went back to pretending that everything was normal and not talking about Mom's illness. But at that moment, it suited me fine. It was much easier to get on a plane pretending that her dementia wasn't real. Hell, if Stevie and Dad do it all the time, then why can't I?

I look up as the door clicks open, and to my surprise Stevie walks in. He's out of drag, but I can tell by his red face he's come back from a show. He always scrubs his make-up off like he's scrubbing red wine out of a carpet, and it means his face holds a pink tinge for a few hours afterwards. His hair used to be a clear giveaway, too, having a life of its own after sitting under a wig and hot, bright lights for hours, but since he shaved it and bleached it blonde, it's much tamer.

'What are you doing here?' I say, getting to my feet and grabbing the suitcase he's lugging behind him.

He shoots me a death look, which makes it clear that he's spent the last however many hours sitting on a Megabus. 'I live here?' he says, like it's the most obvious thing in the world, which I suppose it is.

'I thought you'd be at a show,' I say, kicking the door shut as he stumbles in and throws himself on the sofa next to me.

'I was,' he replies, his voice muffled by the cushion his face is squished against. 'It was a lunchtime show, in Manchester.'

'Cool.'

'Not cool; it took seven hours to get back. The traffic was so bad.'

Stevie started drag a few years after he moved to London. I'm not sure whether he'd always wanted to be a drag queen, but he always loved dance, music and performing. He's exceptionally creative, so really, when he told us that he'd started performing as Stevie Trixx, it felt like a natural fit. It was like all of his talents had been combined into one.

'Are you okay?' I ask, peering down at him as he stares mindlessly at the ceiling.

'I'm so tired,' he groans. 'I've worked the past ten days straight.'

He lifts his head slightly so he can see me. 'How's Mom?'

I think back to her in the hospital, making everyone laugh and chatting to all the nurses and fellow patients like they'd known each other for years.

'Exactly how she always is,' I say after a pause. 'Acting like nothing had happened.'

Stevie drops his head back onto the cushion. 'I'm glad she's okay.'

'She misses you,' I say, unable to help myself. 'She was asking all about your shows.'

Stevie unlocks his phone. 'Yeah, I'll send her some pictures or something. I miss her too.'

I sigh inwardly. There is no point trying to push Stevie any further on this. It'll only start an argument – and for what? He knows I think he doesn't speak to Mom enough and I find it extraordinary that he seems to not want to speak to his own mother. Who also happens to be the kindest, most supportive person in the world.

But, like I said, there is no point in saying all that. It's not like I haven't said it before.

'I missed you,' Stevie mumbles, his eyes fixed on his phone.

'Yeah?' I say, taken aback.

'The flat is too quiet when you're not here,' he continues. 'I'm glad you're back.'

'Well, I'm glad to be back,' I say automatically.

Stevie flings a floppy arm towards me and pats my arm, the closest we'll get to physical affection.

'Are you sure you're all right, man?' I say. 'Was it a bad show?'

He shakes his head, not looking up from his phone. 'Just tired, feeling a bit drained.' I nod, getting to my feet. Stevie looks up at me, his eyes widening. 'Where are you going?'

'I was going to take a shower and go to bed,' I say. 'Why?'

'I thought you might want to watch a film with me or something.'

I look at him, feeling like I'm back looking at six-year-old Stevie, asking if I'll play hide and seek with him after school. 'Yeah, of course,' I say. 'And have you eaten?'

He looks up at me and I know the answer.

'I'll order us some food,' I laugh, ruffling his head as I walk towards the kitchen.

'I'll do it,' Stevie calls after me. 'I can't have you getting robbed again by a shitty burger joint. I'm supposed to be looking after you.'

I poke my head out of the kitchen, frowning at the back of his bleached head. 'I thought I was meant to be the one looking after you.'

He waves a hand at me, scrolling through Just Eat. 'You look after enough people already, Nate.'

Chapter Seventeen

Annie

As I crash through the door of our flat, I make the mistake of glancing at myself in the hallway mirror and feel the instant surge of dismay I get every time I look at it. Penny put it up and she's about two inches shorter than me, so when she looks in it she can see her lovely sunny reflection beaming back and then leave the house with the comfort of knowing that she's about to have a great day. When I look, I only catch sight of my chins and neck and leave the house knowing that if I walk into Waitrose at Christmas then some tweedy toff might mistake me for one of the turkeys.

I fling open the suitcase in my room and start chucking things inside it. Clothes, make-up, pyjamas. I have about forty minutes until I need to leave the house to get the train back to Mum's and Dad's house.

'Hello!'

I look round to see Penny and Tanya standing at my door, both looking a little pink-cheeked and suspicious. They climb onto my bed, Penny immediately burrowing her way under the covers like she always does (she says I have the best bedding in the flat, which is true) and Tanya perches alongside her, in a far more respectful manner.

'Hey,' I say back.

'What are you doing?' Tanya asks. 'Are you leaving us?'

'Just for the weekend.' I reach out and grab an electric-blue jumper I knitted last winter, swiftly throwing it into the suitcase. 'Apparently I've been invited to my cousin's christening.' I look up at them both. 'You don't want to come, do you? Mum's doing a stew tonight.'

Penny groans. 'I'd love to, but I'm seeing Mike.'

'I've got plans tomorrow,' Tanya says apologetically. 'You'll have fun, though. Tell your parents I say hi.'

'Me too.'

I smile, taking a handful of socks and lobbing them onto the pile of clothes. 'I will.'

'And before you go,' Tanya adds, the suspicious look back on her face, 'we've got something to tell you.'

'We've been doing some detective work,' Penny grins.

I raise my eyebrows at them. 'What does that mean?'

I'm not sure I like where this is going.

'Well,' Tanya starts, clearly desperate to share. 'We were both sad about your missed opportunity with American Boy.'

I feel a pang in my heart.

For God's sake, get a grip, heart. You've met him once, for ten minutes!

'And about him leaving without a trace and you never seeing him again,' Penny adds.

'So, we thought we'd help you find him,' Tanya bursts, practically bouncing up and down at the idea.

I laugh. 'How are you going to do that?'

'Well, that's what I said,' Penny replies. 'But then Tanya had the most brilliant idea.'

'The guest list!' Tanya cries. 'His name must be on it. So, I spoke to my friend Yaz who was on the events team, and she gave me the list. All we have to do is find your guy on Instagram and bam! We've got him!'

I stare at her. Crikey, Tanya is wasted in PR. She should be a detective.

'Is that allowed?' I say. 'What about GDPR?'

Penny huffs dismissively. 'Nobody cares about that, Annie.'

'I think they do.'

'Nobody cares if it's in the name of love,' Tanya cries, beaming at me.

'And if he does care, then you can just block him,' Penny adds and Tanya nods supportively.

I'm about to protest again that this is a ridiculous idea, but curiosity begins to tickle behind my chest. Is American Boy's name on that list? Could it really be that easy to find him? What if it is? What if he's the love of my life and this is my happily ever after?

'Oh, look at her face!' Penny gushes. 'She's totally planning her wedding right now.'

'I am not.'

I will wear white and have a huge veil and my bridesmaids will be dressed in blue.

No, green.

No, all different colours! To match the autumn leaves!

'I don't know,' I mumble, feeling a frisson of embarrassment as I catch their excited expressions. 'Is this not a bit cringe?'

'It's romantic!'

'Everything about dating is cringe, Annie,' Penny says, pulling another pillow from the back of my bed and placing it behind her head. 'Do you find Hinge less cringe?'

Hmmm. She has a point.

'Just let us try and find him,' Tanya says. 'Then you can decide whether or not you're going to message him.'

'You're not going to message him first?' I ask sternly.

Tanya looks as if I've asked her if she's about to shoplift. 'Absolutely not!'

'Penny?'

'Guide's honour,' Penny says, holding three fingers up towards me.

'Okay,' I shrug. 'Fine. Go and internet-stalk to your heart's content.'

Tanya claps her hands together excitedly. 'I'm so glad you said that, because I've already started.'

'What?' I gape at her. 'Tanya!'

'Only with the first guy!' she says, going pink again. 'Is this your American Boy?'

She turns her phone to me and I see a man sitting on a sun lounger, with six women in bikinis draped around him, looking like they're in the advert for the next *Wolf of Wall Street* film.

This is going to be a long weekend.

*

Two hours later and I'm squashed into my corner seat on the train, using my bag as a pillow, watching as we chug deeper into the countryside and further away from the bright lights of the city.

Outside, the rain is lashing down, leaving little trails which wriggle down the window before flying back off again. The cloak of darkness, which appeared at 7 p.m. in September and has been gradually spreading itself earlier across the sky each day, is firmly in place, giving you that magical feeling of it being the middle of the night or the early hours of the morning. I know everyone moans about the nights being so dark in winter, but I love curling up on my sofa under a blanket and feeling like I'm hiding from the world. Of course, I love summer too. I love the pub gardens and the smell of sun cream and the feeling of frolicking across Hyde Park flinging a frisbee at your friends which you're all not in the right state to catch after a bottle of rosé. But you can't beat autumn. It makes me feel safe.

I know this isn't the coolest thing to say, but I love hanging out with my parents. It doesn't take much for me to throw my weekend plans out of the window and spend two days in my childhood home, with its big windows and squashy, plump sofas. The house always smells of delicious food – there's simply no comparison with the food smells in our flat. Neither Mum nor Dad is Gordon Ramsay, but the smell of lasagne or roast chicken sails around my body and gives me a hug as soon as I walk through the door. Like the ribbons of steam floating from the oven are wrapping their arms around me and giving me a little squeeze.

After the train arrives at Moreton-in-Marsh, I lug my suitcase onto the platform and watch the machine swallow my ticket as I push my way through the barrier. Just like clockwork, I spot my dad immediately. He's sat in the Volvo, tapping the steering wheel as Mumford & Sons blares out of the speakers. Every birthday party, trip to the pub, swimming class or school disco . . . It was always Dad in the Volvo ready at the end of the night, parked outside ready to pick me up.

He spots me and gets out of the car, even though I try and wave for him to stay in his seat. I'm thirty-two and he still feels the need to show me how to open the boot.

'Hi Dad,' I beam. He's wearing his favourite green fleece and jeans. As he hugs me, I smell the trace of a freshly baked cake on his skin.

'Hello, champ!' he says, giving me a little shake. He takes my bag before I can protest and drops it into the boot. Cereal bar wrappers, a coffee cup and the *Sunday Times* greet me as I climb into the front seat. You can usually guess where my dad has spent his day by following the Tunnock's Caramel Wafer wrappers.

'Right,' he says, clicking the car into first gear. 'How are you doing?'

'Fine,' I say, making myself comfy as we start to make our way home. 'You?'

'I saw your latest costume!' Dad says, ignoring my question, like he always does when I ask how he is. 'It was fantastic! Was the lady pleased?'

I smile. We had another commission come through earlier in the week for a polar bear outfit. The brief was 'cool meets gross' and I went all out. I made an amazing catsuit, using white, pale blue and glittering silver fabric and an incredible bear headpiece, with a furry mouth that was stained brown and red from fake blood.

'Loved it,' I smile.

'They always do!' Dad reaches forward and shakes my leg. 'Mum couldn't believe it. She showed all the neighbours.'

I try not to roll my eyes. Mum and Dad wanted more children, but for one reason or another I was the only one who appeared, which means their 'my child is the best' radar is slightly broken. And by that, I mean it's completely out of whack. Don't get me wrong, they were never the type to shove me on stage and force me to audition for *The X Factor*, and then scream at the producers if I didn't get in. They let me do my own thing, but everything I did, in their eyes, was fantastic. Every mud pie I made was the yummiest, every drawing the prettiest, every song I sang the most tuneful. Now, as someone with the musical talent of a toilet brush holder, can you imagine their level of pride and intense 'look how brilliant my daughter is' when I do something I'm actually good at?

It's lovely to have such supportive parents, but it makes me feel a bit uncomfortable when they boast about me to their friends and neighbours, and I can see the thought bubbles popping up above their heads.

It really isn't that impressive. She's a thirty-something adult who makes costumes in her spare time. It isn't even her job.

Can you imagine how embarrassing it is when they do it in front of people like Tanya and Penny? Penny is a *scientist* and Tanya is responsible for half of the fashion stories you read in the papers and see online. I tried saying this to Mum once, but she got all emotional and told me that the world had enough doctors, but there was only one of me. I wanted to point out that if the world was on fire and we were escaping to Mars, I *think* they'd choose a doctor for their new society over a Halloween costume maker, but I stopped myself. She was already on the verge of tears by this point and I knew I was dangerously close to pushing her into a rant about the importance of the arts and how the government should be doing more to support them.

'Here we are then . . .' Dad says, as the car crunches over our drive. I feel a warmth spread through my chest. Our house is like something you'd see in a fairy tale. It's a fat, squat cottage with vines snaking across the front, sprouting pink and white flowers in the spring and catching pockets of snow in the winter. It has a winding garden path, surrounded by plants (and, in October, Halloween decorations), and a red front door that Mum painted herself to bring the place 'some colour' when they first bought the house.

As I get out of the car, Mum flings the front door open and waves enthusiastically. I laugh. For goodness' sake, why does she always act as if I'm the prodigal son returning from the war? I literally spoke to her three hours ago.

'You made it!' she cries, bundling me inside as soon as she gets her hands on me.

'Of course I made it,' I say, grinning. 'I came from London, not the Wild West.'

'My driving isn't that bad,' Dad says, giving me a wink.

'Come on through!' Mum says, and I follow Dad into the kitchen. Three big pans are bubbling away on the Aga, and Mum is swigging from a glass of red wine while she stirs one of them with a wooden spoon. As always, the smell of the kitchen lifts me slightly off my feet.

I sit down on a chair as Dad flicks the kettle on, holding a bottle of wine up to me questioningly.

'Tea is fine, thanks,' I smile.

'Dinner will be ready soon,' Mum says. 'While we wait, why don't you try on that dress I made?'

I unravel my scarf from my neck. It's multicoloured; I made it from the scraps of wool I had left over last Christmas. I wasn't sure if it looked a bit mad, but when Tanya saw it she asked if I'd got it from Chanel. She was a bit drunk at the time and had just come back from her work Christmas do, but I still took the compliment. Not that she ever repeated it when sober.

'Let the poor girl sit down for a minute,' Dad chides, and Mum rolls her eyes.

My parents met when they were seventeen. Seventeen! If I'd married when I was seventeen, I'd have ended up with anyone who held any resemblance to John Paul from *Hollyoaks*. They met in college and, apparently, instantly knew that they'd found the *other half of their soul*. And yes, that is what I've seen them write in their anniversary cards to each other.

I know that they were secretly hoping that I'd also find 'the one' when I was young and spend my twenties travelling the world and being in love, just like they did. They'd never admit it – but I know they're desperate for me to meet someone. God knows what they'll do the day I finally bring someone home for them to meet. I'll have to sedate them in some way, or try and time it to be in January when they're ploughing through their annual 'I am never drinking again' month.

'How's work?' Dad smiles at me as he puts a steaming mug down on the kitchen table. 'How's Pam?'

'Is she still smoking at her desk?' Mum grins.

Last year, Penny, Tanya and I had to move out of the flat for six weeks while our landlord finally got round to tackling the mould that was skirting around our walls like condensation on a shower screen. Penny moved in with Mike (and his three housemates, who all sit on different parts of the hygiene scale) and Tanya moved in with someone from work. I came home, not that I really had much choice. It's not that I didn't have any other friends that I could ask. It was more that if my mum had found out that I'd needed somewhere to stay for six weeks and not come home . . . Well, let's just say that she would have been dressed in black for the rest of her life to mourn the loss of her daughter, who chose a friend's sofa over her childhood bedroom and home-cooked meals.

Anyway, I didn't fancy commuting to London every day, so Pam let me work from home while the work was going on. I organised all the viewings with houses and schools and spoke to any prospective clients before matching them with someone in the team who was based in London. On paper, it sounded great. A clean, warm house for a month. A fully stocked fridge and washing that's lavished in fabric softener.

In reality, Mum and Dad saw it as their chance to see me 'in the real world' and made no effort to hide the fact that they were desperate to watch me work so they could look at each other adoringly and praise themselves for creating a functioning adult. Pam met them over Zoom, as they insisted on 'popping in' to the kitchen every time I was on a call to eavesdrop, and – if they had their way – get involved. I mean, thank God I don't work in sales. They'd be standing behind me demanding the client take the deal before they ring up their parents and tell them what's what.

Luckily, my parents seem to love Pam even more than I do. And the feeling turned out to be mutual. They are a similar age, so can chat for ages about ABBA and EastEnders. I got very little work done that month.

'She's all good,' I smile. 'She liked my costume for Halloween.'

'So she should!' Dad says loyally. 'Actually, did you hear back from Atif?'

Mum's brow knits. 'No, I didn't, I'll send him a message.'

I try not to groan. Atif is the editor of our local newspaper, where Mum spent my entire childhood emailing the team pictures of me in my costumes, until one day she met Atif's wife at the bakery and somehow managed to wangle his phone number out of her. I'm sure Atif rues the day that he woke up with a penchant for sourdough.

'Why are you messaging Atif?' I ask, already knowing the answer.

'For his Halloween piece in the paper!' Dad says. 'He always loves to include your picture.'

'No, he doesn't.'

'Yes, he does! He told Mum, didn't he?'

'Yes!' Mum chirps back.

I roll my eyes. There is no point telling her that Atif is just being polite.

'Now, what's next?' Dad smiles at me. 'Have you got any more orders in?'

I take a sip of my tea and feel myself warm at the sweetness. Dad always puts a spoonful of honey in it, even though I told him that I gave up the habit years ago.

'Just the gremlin one that came through the other day,' I say. 'I've nearly finished.'

'Fantastic,' Dad beams at me. 'I can't wait to see it.'

I smile, picking up my phone which has burst into life at the sudden influx of signal and is vibrating wildly.

My three-way group chat with Tanya and Penny is going ballistic. For a second, I fear that they may have spotted a mouse again and they're demanding I come back to London to sort it out (last time, they both hid in Tanya's room for hours one night squealing whilst I chased it out of the house and promised that I spotted where it went and carefully – and securely – blocked its entrance. Reader: I have no bloody idea where it went, but I was so delighted that it had disappeared and they'd stopped screaming that I was prepared to swear on the Bible if it meant I could go back to bed).

But when I open the messages I see that Tanya and Penny are sending me endless photos of men's Instagram profiles.

Annie – we're trying to work out which man is the most likely to be your type. It's quite tricky without you here, but Penny has come up with an equation!!!!

I grin as I look at the seven emojis Tanya has sent along with her message. Tanya is the most glamorous, suave person that I know, until she writes a WhatsApp message. Then she may as well be christened Judy from Accounts.

Male, aged between 18 and 40.

I nearly drop my phone. Eighteen! What does she take me for? I could be his mother!

I mean, I would have been fifteen, but still.

American looking, nice man x the likelihood that Annie will find him attractive considering his type is a woman dressed as a bat.

I raise my eyebrows as I read Tanya's following message.

Isn't it BRILLIANT?

I mean, that makes absolutely no sense. They've clearly cracked open the champagne Tanya was gifted by a client last week.

We will shortlist and show you when you get back. We're so excited!

I take a deep breath and send up a silent prayer.

Please God, don't allow my friends to message these poor, unsuspecting men asking if they're a) American and b) like female bats.

Chapter Eighteen

Nate

'Here he is, back from the States!'

I look up from my desk and see Brian peering at me in between the forest of plants. He's wearing a green corduroy shirt and his unruly hair is springing out of the top of his head. It somehow looks wilder than it did the last time I saw him.

'Hey, Brian,' I say. 'Sorry for taking off like that.'

He waves his hands at me. 'It's all good. Is everything okay now?'

An image of Mom and Dad flits into my mind, waving at me from the front door as I climbed into my taxi to go back to the airport. Mom was leaning into Dad's shoulder, beaming at me, looking exactly as she always does. Just like nothing had happened at all.

'Yeah,' I say, after a beat. 'All fine, thanks.'

'Good!' Brian cries, slapping his hands together and making me jump. 'I need to speak to you about stories.'

He walks round to my desk and takes the spare chair, plonking himself down and using his feet to drag himself towards me. I feel myself brighten. Finally, I'll be able to experience London properly if I'm being sent on actual *experiences* for work.

'Great,' I say. 'I can be flexible with days. I used to work weekends quite a bit in New York.'

'Weekends?' Brian scrunches up his face in confusion.

'Yeah, if any of the events are on a Saturday or—'

'No, no, not them,' Brian says dismissively. 'All those events are taken by the rest of the team.'

'Oh.' My face falls. 'Well, what do you want me to write about, then?'

'You tell me!'

He rests his elbows on his knees and looks at me expectantly.

Damn. After our first conversation, I was really hoping he'd forgotten about this wild idea that, as a writer, I should just be able to think of brilliant stories on the spot.

'I wasn't expecting to . . . let me brainstorm and get back to you,' I say.

'No need!' Brian says at once. 'Let's just brainstorm some ideas now.'

I try to stop the alarm from showing on my face. It's like a six-word horror story: *let's just brainstorm some ideas now.*

'Right,' I say, realising that he's waiting for me to say something. 'Sure.'

I glance around as Helen from HR swans past, desperately hoping that she will distract Brian in some way and save me. One thing I've already noticed about Brian is that he is a professional procrastinator. He spends all of his time flitting from one desk to the next wanting to chat about nothing in particular. I've yet to see him open his laptop, let alone sit at his desk, since I started here.

'I'm looking for something fresh and fun,' Brian says, leaning back in his seat. 'So, what you got?'

I blink at him. I cannot think of a single fresh or fun thing.

'Well,' I say, as the thought drops into my mind. 'I'm going to my first football game next weekend with my friend, Remy. I could write about that? My first sporting experience as a New Yorker in England?'

Brian pulls a face. 'Who's playing?'

'Chelsea . . .' I begin, already knowing where this is going.

'Versus Man City? Fuck, no. Nobody wants to read about that.'

I press my lips together, fighting the urge to question whether he'd be more excited if I said it was a Tottenham game.

'What else? What did you do at the weekend? Tell me about that.'

I think of Dad's face when he picked me up from the airport. Mom's reassuring smile as she helped me find clothes to wear from my childhood bedroom. My chest spasms.

'I went to a party,' I say.

Brian snaps his fingers. 'Okay, a party. What else?'

'What do you mean?'

Isn't a party enough?

'What happened at the party? Tell me about it.'

I push my fingers through my hair. 'I'd rather it not be a story about my life,' I say. 'I usually review events.'

'We're just spitballing!' Brian says, holding his hands up innocently. 'I'm just trying to get the ball rolling. Tell me about this party.'

I sigh. 'Fine. It was a masquerade ball for Halloween, launching a big perfume.'

'Fancy! Hey, Helen.' Brian waves his arm at Helen who is walking past again and beckons her over. 'Nate went to a *ball* last weekend.'

Helen raises her eyebrows at me. 'Get you.'

'So, what did you dress up as?' Brian asks.

'I didn't,' I say. 'I just wore a mask and a suit.'

'You didn't dress up?' Brian repeats. 'On Halloween?'

'Some people did,' I say. 'There was one girl dressed as a bat.'

As soon as I say it, the image of her pops into my head. Her dark, shimmering eyes and that big laugh.

'I saw that,' Brian grins, turning to Helen. 'Did you see that?'

I frown as, to my annoyance, Brian has started giggling. 'Saw what?'

'That look! Tell us about the bat girl, then.'

'There is nothing to tell.' Honestly, this man is like a child.

'He's going red!' Brian chides. 'Go on, tell us.'

'I had a drink with her.'

'And?'

'And it was nice.'

'*And?*'

'And nothing!' I cry, trying my very best not to explode at him as I turn back to my laptop. 'I had to leave, I didn't get her number or her name. It was a ten-minute conversation, if that. It was nothing.'

Silence falls across the office and I click through my emails, hoping to signal that the conversation is over. When I glance up, I spot Helen and Brian beaming at me smugly.

'What?' I snap.

'There's the story!' Brian says triumphantly, slapping his knees and getting to his feet.

'There is no story,' I say, bewildered. 'Nothing happened!'

'Oh!' Kayleigh says, excitedly turning to Brian. 'We could do like a "Are you my Cinderella?" type story! We could include Nate's picture and try and find her!'

Brian clicks his fingers into two guns towards Helen. 'Love it. Let's do it.'

'Do I not have any say in this?' I say indignantly.

'Not unless you can come up with a better idea,' Brian grins, sauntering over to the finance department.

'Brian,' I start, 'I really—'

'Nate, relax!' he calls, picking up a ping-pong bat and twirling it in his fingers. 'What's the worst that can happen? Gary, take a nice picture of Nate, will you? And let's stick it on the socials and see what happens.'

'"Have you seen this man? Tall, dark and handsome, Nate Simpson is our New York heartthrob trying to find his Miss Right. Were you at a masquerade ball on Saturday 31st October? Did you have a drink with Nate? If so, we want to hear from you . . ." Why have they made it sound like you're a convict on the run?'

I pull two beers out of the fridge and hand one to Stevie, flopping down onto the sofa and groaning.

The rest of my day was an absolute nightmare. Everyone in the office was so excited at playing the role of matchmaker that they all abandoned their laptops to help choose the best photo of me and write my dating bio before plastering it all over social media. We spent the entire afternoon watching to see if any woman came forward who might be Bat Girl.

Spoiler: nobody did.

'I know,' I say. 'And they're supposed to be writers. They all thought it was great.'

'Do you think she'll see it?'

'I really, really hope not.'

Stevie laughs, scrolling through the article on his phone. 'What would you rather? A hundred girls get in touch that you have to date with your boss in the corner, or nobody messaging at all?'

'Nobody,' I say at once. I want Brian as far away from my love life as possible.

'But what will you write about? Don't you have to, like, write something to be a writer?'

I give him a warning look. 'You're not allowed to say that. That's blasphemy to writers.'

Stevie grins and sips on his beer. The football has been lightly yelling at us from the television for the past thirty minutes. I realised, if I was going to spend my Saturday with Remy going to an actual football game, then maybe I should watch a game to try and understand the rules. I said this in passing to Stevie, which led to a full lecture on football culture and how important it was that I cheered for the right team, depending on where I was sat. Also, from the way that Remy invited me, I gathered that giving me his spare season ticket was like handing me the golden keys to the palace, so I needed to treat it with respect.

I've also decided I'll go to Aunt Tell's on Sunday.

'Do you know what's going on?' I say to Stevie, pointing at the screen with my beer.

'Yeah, of course,' Stevie nods. 'I understand football, I just don't like it. That's Marcus Rashford.' He gestures towards a Black man in a purple kit. 'Everyone knows who he is. He's a national treasure.'

'Marcus Rashford,' I repeat, resisting the urge to write the name down so I can revise later.

'How's Mom?'

I look round, slightly surprised. Stevie is still staring at the TV, but I notice a slight change in his expression.

'She's good,' I say. 'I think I'm going to try and call her this evening if you're around.'

He shakes his head. 'I'll leave you to it. I think I'm going out later.'

Shock. 'Where are you going?'

'I think . . .' Stevie says, pulling his phone out of his pocket and opening an app '. . . I'm going on a date.'

He turns the screen and shows me a man with long, dark hair and an eyebrow ring.

'Nice.' I look down at my phone. It hasn't made a sound

since Mom rang me yesterday, apart from one text from Remy sending me a video of a man accidentally falling into a swimming pool.

'I'll stay with you until the end of the game, though,' he says, grinning at me. 'I need to make sure you don't get beaten up on Saturday.'

I roll my eyes. 'It won't be that bad.'

'No,' he says, putting his phone away. 'It's fun. Apparently.'

My stomach lurches as I spot an email from Brian popping up on my phone titled: *I think I've found her*.

'Oh God . . .' I mutter, showing Stevie my phone. Before I can stop him, he grabs it out of my hand. 'Give it back! How do you know my password?'

'You've had the same password since you were eleven,' Stevie says, turning his body around on the sofa to face me.

'Don't send anything back, that's my boss.'

'Oh wow.' Stevie lets out a long whistle.

I groan. 'What? What's he sent?'

'I think this is the shortlist. Forty women have replied.'

'Forty!' I nearly drop my beer.

Despite myself, my heart lifts slightly.

What if she's there? What if it really is going to be that easy?

'And they've sent their phone numbers. Right,' he pulls his long legs up to his chest, 'you're going to pick one and go on a date tonight. We can do a double date, it'll be fun.'

'No.'

'If you don't pick, I'm going to pick for you.'

'Fuck off.'

'So, what did this girl look like?' he says, narrowing his eyes as he scrolls freely through my phone. 'I'll whittle it down.'

'Urgh. I don't know.' I push my thumb and forefinger against my forehead. 'Do we have to do this?'

'Yes. What was her ethnicity?'

'White.'

'Hair colour?'

'Dark.'

'Long or short hair?'

'Long.'

'Right . . .' He swigs his beer. 'That narrows it down. You have fifteen women to pick from. How old do you think she was? Was she older than sixty?'

'No!'

'Okay . . . that takes out you, and you . . .'

'I need another beer.' I go to get up when the TV erupts and the screen is filled with Marcus Rashford, his arms in the air towards the crowd and his teammates leaping on his back, jostling him with animalistic joy.

'I told you he was good,' Stevie says knowingly. I give him a shove as I take his empty beer and walk towards the fridge.

'Do you want to pick her or shall I?' Stevie calls after me. 'Ohh . . . she looks nice. I think she's my favourite.'

'Well, let me look,' I say, kicking the fridge door shut and grabbing the bottle opener. 'She may actually be there.'

'You are into this!' Stevie says triumphantly. 'God, you're such a romantic it's sickening.'

I hand him a beer as he turns the phone to me. 'Contestant number one, Jane.'

I study the picture. It's a woman who looks roughly the same age as me with curly hair and lots of eyeliner.

'That's not her,' I say. 'She didn't have curly hair.'

'She could have straightened it.'

I roll my eyes. 'Fine.'

'Contestant number two, Hayley.'

He turns the phone towards me again and I swat it away. 'Stevie, I don't want to sit through each girl. She's not going to be there, and even if she is I won't recognise her. She was wearing a mask and it was dark . . .'

'Okay, okay,' Stevie says in a horrible, superior voice. 'Calm down. You don't have to do it.'

I feel a wave of relief as I sink into the back of the sofa.

'Thank you.'

'I'll choose for you.'

'Stevie!'

'Jane is free tonight, I'll ask her to meet us at Simmons at nine and see if Jason is free. This is going to be fun.'

I slug my beer.

I instinctively feel it won't be.

Two hours later and I'm sat in a bar opposite Stevie, who has almost finished his second Heineken and we only arrived twenty minutes ago. Simmons is small and dark, with high tables and loud bartenders, shaking cocktails over their shoulders and slamming shots down on the sticky bar. The room is cast in blue light, and the walls are covered in different posters.

'Is this what life is normally like for you in London, then?'

I ask. Stevie looks up from his phone. He's been watching the Formula One highlights since we arrived.

'What do you mean?'

I pick up my beer and gesture to our surroundings. 'How many dates have you brought here?'

He puts his phone down, raising his eyebrows. 'Are you judging me?'

I laugh. 'No! If anything, I'm jealous.'

'So, you can be honest with me. How much are you hoping that tonight is this Bat Girl that you keep talking about?'

'I do not keep talking about her,' I mutter into my pint.

'You do in your sleep.'

'Shut up.'

'Our walls are thin.'

'You're telling me!' I guffaw and Stevie gives me a wicked grin.

I take a swig of beer. 'It isn't her. I'd recognise her from the pictures.'

Stevie huffs at me. 'Wasn't she wearing a mask?'

'Yes, but . . .'

'Anyway,' he waves his hand at me, 'so what if it isn't her? Jane might be really nice.'

'I'm sure she will be.'

Stevie rolls his eyes at me. 'God, you're impossible. Oh! There's Jason.'

I peer round and spot a burly, long-haired man in a T-shirt, looking around the bar. Stevie walks over, leaving me with my beer.

I pick up my phone and check my messages. Jane and I

Falling For You

had been messaging to arrange meeting here, so I'm hoping she'll text me when she arrives. With any luck, she may be pleasantly surprised by how I look in real life versus that terrible photo of me that Brian took in the office. If she arrives at all, that is.

Or she arrives, sees me, and then leaves.

God, what am I even doing here? Why did I let Stevie talk me into this? Why—

'Nate?'

I look up from my phone and spot Jane. I recognise her immediately from her photo. She has bright eyes, curly hair and a big, toothy smile. She looks lovely, but she's not Bat Girl.

'Hey,' I say, getting to my feet. 'Jane?'

Do I hug her? Or is that weird? Shake her hand? Wave? No, hug. I should hug. It would be rude not to hug. Just hug her, for God's sake.

She nods, the opportunity for me to hug her naturally sailing past us.

I'm glad Stevie wasn't here to witness that.

'Would you like a drink?' I ask, moving towards the bar. Jane nods and follows.

'I appreciate you coming,' I say. 'It's a bit of a weird one, isn't it? Meeting like this.'

I feel a light spasm of alarm as the thought dawns on me. Why is she here when the advert clearly said I was looking for someone, and she knows it's not her?

I flag down the bartender and order a beer, and then let Jane order herself a glass of white wine.

Maybe she met someone at the party like I did but was too drunk to remember.

'So,' I turn to her, 'did you enjoy the party?'

'What party?'

I keep the smile on my face. 'The Halloween party? The masquerade ball?'

She frowns, taking her glass of wine from the bartender. 'I don't know what you're talking about.'

'Oh.'

'My friend said you put an ad online saying you wanted to go on a date. She applied for me.'

Ah. 'Oh,' I say. 'Right.'

'I thought it would be fun.' She smiles at me. 'A different way to meet someone, you know?'

'Sure,' I nod, taking a sip of my beer.

Come on, Nate. You're on a date with a cute girl. You knew it wouldn't be Bat Girl, it's impossible you'll ever see her again. Just let it go.

The next day I wake up with a new sense of purpose. Jane and I had a nice enough time, but we left after an hour or so of polite small talk and a brief hug and I was back at the flat by eleven. Stevie disappeared with Jason, and I didn't hear him come in until the early hours of this morning. But when I wake up in my boxroom, with a fresh, clear Sunday stretching out in front of me, I know that I can finally do what I came to London to do.

Today is the day I'm going to go and find my Aunt Tell. Speak to her about Mom and convince her to come back to New York to visit.

I get up, take a shower and start to plan my journey down to Epping. The sky is a bright, powder blue and the sun is blazing out from behind the clouds, but there's a crisp chill in the air. I wrap a scarf round my neck and step out of the front door.

My mom is a New Yorker through and through. She grew up outside of Manhattan with just her mom and sister in a small apartment above a store. She met my dad waiting tables at a restaurant downtown, and they never looked back.

Aunt Tell's early adult years were spent moving to London to follow her dream of becoming an actress. She came here when she was twenty-five and has been performing in theatres ever since. I used to joke with Stevie that he must take after Aunt Tell and I must take after Mom, but he didn't like that.

I take a train to Epping and emerge from the station onto a suburban street. Taking in a lungful of icy air, I begin my walk to Aunt Tell's house, my phone shouting directions at me every thirty seconds or so.

If all goes to plan, I should be able to go back to New York by the end of the month. I'm trying not to think too much about why Aunt Tell has been ignoring my messages and calls for the past six weeks or so. I've sort of put it down to some whimsical idea of all of my emails getting lost in cyberspace or I somehow have her wrong number (even though I totally don't). We'll both just pretend it never happened.

'Turn right,' pipes up my phone. 'Then in four hundred yards, the destination is on your left.'

I look up from my phone, feeling my eyebrows raise as I take in the row of grand houses all sat next to each other like perfect dollhouses. In short, they are all enormous. I can't believe Aunt Tell lives in a house like this.

I count the numbers on the houses and stop walking as I reach number 30. It's not quite as big as the house next door, but with its smooth white plaster and crisp black window frames, it's pretty much the smartest. And still way too big for just one person.

I walk up the drive, noticing her shiny car, and then raise my hand to the ruby-red door. A Christmas wreath is looped round the door knocker, far too early in my opinion, with little fairy lights twinkling around it.

I hold my breath as the knock reverberates through the door. I haven't seen Aunt Tell in years. She might not even recognise me. I know Mom has said that she sends pictures, but I've got no idea what pictures or from how long ago.

The door swings open and my eyes widen as they land on Aunt Tell.

She is a small woman, with honey-blonde hair curled above her head in a large quiff. Her eyes are shadowed with dark make-up and her thin lips are coated in a shimmering pale pink. She's wearing a floral dress and an eccentric scarf. As soon as she sees me, her mouth falls open like she's seen a ghost, and before I have time to recite the lines I had rehearsed on my way over, I'm pulled into a hug.

'Oh Nathaniel!' she cries, clasping my head and rocking me from side to side. 'It is so good to see you.'

I shuffle slightly in my seat, wating for Aunt Tell to reappear with the coffee. I'm perched in a large armchair which has a golden trim and is upholstered with a rich purple velvet. It looks like a chair that's there for decoration rather than sitting on. But she insisted.

After what felt like hours, Aunt Tell finally let me go and bustled straight into her house, commanding me to follow. Her hallway had black and white squared tiles, a glittering chandelier and a sweeping wooden staircase. On the walls were photos of her, looking furious or gobsmacked, mid-scene in various acting roles. The odd picture had her clutching a bouquet of flowers, one hand to her heart, beaming at an adoring audience. I noticed there weren't any pictures of us anywhere. Aunt Tell has never been married or had any children. We are the only family she has, and it's like we don't exist.

Which makes sense, considering she's been ignoring me for the past six weeks.

But she seems so happy to see me! She hardly greeted me like someone she was trying to avoid.

'Here we are!' she coos, placing two china mugs down on golden coasters and beaming at me. She is practically glowing.

'Great,' I say. 'Thank you. Sorry for just dropping in like this, I tried to call, but . . .'

But you never answered.

'It's a lovely surprise!' she says at once, placing her hands on her lap and staring at me. Her eyes are wide and, unlike Stevie, her American accent is as strong as mine, even though she's lived in the UK for half of her life.

I smile, taking a sip of my coffee.

This is the part where I ask Aunt Tell straight whether she can come back to New York, say how Mom isn't doing so good and that she misses her. How seeing her will do Mom the world of good. But when I look up at Aunt Tell's hopeful face, something stops me.

'My goodness,' she sighs. 'I haven't seen you since you were yay high.' She holds up an arm. 'I can't believe this handsome man sat in front of me is my little Nathaniel. I say all of your names, you know. Right before I go on stage each night, I bless each of you.'

I pause, unsure of what to say.

'At the theatre!' she continues, reading my silence. 'When I have a show! Before I go on I say, "God bless Linda, Paul, Nathaniel and Stevie. God bless them all."'

'Oh,' I say, realising that I couldn't stay silent a second time. 'That's nice.'

'It helps keep me calm, thinking of all of your faces.' She smiles, picking up her coffee cup. 'I've got a show tonight – you should come!'

She leans forward excitedly.

'Oh,' I say. 'I can't stay. Sorry, I—'

'I'm playing Beth in *Paula's Race Car* at the Pheasant,' she says, as if I haven't spoken at all. 'It's the other side of town and it's terrific fun. We're halfway through a six-month run.'

'Congratulations,' I say. 'I was actually hoping to speak to you about Mom.' I look at her steadily, ready to catch a reaction, but her beaming expression stays put. 'I was wondering if you had plans to visit her anytime soon.'

'Visit her?' She blinks her heavy eyelashes. 'Back in New York?'

'Yeah.' I sip my coffee. 'I know she'd love to see you.'

'And I'd love to see her!' she cries, her hand flinging to her chest. 'My darling sister.'

I watch her, my mind scrambling to work out what she means.

'Great!' I say after a pause. 'Well, I'm planning to go back to New York soon. I'm only here for a few months, so can I tell Mom that you'll be in touch to arrange a visit soon?' I try and keep my eye contact with her, but she looks away and starts busying herself with the empty coffee mugs.

'Of course! Now, I'm sorry, Nathaniel, but I must ask you to go. I need to get ready for my show. But this was such a wonderful surprise – please come and visit me again soon.'

And before I know it, I'm shooed out of the front door back onto the streets of Epping.

'But you'll call Mom?' I blurt, moments before she shuts the door.

'Of course I will, darling! See you soon!'

And as the door slams, I'm left with three thoughts.

1. She must be the weirdest woman I've ever met.
2. I need to apologise to Stevie for comparing him to her.
3. She's lying.

Chapter Nineteen

Annie

I hold up the swamp-green fabric to the light, squinting as I peer at the hem. The material has an elasticity which is perfect for the cinched-waist look of the design that I am hoping for, but it makes it pretty tricky to keep the hemline neat.

I curse under my breath and pick up my metal stitch unpicker. There is no way that the client would notice that the hem ever-so-slightly veers off to the right, but I'll know. And I like everything I work on to be perfect.

Once I had asked Mum if we could make our own clothes, it was like we opened a door into a new world. Mum's career as a print designer meant she was naturally creative, but she'd never even thought of making her own clothes, let alone tried it. But all it took was several Saturday afternoons poring over books in the library, rewinding clips of television shows and picking the brain of Esme, the woman who ran our local fabric shop, and we were hooked. Where most teenagers were out drinking or hiding from their parents at the weekends, I couldn't wait to spend Sundays with Mum. We'd design the item together, whether it be trousers or a dress, whatever I fancied really, and then go out and pick the fabric and spend the rest of the day cutting out the pieces and stitching them all together.

Dad would normally be in the kitchen, cooking us up some form of roast, and the evening would end in a fashion show, where Mum and Dad would 'rate' the outfit. I mean, they always gave it a ten, but insisted on doing it anyway. By the time I was eighteen and getting ready to go to university, I had an entire wardrobe filled with my own clothes, and a lot of them I had made from scratch by myself.

I place the fabric back under the sewing machine and slowly press my foot down on the pedal.

All in all, the christening was fine. A standard event with our extended family and friends, lots of chat about mortgages and promotions, engagements and babies. All of which I couldn't really join in with, but it was fine because everybody loved my dress (I ended up wearing a dress I'd made last year) and kept asking where it was from. Which made Mum prouder than she'd be if I announced that I was closing on a six-figure townhouse in Camden, was about to start my new position as Managing Director at the Bank of London and was pregnant with triplets with my gorgeous, highly successful husband.

I got back home to Clapham about three hours ago, and have been glued to my sewing machine ever since.

I hear a half-hearted knock at my bedroom door as it creaks open, but I keep my eyes firmly fixed on my hem. I will not mess this up again.

'I brought you a tea.'

In my peripheral vision, I see Penny sit down on my bed and place two cups of tea on my bedside table.

'Thank you.'

'Well, Tanya made it. I just brought it in.'

Right on cue, Tanya bustles through the door and climbs onto the bed next to Penny.

'How was your weekend?' she asks. 'How are your mum and dad? Ooooh . . . what are you working on?'

I narrow my eyes as the needle skims the final piece of fabric, and then finally turn to face them, letting out a sigh of relief.

Done. Perfect.

'Another commission,' I say. 'This one is a gremlin for an eighteenth. This is the body piece.'

I hold it up so they can see and Tanya reaches forward, fingering the fabric.

'It's beautiful. I love it.'

'Thank you.'

'You seem to be pretty busy with commissions!' Penny says, and I can hear the hope in her voice.

'Not busy enough,' I say, reading her mind. 'But yeah, it's nice that we've got a few more coming in. How are you guys?'

'Good now,' Penny says, tucking her feet under my duvet. 'Yesterday was awful.'

Tanya pulls a horrified face at me and I grin. 'Yeah, I figured from your messages that you'd opened that champagne.'

'And the rest!' Tanya cries. 'We had so much prosecco. God, it was so bad, we could barely move yesterday.'

I smile, taking a sip of my tea.

'But,' Tanya says, blowing the steam away from her cup, 'we actually have good news.'

I raise my eyebrows at her.

'We found American Boy.'

Immediately, I feel my heart lift.

I've really tried to shake this. I only met him once for a very brief conversation. There is no reason why I should still be thinking about him – it's ridiculous! Also, London is a huge city and the chances of us ever meeting again are near impossible.

Unless Tanya and Penny really have found him . . .

'Look at your face,' Penny grins. 'I knew this was a good idea.'

'How have you found him?' I say, ignoring Penny's stupid grin. 'How do you know it's him?'

'It was quite easy, actually,' Tanya says. 'It was just a process of elimination.'

'He had to be on that list somewhere,' Penny says. 'So it was just a case of narrowing the names down.'

'It took a lot of research,' Tanya adds. 'We thoroughly looked through all of their Instagram profiles.'

'You didn't message any of them, did you?'

'No,' they both say in unison, their expressions serious.

'Okay,' I say, turning round on my chair to face them. 'Show me.'

Tanya and Penny share a grin as Penny pulls out her phone.

'Okay, caller . . .' she says. 'Is this your American Boy?'

My heart jumps into my throat as she hands the phone to me. She's showing me an Instagram page, and my eyes wildly scan through it, trying to find his face. Have they found him? There are a lot of pictures of London and skylines, but eventually I find a picture of him and . . .

'Guys!' I cry, outraged. 'I don't think this guy is single! And I also don't think he's into women . . .'

It's a picture of a tall blonde guy. He's wearing a sequinned unitard and is kissing the man next to him, fully on the lips.

'Well, we thought that at first,' Penny says, as though it's no big deal at all. 'But he was the only American guy we could find! He wasn't even on the guest list – he was tagged in a picture from the night.'

'And we thought he could be bisexual!' Tanya says quickly, desperate to keep the fantasy alive. 'He's American, it says so in his profile.'

I scroll through the pictures. 'He's definitely not bisexual.'

'How do you know that?' Penny arches an eyebrow at me. 'You're just making an assumption based on his photos.'

'No,' I say, turning the phone to face them, 'I'm making an assumption based on the "I'm gay, I'm great, I'm gorgeous" T-shirt he's wearing.'

'Oh.' Tanya bites her lip. 'We didn't see that.'

I roll my eyes, but I can't help but laugh. 'You got me then,' I say. 'For a second I really thought you'd found him.'

'We looked through every guy on the list,' Tanya says earnestly. 'It took us hours.'

I feel a pang of guilt. 'Well, thank you. I guess he has just disappeared into the ether.'

'Or maybe you imagined him,' Penny says helpfully, and I give her a look.

'I'm not that desperate.'

'Yet.'

'Shut up.'

'I know what will cheer you up,' Tanya says. 'They're hosting another speed-dating session down at the Clapham Arms next Saturday.'

Penny groans. 'That's not fair, I want to go.'

I smile. Speed dating has become a bit of a weird tradition between the three of us. We first went at university when we were all still single. Tanya had been unceremoniously dumped by some loser called Euan, and Penny found a local speed-dating session that same night. We got pissed and decided to go, and it turned out to be one of the funniest nights of the year. We all put on different accents and set ourselves stupid challenges (I had to see how many times I could say the word 'peacock' and Penny had to convince everyone that she thought she was a real wizard). By the end of it, Tanya could barely remember Euan's name.

'Can't you come and just make up a persona?' I ask.

Penny scrunches her nose. 'That feels a bit unethical.'

'Or,' Tanya says, her eyes wide, 'why don't you *and* Mike go and you can pretend you don't know each other and then, like, sexily meet at the end . . .'

Penny kicks Tanya from under the covers. 'Stop getting turned on about me and Mike, you weirdo.'

Tanya laughs. 'Well, I'm definitely going. Annie?'

'Yeah,' I grin. 'Count me in.'

Chapter Twenty

Nate

'Here you are, then.'

I look up as Remy hands me a plastic pint of yellowy, foamy liquid. I take it in my gloved hands and immediately take a sip.

We arrived at Stamford Bridge about an hour ago. I met Remy outside Fulham Broadway station at nine in the morning, just like we'd planned the week before. I was surrounded by a sea of football fans, all swarming out of the station, chanting and jostling each other in their blue football shirts, and I suddenly felt a bit like an alien in my green sweatshirt.

As soon as we got into the stadium, I ran to the merchandise stand and bought the first Chelsea shirt I could see, blaming the eye-watering cost on the conversion rate. I pulled it on over my sweatshirt and immediately felt like I'd put some armour on. I may not fully understand the rules, but at least I was now blending in with the crowd.

Remy was wearing his flat cap, jeans and a blue Chelsea football shirt. He held his hand out for me to shake as soon as he saw me. Now we're sitting in our cold plastic seats waiting for the game to start.

'Big game, this,' Remy says.

'Yeah?'

He nods, taking a sip of his pint. 'If we win this, we're back to the top of the league.'

I pull a face, hoping I'm hiding the fact that I have pretty much no idea what any of that means, even though I was trying my best to research it on the subway over.

I take a sip of the crisp lager and feel a chill race under my skin. The stands are beginning to swell with people, either dressed in blue or red. Everyone is buoyant and bubbling with excitement.

'Thanks for this,' I say to Remy, gesturing to the stadium.

He nods into his pint. 'No problem, mate. Had the spare ticket, it's nice for you to experience it properly.'

I tuck my free hand into my pocket.

'Have you recovered from squash, then?'

'Only just,' I laugh, sticking out my left leg. 'My calves were absolutely killing me after.'

Remy smiles. 'You'll get used to it.'

'Have you been back since we played?' I ask.

He takes another sip of his pint, watching as the crowds continue to jostle into the stands, all carrying their pints and chatting animatedly to one another. 'No, I only go on Saturdays. It's too much with my job otherwise and, you know, we're here today.'

I pull my jacket closer around my body and glance at Remy. The weathered skin on his face is prickled with the shadow of beard, his small eyes are creased and surrounded by deep lines and his shoulders are hunched up to his ears.

'You're a journalist, aren't you?' he says.

I pause.

'More of a writer,' I say. 'I write for *Take the Time*. It's a magazine that covers different events. So I basically get sent to events and then have to review them.'

'Get you.' Remy raises his eyebrows, impressed. 'You get to go to some swanky events, then? Where has my invite been?'

I grin. Remy would be the perfect person to take with me to any of the events.

'I haven't been invited to any whilst I've been in London,' I say. 'At the moment they want me to write about my love life.'

'Oh yeah?'

'It doesn't exist,' I say, before Remy can get any ideas. 'So, yeah, I'm not writing anything at the moment. But I'm meant to be. I don't know how long they'll keep me here when I'm not writing anything.'

Remy slaps his hand on my shoulder and gives it a shake. 'Well, you're in luck, my boy.'

I glance at him, trying to stop my pint from tipping all over the floor.

'Remy, I'm flattered, but you aren't my type.'

He chuckles. 'It's speed dating tonight. I signed you up after squash last week.'

I'm about to argue when I see the mischievous glint in Remy's eyes. This will be the third time he's taken me somewhere since we've met, and each time it's been fun.

Also, I desperately need to meet someone else so I can stop thinking about Bat Girl. It's pathetic.

'Well, there go my Saturday night plans!' I laugh, giving his shoulder a shake back. 'What about you, then?'

He looks up from his pint. 'What about me?'

'Have you got a girlfriend? Wife?'

That small smile comes back again, but it vanishes almost as soon as it appears.

'Nah, not for me,' he says. 'Not for a long time.'

I stare down at my phone, battling the feelings of self-loathing as I scroll through the list of women (and men) that Brian has sent through in response to the embarrassing 'Have you seen this man?' advert.

I wasn't lying when I said that I wanted absolutely nothing to do with it. But when I got back to the flat after the game, Stevie was out and so, after an hour of mindlessly plodding around, I couldn't resist any longer. Just in case she was there, somewhere on that list. Which, of course, I knew she wouldn't be. And even if she was, would I recognise her? All I remember about her now is her deep, dark eyes and how she made me feel.

How she made me feel? Urgh, get a grip, man. You met her once.

I turn my phone over decisively. Remy advised me to book a taxi to tonight's speed-dating event in Clapham. Initially, he tried to explain how to get the train there, which I thought I'd manage, but when I asked him to repeat the directions I'd obviously pushed him over the edge and my incompetent, lost-male New Yorker charm had well and truly worn off.

On my journey back to the flat, I did think about messaging Aunt Tell, just to follow up on our conversation about her reaching out to Mom. But as I regained signal upon leaving the subway station, I saw she had messaged me first.

Darling Nathaniel, I am so sorry I ended our meeting so quickly, it was lovely to see you. I've put two tickets aside for my show, any night of the week! Would love to see you there. Big kisses.

I'd thought she was desperate to get me out of the house and never have to face me again, but now she wanted me to go and see her show. Why?

I've ignored the message for now. God only knows what Stevie will say if I ask him to schlep across London to see Aunt Tell in a show.

I'm about to get in the shower when my phone starts to vibrate. At first I think it'll be Brian with a fresh batch of single women for me to scroll through, but then I see Mom's name appear on the screen.

'Hi, Mom,' I say, as her sunny face pops up. Her dark hair is twisted above her head and she's wearing a thick jumper.

'Hello, Nate,' she beams. 'It's snowing in New York!'

She turns the camera round so that I can see out of the kitchen window, and I feel a sudden pang of longing as I spot white florets of snow spiral down from the sky. It's Thanksgiving next weekend and I had planned on going home, but then Mom had her fall and I spent all the money I'd saved on the emergency flights, so now I can't afford to go back until Christmas. It's the first Thanksgiving I've spent without my parents, and Stevie is working all weekend as usual. I'm trying not to think too much about it.

'So it is,' I say. 'Is it settling?'

'Oh yeah!' She turns the camera back to her face. 'How are you doing? How's Stevie?'

I feel an instant frisson of annoyance. I guess Stevie hasn't called her this week, then. Again.

'All good here,' I say. 'How are you?'

'All fine,' she nods. 'Your dad and I are just prepping for Thanksgiving. What are you going to do with yourself?'

'Oh, you know,' I say, trying to keep my voice upbeat. 'I've got a few offers.'

I can't tell her that I have no plans and nothing on the horizon.

'Have you been down to the country yet?' She smiles. 'Have you seen the house?'

I lean back in my chair. She's talking about the house in *The Holiday*. A little cottage nestled in between curving trees and strings of ivy, with a winding path and a wooden fence. She always used to tell me that was her dream house.

'Not yet.' I smile back at her.

'I've looked it up,' she says, the camera angle suddenly changing as she puts the phone down on a desk and all I can see is the bottom of her chin. 'And it's based on an area in the Cotswolds.'

'Right.'

'You have to go find it, Nate.' She picks the phone back up and glimmers at me. 'You can't go to England and not see *the house*.'

'Maybe I'll see it and buy it for us,' I say.

Mom laughs. 'Wouldn't that be nice?'

We sink into silence and I sigh, looking around at the thin white walls of the flat. Worlds away from the fat little cottage that we love talking about.

'I better go, Mom,' I say, trying to shift the heaviness in my chest. 'I'm going out tonight.'

'If you meet Keira Knightley, tell her I say hi.'

I laugh, rolling my eyes. 'I will.'

'And send Stevie my love.'

I pause, the laugh evaporating. 'I will.'

Chapter Twenty-One

Annie

'You look so great.'

I smile gratefully at Tanya. After the debacle of 'finding American Boy', Tanya and Penny put in a lot of time hyping me up to make up for trying to matchmake me with a gay man (which, let's be honest, would probably be quite fun, but not what I'm looking for). Penny went to Mike's house, even though we both tried to persuade her to come and just sit at the bar, but she did help us get ready first and vowed to be back later that night so she wouldn't miss out on any gossip. I'm wearing my low-cut burgundy jumper with strings of glitter sewn in that I made earlier this year, along with my jeans and boots. Tanya is wearing a violet dress, tights and pumps.

The bus bumps over a pothole and we both bob up and down.

'So,' I say, grinning at Tanya as the bus gets closer to the pub. 'What are we doing tonight?'

Tanya looks thoughtful. 'Well, do you actually want to meet someone there?'

'There won't be anyone there,' I say at once. This is not my first rodeo.

Tanya laughs. 'Okay. Let's do accents, then.'

I groan. Accents are by far my worst skill.

'Oh God. I definitely won't meet anyone if I do that. What do you want to do?'

Tanya pauses, thinking, and then claps her hands together.

'Oh, Scottish! I've just finished watching *Outlander*. I can pretend to be Claire.'

'Can you actually do a Scottish accent?'

'Yeah. Listen to this: hello, my name is Tanya.'

'That's a no, then.'

She hits my arm and we both laugh as the bus turns towards the street that the Clapham Arms sits on. I reach forward and press the bell.

'Oh, I'm so excited,' Tanya says as we clamber to our feet and stagger down the stairs. 'We haven't done this in ages.'

'Shall we get a Chinese after?'

'Definitely, but don't tell Penny,' she says as we thank the driver and hop off the bus. 'She's jealous enough as it is.'

It's a cold, crisp night and our breath puffs out in front of us like little clouds.

The Clapham Arms is a small pub sandwiched between a Costa and a charity shop on Clapham High Street. It's a Tardis inside, with a squashed bar stacked with every bottle you can imagine, which stretches back a surprisingly long way. It's like climbing into a rabbit hole: on the outside it looks so cute and dinky, but once you're inside suddenly *you're* the cute and dinky one. We've been here a few times over the years. The garden catches the early afternoon sun and, if you go at the right time, is the perfect place to cradle a cider and lightly sizzle your skin.

Tonight, the right-hand side of the pub has been transformed into an arena for dating. All the tables have a limp rose in the middle, and a small tea light flickering hopefully. Singletons are milling around the bar, chatting with friends and stealing glances at the other spectators. Tanya links her arm in mine as we walk straight to the bar. We're greeted by an older man in a flat cap holding a clipboard.

'Good evening, ladies,' he says. 'Are you here for speed dating?'

'Yes, please,' Tanya smiles. The man ticks a few boxes.

'You've got the last couple of spaces. We'll start in a few minutes if you want to get yourselves a drink. There's a special offer on cocktails tonight.'

He gives a knowing look towards the barman and we thank him, slotting ourselves in the only gap available. The bar is bustling with chatter, and the pub smells like a potion of woodsmoke, beer and coffee. Even if a pub only makes one coffee a day, the smell latches onto the walls, adding a certain level of sophistication that you don't get in a nightclub. The type that says: we also serve Yorkshire puddings.

'Okay,' Tanya turns to me, 'what shall we have?'

'Are we going to sit next to each other?'

'Oh no.' Tanya pulls a face. 'If we do, we'll have to date the same guy one after the other. You'll put me off.'

I laugh. She has a point. Also, Tanya is easily the most beautiful person in the room. The last thing I need is to be the afterthought of each date as they move from her to me.

'Okay,' I say. 'No point sharing a bottle of wine, then.'

'Unless we can split a bottle between two wine glasses?'

I look around the room. It's a good turnout, and some of the men here are actually quite attractive.

'Sure,' I say.

Tanya leans over the bar to get the barman's attention and I run my fingers through my hair. I haven't had a proper boyfriend since Tyler – not that I'm really sure he was ever my boyfriend in the first place. He was more like a guy I dated for six months, until he found someone better at a club while I was at the bar getting us some drinks. The cold realisation that our weekends spent holding hands down the street, sharing dinner or rolling around in bed together meant a lot more to me than they ever did to him hit me like a bucket of water to the face. The whole thing knocked my confidence in a way I hadn't expected. It wasn't that I felt like crawling into a hole and never letting any man see me again because I was so hideously unattractive, more a solemn acceptance. Like, fine. I'm not attractive. Guys don't fancy me, they're always looking for the girls who are naturally beautiful, confident and sexy. So, I'll stop bothering. I'll focus on myself instead. I'll go full 'me'. I'll wear the bright clothes and the baggy dresses, and I'll throw every pair of heels I hate into the bin, even though I used to stuff my feet into them because that's what everyone else was doing. It's like I went into full self-defence mode. Like, I don't care if nobody fancies me because

I don't *want* anyone to fancy me. It was easier to focus on myself and hide behind this magnificent steel wall than put myself out there again.

Don't get me wrong – I've had the odd date, snogged strangers on a dance floor and spent evenings flicking through Hinge with Tanya and Penny, but that's as far as it has ever gone. I never see anyone more than twice; that's quite enough for me.

Except, since I met American Boy, I'm not sure if it *is* enough. I felt attractive and empowered talking to him even though I was being my full, weird self in my bat costume. It was something I hadn't expected to feel. I'd given up searching for that feeling because I'd convinced myself that I didn't want it anyway. But with him, it felt quite nice. Like someone had flicked a switch inside me.

Tanya puts a glass in front of me and starts to glug the white wine into it. Once it's teetering over the lip of the glass, she stops and I take a quick sip.

'Okay,' Tanya says. 'Let's sit at opposite ends. I'll sit in that corner,' she points with her wine glass, 'you go over there.'

I nod. 'Deal. And if it's all going terribly?'

'Then we'll have a great story to tell Penny later, and remember, Scottish accents!'

Tanya winks at me as the man with the clipboard begins to shepherd everyone into seats. He's perhaps in his fifties, with olive skin and small, kind eyes that crinkle at the corners.

'Okay, everyone. I'm Remy and I'll be your host tonight,' he says. 'Ladies, if you take a seat and the gents will rotate. You have two minutes to make a good impression, and when you hear the bell you must move on. Ready? Take your seats, gents.'

I take a sip of my drink as a tall, dark man sits in front of me.

The bell rings.

'Fancy seeing you here.'

Chapter Twenty-Two

Nate

I don't believe it.

Since the moment I hung up the phone to Mom, my afternoon has been a disaster. First, the cab dropped me at the wrong pub, and I only realised when I called Remy as he was nowhere to be seen. Then it rained and I had to do a ten-minute walk to the correct pub, so I arrived with a minute to spare. Of course, I didn't have an umbrella (why would I need one if I was getting a cab?) so I turned up damp, slightly sweaty and late.

And now I'm sitting opposite this girl.

This girl who won't stop talking about *Love Island*.

'It's really good – you should watch it! They have loads of series online. Series four is the best, though. Honestly, it's so good.'

I've been here for about ninety seconds and have said four words. They were: 'Hey, how are you?'

She hasn't even given me her name. A common occurrence for me, it seems – why am I unable to ask a girl her name? She's a redhead and petite with big shoulder pads and even bigger eyelashes. She's cute, but I cannot gauge whether this date is going well or if she just wants someone to listen while she talks about *Love Island*.

'So,' I say, desperately trying and failing not to interrupt her. 'What do you do?'

Her face falls and I feel a stab of embarrassment.

Well, who can blame her? It's hardly the most exciting question.

'I work in marketing,' she says flatly. 'You?'

'Ah!' I reply. 'I'm a writer.'

We fall into silence and I want to kick myself.

Argh. I should have just let her carry on talking about *Love Island*. I glance over my shoulder at Remy, who is sitting at the bar with a pint. He gives me a wink.

Right, come on, Nate. You can do this. You've chatted up women before. There was even a time when you felt like you were pretty good at it.

'And what do you—'

I am interrupted by the shrill bell from behind the bar, jangling loudly.

'Right,' I say, as all the men around me get to their feet. 'Well, it was nice to meet you . . .'

I trail off, waiting for her to tell me her name, but she's pulled out her phone.

I shuffle over to the next seat and plonk myself down opposite a girl with the largest glass of wine I've ever seen.

It's funny; as our eyes meet I feel a little tug behind my chest. But then she opens her mouth and starts speaking.

'Hallllooooooooooo, hoo are ye?'

I blink at her, my mind spiralling with panic. Oh God. I have absolutely no idea what she just said.

I take a sip of my beer and nod. It's fine, it's just a different accent. I'll get used to it in a second.

'Ah ye dyau?'

I blink. Nope, I still don't know what she said.

'Sorry,' I say, after realising that she's waiting for me to reply. 'I didn't get that.'

Her face changes and so, incredibly, does her voice.

'You're American?'

'Er . . . yeah,' I say. 'You're . . . sorry, where are you from?' I don't even want to guess where that accent was from.

'London,' she says at once, the weird accent now completely gone.

'Has your voice changed?'

'Yes. Sorry, where were you on Halloween?'

I can't help it, I roll my eyes.

'Oh yeah, here we go,' I laugh. 'Have you seen this man? Where were you on the night of 31st October? Who showed you this – was it Remy?'

'Who?'

'The guy at the bar.' I turn in my seat and catch Remy's eye. 'Yeah, very funny.'

I turn back to her, still laughing, but she's looking at me blankly.

'No,' she says after a pause. 'What did you do on Halloween?'

I open my mouth to reply when the bell rings again and, like clockwork, all the men spring to their feet.

'Nice to meet you,' I say, but she's already pulled out her phone and is manically messaging someone.

Another girl from London I met without getting her name. This is becoming a habit.

Chapter Twenty-Three

Annie

Penny: Are you sure it's him? Did you ask him?
Annie: I tried! He was acting weird.
Penny: Maybe he's just an American with dark hair?
Annie: Maybe, but I just felt—

'Do you?'

My eyes snap up from my phone and I realise with a jolt that the guy opposite me has been talking this entire time.

Shit. I barely noticed him sit down.

I could just nod, that's the safest thing to do.

But what if he asked, 'Do you want a threesome right now with me and the barman?'

'I'm so sorry,' I say, turning my phone over as it vibrates again. 'Can you repeat that?'

'No worries,' he smiles. 'I asked if you like music.'

Oh, I totally could have just nodded to that.

'Yeah,' I say, 'do you?'

The guy starts talking again, but my eyes wander off. The American guy is sitting opposite the girl next to me, chatting freely. He hasn't even given me another glance.

Is it him? Or am I just going mad? Am I so desperate to see

him that I'm just pinning my hopes on any random American? What am I going to do next – start fantasising about Donald Trump?

(Spoiler alert: no.)

'Anyway, my name is Blake.'

I look back at the guy opposite me. Thankfully, I'm pretty sure he hasn't noticed my glazed expression for our entire date.

'I'm Annie.' I smile back as the bell rings and he gets up and moves. The American guy moves another place further away from me just as my phone vibrates again.

Penny: I took this video on the night you guys met. I just remembered. Is this him?

It's a screenshot of me facing American Boy, trying to break free of the bat wings stuck in his suit. I zoom in with my fingers. The picture is dark and blurry, and his mask is covering half of his face. All I can make out is that he's dark and has a beard. It could be anyone.

The bell rings again and I look up in alarm, suddenly worried I've ignored another guy for a solid two minutes, when I notice the man in the flat cap has started speaking.

'Let's have a drink break; I can see too many empty glasses.'

I get to my feet before the next guy can sit down and march towards Tanya, only to see that she's still in full flow with a red-headed guy with a topknot. I stand stupidly on the spot and then my eyes find American Boy, on his phone. Fuelled by half a bottle of wine, I charge over.

'Sorry, but where were you on Halloween?'

He looks up at me from his phone, amusement playing on his face.

'Am I going crazy or has your voice changed?'

'Were you at a masquerade ball?'

It feels like a lifetime passes whilst I wait for him to answer. Embarrassment flares up my body as I fight the urge to run away and pretend none of this ever happened.

What are you doing? Even if this is the right guy, he left you. He literally ran away! And now you're confronting him? In person?

He turns his body to face me.

'Were you?'

'I asked you first.'

I see his eyes spark. 'Were you dressed as a bat?'

Something inside me glows. It's him. I was right.

I was right.

'Were you the person with the worst costume in the room?'

He raises his eyebrows in mock offence. 'Were you the person who stabbed me with their costume?'

I put my hand on my hip, fighting the urge to grin at him. 'Were you the person who rudely left halfway through a conversation without even saying goodbye?'

He rubs his chin. 'Yeah,' he says. 'That was me. I'm sorry about that.'

'You didn't even tell me your name.'

He meets my eyes and my heart pulls. 'It's Nate.'

I smile at him. 'Hi Nate. I'm Annie.'

'Is it too late for me to ask you on a date?' He holds my gaze steadily.

I pause, looking around the room. Tanya is still engrossed with ponytail man, looking pretty happy.

'Right now?' I ask.

'No, not now!' Nate laughs, and then reads my expression. 'Unless you want to? Yeah, now is good. Not here though, right? I want more than two minutes this time.'

'Okay,' I say, pulling out my phone and sending a message to Tanya. 'Let's go. I know a place.'

'I can't believe this is where you've taken me for our first date.'

'You said you'd never tried British cuisine!'

'Yeah, but *this*? Is this really the best London can do? What about Gordon Ramsay?'

'He'd love a kebab. I mean, it's technically Turkish but trust me, it's part of our culture.'

Okay, so I didn't leave the Clapham Arms with the intention of taking Nate to a kebab shop, but the temptation was too great to ignore. He started babbling about how he moved to London to experience life here and then admitted that he'd never had a Saturday night kebab.

I mean, he was practically asking for it.

We step forward in the queue. I glance back at Nate and swallow a laugh. He looks horrified.

'I'll order for us, shall I?' I grin, taking Nate's silence as a yes. 'Two lamb shish, please.'

The guy behind the counter nods as I tap my card on the machine. Nate jumps in alarm. 'Oh no, have you just paid? This is getting worse by the second.'

I laugh. 'What do you mean?'

'Well, I'd never take a woman on a first date to a kebab shop, let alone let her pay.'

'I wanted to pay.'

'So did I!'

I pull myself up onto one of the stools and place my bag on the table. It's a tiny kebab shop, with lurid yellow lights and brown tables. In about three hours, the place will be overflowing with drunk, famished Londoners. But for now, it's just us eating in.

It's funny. I wasn't sure I'd be able to recognise him in a line-up of men. It was so dark when we met and he was wearing a mask. And it was over just as quickly as it had begun. But tonight it was like as soon as I set eyes on him, my body seemed to know who I was facing before my brain did. Something just switched inside me, and that was that.

He's better-looking than I remember. He has dark, thick hair which is curly and close to his head and a beard that runs across his strong jaw. His eyes are green and sparkling, and his arms are covered in strings of tattoos.

He's gorgeous.

I hop back off my seat as our order is ready and pass him the yellow polystyrene container. I snap mine open and look down at the sea of school-bus-yellow chips, shredded salad and layers of meat. I catch the look of horror on

Nate's face as he takes in his own portion and burst out laughing.

'What?' He laughs nervously.

'You look like I'm about to give you poison.'

'I'm worried you are.'

'It's nice!' I say. 'Everyone in London loves it. Trust me, it'll be rammed in here within a few hours.'

He picks up a cut of meat dubiously and drops it back into the box.

'Just try it,' I say. 'What's the worst that can happen?'

'It'll give me food poisoning?'

'Then you get a day off work and can binge-watch *I'm a Celeb*. That sounds pretty good to me.'

I read his expression. 'It's a British show. It's good.'

'As good as cups of tea and kebabs?'

'No,' I grin, stabbing my kebab with my fork. 'Nothing is as good as tea and kebabs.'

I take a bite, letting out an involuntary groan, and then immediately feel myself giggle.

Nate smiles at me. 'What?'

I shake my head, trying my best to chew and swallow the mouthful as quickly as possible so as not to choke in front of him.

'Is it me?' Nate laughs, looking down at himself. 'Have I said something?'

For some reason, this makes me laugh even more. I shake my head and turn my back to him.

'Oh God, now you can't even look at me!' he exclaims. 'Am I that bad at dating? I'm just sitting here!'

I take a deep breath and swallow the mouthful of kebab. It chugs down my throat in a big, congealed blob. 'Okay,' I say, turning back to face him. 'Sorry about that.'

'Are you going to tell me what you were laughing at?'

'No,' I grin. 'Try your kebab.'

He holds my gaze, challenging. 'Not until you tell me what's so funny.'

'It's nothing.' I roll my eyes, laughing.

'I'll be the judge of that.'

I unscrew my bottle of Coke and take a swig. 'Okay, fine. I was laughing at how unsexy I was, taking a huge bite of kebab and groaning like I'd never eaten before. It's probably not the best way to behave on a first date, and it just made me laugh.'

We both look round as the door swings open and three lads bustle in.

'I thought it was sexy.'

I'm pulled back to the moment, and I catch Nate's eyes. I grin. 'There isn't a sexy way to eat a kebab.'

Nate peers down at his open carton of food questioningly. Before I can register what he's about to do, he picks up the kebab and takes a huge bite, rolling his eyes to the back of his head and groaning. The three guys at the counter look round and I reach forward and thwack him, a squawk of laughter shooting out of me.

'Oh my God,' Nate manages, covering his mouth with his hand. 'This is really chewy. How do you swallow this?'

'You took a huge bite!' I cry.

Falling For You

He holds up a hand to me and chews frantically, before eventually swallowing.

'Okay,' he says. 'I get it. That wasn't sexy.'

I beam at him, trying to work out why it felt like the sexiest thing I've ever seen.

Chapter Twenty-Four

Nate

I've found her. I can't believe I found her. She's even better than the version of her that I'd made up in my mind. She is funny, she is gorgeous, she's *fun*. And somehow, she seems to find me fun, too. It wasn't just a fluke on the night we met that I felt like our conversation was the best I'd had since I got to London. It feels easy with her. It feels like the most normal thing in the world.

She takes another huge bite of her kebab and catches my eye, immediately giggling madly again.

God, I love the way she laughs.

She waves her hand at me and turns her back on me again.

'Sorry,' I say. 'It's fine, I'm not laughing at you. I told you, I think it's sexy.'

I see her back hunch over as she laughs even harder and I battle with the urge to make her laugh as much as I can without making her choke.

Eventually, she turns around to face me.

'You've barely eaten yours,' she says, looking down at my damp kebab. 'Don't you like it?'

'No comment.'

She gasps. 'How can you not like kebabs?'

'Shh!' I lean forward and grab her hands. 'Keep your voice down. I'm still on the run from all my colleagues after telling them I don't like tea.'

Her eyes shine at me, and she doesn't take her hands away. 'Gosh, I wonder if I should even be seen in public with you.'

'You're not the first person to wonder that.' She laughs again and my chest lifts. 'So,' I say. 'Where is the bat costume? I almost didn't recognise you.'

She raises her eyebrows at me. 'You *didn't* recognise me! If I hadn't come up to you then we'd have walked into the abyss, never to see each other again.'

'Well, I was looking for Bat Girl.'

'She only comes out on special occasions,' Annie says from under her lashes, and then immediately bursts out laughing. 'Can we pretend that didn't happen? God, why am I so cringe?'

'I think you're great.'

'You don't know anything about me,' she says, her cheeks still tinged pink. 'I could be a serial killer.'

'Is that why you've taken me to a kebab shop?'

She laughs, hitting me lightly on the arm.

'I know that you're talented,' I say after a pause. 'I know you're funny and interesting. I know that you're gorgeous.'

Her eyes flick up at me. 'Whatever,' she mumbles. 'Oh!' she snaps her fingers, putting down her kebab. 'Before I forget, Mr Cinderella, is this yours?'

My eyes widen as she pulls out my ring from inside her purse. It gleams up at me from her open palm.

'Yeah,' I say, feeling myself soften with relief. 'I thought I'd lost it.'

She smiles, handing it over to me. 'I kept it in my purse in case I . . .' She trails off, her cheeks turning pink.

'In case you walked past a pawn shop and needed some cash?' I finish, grinning.

She laughs. 'Yeah, exactly. Whose is it, then?' She gestures down to the ring.

'It's mine.' I blink at her in mock confusion. 'I don't go around stealing jewellery from people.'

She rolls her eyes at me. 'Who gave it to you?'

I place the ring on my pinkie finger. 'It's my mom's. My brother used to borrow her jewellery when we were kids and I got jealous one day, so she gave me this.'

She tilts her head. 'Aw, that's nice. Is your mom back in New York?'

I feel my heart wrench and for a second I'm pulled out of this bubbly, exciting moment with Annie and back into the kitchen with Mom.

'Yeah,' I say. 'She's not well, she . . .' I look up, catching myself. 'Sorry, I don't know why I'm telling you.'

She leans forward and takes my hand, sending a frisson of electricity through my body. 'I'm really sorry to hear that. My parents are my whole world, I can't imagine one of them being sick.'

I give a rough laugh. 'Yeah. It's not the greatest experience.'

'I bet.'

'It's no kebab, anyway,' I joke, looking down at my sweaty yellow box. 'Do your parents live in London?'

She shakes her head, swallowing her mouthful, and lets go of my hand. 'No. They're in the Cotswolds in my childhood home. It's not too far from here. It's probably the most typically British place you can go to. Like, I think some of *The Holiday* was filmed there.'

'I love that film.'

She laughs. 'Why doesn't that surprise me?' She watches as I close the lid to my kebab, defeated. She smiles. 'Well, if you're not enjoying this part of our British culture, I feel like I should show you another staple.'

They do say that if you want to experience a city properly, you should get a local to show you around. You'll see the hidden bars, the restaurants serving the best foods, the secret entrances into the parks where you'll get the best view of the city.

Or, in my case, the sweatiest carpeted nightclub in the world.

'Welcome to Infernos!' Annie yells over the music, which is pumping out a heavy bass version of a Nicki Minaj song. The place is filled with young people, all flailing their limbs around and dancing wildly, clinging onto plastic glasses filled with luminous liquids. Some people are in tiny dresses, others in tracksuits, but everyone looks as if they've come to a place where nobody else can see what they're doing. And that particularly goes for the couple pressed up against the wall in the corner.

'Cool!' I manage, as it's the only thing I can think of to say. I haven't been to a nightclub in *years*. For *Take the Time* magazine, I've mainly been sent to bars, art galleries and posh restaurants.

They'd never dream of sending me to a nightclub. Not that I wouldn't go, but I don't think I'd be let in. I'm too old!

Or so I thought.

'Let's get a drink,' Annie says, grabbing my hand and pulling me towards the bar. I follow her mindlessly. Now we're standing up again, I notice our height difference even more. She's about a foot shorter than me. Since I realised who she was I've started noticing all sorts of things that I didn't see when we first met. Her long, dark hair. Her big brown eyes and turned-up nose, her slightly crooked teeth and heart-shaped lips. But the way I felt when I spoke to her felt the same as the first time. It wasn't just a weird feeling of the moment. It was real. She was real.

'What do you want?' Annie yells and I bend down to try and get closer to her. 'To drink?' she adds.

My mind goes blank. 'Rum and Coke?' I offer. 'Whatever.'

'And a shot!'

I shake my head, but then realise that it wasn't a question and she's already leaning over the bar, shouting our order at the bartender. A moment later he reappears with two glasses, and two neon shots. Annie hands me one and I don't bother arguing, knocking it back instantly.

'Okay,' she says, taking my hand again. 'Let's go.'

For a moment I'm worried she's about to drag me onto the dance floor. If she thought that eating a kebab wasn't sexy, she has no idea what my six foot three, awkward limbs are capable of. Thankfully, she leads me to a space next to the fire exit, which seems to be quieter. She shimmies onto a banquette and I follow her.

'Cheers!' she cries, and we knock glasses. 'You can't experience London properly without coming to Infernos.'

I look around dubiously. 'Really?'

'Margot Robbie comes here!' she adds earnestly. 'You're not a snob, are you?'

'No,' I laugh and shake my head. 'This just isn't what I'd normally plan for a first date.'

'What would you plan, then?' She grins at me, her eyes sparkling again.

'Well,' I say, racking my brains for something impressive to say. 'To start, I would take you out for dinner.'

'We've just been for dinner,' she says.

I go to argue but can't help myself, her smile is infectious. 'Okay, fine. Well, then I'd take you for drinks.'

She holds up her drink at me, raising her eyebrows. I roll my eyes and she laughs again.

'And let me guess . . .' she says, leaning closer to me. 'Then you'd take me somewhere to go dancing to shit music, with sticky floors and sweaty strangers.'

I run my fingers through my hair. She's so close to me now that I can smell her perfume. It's sweet and floral. It's lovely. Everything about her is lovely.

'Fine,' I say, holding up my hands. 'You've got me. This is the perfect date.'

I glance down at her lips and then back at her eyes. Then, before I can think about it too much, I pull her in and kiss her.

If I thought I felt sparks before, that was nothing compared to how I feel now.

Chapter Twenty-Five

Annie

'Penny, Penny, Penny, Penny. Tanya, Tanya, Tanya, Tanya!' I cry, running in between their doors and knocking wildly. 'Wake up!'

Tanya appears first, her eyes wild with alarm.

'What is it? Are you okay? Is it the mouse?'

I beam at her. I can't help it. I've been grinning like a madman since last night, since I realised that I'd actually managed to find him.

'What the fuck?'

I turn to see Penny, her eyes barely open. She looks like she's just come out of hibernation. 'Annie, it's like eight in the morning.'

'That's not early.'

'It's a Sunday!'

'I need to talk to you both,' I say, the words falling out of my mouth. 'I've made us all a tea. It's in the living room.'

As we walk through, Tanya eyes me suspiciously. 'What time did you get in last night? I didn't hear you. Who was that guy you left with? Your message was so mysterious! Are you okay?'

'I'm great!'

Penny stumbles past us, immediately crashing onto the sofa. 'I'll listen with my eyes closed,' she mumbles as I bounce after her.

Tanya picks up her tea and I drop down into the beanbag, which swallows my body at once.

'Okay . . .' Tanya says slowly. 'You're weirding me out a bit. What's going on?'

'Guess who I saw last night?'

'Peter Andre,' Penny says, her voice muffled by her pillow.

I roll my eyes. 'No.'

'Oh!' Tanya sits up a bit straighter. 'Rod Stewart?'

'Boris Johnson?'

'No and no.'

'Our landlord?'

'No!' I cry, swatting away their guesses with my hand. 'American Boy.'

It takes a minute for the penny to drop, and then I see Tanya's mouth drop. Penny peels her eyes open and smiles.

'So it *was* him.'

'What, was he there?' Tanya gapes at me. 'Did I date him? Is that who you ran off with?'

'Yes, no and yes.'

Penny slowly pushes herself up to sitting straight on the sofa, a big tuft of her blonde hair sticking out vertically. 'I need more information,' she says, picking up her mug and wincing as it singes her hands through the thin china.

I reposition myself on the beanbag and tell them everything. We ended up staying in Infernos until the lights came on, dancing and yelling lyrics at each other and laughing. There was so much laughing. And *so much kissing*. I haven't kissed someone like that since I was a teenager.

'Sorry.' Penny holds up a hand. 'You took him to a kebab shop and then to Infernos? Are you mad?'

'He kept talking about how he really wanted to *see London*,' I say.

'That's a red flag for me,' Penny says.

'He loved it!'

'Even more of a red flag.'

'Hang on, wait,' Tanya says, interrupting us both before we can start one of our bickering matches. 'You kissed?'

I beam. 'Yup.'

'And what next? A second date? How was it left?'

'He asked to see me again and then said he'd message me.' I turn over my phone and it blinks back up at me, blankly.

'But nothing yet?' asks Penny.

'No.'

'Well, it's only first thing in the morning,' Tanya says fairly. 'I'm sure you'll hear from him soon.'

I hold the phone, basking in my warm glow. 'I'm sure I will too.'

Potential reasons why I haven't heard from Nate:

1. He's lost his phone. He dropped it down a gutter on the way home, never to be seen again, and has absolutely no way to find me.

2. He was so horrified at Infernos that he's moved back to America.
3. I'm a terrible kisser (worst one, please don't let it be this one).
4. He's dead.

I twiddle my pen between my fingers and glance up at the wall clock which hangs opposite the entrance to our office. It's steel grey with shiny hands and crisp, neat numbers. It's almost the only thing in the office that I let Pam choose – except for her office chair.

My eyes flit back down to my phone, laid next to the keyboard on my desk, silently taunting me, just like it has been for the past two days.

Two days! It's been two days since we went on our date and he still hasn't texted me. Why? What could he possibly be doing?

I would text him, being a modern woman and all that jazz, but at the end of the night I was being all aloof and hard to get and acted like I wasn't fussed about getting his number so left without it.

I *am* fussed. Of course I'm fussed! Although it's probably a good thing that I don't have his number, or he would have received a desperate, dreadful message begging him to see me again and promising that I'm not actually that bad at kissing.

Or, worse, a stern message giving him a piece of my mind which would be chased immediately with a terrified 'sorry, wrong number lol!' which would then live in my head, rent free, for the rest of my sorry little days.

Argh! I hate dating. Why do I ever trick myself into thinking it's fun and sexy and spontaneous? When really, it's a torturous game of chess where everyone seems to know the rules apart from me. I don't even have a sodding board. I should just stay at home and make jumpers and costumes and stitch myself a felt boyfriend instead.

I look up in alarm as I hear the zip of a lighter and spot Pam holding an open flame inches from her face.

'Pam!' I scold. 'The fire alarms!'

Pam jolts like I've pulled her out of a trance and shakes her head. 'Thanks, love,' she mutters in her gravelly voice. 'Why are you here?' she adds, almost as an afterthought. 'Don't you have some properties to look at today?'

It's just me and Pam in the office. Every now and then, you can hear the finance wankers on the floor above us making a loud cheer or yelling something across the floor, but otherwise it's just silence. I wiggle my mouse and watch my laptop come back to life, pulling the email I've been ignoring right back to the centre of my attention.

'Not until this afternoon,' I say. 'I've got to deal with a list of essentials first.'

After much deliberation, I managed to get a client to agree on a five-bedroom house in Knightsbridge (they acted like I was trying to trick them into signing a six-month tenancy agreement for the London Dungeon). A few years ago, I would have cracked open a celebratory bottle of prosecco and given myself a big pat on the back. A hard job well done. Congratulations to me.

Now that I am older, wiser and jaded, I know that difficult

clients are like leeches. They suck the life out of you and are incredibly difficult to shake off.

So, as expected, after signing the agreement, the expected list of 'essentials' came through. And it's my job to source all of these items before they arrive, make sure they're ready for them in their house and time the whole process so that the oven pings with a fresh loaf of bread moments after they turn the key for the first time.

I'm exaggerating, but I'm sure they'd gladly take me up on the loaf of bread if I offered it and see it as no big deal whatsoever.

But this is why Pam and I have stuck together all these years. Pam sorts the logistics, she schmoozes the clients and negotiates the rates, and then she passes it over to me. She knows that I'll source whatever weird and wonderful request the client has, and that I won't rest until everything is perfect. Which is why so many clients come back to us. We're the best. We are the dream team.

Pam lets out a groan, arching her back and resting her hand below her shoulder blades.

I frown. 'Are you all right?'

Her face contorts but she shakes her free hand at me, the unlit cigarette still clasped between two fingers.

'How long have you been sat in that chair for?' I ask. 'Have you even moved today?'

Pam is always here before I get into the office, and I've never really had a firm grasp of what time she leaves the office every day. When I first started working with her, we were based in her house, so obviously she stayed there longer than I did and worked insane hours. But since we moved to an office, I was hoping I might get in before her and have time to make her a coffee and toddle around by myself for a bit. Two years on and it feels like nothing more than a pipe dream. I get in for 8 a.m. every day, and each time I walk in to see Pam craned over her laptop, her nose almost touching the screen and her eyes squinted behind her thick glasses. Cigarette in hand, coffee half drunk.

'What?' she barks, letting go of her back and hunching over her keyboard again.

'Come on!' I say, getting to my feet and marching over to her desk. 'Get up. You need to move your body. You're getting stiff.'

She rolls her eyes at me. 'I'm fine.'

'Pam,' I place my hands on my hips, 'you already refused to use an ergonomic chair. If you don't let me help you, I'll report you to HR.'

She snorts. 'I *am* HR.'

'Exactly.'

She catches my eye, a naughty smile on her face like she's a child who's been caught snaffling ice cream. After a moment, she thrusts a tanned hand in my direction and I pull her to standing. She groans again, grabbing her back.

'You need to stop working so much,' I say, leaning forward to grab her as she rests on her desk for support. 'When was the last time you had a massage?'

She shakes her head. 'I don't have time for that. I'm fine, Annie. Just a crick in my back.'

I press my lips together, ignoring her knowing smile.

'Well, just stay standing for a minute and do some stretches. Like yoga,' I say, aware that I know absolutely nothing about yoga. 'It's important that you move your body.'

Pam nods at me, batting me away and closing her eyes. At least I got her to stand up and spend a few minutes away from her laptop. That's more than I'm usually capable of doing.

'If you do go travelling to India then you'll need to know how to do yoga,' I say, giving her a knowing look. 'Penny always talks about going there for a month to become a qualified yoga teacher.'

I mean, a typical Penny thing to do. Not only is she a scientist with a PhD, but she also runs marathons and casually wants to become a qualified yoga teacher, as if she isn't impressive enough already.

Pam twists her back and winces as it cracks. 'If I do go to India, I won't be doing any of this shit.'

'It's not shit!'

Her back cracks again and she lets out a groan before dropping back into her seat. 'Are you happy now? I've had a stretch. I'm fine.'

'Oh,' I say, catching sight of my swollen rucksack. 'Before I forget . . . I've got a surprise for you. Close your eyes and put your hands out.'

'Why?' She eyes me suspiciously.

'Just do it,' I say. 'Please.'

Pam rolls her eyes but she does comply, holding one limp hand in my direction. I unzip my rucksack and pull out a scarf. It's one I've been working on for a few weeks.

It's knitted with four different shades of green wool that I found at a charity shop, along with an amber thread from the bottom of my sewing kit. I place the scarf in her hands and Pam smiles as soon as she feels it.

'Can I open my eyes now?'

'You can.'

Pam opens her eyes and her face lights up. She sits back in her chair so she can hold the scarf with both hands, running it through her fingers before winding it round her neck. 'Oh, it's lovely. So soft. You're very talented, Annie.'

I feel a warm glow. 'It was nothing.'

I really struck gold when I stumbled across her job advert all those years ago. Pam swears a lot, she doesn't like small talk and she refuses to go to the pantomime with me every Christmas, but she's my biggest fan. I could knit her an all-in-one sleepsuit for the summer and she'd wear it, even if it meant drowning in her own sweat.

I go back to my desk and, to my annoyance, feel myself glance expectantly down at my phone. It stares back up at me, motionless. Like the arrogant little shit it is.

Oh my God, this is going to drive me *insane.*

'Right,' Pam says, getting to her feet. 'Annie, I'm going to go and meet a client for lunch. Can you man the phones for an hour or so?'

'Sure,' I say at once. 'Of course.'

I wiggle my mouse again to bring my laptop back to life when, next to me, my phone vibrates. I almost fall off my seat.

It's Nate. He's finally messaged me.

Falling For You

I scrabble to open it, adrenaline flying through my veins. As I read the text, my heart sinks and I feel a cold wash all over my body.

Right. Well, that's that, then.

It's over.

Chapter Twenty-Six

Nate

I stare at my phone. It stares back at me silently. I'd been waiting for it to ring for hours, and then for the last forty minutes I've been sat, simply watching the blank screen.

After my date with Annie, I spent hours floating around like I was walking on air. Finally, London seemed a bit brighter. I started being able to see the London that I'd watched on TV all those years. I saw the smiling people, the couples kissing, the Christmas lights twinkling. I even laughed when a red bus skirted past me and splattered rainwater up my legs. I loved it here! I'd never had a feeling like this in New York. I don't know if I've experienced this feeling in my entire life.

The morning after our date, I woke up to find Stevie knocking at my door with a paper cup of coffee. For the first time since I'd moved in, he was here to wake me up and help nurse my hangover. He perched on the end of my bed and made me recount all the details about the date, who Bat Girl really was and how things were left. When I told him I got her number, he insisted that I had to wait two days to message her. Apparently, that was the unwritten rule of dating

Falling For You

Londoners. Any earlier and I'd give her 'the ick'. If I hadn't given her the ick by my dancing, he added unnecessarily.

Needless to say, I wanted to message her right away. I wanted to knock on her door and take her out for breakfast. Ask her where else weird and wonderful she could take me in London, what other stories she had, what other costumes she was planning to make. I wanted to know absolutely everything about her. But I took Stevie's advice. He knew much more about dating than I did as he had far more experience (I came back with that one which, annoyingly, he took as a compliment).

I spent two solid days in my bubble. Work didn't even feel that bad. Hell, I laughed when Brian showed me the new batch of people who had written in for the Miss Cinderella story. I told him I'd been on a date with Jane, which seemed to be dull enough to satisfy his appetite for gossip, and let him decide that perhaps I was better writing about the latest exhibitions in the London museums. Which was fine by me – I thought maybe I could take Annie with me. I hopped, skipped and jumped around London. I felt ten pounds lighter.

And then I woke up this morning to one, singular word on my phone and it was enough to make my blood turn to ice.

Help.

It was from Mom. She sent it at four in the morning, which would have been late at night for them. I called her as soon as I saw it, but she didn't answer. Then I called Dad; he didn't answer either. The sensible part of my brain tried to tell me that it was late for them; the reason they weren't answering was because they were sound asleep, tucked up in their pine bed and floral bedcovers. But the ugly, irrational side of my brain sucked the silence of the morning up like gasoline.

Maybe they aren't answering because something has happened. It's too late now. If you'd answered at the time, then you could have been there. If you hadn't left New York then you could check on them; you could even have been with Mom when she messaged. But you're not. You're here and something has happened to her, and now nobody is speaking to you.

It's been swirling around my body for the past six hours, ripping every part of joy out of me and extinguishing every spark that had been flickering for the past two days. All that's left in me is cold, dark fear. I messaged Brian to say that I needed to work from home, and I've just sat staring out of the window ever since. I messaged Annie too.

Hey, sorry I've got a lot going on right now. Have a good week.

It's hardly the message I'd wanted to send, but I didn't want to leave her in silence and I didn't know what else to say.

I haven't told Stevie. He left to go to a gig before I'd gotten up, and there is no point worrying him. I'll tell him once I know what's going on. Once Mom calls me.

If she ever calls me.

I lean my head against the back of the lumpy sofa. I tried going on a walk earlier to take my mind off it all, but all it did was make me constantly worry that my phone may lose signal or ring without me hearing it, and I'd miss another message.

Why would she be asking for my help? She should be at home with Dad, safe. What could possibly be wrong?

I almost jump out of my skin when my phone vibrates. I snatch it from the coffee table and deflate as I see Stevie's name on the screen.

'Hey, man.' I told myself that I wasn't going to tell Stevie about the message until I knew what was going on. But the more time that has passed, the more scared I've become. This was my plan based on the idea that Mom or Dad would call as soon as they woke up. But what if something worse has happened? What if they aren't able to call me, and we don't hear from them for days? Or not at all? The thought of it makes me feel sick.

'Listen,' I say, interrupting Stevie as he starts chatting about his journey up to Sheffield. 'I've got to talk to you quickly. I'm sure it's fine, but I got a weird message from Mom this morning.'

Stevie is silent down the phone for a moment and I can hear my heart thudding in my ears. 'What does that mean?' he says eventually.

'Well, nothing,' I hear myself say. 'I'm sure it's all fine.'

Why am I saying this? I don't know if it's fine. I don't know anything.

'For fuck's sake, Nate,' Stevie snaps. 'Just tell me what's going on.'

'She messaged me in the middle of the night.'

'Saying what?'

'Saying "help".' I force myself to say it, even though it's enough to make me want to throw up. It sounds so much worse when I say it out loud.

'Help?' Stevie repeats. 'What do you mean?'

'I don't know,' I say, running my fingers through my hair. 'That's literally all it said. But I'm sure everything is fine.'

'Stop saying that!' I flinch as he shouts down the phone. 'You can't possibly know that everything's fine. Don't patronise me.'

'Well, I don't know what to do!' I exclaim, a bolt of rage piercing through me. Does he have any idea how much I wish it was someone calling to tell me that they're sure everything is going to be okay, instead of it being me? *Why does it always have to be me?*

'Have you spoken to her? Or Dad?'

'Of course not,' I say, failing to hide the anger in my voice. 'I'd tell you if I knew more, wouldn't I?'

'Well, try and call them, then.'

'What do you think I've been doing all day?' I shout, getting to my feet and throwing my arm in the air. I wince as my wrist knocks the lampshade and glass splinters around my fist. I take a deep breath as the pain slices through my hand.

'Look,' I start again. 'I'm telling you all I know. As soon as I hear something I will call you, I promise.'

But the line has gone dead. Stevie has hung up.

I chuck the phone onto the sofa and storm into the kitchen, grabbing sheets of kitchen roll to wrap round my hand. Specks of dark blood swell through the white squares and I curse, sucking the cut as I rifle through Stevie's cupboard. Of course he doesn't have a first-aid kit, or anything mildly similar to one. He's a child. He's a child who's been hiding in London for the past ten years with his head in the sand, ignoring everything that's going on around him. His family, his responsibilities . . . they've all been things I've had to pick up.

I wince as blood seeps through the paper towel and feel a dart of panic.

Shit. I think I've really cut myself.

I'm about to run my hand under the tap when I hear the faint jingle of my ringtone. I dash into the living room and snatch up my phone, answering it before I've even clocked who's calling.

'Hello?'

'You all right?'

I recognise the relaxed rhythm of Remy's voice instantly and before I can compose myself, I hear myself blurt, 'Remy, do you know where the nearest hospital is?'

'Here you are, lad.'

I glance up as Remy hands me a polystyrene cup. I hold it with my free arm, my other still held aloft, as instructed by the frazzled nurse who bandaged me up and told me to stay put until she got back. That was about thirty minutes ago.

'Thanks,' I say. 'Sorry.'

'Stop apologising.' Remy hadn't asked why I needed to go to hospital. He just wanted to know where I was, and then twenty minutes later showed up in his black cab and told me to get in. He only asked me two questions: if I was okay, and if I'd been in a fight. I heard myself answer no to both of them, before hurriedly adding that I was fine really and that I was probably overreacting. I said this while I had an entire roll of kitchen roll on my lap, which was thinning out by the minute as it sucked up my blood like a thirsty sponge.

I jump as my phone vibrates next to me. I grab it, only to see a pointless email from Deliveroo. It makes me so angry that I almost launch my phone across the room. Remy catches my expression and raises an eyebrow.

'Are you sure you're all right?'

'Yes. I'm fine.'

He looks pointedly down at my phone. 'What's that about, then?'

'What's what?'

'Who are you waiting to hear from? You're not wound up about that girl, are you?'

In the middle of my desperate worry about my mom, my anger that they still haven't called me back even though they will have been awake for hours, my embarrassment at having to call Remy for help and my slight self-pity for my slashed hand, I feel a spark of excitement as Annie's face pops into my head.

'That girl?' I echo.

'The one from the speed dating – the one you left with.'

I shake my head and wiggle my fingers as pins and needles creep over them like tiny, prickly spiders.

Remy takes a sip of his coffee. 'She seemed nice.'

I spot the twinkle in his eye and can't help but smile.

'What's your story then, Remy?' I ask. 'Why are you spending your weekends hanging out with me? Do you have someone at home?'

Remy shakes his head. 'Oh no, not me.'

'I bet you know all the tricks.'

He smiles, his lips pressed together. 'I know a few.'

'Well then, what? Are you dating someone? What's going on?'

He gives me a look and places his coffee on the floor. 'Nothing, mate.'

'Why not?'

He shrugs coyly. 'Who knows, eh?'

I knit my brow when an idea pops into my head. 'Do you like theatre?'

He frowns at me. 'Theatre?'

'I've got tickets to a show if you want to come. My aunt is in it. She's the one I'm trying to get to visit my mom. I thought going to see her in her show might get me in her good books.'

He smirks and then cocks his head. 'Sure. Why not?'

He leans his elbows on his knees and looks straight ahead. We drift into silence.

'I'm waiting for a call from my mom,' I say eventually, feeling too tired to try and cover it all up with a fake smile and a lame story. 'I got a weird message from her last night. I haven't been able to get hold of her since.'

He glances up at me. 'I'm sorry to hear that, Nate.'

I'm about to make a light comment about how it isn't so bad, but I can't bring myself to do it.

'Nathaniel Simpson?' I look up as the nurse reappears and gestures for me to follow her.

'Want me to hold your hand?' Remy grins.

I give him a shove on the shoulder as I get to my feet. 'I think I'll be okay. You can go home, though,' I add. 'You don't have to wait for me.'

He picks up his coffee and nods his head. 'I'll be here, Nate. Don't worry about it.'

The nurse spent twenty minutes threading tiny stitches through the cut on the palm of my hand. The needle pierced both sides of flesh and weaved them back together, and it all felt so small and minor that I felt pathetic for wanting to cry out in pain.

As good as his word, Remy was still waiting on the plastic chair where I left him when I came out with my newly bandaged hand. We climbed into his cab and he drove me back to the flat. I tried to offer him some money, but he just said that I could buy him a pint next time we were both at the pub. I said I'd buy him two, and an ice cream at the theatre. He laughed at that.

I've been lying in bed, staring at the ceiling and feeling completely tormented for the past few hours. When I got out of the hospital, I was convinced I'd have a message from Mom that had somehow gotten lost within the poor signal of the building. But there was nothing there. It took all my strength not to lose my mind. Annie hasn't messaged me back either, but I can see that she's read it. I want to message her again, but I'm so exhausted from the past twelve hours that I feel like my brain isn't working properly. I can't think of what I'd say, and we had such a great time on Saturday. It was so fun and free, I don't want to burden her with all of my bullshit. She was my escape from it all.

I heard Stevie get in about an hour ago and go straight to his bedroom. Even though he'll assume I was asleep, I thought he might come and wake me up to see if I'd heard anything. I'm sort of glad he didn't. I don't think I could bear to tell him that not only had I not heard anything at all, but as time went on, I was rapidly losing faith that it would all be okay like I promised. Because he was right – how would I know?

I roll onto my back and close my eyes. I force myself to focus on my breathing, the only thing I feel like I can control right now.

In, out, in, out, in, out, in—

I jump as my phone vibrates next to me and I finally see Mom's name flash up on the screen.

'Mom,' I cry, pressing the phone to my ear. 'Mom? Are you okay?'

As soon as I speak, Stevie comes crashing into my room, wide-eyed. He'd obviously heard my phone through our paper-thin walls. I switch the phone to loudspeaker. He glances at my hand in confusion and I shake my head, mouthing, 'I'm fine.'

'Oh!' Mom's voice spills through into our deathly silent room. 'Hello, love!'

Stevie hovers at the doorway. My heart climbs into my throat. She sounds . . . okay. She sounds like Mom.

'Are you okay?' I say. 'I got your message yesterday, but I was asleep. I've been trying to get hold of you and Dad all day.'

The phone makes a scuffling sound as Mom walks through the house. 'Oh yes, I'm fine,' she says. 'How are you?'

I make the mistake of looking up at Stevie. He looks murderous.

'Fine,' I say carefully. 'Mom, you texted me saying "help" yesterday. Are you all right?'

'Did I?' Mom says. 'I don't think I did.'

My heart sinks. She doesn't remember.

Stevie storms out of the room, throwing his arms in the air. I wince as I hear his bedroom door slam.

'Yeah,' I say, leaning back onto my bed as a wave of exhaustion hits me. 'You did.'

'Oh,' Mom says after a pause, and then she laughs lightly. 'That must have been a mistake. How are you, sweetie? How's Stevie?'

I place a hand over my face as a cold mixture of fear, relief and panic begins to take a hold of my body.

I inhale deeply. 'How was your day?'

Chapter Twenty-Seven

Annie

'So here we have a property that I really think you'll like.'

I hear my voice tighten as I repeat the same sentence I've been parroting to this client for the past six weeks.

Melissa Dumfry is the Head of Sales at a global, multi-million marketing company and is about to relocate to London for eighteen months. They've given her a budget of thirty thousand pounds *a month* to cover her expenses, and I know that's moving over from a one-bed apartment in New York. So far, I have shown her eight properties. Eight! All dotted across different parts of leafy London, from the white-bricked Georgian to the terraced Victorian. She's seen – and hated – them all.

I need her to agree on a property by the end of this week. Partly so I meet the deadline set by the client, and partly so I don't murder Melissa the next time I see her pout as if something has just collapsed and died under her nose when I say something like: this property only has one communal swimming pool.

Today, I'm showing her a three-bedroom flat in Knights-bridge. It's right behind the Victoria and Albert Museum and in its own gated community. It's on the third floor of a block of flats (an immediate red flag that I managed to skirt over by distracting her with the enormous lift) and spans over two thousand square feet. It's decorated in creams and light, speckled greys with fat, plumped-up sofas and towering double beds stacked with firm cushions, crisp white sheets swept over each mattress.

Looking around these ridiculous houses is one of my favourite parts of the job. Our clients range from all over the world, all with different needs and definitions of what the word 'essential' means, but they all have one thing in common: their budgets. I worked out pretty quickly that if you work for a big enough company, then they're prepared to chop off their left foot if it means that you'll agree to relocate. I mean, honestly. These people are being put up in the best properties London has to offer and act as if they're doing their CEO a favour.

Melissa skims past me in the reception as the lift pops open and we both step inside. We glide up to the third floor and I can't help but look at our reflections in the mirror as we stand next to each other. Melissa is tall and sleek, with dark skin and thin, long limbs and glossy hair. She's wearing a granite-grey coat that falls down her body and shiny snake-skin boots. Her make-up is subtle, only the tint of a pink lip and the slight flick of a mascara wand, but expertly applied. She is the definition of well put together.

Standing next to her, I look like her child.

Today, I'm wearing one of my favourite dresses. I made it out of an incredible Indian-inspired fabric. It's punch pink, with illustrations of round trees with birds nestled inside them, painted with a thin gold thread. It's silk, so not overly warm in this weather, and I've paired it with one of my oversized cardigans, which is bright orange and hangs off my shoulders with big, billowy sleeves and reaches the backs of my knees.

During the first month I worked for Pam, I could barely scrape enough together to pay for the bus every day. But as soon as I got paid, I went to Matalan, pulled everything 'smart and sensible' off the shelves and bought it. I'm talking neat grey trousers, navy pullovers and crisp white blouses, all finished off with black, buttoned-up shoes.

I wore my new outfit the following Monday, feeling pretty proud (albeit incredibly uncomfortable and slightly depressed at the disappearance of my personality in my horrible new clothes). Pam didn't say anything to me all morning, staying hunched over her laptop like always. It wasn't until I was leaving for the day that she muttered, 'Oh, by the way, Annie. What the fuck are you wearing?' I started giving her a babbling answer about my new 'work clothes' when I took a moment to notice what she was wearing. Loose-fitting cotton trousers, baggy shirt and big, jangly earrings. She didn't look like she was about to march into a boardroom and shake hands with Alan Sugar. She said I could wear what I wanted to work, and anyone who judged us based on what we were wearing wasn't the right customer for us anyway.

So, here I am, in all my colourful glory. I've learnt to ignore the looks of surprise when the especially wealthy clients meet me for the first time. If I'm feeling particularly brazen, I'll even take it as a compliment.

The lift pings, and the doors slide open right into the living room of the flat. It's bright and airy with wooden floors, high ceilings and an enormous TV built into a bookshelf.

Outside, the crisp white sunshine is pouring through the floor-to-ceiling windows. In the distance, you can see clusters of spiky, naked trees, completely free of their leaves now, housing several pigeons perched happily on their branches.

'Right,' I say, springing into action. 'Here we are. I'll leave you to have a look around. Come back to me if you have any questions. I do think this one has had a lot of interest, though, so we need to act fast if you think it's the one for you.'

I think I say this line about eight times a week, and every time I say it I feel it float into the air with less and less weight. These people are too important to care about deadlines. If they want something, they'll get it.

Melissa thanks me and glides through the apartment. I flick open my folder and look down at my next appointment this afternoon. It's with a new client who has a family of four that are being brought over for their new position in London. This means I'll need to organise schools, childcare, and inevitably find a place with a big garden in the centre of London.

I sigh and take out my phone, feeling increasingly annoyed as it stares blankly up at me.

It's been six days since my date with Nate, and three days since he sent me that cold, dismissive message, and I haven't heard from him since. I mean, I thought the date went well.

We spent the entire night together, laughing and chatting, but I've never received a more obvious 'I'm fobbing you off' message than the one he sent me. Was he faking it the entire time? Humouring me? It makes me feel a bit ill.

I didn't reply to his message, obviously. What was I supposed to say? The only smidgen of power I had left was to leave him hanging.

I take a deep breath and drop my phone back into my bag.

Penny's been with Mike since we left university and Tanya isn't fussed about men and dating, which is probably a side effect of being so beautiful that having men drop at your feet on a daily basis makes dating feel a bit tedious. This means that they are both fully enraptured by my potential new romance and have been picking apart Nate's message since the moment I sent them a screenshot of it.

It also meant that when I got home last night, they couldn't wait to find out if I'd heard anything more. And when I said I hadn't, they started their conspiracy theories, the excuses and then, inevitably, the bitching. What a bastard, he doesn't deserve you, men are pigs. You all know the words, sing along if you wish.

I think I've felt every emotion possible this week. The hope, the giddiness, excitement, desperation, disappointment . . . and now, anger.

I'm not just angry with Nate for ditching me, I'm also angry at myself. Like, hello? You knew this would happen. This sort of thing happens to me all the time, but did it stop me from spending days twirling around the flat like Anna from *Frozen*? No. You'd think after Tyler I'd have learnt my lesson and not got so bloody carried away. It always leads back to here. Hello disappointment, my old friend.

My bag vibrates and I look down to see a message from Mum pop up.

We can't wait to see you tomorrow!

I smile. It's Dad's birthday, which means I'm going home to celebrate with them. Mum did invite Penny and Tanya, but it's just me going.

I said I'd go down on Saturday and stay the night. My train is booked, all I need to do now is pack.

I hold my breath as I hear Melissa walking back through the apartment. Is this it? Have we finally found the one? Or will she be pulling her staple face of disgust?

I look up as she enters the room. To my annoyance, her nose is turned up.

'How was it?' I say, acting like I can't read her obvious disdain.

'Not for me,' she says in one breath, her chin high in the air. 'I'll need to see something else.'

I squash down the irritation that seethes under my skin. 'Of course,' I smile. 'No worries at all.'

Chapter Twenty-Eight

Nate

I've only seen Stevie once since the phone call from Mom as I came home from work and he completely blanked me, then went out shortly after. I know he's not really annoyed at me; he's annoyed at well... everything. Mom, her message, the panic it put us through. But neither of us can be annoyed at Mom about it – that's just cruel. So, it's easier to be annoyed with me. Whatever, I'm annoyed with him too. He's acting like a child.

We're brothers, we've fought before. But being ignored in a tiny flat which is too small for two regular adults, let alone two men who tower over six foot, is a new level of awkward. I knew he wasn't working tonight, and since I still haven't heard back from Annie, I had no choice but to go out.

Which is what has led me to the theatre, squashed next to Remy, who I suspect much like me is questioning the life choices he has made that have brought him to this moment.

It's not that Aunt Tell isn't good. I mean, she's been a professional actor her entire adult life. You don't get to do that unless you're talented. Look at the size of her house! I think it's more that this may be the most depressing play I've ever seen and Aunt Tell died in the first seven minutes. She could have mentioned that when she offered me the tickets.

But I do feel like the universe gave me these tickets as a helping hand. Aunt Tell clearly has no intention of speaking too deeply about Mom, so I thought if I did her a favour, saw Tell in the environment where she's happiest, then maybe she'll know I come in peace. Even though really, I come with quite a stern invitation and an unwavering need to get her to agree to come back to New York. But you know, peace too.

I'm trying not to think too hard about how I've screwed things up with Annie. Every time I check my phone, I hope to see a message from her, in her bright, fun voice, so that we can go back to how we were in that club in Clapham. But there's nothing. And who can blame her? I've hardly been a stand-up guy so far, have I?

I know I could message her again, but what would I say? I don't want to burden her with all my baggage. Not when we had so much fun together.

Remy shuffles in his seat and I hide a smile. These seats are way too small for us, and I know this is hardly Remy's idea of a great night out. But he didn't even flinch when I mentioned going. He's a good guy.

I jolt to attention as the audience start to clap and I realise that the play must have come to an end. Aunt Tell takes centre stage, throwing her arms into the air before cupping them to her chest and dipping into a deep bow. She gets the loudest cheer of them all.

'Thank you for coming with me to this,' I say to Remy as the claps fizzle out. The lights come on and I start hearing the snaps of the theatre seats as people get to their feet.

Remy raises his eyebrows at me, a small smile playing at the corners of his mouth. 'I didn't realise you hated squash that much.'

He groans as he stands and clicks his back.

'I definitely owe you a pint,' I say. 'Do you mind if we stay behind and say hi to my aunt? It won't take long. I said we'd meet her at the bar.'

Remy nods as we start to pick our way through the crowd. My hand throbs as it drops to my side. It's still wrapped up in layers of bandages.

As we walk down the stairs of the theatre, I spot that the bar is practically empty as the crowd swarms towards the doors, back onto the icy, quiet streets of a Thursday night. The bartender clocks us as we walk forward, and I can almost see his fight not to roll his eyes at the possibility that his shift won't be finishing in the next five minutes.

'Is the bar still open?' Remy says, peering over the bartender's shoulder.

'Yes,' the bartender says, disgruntled. 'We close at eleven.'

'Great,' Remy nods, 'I could do with a drink.'

'We're just meeting one of the cast members,' I explain. 'We won't be long.'

'Nathaniel!'

I look up as the excited voice of Aunt Tell pours through

the room like heavy cream. She sashays towards us, her face still thick with show make-up, wrapped in a heavy coat. She throws her arms around my neck – nearly breaking my back as she pulls me down to her level – and gives me a huge squeeze. I'm not sure if I'll ever get used to her treating me like her long-lost son when she's been ignoring me for the past couple of months.

'Hi Aunt Tell,' I say as she lets me go. 'Well done on the show – you were great. This is my friend, Remy.'

Aunt Tell turns to Remy and dips her chin. She holds out her hand and he takes it, giving a little bow.

'You were fantastic,' he says earnestly. 'What would you like to drink?'

Patches of pink form on Aunt Tell's cheeks and she shimmies her shoulders in a way I've never seen an adult do.

'Ooooh! Champagne, please!'

Remy doffs his flat cap and turns back to the bartender, who now looks thoroughly pissed at the realisation that he'll be working right up until 10:59 p.m.

'You enjoyed it, then?' Aunt Tell coos, putting a hand on my arm. 'You really liked it?'

'Yes,' I say at once. 'You were great.' That bit isn't a lie, at least.

'You are too kind.' She cups her chest, turning to gaze at Remy, who gives her a wink over his shoulder.

'Listen,' I say, keen to steer the conversation before Aunt Tell is completely swept away by Remy. 'I spoke to Mom today. She—'

'Your darling mom!' Aunt Tell cries, her hands back at her heart. 'How is she?'

I pause. She's fine . . . considering she's dealing with early onset dementia.

'She was asking about you,' I say, avoiding the question in order to keep things light. 'I was thinking maybe you could come back with us at Christmas to visit.'

'Sounds wonderful,' she says, but as Remy turns back with her champagne, I can tell she isn't listening.

'Really?' I press on. 'Shall I book us some flights, then? I'll just need your passport details.'

'Sure, honey,' she says absent-mindedly, her glittering eyes fixed on Remy. 'So, tell me, what did *you* think of the show?'

I hop from one foot to the other as the subway rockets around the corner, snaking through the underground passages. Mom called earlier this afternoon, and we ended up chatting my entire lunch break. Everything has slipped back into normal conversation. How are you? How was your day? Was work okay? How's Stevie? I debated messaging Dad, telling him about the message from Mom, but I couldn't bring myself to do it. If he didn't already know, then why would I tell him? All it would do is scare him, and he's scared enough as it is. I know that. I've just run away from it.

Guilt hammers under my chest and I close my eyes for a moment.

The train pulls up at Camden and my eyes open as

I knock into the man next to me. I mumble an apology, squeezing my way off the tube to start the quick walk back to the flat. The air is cold, whizzing past my face and leaving speckles of ice behind, ready to nip and pinch at the tips of my ears and the tops of my cheeks. The Londoners are fully buried in their scarves now, with only their narrowed eyes poking out at the top, scanning the sidewalks for any gaps in the crowds that they can skirt through. I weave my way through the throng of commuters, pulling my coat tight to my body. Sure, it's cold, but it has nothing on New York winters. Brian and Helen were chatting excitedly with a few others today about how it might snow at the weekend, but that's one part of England that I haven't been swept away by. You don't know snow until you've been to America.

I hop up the final steps of the building and push my key into the lock, giving the door a swift kick to force it open. 'Hello?' I call out, pushing the door shut and unravelling my scarf.

'Hi.' Stevie's voice comes from the kitchen, carried by the splats and crackles of something in the frying pan.

Okay, so he is talking to me now. That's something.

I drop my bag and walk into the kitchen. Stevie is frying an egg.

He looks up from the hob. 'Want one?'

I shake my head. 'Nah man, I'm good.'

I don't know if it's my mind playing tricks on me, but Stevie looks thinner than he did a week ago. His eyes are circled by deep, dark rings and his cheekbones are jutting out under his greyish skin. His mouth is pressed together in a line, like he's fighting desperately not to let out all the angry words that are buzzing inside his mouth.

He nods, flipping his egg onto a piece of bread and following me into the living room.

'I saw Aunt Tell the other day,' I say, watching closely for a reaction.

He scowls, dropping down onto the sofa. 'Why?'

'Mom talks about her a lot.' I shrug. 'I was hoping I might be able to persuade her to visit her back home.'

He scrunches up his face, his eyes fixed on the TV. 'She won't do that.'

'Why not?'

'She's too selfish.'

I focus on the TV as two cheery presenters sit on a sofa and interview a sad-looking elderly man.

He glances at me. 'What have you done to your hand?'

'Ah,' I say, looking at my bandage. 'I punched your light. I'll get you a new one.'

He frowns. 'Are you okay?'

'Yeah, fine.' We fall back into silence and I sit down next to him. 'Are you working tonight?' I ask.

Stevie shakes his head.

'This weekend?' I press further. He stuffs his sandwich into his mouth as the theme tune for *Bargain Hunt* starts up and shakes his head again.

'Did you want to do something?'

'What do you mean?' he asks, his mouth full of congealed bread and his eyebrows still scrunched together angrily. I feel myself bristle.

Why does he have to be so angry all the time? And with me? I'm just asking if he wants to spend time together.

'Well, it's Thanksgiving,' I say, trying to keep my voice light.

'They don't celebrate Thanksgiving here.'

I bite the inside of my cheek, forcing myself to take a deep breath. 'Yeah, but we do,' I say slowly. 'I could cook us up a Thanksgiving dinner. I can try and make us some yams?' Stevie doesn't say anything, but just cocks his head to the side non-committally. 'We could call Mom and Dad,' I continue. 'We could try and time it so that we eat at the same time and FaceTime them or something. Pretend we're all together.'

Stevie swallows his mouthful. 'What's the point?'

I can't help it now; the hot anger I've been trying to keep at bay bubbles up inside me. 'What's the point in having dinner?'

'You know what I mean.'

'No,' I say flatly. 'I don't.'

He glares at me, leaning forward on his elbows. The only light is from the TV, which is flickering madly as the adverts pop through the living room. 'Forget it,' he says, getting to his feet.

'It's nice to call Mom and Dad on Thanksgiving because they're our *parents*?' I snap, finally losing control. 'What's wrong with that?'

Stevie doesn't answer, walking into the kitchen. But now

the anger is out I can't control it; it's like everything I've kept in my bubbling, angry jar for the past month is now free. It's exploding through my body, making the blood under my skin hot and my heart race.

'No,' I say, getting to my feet and following him. 'Don't walk away from me, Stevie. You have something to say. Say it. What's wrong? Why don't you want to speak to Mom?'

'Because she's not there!' he cries, spinning round to face me. 'You saw her the other day! She put us through hell and then couldn't even remember. There is no point in talking to her.'

I stare at him, anger buzzing through me. 'No point?' I repeat. 'No point in speaking to your own mom?'

He looks at me squarely in the face and although his jaw is tight and jutted forward, I can see the glimmer of fear behind his eyes.

'No,' he says eventually, dropping his plate on the side with a clatter. 'There is no point.'

'Stevie,' I say. 'You don't mean that. You—'

'I'm not doing it, Nate,' he says, going into his room. 'I'm just not.'

I open my mouth to reply but it's too late. He's slammed the door.

I spend the rest of the evening sitting on the sofa, watching garbage on TV. Two people scream at each other in *EastEnders*, a stand-up comedian promotes their new show on a red couch and finally the sombre ten o'clock news rolls around before I pull myself up off the sofa and into bed.

Stevie stays locked in his room, not even coming out to go

to the bathroom. I debate knocking on the door and forcing him to talk to me, but I'm worried what I might say. The red mist of anger still hasn't fully faded from behind my eyes; one wrong thing said or a look thrown in my direction and who knows what we might end up yelling at each other.

As I lie in bed, the weekend stretches before me like an ominous blank page. Stevie will be in, and I'll end up spending half the time locked inside my room waiting for him to go out so I can relax in peace, and the other half sat on the sofa wondering if he's secretly hoping the same.

In the end, I message Remy, hoping that he might be at a loose end or wanting some company to watch another football game, but he's up in Leicester for the weekend visiting his parents. I even debate messaging Aunt Tell, but decide against it. I don't want to spend the weekend around her weird, buzzing energy. It's hardly the way I usually spend Thanksgiving.

After a few hours of wallowing in my own pit of worry and self-doubt, I pull out my phone and do the one thing that Mom and I spoke about doing when I came to London. I google where *The Holiday* is set and book a return train ticket for the next day.

My hand stings and I look down at the bandage still tightly woven around my hand, although a little frayed and peeling away at the edges. I take a sip of my pint. I thought I'd try a Guinness this time. It's not bad, but hardly as delicious as it looks when it's poured and you're made to believe you're about to drink something like thick, creamy hot chocolate.

So, here I am, sitting in a cosy country pub. It's all a bit wonky and looks as if a child has given it a big squeeze when all the bricks were still wet. There are flickering yellow lamps and lots of thin bar towels. A gaggle of people are huddled around a dartboard in the corner of the room, cheering every couple of minutes and slapping each other on the back, and there's a glossy black Lab stretched out in front of the roaring fire which is feeding a warm, smoky smell throughout the pub.

It only took two hours on the train, and as I stared out of the window and watched the world around me slowly get less grey, I felt the chains around my chest loosen too. At one point, I felt so far away from my problems that I nearly let myself message Annie. This time last week, we were about to have our first date together. Well, first if you don't count the ten minutes of chat at the Halloween ball.

I can't message her now. I mean, what would I say? Sorry I sent such a weird message; I thought my mom was in danger so I didn't really have any working brain cells to send you a proper message, and then I spent the rest of the week either yelling at my brother or preparing to sell my organs if it meant I could go back home and make sure she's okay?

Annie was so fun and carefree last week, and so was I. That Nate was fun. Nobody wants to hang out with this Nate. Even I don't want to hang out with him.

I sigh, taking another sip of the Guinness.

My train arrived at midday, and I've spent the afternoon wandering around the cobbled streets and going into quaint, tiny tea rooms and along paths by flowing rivers.

The Cotswolds is not too dissimilar to London, but it's like a version of London with a layer pulled back. Everyone walks a bit slower and smiles at each other. The bartender at this pub asked how I was and seemed quite happy to chat to me when he picked up my New York accent, and even gave me tips on what to see in the area. By this point, it was only a few hours until my train back to London, but I still lapped it all up. Maybe I'll come here again, for a proper weekend.

I took a crossword from the bar and set myself up by the fire, being careful not to disturb the black Lab, whose name I learnt was Bessie, and I've been sat here ever since. It feels quite easy to hide from all your problems when you're sitting in a place like this, where the only thing you have to think about is what six down is, nine letters: ARCHETYPE.

I take out my phone and send a picture to Mom, being sure to capture the roaring fire in the background and the framed black and white photo of the local cricket team, all proudly resting on one knee and smiling up at the camera. She'd love it here. I'll bring her one day.

As I click 'send', I notice the weather app on the home screen and I start, quickly getting to my feet.

Shit. I'd forgotten about the snow.

'Sorry,' I say to the bartender. 'It says it's meant to snow tonight, is that right?'

He blinks at me as we both silently question why I'm asking him, as if he's the weatherman.

'Think so,' he says after a pause. 'Are you staying here tonight?'

'No,' I say. 'I'm going back to London.'
'How?'
'By train.'
He picks up a glass and starts cleaning it with a rag, looking doubtful. 'Good luck, fella.'

Chapter Twenty-Nine

Annie

I madly start throwing clothes into my open suitcase, the flurry of white specks taunting me in my peripheral vision from my bedroom window, only visible under the streetlights thanks to the 5 p.m. darkness. I'd got totally caught up in an outfit I was creating. We had another commission come through this week, this time for a toad. I found an incredible green, glittery fabric which looks wet to touch when the light bounces off it, and I spent all afternoon sketching out different silhouettes. Well, up until about five minutes ago, when I looked up and realised that it was *actually snowing* and I'd have to leave London *immediately* in order to get a train before they are all inevitably cancelled as our entire civilisation collapses like it does every time we get any more than four specks of snow.

Like, it's not even December yet! Why is it snowing?

I hear a knock on the door. 'Yup?' I call out.

I need to pack a phone charger, laptop and laptop charger just in case I get stuck there because of the snow (seems ridiculous, but entirely possible). In which case, how many jumpers should I bring? Is five excessive?

'Hey, have you got a minute?' My head snaps up to see

Tanya and Penny perched on my bed. I stare at them. Their heads are slightly low on their shoulders, an identical look of worry painted on both their faces.

'Yeah?' I say. 'What is it?'

'Maybe sit down,' Tanya says and I immediately drop into my desk chair, my heart jumping around my body.

'What's going on? You're scaring me. Who's dying?' I wait for Penny to laugh and call me a drama queen, and when she doesn't, I feel like I might be sick. 'Oh my God, it's serious, isn't it? What? Just tell me.'

'I'm moving in with Mike.' Penny blurts it out, as if all the words have collected in her mouth and have fallen out in one go.

I pause, a jumble of confused feelings pushing their way through my body. 'Congratulations!' I say, getting up and hugging her. 'That's great, but . . . oh, but . . .' I trail off as realisation dawns on me. 'You're moving in with Mike? So, you're . . . you're moving out?'

Penny nods and out of nowhere I feel a lump in my throat.

Oh my God, I can't cry. This is a huge deal for Penny. It's exciting. I need to be excited.

But it's just . . . Penny and I have lived together for the past ten years.

'That's great!' I say, although now my voice is all weird and stretched, like it's two octaves too high. 'I'm so excited for you.' I turn to Tanya and hit her on the leg. 'Who are we going to get to fill the boxroom, eh? No nutters!' I laugh too loudly and then realise that I'm the only one making any sound. I was so focused on Penny that I'd barely looked at Tanya, but she's pulling the same expression as Penny.

Gosh, she looks more upset than I do. 'Hey,' I say, giving her hand a squeeze. 'It's okay. We'll still see Pen all the time, and we can get her to make us loads of batches of stew before she goes so our freezer is full, right, Pen?'

'I'm moving to Paris.'

Just like Penny, Tanya's confession comes out in a weird, frantic burst, but this one hits me like a cold bucket of water.

'What?' I manage.

Penny has been with Mike for years. I always knew the day would come where Tanya and I would be left to our own devices for a few years, until we both eventually settled down when we were *both ready*.

'Paris?' I say stupidly. 'Why?'

'She's been offered a job,' Penny says, and I notice that she's put her arm around Tanya's shoulders supportively and I feel a horrible pang of guilt. She's not hearing this for the first time. She already knew.

Oh my God, have they rehearsed this without me?

'A job?' I say, after realising that I've been silent for too long. 'What job?'

'It's in the Paris office,' Tanya says in a small voice. 'I'll be heading up their PR department. It's quite a big deal.'

'It's a huge deal!' Penny says loyally, giving Tanya's shoulders a shake, and it's only then that I notice I haven't even said anything positive yet.

'That's amazing!' I utter. 'Wow, Tanya. That's huge.' I reach forward and give her a hug, but it's all limp and cold, not like the warm, hard hugs that we normally give each other. 'So . . . wow,' I say when I sit back down. 'You're both moving . . . That's amazing, it's great. I'm so happy for you both.'

And the thing is, I do mean it, but my voice is weak, like it's been stripped of all emotion.

'We're really sorry!' Tanya cries. 'We don't want to leave you!'

I look down at my hands, feeling a flush of embarrassment. 'Haha,' I say in a weird, fake laugh. 'I'm not your child, Tanya.'

Even though I do feel like one, quite a lot of the time.

'No!' Tanya says quickly, her face flushing. 'Of course not. I just—'

'It's not for another month or so,' Penny says.

My stomach lurches. 'Have you told the landlord?'

She shakes her head earnestly. 'No, but Mike has found a place for us to live, so I do need to tell them soon.'

I turn to Tanya. 'When do they want you in Paris?'

'As soon as possible,' she manages.

And then it hits me. I'm not just being told that my best friends are about to do something amazing and exciting, something that I have no version of; they're also telling me that the three of us are about to split up and, for the first time in ten years, we're not going to live together. We're not going to live in our flat. We're all going to move out. *I'm going to have to move out.*

Shit. Where am I going to live?

'Okay,' I say, turning back to my suitcase to try and hide

the fact that my eyes are suddenly brimming with tears. 'Well, you can tell him tonight if you like.'

'Annie . . .' Penny says. 'Don't be like that.'

'I'm not being like anything!' I say, trying to sound bright. 'I've got to get a train back home before the snow gets really bad, and if you both need to move out quickly then we might as well get the ball rolling.'

'Are you okay?' Tanya says, the desperation in her voice so heartfelt that it almost makes me melt into a puddle on the floor. But instead, I turn to them, a horrible, painful smile forced on my face.

'I'm fine!' I say. 'No, I'm great. I'm really, really happy for you both.'

I loll my head against the train window and feel my skull rattle against the glass. I left as quickly as I could, stuffing my suitcase and forcing it shut, then running out of the flat, leaving behind a string of excuses about how I had to make this train, it was the last one that was running for the day, and if I missed it then I'd miss Dad's birthday.

All of it was true, but that wasn't what I was really saying. Really, it was more like: I've got to go, I can't stand to be in the flat for a minute longer otherwise I'll burst into tears and ruin your lovely, special moment with my selfish fear about what the hell I'm going to do now and you'll never believe me when I say I'm really happy for you both, even though I really am. Really.

The worst part is, I didn't see this coming. I knew that Penny would move in with Mike at some point, but I tucked the thought away and assumed it would happen in like . . . ten years. But not ten years, because by then we'd all be in our forties, but like, when we're thirty-something . . . even though we're all thirty-something now.

And as for Tanya, I knew she was fantastic at her job. She always has been. I knew her PR firm has offices all over the world and she's always wanted to travel more. But I never considered that might result in her getting snapped up by a different branch of the firm and leaving the country. But then, why not? It seems so obvious now. All of it seems so bloody obvious, and yet I *never* considered any of it. I was too busy in my little bubble, pratting about and making costumes. What is the matter with me?

The train starts to slow down, approaching my stop, and I get to my feet, hauling my suitcase off the top rack. The snowflakes have steadily fallen thicker as the evening has gone on, and the further the train has pulled into the countryside, the more it feels like we're being drawn inside an enormous feather pillow.

I heave my suitcase down onto the platform with a thud, wincing as the icy air hits my face and the snowflakes cling to my eyelashes. It's a ten-minute walk home from the station, and as I decided to get an earlier train, I told Dad not to worry about picking me up. My suitcase is on wheels, and anyway, I need the time to collect myself before seeing Mum and Dad. If I saw Dad right now, I'm worried I'd burst straight into tears.

I stop at the ticket barrier and start fumbling for my ticket. My hands grasp at my empty, gaping pockets and I curse under my breath.

Where is my ticket?

I sidestep out of the way of the queue of people, looking around as I debate whether to beg the station staff to let me through or jump the ticket barrier and make a break for it, when my heart stops.

It's him. Nate. Stood on the platform.

He . . . What is he doing here?

I peer at him. The snow is falling thickly now and it's hard to see . . . but as I walk closer towards him, my heart starts to race. Oh my God, it's him. It's definitely him. The guy who ran out on me, and then well and truly fobbed me off. Should I say something? Or just go? No, Annie, hold your head up high and leave. He is not worth your time. He is—

'What the fuck are you doing here?'

Or, you know, just shout at him.

Nate's head jolts up and he looks so shocked to see me that I almost laugh. '*Annie?*' he cries. 'What are you doing here? Hi!'

'Remember me?' I say. 'I'm the girl you keep trying to lose?'

He blinks at me. 'Trying to lose?'

'Yeah.' I pull my hat closer to my ears. 'First you run out on a conversation with me without saying goodbye, and then you fob me off after we have an actual date.'

'Fob you off?' he repeats. 'I didn't do that, did I?'

'Yes, you did! We had a great time and then you just palmed me off with a shitty "sorry I don't want to see you again".'

God. Way to play it cool, Annie.

'Ah,' he presses his thumb and forefinger against his

eyebrows, 'you're right. I didn't mean it like that. I'm sorry. I suppose I've blown it now, haven't I?'

'Yes,' I say at once. 'You have.'

He nods, the playful spark in his eyes that I saw last time we were together nowhere to be seen. He drops his chin. 'Understood.'

This is the part where I turn on my heel and storm off, with my last shred of dignity and an impressive story to tell my friends. But something stops me. He looks so sad.

'You haven't answered my question.'

He looks up. 'What question?'

'What are you doing here?'

'Ah.' He tucks his hands in his pockets and then looks up at the blinking announcement screen. 'Well, I think I live here now.'

'In Gloucestershire?'

'On this platform.' He gives me a goofy smile and I feel myself soften.

'Are you going to give me a real answer?'

'Oh, it is my real answer.' He runs his fingers through his hair. 'I thought it would be fun to come down here for the day and escape London – it's where *The Holiday* was filmed and Mom insisted that I went and found it while I was in England. She's not doing so good, so I thought it would cheer her up if I sent her some pictures. But it turns out that you people can't deal with snow and all the trains home are cancelled, and I have zero signal to get a taxi, so now I'm stuck here . . .' He pushes a small patch of sludge with the tip of his shoe. 'On this platform, at one with the pigeons.'

I look around. Sure enough, we're now the only people standing on the platform. The snow is spiralling out of the sky, hitting us in all directions, and in place of where the trains are normally announced are the flashing, ominous words: NO TRAINS.

'Come on,' I say, cocking my head as I turn on my heel.

He looks up. 'What do you mean?'

'I can't just leave you here,' I say, nerves tickling at my body as I hear the words before I register them. Shit, am I really going to do this?

'No, honestly. It's fine.' I turn back around and see him standing in the same spot, his hands firmly pressed in his pockets. 'You're right, I've been an asshole. You don't need to help me.'

I raise my eyebrows at him. 'I'm not going to just leave you out here in the snow, am I? I'll find you somewhere to stay.' I start walking towards the exit, finally locating my train ticket in the depths of my pocket, but he doesn't follow me.

'I've tried,' he says lamely. 'It's just, the signal here is so bad and my phone . . .'

'Are you still standing there?' I place a hand on my hip. 'I'll help you, now hurry up. It's freezing.'

'Really?' he says. 'You don't have to . . . I'm sure I can . . . thank you so much.'

I laugh wryly as he finally catches up with me. 'Don't thank me yet. You have to meet my parents first.'

Chapter Thirty

Nate

It's like I've stepped into a fairy tale. The sky is white with thick, silent snow falling around us like powder and sitting on top of the sidewalk like icing sugar. All the noise I could hear earlier of cars, clinking pint glasses and laughter has vanished. It's like it's only me and Annie left in the world, making our way down yet another street full of cottages with thatched roofs and square windows, sparkling yellow with the life and light of everyone inside them.

And then there's Annie. I couldn't believe it when I turned around and there she was. I'd been stood on the platform for hours, silently panicking. My train had been cancelled, as had the ones before and after it, and my phone was playing a game of cat and mouse with the single bar of signal it managed to pick up all day. There were no Ubers around, and the taxi office at the front of the station was closed. I was paralysed, trying to work out whether it was better to wander back down into the town and see if a pub would take me in for the night, Mary and Joseph style, or to stay put in the hope that a train may turn up or someone who ran the taxi rank. Basically, I was waiting for a miracle. And that's when Annie showed up.

With everything that has happened this week with Mom and Stevie, I'd almost forgotten how it felt to be around Annie. How I felt lighter, freer, a bit brighter. My smile was bigger, always waiting to grow on my face, my eyes constantly looking for her. I can't believe I didn't message her again. Why didn't I message her?

But it doesn't matter now. Even though she's saving me from sleeping on a bench in the snow, I've ruined it. Someone like Annie doesn't need to be with a flake like me. She deserves someone who knows how brilliant she is.

Well, *I* know how brilliant she is. I've never been so sure of anything in my life.

She catches my eye and laughs. 'Will you stop it?'

I can't help it, I laugh too. 'Stop what?'

'Looking at me like that.' She pushes her hands into her pockets. 'I can see you.'

'Sorry. I'll play it cool.' I force myself to look forward. She steals a glance at me and I can't help it, I look at her again. We both laugh and she pushes me with her elbow.

'I bet this is your dream,' she says, and for a moment I'm about to spill out that yes, this is exactly like my dream, until I realise that she's talking about our picturesque surroundings. 'You don't get more quintessentially British than the Cotswolds.'

'You're right,' I say. 'That's why I came here for the day. I can't believe you grew up here, you're so lucky.'

Another wave of snow sprays us both in the face and we

wince. The snowflakes stick to my eyelashes and I notice the tip of Annie's nose has turned pink.

'Go on, then,' she says.

'What?'

'Tell me what the fantasy is.' She grins at me. 'I want to know what your perfect British life would be and how realistic it actually is. You do know that we don't all have magic umbrellas or eat marmalade sandwiches?'

'I hope not,' I say, giving her a look. 'Marmalade is disgusting.' She laughs and I scan along the street. At the end, there's a house set further back than the others. It has a small garden path with stones leading the way like lily pads up to the cottage made of warm, golden stone, and strings of ivy weaving around towards the uneven tiled roof. It looks just like the *Holiday* house.

'This,' I say, nodding towards the house. 'I'd live somewhere like this. I'd be happy—'

'And in love?'

I feel a warm glow in my chest. 'Of course. Isn't life a bit better when you're in love?'

Annie snorts and I look round at her. 'Sorry,' she says, trying to hide her smile. 'I just don't know if I can deal with how cheesy you are. You're like a cartoon character.'

'Maybe I'm just saying what everyone else is too cool to say.' I raise my eyebrows at her and she cocks her head.

'Go on, then,' she says. 'What's in this house? A wife?'

'Yup,' I nod, pushing my face further into my scarf. 'Some kids. A big study filled with books.'

'Sounds nice. A sewing machine?'

I smile. 'Yeah, of course. A whole room full of clothes and fabrics and . . . needles. I don't know, whatever you need to sew.'

She laughs. 'A fire?'

'Definitely, and a big dining table.'

'And a cat?'

'No.' I scrunch up my face. 'A dog.'

'Ah.' She kicks a patch of snow and pulls a face of mock disappointment. 'You've lost me there, I'm afraid.'

'Who said you were invited?' I tease.

'Wasn't I?' She gives me a knowing look.

I smile and shake my head. 'I think you belong there with me. Who else will keep the room with the sewing machine alive?'

She nods and points over a small bridge. 'My parents' house is just over here.'

I smile, tucking my hands into my pockets.

What I don't say is: who else would I be in love with?

Chapter Thirty-One

Annie

Oh God, I can't believe I'm about to do this.

After *years* of hints, drunken questions and downright blackmail (if you get married before I turn sixty, I'll get Dad to pay for a bar. Please, Annie. I just want to look nice in the pictures!), I am willingly bringing a man home for them to meet.

And not only that, I'm doing it with absolutely no warning. Not only have I not told my parents that I'm bringing Nate round; I haven't even told them that he *exists*.

I did debate calling them once me and Nate started walking home, but I knew that no matter how much notice I gave them, it wouldn't be enough to stop Mum from *exploding* with adrenaline. So I thought the best bet was not to say anything and let them find out when Nate appeared on their doorstep. At least then Mum might behave herself a bit more. I hope.

I'd planned on being annoyed at Nate for the rest of my days. I was ready to write off our amazing date as a weird one-off, never-to-happen-again experience. Like a spontaneous night out with your friends that was amazing, but you know you could never recreate it so everyone just promises to never try.

But then he was right there, standing in front of me. I was angry at first but it just faded away, and after sixty seconds of us talking I was back in Infernos, laughing opposite him as we danced like we were the only two people in the club. It felt impossible to stay angry with him, unnatural even. Like something inside me was going: *no, this isn't the right feeling to have with him. It's not anger, it's something else. It's something better.*

Also, I was hardly going to leave him to freeze to death.

I glance up at him and feel a pang in my heart. He looked different when I saw him on the platform. I don't know if it's because he was freezing and lost or if it was something else, but he just looked . . . different. Slightly smaller, slightly less bright. I couldn't leave him, I just couldn't.

Although I have a feeling I'll regret this generosity of spirit in approximately ninety seconds.

'Okay,' I say, turning to Nate as I pull out my keys. 'There are some things I should warn you about my parents.'

He looks at me questioningly. 'Right?'

'They can be a bit . . . intense.'

'Intense?'

'They're great,' I add quickly, worried that I'm painting them out to be nudists or role-play addicts. 'They're just a bit . . . intense.' I glance at the upstairs window and to my alarm spot Mum, gawping down at us both.

'You've already said that.'

'I know, but I can't think of any other way to describe them.'

He smiles and squeezes my arm. 'I'm sure they're great.'

I open my mouth to say something else when the door bangs open to reveal my mum and dad. They're both wide-eyed and flushed, and Mum is out of breath from sprinting down the stairs to check that she isn't hallucinating.

'Hi,' I say tightly, eyeballing them both to try and send them a message telepathically.

Don't act weird. He's just a man. You've seen men before. Stay cool.

'This is Nate,' I say. 'Nate, these are my parents.'

I'm about to say their names, when to my alarm Mum throws her arms around Nate's neck and for an awful moment, I think she's about to burst into tears.

'Nate!' she cries. 'Hello! We've heard so much about you!'

I stare at her, horrified. She didn't even know he existed until about eight seconds ago!

I turn to Dad, hoping he'll bring some sanity to the table, when to my horror I realise that his eyes are shining.

'We're so pleased to meet you, Nate,' he says gravely, shaking his hand as if, after years of praying, Nate is finally here to make a bride of their desperate, gremlin daughter.

'Right!' I say quickly. 'Everyone inside, it's freezing. Mum and Dad? In the kitchen, *now*.'

'Oh Annie, he is *lovely*.'

'Mum!' I cry, snapping my fingers at her as she slips back into her I-need-to-buy-a-new-hat trance. 'What did I just say? He's a *friend* who is stuck here because of the snow; I said I'd help him find somewhere to stay. He doesn't know the area, he's American.'

'What football team does he support?' Dad pipes up.

I roll my eyes. Why is that important? 'Just be normal, please?' I say. 'Don't terrify him by giving him the Spanish Inquisition.'

'Fun fact about the Spanish Inquisition—'

'Not now, Dad!' I run out of the kitchen and find Nate awkwardly perched on the living-room sofa. The fire is roaring with brilliant, yellow flames, sending a lovely woody smell through the house.

'Sorry about that,' I say. 'They were just a bit . . . excited. Not that they've ever heard of you before,' I add quickly, wanting to shut down any idea that I've spent the last week doodling *I heart Nate* on the back of my hand.

'Really?' Nate says lightly. 'I told my mom about you.'

'Really?' I blink at him, taken aback.

'She loves romance,' he says. 'She wanted to hear how my dating life was going in London, so I told her.'

'What did she say?'

He smiles, looking down at his hands. 'She wanted me to try and find you.'

'And did you tell her?' I sit down next to him.

'Tell her what?'

'That we found each other!' I say, feeling myself redden.

'Ah.' A shadow passes over his face. 'No. Not yet.'

I push my lips together. God, read the room, Annie. He didn't message you, he hasn't told his mum any more about you. *He isn't into you.* I just need to find him somewhere to stay for the night, do my Good Samaritan deed and then forget all about him. Weird lovely feelings or no weird lovely feelings. That is what I have to do.

'Right,' I say, pulling my parents' laptop out from under the sofa and tapping in their password. 'So, here you go. If you google B&Bs in the Cotswolds, there are loads around here. You can use our landline to call any.' I hand him the phone. 'Let me know which one you decide to book and I'll walk you over to it. There are quite a few that aren't that far away.'

He nods. 'Right. Of course. Thank you, Annie.'

I slap my thighs and get to my feet. 'No problem,' I say, walking out of the sitting room and forcing myself not to look back at him.

'Right!' I say loudly as I walk into the kitchen, forcing Mum and Dad to stop their incessant whispering in the corner. 'What's the plan for this weekend?'

They blink at me, totally still for a second, when Dad launches into action. 'Ah, of course. Well, we thought we may do a nice walk tomorrow and then—'

'Annie!' Mum hisses in her I'm-being-really-quiet-but-I'm-actually-being-insanely-loud whisper. 'What's going on? Is he your boyfriend?'

'No!' I snap, exasperated. 'Mum, we've just been over this – we're just friends.'

'But why?' she cries. 'He seems so nice!'

'You've spent thirty seconds with him.'

'Mother's intuition! A mother *always knows*.' Mum taps the side of her nose and I roll my eyes.

'I think that's about whether your baby needs feeding or burping, not whether your daughter should go out with a guy you like the look of,' I say flatly.

'Excuse me?'

My head whips round to see Nate standing in the doorway. My face immediately burns. Oh God, how long has he been standing there for?

He's holding the phone and looking at us apologetically. 'I'm so sorry,' he says. 'How do you work this? I think I've found somewhere.'

'Found somewhere?' Mum repeats. 'What do you mean? You're not leaving, are you?'

And then everything goes into slow motion, I can feel it about to happen, right in front of my eyes . . . but I just . . . can't . . . quite . . .

'You must stay for dinner!'

. . . stop it.

'Sorry,' I gabble to Nate about forty minutes later, the first moment I've got just the two of us after Mum and Dad barrelled him into the kitchen and refused to let him go. Where did you grow up? What do you do for a job? How are you finding London? What shoe size are you?

Okay, so they didn't ask the last one, but I wouldn't put it past them at this rate.

'Sorry?' He turns to me. 'What for?'

We're both sat up on the stools in the kitchen, looking over to where Mum has been chopping, simmering and adding the final touches to dinner. Dad has poured us both large glasses of red wine and the fairy lights that Mum hangs every autumn are twinkling around us.

'I didn't mean to ambush you into spending the evening with my family,' I say.

And me, I want to add, but I don't.

'If you want to go back to a hotel then that's totally fine. I'll make an excuse for you, say you have to get back to work or something.'

He smiles at me, and sitting this close to him in the light I notice for the first time that he has a dimple in his right cheek that creases when he smiles. I can smell his earthy, manly scent and for a moment I feel myself leaning closer towards him. But I catch myself.

He's not interested, remember?

'Not at all,' he says, 'I'm having a great time. Is this really where you grew up?'

I look around at the kitchen. Pots and pans hang from the ceiling, and behind us is our oak table, stained with years of dinners and parties, little hands clutching onto the wood and drinks spilling over after too much generous clinking. Artwork covers the walls, but also framed photos of the three of us: windswept at the beach, huddled around a Christmas tree, standing at the top of a cliff in Cornwall.

'Yeah,' I say proudly. 'It is.'

'It's amazing.'

I sigh. 'I know. I'm really lucky.'

'It's just like the houses in the films,' he says, leaning back on his stool and looking around. 'My mom would love it here.'

'Has she been to England before?'

He shakes his head, his dark eyes still scanning the room, taking in every nook and cranny. Every wooden chicken, every framed photograph, every speckled plate.

I'm about to ask him more about his mum when, right on cue, my own mum bustles in. For God's sake, has she put lipstick on?

'Right,' she says jovially as she marches over to the Aga, 'I think we're almost there. Where's your father?'

I start to tell her I don't know when she cranes her neck and bellows his name over her shoulder. Nate catches my eye and grins.

'Sorry,' I mumble again. 'I hope your family is as mad as mine.'

'I think they're fantastic.'

'Here we are!' Dad bumbles into the kitchen. Although he hasn't put lipstick on, I can tell that he's brushed his hair. Probably the result of a panicked Mum, who I think would be secretly hoovering upstairs right now if she didn't have a lasagne in the oven.

'I think it's ready.' She smiles at me, her eyes flitting to Nate. She looks as if she's about to burst with happiness. God, if she's like this now, how the hell is she going to behave when I bring an actual boyfriend home?

'I'll set the table,' Dad says, rubbing his hands together and pulling open our cutlery drawer.

'Can I help?' Nate says, swivelling round on the stool. 'What can I do?'

I pick up my wine and shake my head. There is absolutely no way they will let Nate even raise a finger while he's here.

Falling For You

'Nothing!' Dad says. 'You are our *guest*.'

I raise my eyebrows at Nate. 'Just relax,' I say. 'They're not going to let you do anything.'

'I can't just sit here and not help,' Nate protests. 'You're already letting me crash your dinner.'

'Why don't you tell us about your experience in London so far?' Dad says.

'Well,' Nate says. 'To be honest, it didn't really start until I met Annie.'

I nearly spit out my wine. I don't dare look at Mum; she's one shared glance away from bursting into a spritz of confetti.

'Oh?' Dad says, much cooler than Mum as he lays out the granite placemats, setting our brass cutlery down on the long, rectangular table.

'Well,' Nate says, turning back to me and smiling. 'She made quite the first impression.'

'Of course she did!' Mum gushes, and it takes everything in me not to lean forward and thwack her.

'Why's that, then?' Dad says innocently, and he sneaks in a wink towards me which makes me burn with embarrassment.

Mum pulls the lasagne out of the oven, her hands covered in the red gingham tea towel as a cloud of steam billows around her.

'Well,' Nate says, taking a sip of his wine. 'For starters, she was dressed as a bat.'

Mum puts the lasagne on the table with a thud.

'A bat?' She turns to me. 'Annie, were you in one of your costumes?'

I nod. 'It was Halloween.'

'Oh!' Mum holds the tea towel to her chest. 'In the bat costume? Gosh, that was a *fantastic* outfit. Wasn't it, David?'

'One of your best,' Dad twinkles.

'Have you seen any more of them?' Mum gabbles. 'Of Annie's costumes? They are so brilliant.'

'No,' I say, grabbing Mum by the arm as she starts to scurry past me. 'Mum, Nate doesn't need to see every costume I've ever made.'

'I'd love to.'

I'm about to give Nate a warning look when I realise that he's smiling at Mum, and he looks like he's genuinely enjoying himself. He's not mocking me or cringing at how over the top my parents are; he wants to see.

'Really,' I protest. 'Mum, it's fine.'

'How about we eat first?' Dad says, popping the cork of another bottle of red wine.

'Yes,' Mum says, taking a deep breath as she walks back towards our dining table, but not before running her hand along Dad's arm and giving the tips of his fingers a squeeze. They both sit down, and Nate and I follow.

Mum smiles at us both, her face glowing. 'Let's eat.'

Chapter Thirty-Two

Nate

I sit back on the bed and look around the small boxroom. Low wooden beams are propped up in the corner, holding the weight of the room. The walls are covered in a sage and champagne striped wallpaper, with framed photos of Annie as a child, her parents hugging her tightly or carrying her on their shoulders.

It's the house. It's the house me and Mom have spoken about for years. It's like stepping into a version of my childhood that I don't have any more, where the four of us – Mom, Dad, me and Stevie – were all at home, sat around *our* dining-room table. Laughing and poking fun at each other, playing board games and watching TV. We haven't been that way for years. Even when I am back home, the relaxed ease that Annie and her parents have has left my family. We can all be laughing, absorbed in a new series or marching along the streets of New York . . . but it's always there. That faint thread of worry, winding us all together, ready to give a sharp tug if any of us get too lost in the idea that everything is okay and life is how it was before.

'Hey.'

I look up as Annie walks into the room. It's funny, I thought she was beautiful the first night I met her, when she was in her incredible costume. I thought she was more beautiful when I saw her last week, and she was dancing and having fun, flailing her arms around without a care in the world. But now, seeing her in her hoodie and baggy jeans, her cheeks pink from the warmth of the fire and her face bare of make-up . . . I think she's the most beautiful yet.

'Right,' she says, quietly closing the door behind her. 'They're distracted. I think I can get you out now.'

I raise my eyebrows at her in surprise. 'Out?'

'To a B&B or a hotel, if you found one you liked the look of,' she says. 'You absolutely do not have to stay here.'

As we had chatted around the dinner table earlier in the evening, Annie's mom had asked what I was doing in the Cotswolds. When I told her the story, about how I'd come down here for a fun, spontaneous day and would have got stuck here if it wasn't for Annie saving me and helping me find somewhere to stay, they both sprang into action, insisting that I must stay the night and get the train home in the morning. It was far too late to find somewhere else now, and they had a spare room. Really, it would be madness not to and they *insisted*. I knew I didn't have a choice, but I agreed quite gladly.

'Of course,' I say, catching myself. Annie had said she'd help me find somewhere to stay. She clearly didn't invite me to stay with her and crash her family meal and weekend. 'Sorry. You want me to go,' I say, getting to my feet. 'I'll be on my way. Thank you so much for helping me. I really appreciate it.' I glance at Annie and notice her face change. I'm not sure if it's the light, but she looks disappointed.

'No, it's not that,' she says, sitting on the bed. 'I just . . . you came here for a break and my parents have ambushed you into staying with us.'

'I'm having fun,' I say honestly. 'Really, this weekend has turned out better than I could have expected. But you've done more than enough. I'll go.'

'No,' she reaches forward and touches my arm, 'it's fine. If you're okay then of course, stay. Fuck, Mum will kill me if she thinks I've kicked you to the kerb.' I meet her eyes and for a second I'm lost. They're a deep, chocolatey brown, upturned at the corners and framed by feathery, dark eyelashes. 'Stay,' she says, pulling my arm so I'm sitting next to her on the bed. 'Really.'

'Are you sure?'

'Yes,' she nods. She folds her legs underneath herself and runs her fingers through her hair. It takes everything in me not to take her hand, just so I can hold it in mine.

'So,' she says, 'how does all this madness compare to your childhood? Was it just you and your parents?'

I lean so my back is against the wall and shake my head. 'No, I have a younger brother. I live with him now.'

She smiles. 'I always wanted a sibling.'

I stroke my beard, the image of Stevie with his angry, scrunched-up face floating into my mind. Then another image of him, when we were both kids. When he was always laughing, trying to get someone to chase him round the garden and playing pranks on everyone. He used to laugh all the time before . . . well, I guess before Mom got sick.

'What is it?'

I look up at Annie, breaking from my thoughts. 'What?'

'You looked a million miles away there.'

'Ah,' I smile, 'I guess I was. I was just thinking back to my own childhood. Being here sort of reminds me of home.'

Annie watches me for a second. 'Go on, then.'

'What?'

'Tell me about it.'

'Oh,' I laugh, 'it's all very boring.'

She pokes me in the ribs. 'Everyone says that about their own life. I want to know.'

I take a deep breath and dip back into my memory, feeling myself warm.

'Well,' I begin, 'I guess the best way to describe my childhood is to say it was ordinarily extraordinary. It was just like everyone else's happy childhood, nothing particularly spectacular. We spent weekends on bikes or making dens, playing hide and seek or falling off the climbing frame in the park. Dad loves baseball, so he would sometimes drag us all out to watch a game. I think he was disappointed that he had two young kids and neither of them really cared about baseball. Or even had a slight interest in it.'

She laughs. 'I had the same with my mum and cooking. She's tried to teach me everything she knows so many times and I just couldn't care less.'

'Yes,' I raise my eyebrows at her, 'but you love kebabs.'

She laughs louder this time and pokes me again. 'Okay, what else? What about your mum, and your brother?'

I force myself to pull my eyes away from her.

'Stevie was born the most annoying person on the planet,' I say matter-of-factly, 'but we've always been thick as thieves. Nobody used to laugh as much as Stevie did – his laugh was always infectious. He could get away with murder.'

'Used to?'

I raise my eyebrows. 'Hmmm?'

'Sorry,' she says, shuffling herself on the bed, 'you said, he used to laugh . . . does he not any more?'

I sigh. Damn, I hadn't even realised I said that.

'Sorry,' she says quickly, 'that's none of my business. I shouldn't—'

'No,' I interrupt, taking her hand to stop her from flapping it around anxiously, 'it's fine. I just hadn't registered I'd said it. I guess he's just more stressed now . . . we all are, really.'

I start to let go of her hand when I realise she's entwined her fingers with mine.

'Because of your mum?'

I nod, smiling. 'She's the best one out of all of us. Like, Stevie and my dad are great, but nobody shines a light close to Mom's. She'd love this house.' I use my free hand to gesture around the room. 'It's like everything we used to talk about as kids at Christmas. She watches *The Holiday* every year. Like I said, that's why I came here this weekend . . .' I steal a glance at Annie. 'I didn't intentionally follow you home, contrary to what you might think.'

She laughs and shakes her head. 'I thought maybe I'd planted the seed last time I saw you.'

'I think there was far too much vodka for that.' I grin at her and she giggles.

We fall into silence and I lean my head back against the wall, looking down at Annie's hand in mine. Her nails are orange, with little black pumpkins drawn in the corners. I'd expect nothing less.

'So,' I say, giving her hand a shake. 'You didn't tell me earlier that you have a sewing room here. I wouldn't have put it in our dream house if I knew you already had one.'

She smiles. 'It's hardly a sewing room. It just has all my outfits in there.'

'So . . . like a shrine?'

She nudges me with her foot. 'No. But yeah . . . I guess. God, I would never bring a guy back to my parents' house on the third . . .' She stops herself, her cheeks pinching.

'Can I see?' I ask.

'See what?'

'Your costumes,' I say. 'Or the shrine,' I add, grinning at her.

She looks at me for a moment, then sighs loudly and gets to her feet, pulling me off the bed with her. 'Fine,' she huffs. 'I guess this night has been embarrassing enough – surely this can't hurt.' She pushes the door open and looks over her shoulder at me. 'Come on, then. This way.'

We walk down the narrow corridor and up another few steps that lead into a small, oddly shaped room. The walls are plain, but it's filled with colour. Rail upon rail of clothes line the walls, with fabrics folded in different cubbyholes and a bright blue sewing machine sat right by the window.

'Did you really make all of these?'

She runs her fingers across the clothes, pulling some out and peering at them.

'Most of them,' she says. 'Mum makes them too. We sort of run a business together.'

'A business?'

'Yeah,' she says, letting go of a black lace gothic dress which swings back into place, 'making costumes for people who want them. Mainly Halloween, but we have orders come through all year.'

I look around at the clothes. There are soft lilac dresses, enormous headpieces for gory creatures with bulbous yellow eyes and fangs, electric-blue gowns and multicoloured woven jumpers.

'It's amazing,' I say, staring. Little sequins and gems glisten as they catch the moonlight bouncing off the settled snow and landing through the window. 'You're amazing.'

She snorts.

'You *are*!' I press on. 'Why don't you do this full-time? You should be doing this with your whole life, you're so talented.'

She laughs, but I see her cheeks have flushed pink again. 'Because I can't.'

'Yes, but why?'

'Because it wouldn't work.'

'But what if it did?'

'Jesus!' She turns to face me, her eyebrows raised but a full smile spread across her cheeks. 'You watch too many films.'

I shrug, taking a step towards her. 'Maybe.'

She looks up at me, my heart lifting as her big brown eyes meet mine. Her chin tilts and I put my hand on her cheek; our lips are inches away and so I—

'ANNIE! Naaa-aaate! Would you like a cup of tea?'

We jump apart and Annie quickly ruffles her hair, moving towards the door.

'Come on,' she says.

'Do you believe in the universe?'

It's an hour or so later and we're both lying on her bed, facing the ceiling. Annie's shoulder is next to mine, and we've been staring at the glow-in-the-dark stars stuck onto the ceiling with Blu Tack. Annie said they'd been up there since she was a baby, and her mom and dad couldn't bring themselves to take them down.

She gives me a sceptical look. 'Are you about to tell me that you're a flat earther?'

'Just answer the question.' I smile back, shifting my right arm so it's under my head.

'Well, what do you mean?' she asks.

The room is dark apart from the yellowy-green stars above us and the pale light of the moon beaming through the paned window.

'Do you believe that everything happens for a reason?' I say, after taking a moment to put my thoughts in order. 'Like, do you believe that everything that happens is meant to happen?'

She pauses. 'Sometimes, I guess.'

'I do.'

'Yeah?' She glances up at me.

'I think I kind of have to at this point.'

'What do you mean?'

I pause, the flicker of anxiety pinching at my chest as Mom's face pops into my mind. I'm about to push it back down and give Annie some generic reason, but I stop myself. I feel safe with her. 'You know I told you my mom isn't well?' I say, keeping my eyes fixed on the stars. 'Well, she's the best person I know, and she started getting sick a few years ago. Sometimes, believing the universe has a big plan for us all is the only thing that keeps me sane. Although fuck knows why Mom having dementia needs to be part of any plan. There is no bright side to that, it's only shit. She doesn't deserve it.' I sigh, and then I feel Annie's hand fold into mine.

'I'm really sorry, Nate.'

I run my fingers through my hair, feeling a weight lift off my chest. I haven't ever said that out loud to anyone.

'It's why I sent you such a weird message last week . . .' I admit. 'We'd had a bit of a scare. She's fine, but I . . . I don't know.'

She squeezes my hand and I glance at her.

'This is my issue with the universe,' she sighs, 'like, it's fun to believe in it when everything in your life is going well, but what about when it's not? There are so many awful things happening all over the world, every day. If the universe is here to look after us all and it has a plan for everyone . . . why do some people get a plan like that and others get, you know . . . nice plans?'

I digest the weight of her words when she sniggers.

'Sorry,' she says, 'that was really depressing.'

I shrug. 'It's true, though.'

'Ask me another question,' she says, shaking my hand, 'quickly, before I kill the mood entirely.'

I furrow my brow. 'Err . . .'

'Come on, anything.'

'Okay,' I say, 'I've got it. What other dreamy men did you meet at the speed dating? I'm sure they were all falling all over you.'

She snorts. 'Hardly.'

I frown at her. 'I'm being serious.'

She keeps her eyes locked forward, but I notice her mouth purse. 'Guys don't really look at me that way.'

'They definitely, definitely do,' I scoff.

She shakes her head. 'No, they don't. And that's okay, I'm not saying I'm ugly or anything, like, I'm fine. But I'm just a "filler girl", you know?' She catches my expression and laughs. 'I'm fine with it, it's something I came to terms with a long time ago. Really, I don't care.'

'I've never heard such rubbish,' I reply. 'What even is a "filler girl"?'

She shrugs. 'Someone there to fill the gap until someone better comes along. It's fine!' she says again, laughing. 'I don't care. Like, it's cool.'

'It's baloney is what it is!' I say in my thickest New York accent, which makes her laugh loudly. 'Where did you even get this from? It was a guy, wasn't it? God, we're the worst. What's his name?' I sit up and pretend to roll up my sleeves. 'Give me his name so I can track him down and give him a piece of my mind.'

She pulls me back down onto the bed. 'You are such a drama queen.'

'And you are misinformed. There is no way you are anything less than first choice – any guy would be lucky to have you.'

She puts her hand on her face and groans, but she's still laughing.

'What about you, then? Have you been dating much since you've been in London?'

I shake my head. 'Not unless you count hanging out with a fifty-something-year-old-man dating. Sorry,' I hold up my hand, 'I still can't believe you think you're a "filler girl"!'

'Oh, I wish I'd never said anything,' she says, grinning. 'Come on, let's talk about the universe again. Tell me how you think we were destined to meet or something.'

I raise my eyebrows. 'Do you think that's such a ridiculous idea?'

She pauses, and then rolls onto her side so she's facing me, her arms tucked under her head. I copy her. For a moment, we just look at each other.

'I don't think it's a coincidence that I keep running into you,' she says softly.

She's so close to me now that I can smell her. She smells like roses and carries the warm, comforting smell of the fire.

I move my head so I'm looking into her eyes.

'Well, why else would I keep seeing you, if the universe didn't want me to?'

She raises her eyebrows at me, but her lips are stretched into a smile. 'Oh yeah?'

'Yeah, I do think I was meant to meet you,' I say, fully moving my body over now so that our noses are almost touching.

Her smile broadens. 'Why's that?'

I think about answering, giving her some poetic ramble about life and love and what I make of it all.

But I decide to kiss her instead.

Chapter Thirty-Three

Annie

Okay, so there were a few things I was expecting to happen this weekend. I was expecting a nice meal with my parents, a good night's sleep in my childhood bedroom and an overall morale boost about life in general, and to leave with a Tupperware of cake under my arm.

I was not expecting to have sex with Nate.

I catch eyes with him and immediately laugh, as I have done every time he's looked at me since we woke up this morning. It's funny; as soon as he kissed me, it was like I couldn't stop myself. It broke down a barrier I hadn't even known was there. Last night, I ran my hands all over him, pressing his chest into mine and kissing him hungrily. His firm hands cupped my body, held my face and gripped onto me like he never wanted to let me go. It was different to anyone else I had been with; it felt like we were meant to be together.

I know. Someone pass the sick bucket. But it's true.

And then the next morning, I couldn't stop myself from holding his hand, putting my arm around his waist or laughing as he kissed me. I didn't even care that Mum and Dad were practically somersaulting off the walls when we walked downstairs, hand in hand. It just felt like the most natural thing in the world. Like my hand was meant to be in his. It's where it belonged.

Thankfully, the snow seemed to have evaporated overnight, leaving behind only a scattering of silver icicles, which meant that the trains were back on. The four of us had breakfast, Mum pulled out a fresh loaf of bread and we all sang happy birthday to Dad over flickering candles that proudly stood atop a glistening, gooey chocolate cake. We had coffee and cake, toast and jam, and in that moment it felt as though I didn't have any problems at all. Tanya and Penny hadn't just told me that they were moving out; I wasn't going to have to find somewhere else to live; a flat share with strangers wasn't looming at me from around the corner. Or if it was, it didn't matter. None of it mattered.

'Will your brother be in?' I ask Nate, as the train pulls up to Paddington. He picks up my bag before I can protest, swinging it round his broad shoulders like it's filled with feathers.

He shakes his head as we make our way through the station. 'Unlikely, he's out a lot.'

'Oh yeah?' I grin. 'Out with the ladies?'

Nate smiles to himself. 'He's gay, so more likely to be out with the guys. He works a lot, too.'

I nod as we weave between the crowds and jump onto the tube. 'What about you?' I say, trying my best to sound nonchalant, even though it's a question that's been buzzing in my mind since he kissed me.

Falling For You

'What about me?'

'Are you out with the ladies much?'

I feel myself burn with embarrassment, but it's something I've been trying to ask him all day. Was last night something he does with lots of girls? He doesn't seem that way . . . but I've been wrong about that before. And fuck, I feel like I've given my heart to him now. I don't know what I'd do if I was one of many.

Nate laughs, giving my hand a squeeze. 'Only you, Annie.' My heart glows.

Only you, Annie.

An image pops into my head of Nate with another girl and I feel my insides squeeze. I quickly shake it out of my mind.

He just told you he isn't seeing anyone else. You have to trust him.

'You look pretty happy about that,' he smiles.

I tuck my hair behind my ear. 'I just . . . well, like I said, I'm not a big dater. So last night . . .' I trail off and Nate swings our combined hands around my shoulders so he's fully wrapped around me.

'It meant a lot to me too,' he says, and before I can say anything he spins me back out so we're side by side again and I laugh.

'Are you rushing back home?' he asks.

I smile, my hand warm inside his. 'I don't have to be.'

'I only live round the corner,' he says. 'Why don't you come in?'

'For a cup of tea?' I tease.

Nate grimaces. 'Not unless you really, really want one.'

I laugh as we walk through the barrier and onto the streets of London. It's like the snow from yesterday never existed; the streets are back to being grey, glistening slightly under the rain. People are hurrying along with their shoulders hunched, their elbows tucked in and their eyes firmly fixed ahead.

'This way,' Nate says, steering me round a corner. 'I thought we could – ah!'

I flinch as a car skirts past us, drenching Nate from head to toe in wet grey sludge. He yelps, jumping back as his trousers cling to his legs. 'Oh my God!' I gasp. 'Are you all right?'

He looks down at himself. 'I'm fine. I . . . are you laughing?'

I can't help it, the giggles bubble up inside me and before I can stop myself, I'm doubled over, trying to hide my face. I don't know what it is, but I can't stop laughing when I'm with him. It's like he just fills me with this happy, excited energy.

'You are laughing!' he cries. 'After I just *saved* you.'

'I'm sorry . . .' I manage between laughs. 'I just . . .'

He rolls his eyes, putting a heavy arm over my shoulders and steering me along the pavement.

'Heartless . . .' he says, giving me a shake. 'Totally heartless.'

We stop outside a chipped blue door, hidden between two buildings. I notice that a fabric shop I love is on the other side of the street. I'm about to comment when Nate pushes the door open.

'After you,' he says, bowing deeply like we've walked straight out of *Game of Thrones*. I laugh, skipping past him and into the dank hallway. 'Right,' he says as we reach the third floor, 'I think I'm going to need to get straight in the shower.' He gives the door to the flat a kick and it pops open. 'Make yourself at home.' He gestures to the living room. 'I don't have any tea, I'm afraid,' he says. 'But I'll make you a coffee if you like.'

I wave him away. 'I'm fine,' I say. 'Go have your shower. I'll be here.'

I give him a look over my shoulder and he grins at me. 'I'll be two minutes.'

I take a look at the flat. It's got the grey, lifeless walls that all rented flats seem to have, but they're covered in bright pictures and swathes of fabric, and the room is full of plants. They have a bookcase, with a few books stacked on top of each other and a . . .

My heart stops as my eyes land on the electric-pink piece of clothing, hooked over the arm of a chair.

A bra.

I step towards it, and as I do I notice some tights hanging next to it. Lipstick on the table.

I pick the bra up.

Why is there a bra here? Whose is it? Nate just told me that there wasn't anyone else. I asked him. He said . . .

He was lying.

My mind races as everything clunks into place.

This is why he didn't message me. He was with someone else. Other girls have been here, with Nate. Like I was *with Nate* last night. Kissing, touching, dragging each other's clothes off . . . He made me feel so special but I'm not, am I? It was all just words to him. Of course I'm nobody special to him, we've only met three times for God's sake. I'm just another girl.

Another, stupid girl.

I'm frozen to the spot, when my eyes land on a note on the table.

I'll be out all weekend. Sorry I was a dick. Call Jane, she'll cheer you up!

Jane . . .

I hear the shower click off, and before I can give myself a moment to think, I grab my bag and run towards the door. I can't be here when he gets out, standing stupidly in his living room all bright-eyed and excited for our day together. He'll laugh off the bra, telling me it was just some girl and it didn't matter because we were just dating, right? It was no big deal, right? And I'll have to stand opposite him and let the realisation wash over me that I still haven't learnt my lesson. Guys aren't serious about me. Not when there is someone better waiting round the corner.

How could I be so stupid as to fall for all this again? When will I learn? What is wrong with me?

I slam the door shut and run down the stairs, trying to fight the panic that's boiling up. I jump on the first bus I see, and send a final message to Nate.

We're not right for each other.

And then I block his number.

I rest my head against my headboard, closing my heavy eyes. They burn as I shut them, as if they're begging me to keep them closed so they can have a break from the tears I've cried in the past hour. I got back at about three this afternoon and have been alone ever since.

The longer I spent on the bus, alone with my thoughts, the more it all made sense.

He ran out the first time we met when his phone rang, he said he was only at the speed dating to help out a friend, he didn't message me back after our first date...

He was never serious about me. Of course he wasn't. He didn't feel any of the feelings I did. I was just one of many girls to him.

I switched my phone off as soon as I sent the message. I knew Nate wouldn't be able to message me, but, worse than that, I couldn't face my parents. I couldn't deal with the excited, bubbly messages that were about to pop through from them both, asking how our journey back was and when we'd be coming to stay again. Saying how much they loved Nate and how *nice* it was to see me *so happy*.

A part of me tried to wonder if I'd got it wrong. Could the bra have belonged to a friend? But a friend doesn't leave without a bra, do they? You only take your bra off with a guy if you're...

My eyes sting. I don't want to think about it.

I wince as I hear a knock on my bedroom door and peel an eye open to see Tanya and Penny poking their heads around. As soon as Tanya sees me, she gasps and runs straight over, throwing her arms around my neck. This just makes me cry all over again.

'Oh my God, Annie! What's wrong?'

'What's going on? Is everyone okay?' I feel a thud next to me as Penny sits on the bed.

'Is it about us?' Tanya says, her arms still firmly gripped

around my body. 'We've been feeling so awful about it all weekend. I'm thinking about not taking the job so I can stay here with you both.'

'And I'll make Mike move in here,' Penny adds. 'It'll be fine.'

I take a deep breath, my face hot from being squashed into Tanya's face, and dab my cheeks with the back of my hands.

'No,' I say. 'It's not that.'

'Well, then what?' Tanya asks, her eyes wide. 'What is it?'

'Hang on.' Penny holds up a hand. 'Do we need tea, or wine?'

'Wine,' Tanya and I say in unison.

'Okay.' Penny scrambles to her feet. 'Don't start without me.'

Twenty minutes later and I've finished telling them the whole story. How I bumped into Nate at the train station, how my parents took him in, how we had dinner together, how we chatted, alone, for hours, how we kissed, how we slept together . . . how I found women's underwear in his flat, strewn across the floor like they'd been freshly ripped off someone else's body. The note telling him to call Jane if he needed 'cheering up'.

'Oh my *God*!' Tanya cries. 'I can't . . . I can't believe that.'

'What a bastard!' Penny snarls, refilling my wine glass.

'And you're sure that's what it was?' Tanya says desperately. 'You're sure the bra didn't belong to another flatmate, or a mate, or . . .'

I shake my head. 'It's just him and his brother, who's gay.

He said it was just the two of them. And he told me there wasn't anyone else, I asked him.'

'Fuck,' Tanya holds her hands to her forehead, 'I just . . . I'm so sorry, Annie. I can't believe it.'

'Neither can I.'

I take a deep breath, but it's no use, my eyes are brimming with tears again in seconds.

'Oh, Annie!' Tanya wails. 'Please don't cry over him, he's not worth it.'

'What can we do to make you feel better?' Penny says, leaning forward and touching my leg.

I shrug, rubbing my eyes. Tanya and Penny look at each other.

'Okay,' Tanya says. 'That's okay. We can sort this. I'll run a bath.'

'And I'll make us a great dinner,' Penny nods.

'We can watch *I'm a Celebrity* tonight,' Tanya adds. 'And I think we have more chocolate.'

'And more wine.'

'Please don't,' I smile weakly. 'You girls don't have to.'

Tanya gives me a warning look. 'It's what girlfriends are for.'

'Oh!' Penny adds, turning on her heel as she's about to leave the room. 'I think I have face packs, and I bought a new candle this weekend.'

I look at her through misted eyes. 'You girls really are the best.'

And then I start crying all over again.

Chapter Thirty-Four

Nate

The thing is, I should know better. I know that life isn't this bullshit you see in films. I mean, fuck. I've lived it for the past five years! From the moment Mom let the bath water run over the third Sunday in a row, the moment she burnt chicken to a charcoaled shell one too many times, the moment I caught her looking at me with genuine fear in her eyes. Like she doesn't quite know who I am, or what's going on. I know how cruel and fucking horrible life can be. And yet, I still let myself fall for the idea that maybe my life could be brilliant. And it was all because of *her* and one weekend we had together.

I angrily fire off another email, my fingers fizzing. I've been in the office since eight this morning, glued to my laptop and avoiding conversation wherever I can.

I got out of the shower and she'd gone, completely disappeared. She'd gone from holding my hand, kissing me in the streets and laughing uncontrollably to just . . . vanishing. Without a trace. I was in the shower for less than five minutes for fuck's sake, what the hell could have happened? All I got was this message:

We're not right for each other.

It was like the final bit of light I had in my life had been snatched away from me. I tried to chase after her, but she was nowhere to be seen. I thought I might hear from her later on in the day, I even tried to call her myself, but all I got was the monotone drone of an unrecognised number. She'd blocked my number. I tried to find her on social media, but she'd blocked me there too. It was like she was a ghost. She'd stripped herself from my life completely; it's like she was never there before.

Except, she was.

I turn my phone over as it starts vibrating and I see Dad's name flash up. I pick it up and walk to the other side of the office, where the desks are empty.

'Hi, Dad,' I say. 'How are you? How's Mom?'

Since her terrifying message landed in my phone a week ago, Mom has behaved pretty much as normal. We've spoken almost every day, we've FaceTimed and she gushed over the photos of Annie's house that I sent her and all the scenic pictures of the Cotswolds. It's like nothing has ever happened. In her mind, anyway. For me, all it did was reawaken the hot fear that simmers under my skin like bubbling lava.

'Oh, she's fine. We're all fine,' Dad says, in the way he always does where I can't quite work out whether he's lying or not. Is she really fine? Or is she fine now, but earlier this morning poured boiling coffee over her hand because she hadn't realised that she'd forgotten to put a mug there?

'Good,' I say, running my fingers through my hair. 'Listen. I think I'm going to come home.'

'Home?' Dad repeats. 'When?'

'As soon as I can,' I reply, turning back to face the rest of the office. Brian and Helen are milling around, holding their cups of tea and chatting to the rest of the team. They won't miss me. They'll barely notice I've gone.

'Really?' Dad says. 'Are you sure, Nate? Is everything okay?'

I press my lips together. 'Yup. Fine. I just want to come back home.'

'Okay,' Dad says after a pause. 'So long as you're all right.'

'Yup,' I say again. 'I'm fine.'

Just like Dad, just like Mom, I'm fine. We're all fine.

I'm going home. There is just one more thing I need to do first.

I rap on the ruby-red door then quickly stuff my frozen hand back into my pocket. I got on the first train to Epping as soon as I'd finished work. I didn't bother calling Aunt Tell to tell her I was coming; she'd sent me her show schedule so I knew she'd be in, and I didn't want to risk her putting on some form of show for me. I don't have time for pleasantries any more. I just need answers.

'Nathaniel!' she gushes as she pulls open the door. 'How are—'

'Why won't you come home and see Mom?'

I'd spent the entire journey thinking of different ways to say this, whether I should be polite or try and coax the answer out of her. But I don't have the energy. I'm sick of people not telling me the truth. I just need answers.

She blinks at me, and I can see the different responses whizzing through her mind. She opens her mouth to speak, but I've got more to say.

'We need you. Mom needs you. I messaged you for weeks, I called and emailed and you ignored me. Then I show up here and you act as if nothing has happened. Why won't you see her? She's your sister! She talks about you all the time and how much she loves you, and you barely even acknowledge her existence. You're here in your big house and your fabulous life and it's like we don't exist. I'm not going to ask you to come see Mom any more, even though she's sick and getting worse by the week, but I just need to know why.'

I break off, my heart racing. Aunt Tell just stares back at me, her eyes wide.

'I see,' she says, her voice hollow. 'I think you'd better come in.'

I step past her, immediately hit by the warmth of her home and the scent of cinnamon and vanilla. She gestures for me to sit in the living room, and I opt for the same plush armchair I sat in before.

'Coffee?' she offers. 'Tea?'

I'm about to refuse when I feel a pang of guilt. I don't want to be rude to her. 'Coffee would be great, thank you.'

She nods and walks into the kitchen, and I look round the living room. A large framed mirror sits on the mantelpiece above a golden electric fire. The curtains are dark green and a thick, heavy velvet and the ceiling is swirled like the top of a cupcake. I hear footsteps and look up, expecting to see Aunt Tell holding a tray, when instead I see . . .

'Remy?' I gape, getting to my feet. 'What are you doing here?'

'Hello, bud.' Remy gives a sheepish smile. 'How are you doing?' We slap hands and give each other a quick hug. 'I'll get out of your hair,' he says, looking at the kitchen as Aunt Tell reappears. 'But let's go for a pint soon.'

He nods at me and gives Aunt Tell a smile. Before I can ask any more questions, he's slipped out of the room and I sink back into my armchair. Aunt Tell puts a floral tray down on the coffee table and sits opposite me.

'He's a fine man,' she muses and I try not to frown.

Remy, you old dog.

We sit in silence for a moment and I will myself not to speak. Eventually, Aunt Tell sighs. 'Well, Nathaniel, I think I owe you an apology.'

I'm about to blurt that she owes Mom an apology, not me, but I stop myself.

'I did receive your messages, but even before then, I knew your mom wasn't well. Your dad had reached out to me a few years ago.'

My head dips. She's known for years?

'And I am sorry I didn't reply. That was wrong of me.' I wait for her to continue, but she stops, taking a sip of her coffee. It seems her apology has finished.

'Right . . .' I say. 'So, are you going to come back and see Mom?'

She shakes her head. 'I can't do that.'

'Why not?' I demand. 'It isn't like you can't afford it. I

know you're in a show right now, but when it finishes? It doesn't have to be Christmas. It—'

'Nate,' she says softly, 'I won't be going to see her.'

'Why?'

'Because I don't want to.'

My coffee cup starts to shake in my hands.

'I love your mom,' she says slowly. 'She's my best friend, and I'd like to keep her in my mind how she's always been. Not how she is now.' My mouth falls open. 'You may think that's selfish,' she continues, reading my mind. 'But it is my choice.'

'Even though you know it will make her really happy to see you? Even though she's asked for you?' I say, my voice shaking.

She looks out through the window and I feel a wall go up between us. I get to my feet. 'Right,' I say. 'Fine. Sorry I bothered you.'

I walk straight out of the door and back onto the chilly street, the words that have been swirling round my brain now hammering at my heart.

Why did I even bother coming to London?

I push my way into the flat. The icy rain has seeped through my jacket, clinging to my curly hair and running over my face. I've been in London for over a month now, and I still don't remember to take an umbrella anywhere.

'Hey Nate?'

I hear Stevie's voice from the living room. We've barely

spoken since our fight, but as soon as I see him I am overtaken by a feeling of needing to protect my younger brother. He's sitting on the sofa, and I wrap my arms around his neck from behind and give him a squeeze. He pats my arm non-committally.

'You all right?' he asks. 'What's going on?'

'Nothing,' I say, letting him go. 'You were right about Aunt Tell, though. She is a dick.' He raises his eyebrows, waiting for me to continue, but I walk to the kitchen and open the fridge. 'Do you want a beer?'

'Go on, then.'

I grab two cans and hand one to Stevie, before flopping down on the armchair opposite him. The TV is flickering, blaring some antiques show that Stevie seems to love.

'You know, you could have saved some time if you'd listened to me in the first place,' he says, clicking open his beer. 'I did tell you she was a dick.'

I sigh. 'Yeah well, call me an idiot.'

'I'd rather call you an optimist,' Stevie says kindly and I soften. He holds his beer can towards me and we knock them together.

'Why do you hate her, then?' I ask. 'You've never told me.'

He shrugs. 'I don't know, man. She's just not like the rest of our family. She's so selfish and self-absorbed. Like, every time I had a friend round from college she'd put on a show for us, but she never cared if I needed real help. She only cared about herself.'

I nod. 'I can see that.'

'I'm worried I'm like her.'

His eyes are still fixed on the TV.

'Like her?' I repeat. 'Stevie, you—'

'I know I'm selfish,' he says, still not making eye contact with me. 'I'm not like you and Mom – you're both so kind and generous. I'm trying to be better, though. I know you're angry with me.'

I press my lips together.

'For what it's worth, I'm angry with you, too.'

'Angry at me!' I burst out incredulously. 'What for?'

He sighs. 'You'll tell me it's stupid.'

'Well, that depends what it is.'

He swigs on his beer and sits up straighter. 'I'm jealous of all the time you got to spend with Mom and Dad while I've been here. Every time I joined a call with you all or saw a picture of how happy you all were together . . . it made me so homesick. I'd have come every weekend if I was able to, but my school was so intense and even after then, I didn't have the money to come home more than once a year. And then Mom got sick and I just . . .'

He rubs the top of his head roughly and I feel a weight drop through me.

'It just got easier not to talk to her. I felt so guilty for missing so much, for being selfish and running away.'

A stone drops through my body. How could I never have realised this before? Of course Stevie is angry. He came to London to follow his dreams and be young and free, and instead life gave him a hand of cards none of us ever expected.

'It's not selfish to live your life, Stevie,' I say. 'None of us could ever have known that Mom would get sick.'

He shrugs and sinks into silence as the TV flickers and a man with a thatch of grey hair smacks a gavel down and everyone cheers.

'So,' I say, after taking a swig of my beer, 'I need to talk to you.'

He arches an eyebrow.

'I'm going home. Back to New York. Things just haven't worked out for me here, Stevie. I thought I could get Aunt Tell to visit Mom, or call her or something, but she won't do it. So I have no need to be here any more. I want to go back home and be with Mom.'

He jerks around, outraged. *'What?* You can't go back, you've only just got here!'

'I know.'

'What about that girl?'

'What girl?' I say spitefully, even though we both know who he's talking about.

'Bat Girl.'

I shake my head, swigging my beer. 'It's over. There is nothing there.'

'Right,' he says slowly, his voice hollow. 'You really want to go back, then? Are you sure?'

'I'm sure.'

'There's nothing I can do to make you stay?'

I lean back into my seat. 'No.'

A siren wails past outside, momentarily flashing our living room with streaks of blue and white light. I glance towards the window. Rain hammers against the pane, the murky grey sky dotted with flickers from the Christmas lights that people have put up, unable to wait a second longer to drape their homes and the street in Christmas cheer.

I'd had big plans for Christmas in the flat. I know Stevie has never bothered to decorate it during the years that he's been here. He's always told us that he's been too busy to come home for Christmas, which I've never questioned too closely, and he spends Christmas Day with a friend. Whenever I called him from New York and we turned our cameras on, I could see his pale flat in the background. No lights, no decorations, no Christmas tree.

When I decided to move here, I knew I was going to have to transform the flat for us both. I'd fill the fridge with Christmas food. I would get us a huge tree and make novelty pictures of our faces squashed on the top of elves' bodies to stick on the fridge. I'd get us some form of hideous singing reindeer that sang every time you walked past it and put it outside Stevie's bedroom door, just to annoy him.

I had so many plans for my life in London.

'I don't want you to go, though.'

I take a deep breath. 'You can come with me if you want.'

I know I'm behaving like a teenager, prodding the bear. We've had this conversation a hundred times and it always ends the same.

Stevie looks away. 'I've got to work, you know that.'

'Just for a weekend?' I offer. 'I'm looking at flights – you could take a week off.'

'No, I can't, Nate. Sorry.'

This is normally where I'd have to fight the anger I feel

whenever Stevie refuses to see or speak to Mom, but this time it doesn't come. I'm so tired, it's like I have nothing left.

'Okay,' I say, getting to my feet. 'Suit yourself.'

'I don't know how to deal with all of this, Nate,' he says, and although he keeps his eyes locked forward, I notice that they're shining. 'She's not who she was any more and I don't . . . I don't know what I'm supposed to do.'

'Just be there, Stevie!' I say, exasperated. 'That's all Mom wants. I mean, man, do you think *I* know what I'm doing? You just need to be there. Go see—'

'I did.'

His words cut across me like a piece of glass. 'What?'

'I did go see Mom. Last year.' He takes a deep breath. 'I came back for a week. You were away with work or something, I don't know. It was just me and Mom. I thought I'd surprise her.'

For the first time, he looks over at me and my heart turns over. It's like looking at four-year-old Stevie again. 'Nate, she didn't have any idea who I was. She was terrified of me. Like, do you have any idea how that feels? For your own mom to be scared of you?'

'What happened?' I can feel my heart racing in my ears.

He scratches his shaved head. 'Dad calmed her down. He tried to make me stay, said she was just having a bad day. But I left. I can't do that to her again. She was so scared of me. She looked at me as if I was about to . . .' He trails off, his voice catching. 'And it's my fault. If I'd been there more over the years, then maybe she . . .'

'She's not well,' I say, forcing myself to say the words that circle around my mind every day. 'That's it, Stevie. It could have happened to me, Dad, anyone. You just caught her on a bad day. When did this happen?'

He shakes his head, swiping the tears from his eyes with the back of his hand. 'I don't know. Like, last October. I asked Dad not to tell you.'

'And you haven't seen her since?'

'No. I message her, though!' Stevie says defensively.

'I get it,' I say quickly, not wanting to start any kind of fight. 'It's hard. Actually, it's worse than hard. It's fucking shit. It's all shit. But I need you.' I move onto the sofa next to him, putting my arm around his shoulder. His head flops onto my chest, just like he used to do with Mom when he was a child.

'I'm sorry, Nate,' he says quietly. 'I don't think I can do it.'

'I'll help you,' I say. 'We'll do it together.'

And for the next hour, with only the noise of the television and the odd screeching siren, we sit there together, hugging, for the first time since we were kids.

Chapter Thirty-Five

Annie

I crash into the office, snatching the tail of my scarf behind me before it gets trapped in the lift. I've run from a client meeting, where I showed them a couple of private schools, and raced back here so I could check my emails and say hello to Pam before the fabric shop closed.

I spent the rest of Sunday crying with Tanya and Penny. We sat and chatted, drank all the wine and then all the tea, ate all the chocolate and devoured Penny's huge, delicious stew. But then I got up on Monday morning and decided that I wasn't going to let Nate ruin another day. He'd already spent the majority of the week before circling around my head, while I was desperately wondering why he'd sent me such a weird message, then he crashed a weekend with my parents *and* ruined an entire Sunday. So, no more. He was not allowed to come with me into this week.

'Hello!' I call, walking through the office. To my surprise, Pam isn't hunched over her laptop like she normally is. I drop my bag, frowning. That's odd – normally, I barely see her move from that space.

'Pam?' I call. She's in the kitchen and jumps when she sees me.

'Are you making a cup of tea?' I say. 'You never get up to make a cup of tea! I haven't been gone that long, have I?'

I grin, pulling a mug down and placing it next to hers, but she doesn't return my smile, just looks at me with a weird, glazed expression.

'Are you all right?' I ask. 'Have you been staring at your laptop for too long? Shall I take you outside for some fresh air?'

I'm teasing her, but the weird, glazed expression doesn't shift.

'Annie,' she says eventually. 'How are you?'

'I'm fine,' I reply at once. 'Are you?'

She nods. 'I'm good. Rodney and I spent the weekend going through things – the business, and the idea of travelling.'

I smile, leaning on the counter, ready for her to start her weekly rant about how Rodney wants to travel the world and she can't leave the business. But she doesn't.

'I think we're going to do it,' she says, giving me a small smile. 'We're not getting any younger, and I do work too much . . . and I love Rodney, I want to do this with him.'

Joy spreads through my chest and I throw my arms around Pam's neck.

'Pam!' I cry. 'That's amazing! I'm so happy for you! Although,' I add, letting her go, 'I don't know how I'll survive without you for a year.'

She laughs. 'I think you'll be great.' I smile, flicking on

the coffee machine. 'And actually, Annie . . .' she continues. 'That's something I want to talk to you about.'

I turn back to face her. 'Yeah?'

'Well, the plan is for us to be gone for a year . . . but I'm going to need someone to take my place while I'm away. And I want to make sure that the right person is here to run it.'

I look at her, my stomach flipping.

Is she about to . . .

'I'd like you to be the acting CEO.'

I run my fingers along the waterfall of fabric. Satins of pearly pink; deep purple; glistening, royal gold. I want to scoop them all up under my arm and take them. Make a dress out of all of them, make a hundred dresses and skirts and jackets.

I always find myself here when I'm stressed. When I moved to London ten years ago, I flitted between fabric shops like a student on a pub crawl, but I ended up gravitating towards this one. When I was a teenager and had just started to make my own clothes, I'd wander into town after school and spend twenty minutes or so admiring each piece in the local fabric shop. Pulling it between my fingers or seeing how it would fall if I wrapped it around my arm. Sometimes Mum would call me and then meet me there. We'd pick a fabric out together and take it home to add to our collection. Our spare bedroom turned into an Aladdin's cave. I loved it.

It's special to me, but as I got older I realised that everyone has one of these places. Whether it be the silence and comfort of a library, surrounded by books and corners you can hide in; the chink of cups and the crisp smell of coffee in the hubbub of a coffee shop; or a walk through a park, where the leaves curl and flex throughout the year, dogs leaping after balls and children running with their arms flailing behind them. Everyone has their own version of their safe space, the place they go when everything feels a bit too much. And a fabric shop is mine, so here I am.

It's fairly near Nate's flat, but I don't care. There is no way he'd come in here, and even if he did, my mind has been replaced with cotton wool. I don't know if I'd even manage to string a sentence together.

My heart burns at the thought of him and I scrunch my eyes, turning to the streams of ribbons floating down from a wooden pole.

I lied to Nate before. I do believe in the universe. Not in the Disney way Nate seemed to, but I do believe that everything happens for a reason. When Tanya and Penny told me that they were moving out and I realised I would also have to move, and I wouldn't be able to afford to live by myself which meant that I'd have to house-share with strangers, I panicked. It felt like my life was being turned upside down *without my consent*. But that's the thing, isn't it? You never get the chance to agree to your life being turned upside down, otherwise you'd never do anything that scared you.

Anyway, when Pam offered me the chance to head the company while she was away, it felt a bit like the universe was offering me a hand. I could take it, I could earn enough money to live in my own flat, maybe even buy somewhere someday. I could stand on my own two feet, properly. Just like Penny and Tanya, I could have a new adventure. But

I know if I did that, then I'd have to let go of my dream of making costumes full-time. I couldn't do both, and if I was running the company, I wouldn't even have the time to take on any commissions. I'd have to let it go, have it as a hobby I could do on a quiet weekend.

My eyes turn to the rows of brightly coloured wool. All squashed together and squeezed into little cubbyholes. I start looking at the saffron yellow, tangerine orange and azure blue, imagining the loud jumper I could knit, weaving all those colours together.

Pam said she didn't want an answer from me straight away and told me to take my time. It took a lot for me not to be the helpful, good girl I've always been and agree to take the job on just because it was what Pam wanted and I am nothing if not a teacher's pet. But Pam shooed me out of the office and told me to take the rest of the day off, probably worried I'd blurt an answer without thinking about it. She knows me too well.

I haven't told anyone yet. Normally, the first thing I do when I hear good news is call my parents and then run to the shop, grab a bottle of prosecco and race home to tell the girls. But I can't yet. I need to make sense of the hot, scary emotions that are snaking around my body first. I need to line them up and work out why each emotion is there and what it's supposed to be doing. At the moment, it just feels as if they're all coiling around my organs and pulling everything too tight.

'Can I help with anything?'

I look round and see Jade. Even though I come in here a

lot, we've never pushed past the customer/staff barrier and into friendship. Which is a shame – she has a fantastic fashion sense. To be fair, it's not very often I come in here like I have today, aimlessly wandering around the shop admiring everything. Normally, I'm a woman on a mission, darting in between appointments or on my way home from work.

'Yeah,' I smile at her. 'I'm just browsing, thank you.'

She nods, and I'm about to ask her how her day is going when the door crashes open. The bell, which usually tinkles gently when someone enters, jangles manically as a whirlwind of a person falls into the shop and clatters towards the counter.

'Jade!' they gasp in an odd mix of American and cockney. 'I need your help.'

There's a loud thud as the man throws his bag onto the counter. I peer over from behind the rail. He's tall, towering over six foot with bleached blonde hair and an oversized bomber jacket – he's the guy who came crashing into the shop last time I was here.

'It's ripped!' he cries, pulling out a garment and showing Jade. 'It's worse than ripped, it's *fucked*! I've got a show tomorrow night and I need this dress!'

I watch Jade examine it, her face pained. I get the impression that she gets this a lot.

'Tomorrow?' she repeats incredulously. 'Stevie, I can't. I've got to run the shop today. It's just me here and I've got commissions tonight.'

'Please!' Stevie begs. 'Jade, I'll do anything!'

'I can help.'

The man's head snaps round at me, his eyes wide. I see his eyes flicker, as if he's about to ask me who I am, but then desperation takes over.

'Really?' he gabbles. 'Do you work here?'

'She might as well,' Jade says, giving me a wink. 'She's a fantastic costume maker.'

I walk towards him and take the fabric from him. It's an emerald-green, thick material with a slight give to it.

'What's it for?' I ask.

'The Wicked Witch of the West,' he says. 'But, obviously, in green. Elphaba style.'

For the first time in days, I feel a spark behind my chest. 'Yeah,' I say, 'I can fix this for you.'

He almost collapses in relief. 'Sorry, what's your name, you fallen angel?'

I smile. 'I'm Annie.'

He throws his arms around me. 'Thank you, Annie.'

So, it turns out, if your body is filled with angry snakes that are carrying burning emotions that you don't quite know what to do with, just go to your happy place and bathe in it. I left the shop with Stevie's measurements, some extra fabric and the promise that I'd deliver the dress back to him by noon the next day. Most of all, I left with a fire in my belly, and guess what? It burnt the snakes. They left. I know they'll come back, but while I'm hunched over my sewing machine, there isn't any room for them. There is only happiness here.

I glance back over at my notebook and check my sketch.

Stevie's costume had a corset, and a billowing, flared skirt with panels of different green fabric with a huge slit up one of the sides. The stitching of the skirt had come undone, meaning it wasn't fully attached to the corset. It's a beautiful dress, but it doesn't scream Wicked Witch of the West. It's more like a ballgown, or a green wedding dress. I did say this, and asked Stevie if he minded if I embellished it slightly, and he said he didn't. To be honest, I think he was so grateful to have me helping him that he would have agreed to anything.

I'm adding a cape with a high, jagged collar and a pair of glistening, evil eyes on the back shoulder. So, when he turns, it will look as if one of the flying monkeys is hidden behind the cape, ready to leap out and rip someone's throat out at the slightest command.

I stretch the fabric under the machine and remove some of the pins holding it in place when I hear my bedroom door open.

'Ohhhh, what are you making?'

It's Tanya, who climbs onto my bed. She picks up my assortment of pillows and cushions and props them behind her, before curling her long legs under her body like a cat and turning to face me.

I furrow my brow as the slippery fabric twists out of place. 'It's . . . a . . . witch . . . costume,' I say, in between pinning the fabric back together. 'I've got to turn it around by tomorrow morning, though.'

'Gosh!' Tanya gasps. 'That's a tight deadline!'

'It's a different type of commission,' I explain. 'It's someone I met in the fabric shop this afternoon.'

'Have you not been at work today?' Tanya frowns.

I shake my head, skimming the fabric under the machine. 'Pam gave me the afternoon off.'

'Are you okay?'

'Yeah, fine,' I mutter. 'She wants me to be CEO while she goes travelling for a year.'

'She . . . *what*?' My eyes are still firmly glued to the fabric, but I can tell Tanya is gaping at me. 'She . . .' Tanya repeats. 'She offered you CEO? What? I mean . . . PENNY!' she yells. 'Come here!'

A moment later I hear Penny stumble through the door, followed by a smell of rich tomato sauce. 'What?' she says. 'I'm in the middle of dinner.'

'Annie has been offered CEO!' Tanya cries, pushing herself to sit up straight.

'*What?*' Penny says. 'Annie, is that true?'

The skirt snaps back again and I throw my head back and groan. God, this fabric is a nightmare.

'Yeah,' I say. 'Pam wants to take off for a year and she offered me the job this afternoon.'

'Wow,' Penny breathes, perching next to Tanya on the bed. 'Congratulations, Annie. That's huge.'

I shrug, suddenly feeling like I might burst into tears.

'What?' Tanya says, leaning forward. 'What is it? Are you okay?'

Why is it that you can be doing quite well at holding in all your horrible emotions, then as soon as someone nice asks if you're okay you suddenly start sobbing like a newborn baby? Does this happen to everyone? Or is it just the emotionally unstable? I'm asking for a friend. Or, well, I'm not. Because that's what's happening to me. Right now.

'Annie!' Tanya cries, pulling me into a hug as Penny leaps up and returns with a box of tissues. 'What is it?'

I take a tissue gratefully and dab my eyes.

'Take a deep breath,' Penny says sternly. I copy her as she breathes in and out, letting the breath shoot out of my mouth in one short, sharp blow.

'What's going on?' Penny says after a moment. 'What's making you so upset?'

'Don't you want the job?' Tanya asks. Her question brings the snakes back, all angry and fast, wrapping themselves around my body.

'Yeah . . .' I say. 'It's a great opportunity. And I love my job.' I take a deep breath. 'It'll mean that I get to live by myself in a nice flat, and I'll maybe be able to afford to buy somewhere someday. I'll set myself up.'

Tanya and Penny look at each other.

'Yeah . . .' Penny says gently. 'That's true. But what else?'

I open and close my mouth, unable to get the words that are swimming in my mind in the right order. Penny catches me glance towards my sewing machine and sighs.

'You're worried you won't be able to carry on with your business,' she says.

I nod, my eyes welling up again. 'I guess . . .' I say, my voice thick as I push the tissue to my eyes. 'I guess I always thought that one day I might do all of this as my proper job, not just as a hobby, and taking on this CEO job just feels like I'm walking away from that.'

'You could still do it, though,' Tanya says. 'You've always done this alongside working full-time, and absolutely smashed it.'

I shake my head. 'I see how hard Pam works. If I take this on, I won't have any time to do it. I won't be able to turn around commissions like this; I'll have to give it up and like, just make the odd costume here and there.'

I make the mistake of looking at Tanya. Her eyes are wide with worry and are shining back at me.

'Why are you crying?' I laugh, poking her with my foot.

She laughs and shakes her head. 'I just want you to be happy, Annie.'

I exhale slowly. 'I need to take this job,' I say. 'It's the right thing to do. It's the sensible thing to do. It's just hard, isn't it? The idea of giving up your dreams.'

'You can always come back to it,' Penny says gently. 'It doesn't have to be forever.'

I shrug and we all sink into silence. I can almost feel Tanya scrabbling around, trying to find a way to fix everything, and Penny, trying to think of a way to make me feel better.

'Shall I make us a tea?' Tanya says, giving my hand a squeeze.

I nod. 'I need to finish making this, though.'

Penny shakes her head. '*You* come before work, Annie. And right now, you need a cup of tea.'

Tanya gets to her feet. 'And there's a new series of *Come Dine with Me*.'

'Come on.' Penny stands up, holding her hand out. 'Work and big life decisions can wait. Dinner can't.'

Falling For You

I let her pull me to my feet and we both walk into the living room. Tanya brings us tea and Penny serves us her homemade spaghetti bolognese as we curl up on the sofa, which is too small for the three of us but we make it work. We sit under a blanket and watch *Come Dine with Me*. As I sit there, all I want to do is reach out and fold this moment into a bottle so I can keep it forever.

Chapter Thirty-Six

Nate

I smile at Remy as he places two pint glasses down in front of us. I've gone back to Hopping Hare. Its light, biscuity taste bounces around on my tongue and warms the inside of my cheeks. I've tried the lagers, I've tried the Guinness, I've tried all the ales (or, at least, I've tried all the ales they have to offer at the Old Queen's Head), and this is the best one.

Remy holds his pint glass up to me and we clink them together.

Remy's wearing his Fred Perry bomber jacket, zipped up to the base of his neck, and faded blue jeans. As always, his grey flat cap is firmly on his head and his salt and pepper stubbly beard is manicured so that it outlines his mouth in a perfect square.

It's Saturday afternoon. The rest of the week dragged by in a horrible, weird blur. I went to work, I sat at my desk, I came home. I've spoken to Mom and Dad every day. Everything has ticked by, just like life always has done. Just fine. Just like my life was before I met Annie. Before we were walking round the streets of her hometown together, laughing with her parents, dancing in that shitty club in Clapham. Before she vanished into thin air.

I push the feelings down. There is no point reliving it. I can't get it back. She's gone, and I'll never know why.

I haven't heard from Aunt Tell, not that I was expecting to. She ignored me for weeks before I forced myself into her life – why wouldn't she ignore me again?

'So,' Remy says, after a few minutes of silence as we both stare up at the flickering television screen. 'Why did you need to see me, then?'

'Can't I just want a pint with you?'

'Sure.' Remy cocks his head. 'But that's not why you called me, is it?'

I take a sip of my pint. Today, the pub is peppered with people. Some of the regulars are propped up at the bar, clusters of families and friends are tucking into cooked lunches and a few children are squabbling over a teetering tower of Jenga. There isn't any football on today (or 'important football', in the words of Remy), so the pub is quieter than usual.

'Well, first of all, I need to talk to you about my aunt.' I give him a questioning look and he grins into his pint.

'She's a nice lady, Nate.'

Hmmm. We'll agree to disagree there.

'We just stayed in touch after the theatre. Just some casual dates. That's all.'

'Okay, sure. I do need to talk to you about something else, though.'

'Is it about that girl?' He smirks at me from over his pint and I flinch.

Fuck, why did I ever tell anybody about Annie?

'No,' I say. 'I'm going back to New York.'

Remy raises his eyebrows in surprise. 'Really? Why's that?'

'I hate it here,' I say at once, the hurt of Annie's name still burning in my chest. I catch Remy's eyes and soften. 'No. Sorry. I don't hate it,' I correct myself. 'I just . . . it isn't what I thought it was going to be.'

'What did you think it was going to be?' Remy says, and the smirk is back. 'Were you expecting to bump into the King?'

I roll my eyes at him. 'I'm not that bad.'

He nods. 'Well, when are you off, then?'

'Soon,' I say. 'I think I'll book my flight tomorrow.'

I'm expecting Remy to have the same reaction as everyone else. The 'oh well, you'll be missed' or, 'I suppose it'll be nice to go back home.' But he doesn't say anything.

'What?' I say, when I can't bear the silence any longer.

He jumps slightly. 'Hmm? Oh, nothing.'

'Yes, there is,' I say, trying not to sound annoyed. 'What is it?'

He glances at me out of the corner of his eye. 'It's just a bit soon to go back, isn't it? I thought you wanted to properly experience life here.'

'I did.'

'And you've been here what, five weeks?'

My cheeks burn. 'Six.'

Falling For You

He shrugs. 'Just pretty soon to make your mind up about a place,' he says. 'That's all.'

I pick up my pint, watching as the bartender drops a crate of tiny glass bottles on the floor with a *thump*. He opens a fridge door and starts slotting them all in place. Orange juices, tomato, apple.

'Yeah,' I say. 'It is quite soon, but it's the right decision for me.'

Remy nods. 'Well, just give me a call when you decide to come and visit.'

We knock our pints together. 'Is this the last time I'll see you, then?' Remy continues. 'Is this the farewell pint?'

I smile, enjoying the way his cockney accent carries his voice. 'It depends when I get the flight. If I get a flight for Monday, then maybe.'

He lets out a whistle. 'Blimey.'

'Or,' I say, as the idea drops into my mind, 'what are you doing tonight?'

He finishes his pint. 'Nothing much.'

'Do you want to come to a drag show?'

Remy raises his eyebrows at me, smiling. 'Are you performing?'

I laugh. 'God, no. Much better than me – my brother. I promise it'll be better than that play.'

Remy laughs and shakes his head. 'Don't let your aunt hear you say that.'

'Is that a yes?'

'Sure. Why not?'

*

'Here you are.'

I hand Remy a bottle of beer and place the tray down on our small table. I got us both a beer and two cherry sambuca shots. I think Remy needs something to settle his nerves, as we seem to be surrounded by screaming hen parties. I asked the bartender to give us a shot of whatever he recommended. I wasn't expecting cherry sambuca, but here we are.

We both knock the shot back and make the familiar 'ah!' sound as soon as it's down. It burns the back of my throat, the acidity and sweetness biting my teeth and storming down my body like a blaze of fire.

Stevie was delighted when I asked for two tickets for his show tonight. Or I *think* he was delighted. Apparently, he's had an 'absolute nightmare' this week, and said hello, yes, you can come, I'll put your tickets with Marina, get me a double vodka Coke, goodbye, all in one breath before hanging up on me. He told me later that the nightmare had involved his costume, but apparently a 'fallen angel' called Annie had offered to help him. I tried to get him to describe her to me, but he was vague and just said she was 'hot and brunette', which hardly narrows it down. But it wouldn't leave my mind. Could it be her, helping my brother? Could it really be that simple?

I have seen Stevie perform before, but I'm ashamed that this is the first time I've seen him since I've been in the UK. It's not that I haven't wanted to, but Stevie is a bit of a slippery fish and getting him to sit down and tell me all the dates that he's performing and where he'll be is impossible.

Not because he doesn't want me to come, but he's so busy and unorganised the last thing he wants to do when he's on the sofa is think about work. But I knew about this one, because he said he couldn't fly out to New York before he'd performed. I got him to agree to a flight next week. We're finally going home together.

Tonight's show is in a small club in Islington. They've filled the dance floor with round tables and erected a stage at the front. I can see Stevie's name scrawled up on the poster alongside the other performers.

STEVIE TRIXX!

Stevie started doing drag officially when he moved to London. But to be honest, he's sort of been doing it his whole life. He's an enormous show-off and loves getting up in front of people on any occasion to perform a dance routine or tell some jokes, and he always loved watching Mom get ready. He used to ask to borrow her jewellery, and if we were ever watching *Dancing with the Stars*, he'd always put on a dress and a pair of her heels and demand that I put on a jacket so we could copy the couples. It's just who Stevie has always been in our family. But I know it isn't as easy for others in his shoes. It breaks my heart to think of people like Stevie living in homes where you're not accepted just because of who you are.

A drag queen walks past us and Remy gapes at her. She has long, slender legs and enormous bouffant red hair which tumbles down her back.

'That's not Stevie,' I say to Remy, before he can ask.

'So . . .' he says slowly. 'Answer something for me, Nate.'

'Sure.'

'And I'm not trying to be difficult, I just want to know.'

I take a swig of my lager. It isn't nearly as nice as the ale we were having back at the Old Queen's Head.

'Stevie is your brother,' he says. 'Right?'

'Right.'

'But . . . when he's wearing all this,' he points towards the drag queen who has made their way to the bar, 'is he still your brother?'

I pull a face at him and he shakes his head. 'No, no, hang on,' he says quickly. 'Sorry. I just mean, is he your brother or your sister?'

I put down my drink. 'So,' I say. 'When Stevie isn't in drag, when he's just Stevie, then he identifies as a man. So we use he and him, and he's my brother.'

Remy pauses for a moment, and then nods.

'When Stevie is in drag,' I gesture towards the drag queen, 'then she's Stevie Trixx. He's playing a character, and that character is a woman.'

I watch the words circle around Remy's mind.

'So when Stevie is in drag . . . she is a she.'

I nod. 'Exactly.'

Remy nods, taking a sip of his beer. 'Sorry, Nate,' he says. 'I just didn't want to get it wrong.'

I clap his shoulder. 'I appreciate that, mate. Everyone is different, though,' I add.

Remy holds his beer bottle towards mine and we clink them together. Moments later, the lights go down, leaving just a pool of light on the stage. Strobes of electric pink and blue strike across the stage and a fog machine starts sending clouds of smoke through the room. Around us, the girls start to scream in delight, throwing themselves in the air and pulling out their phones.

'Please welcome to the stage . . .' a voice booms through the speaker '. . . Stevie Trixx!'

The whole place erupts and Remy looks at me in shock.

I cock my head, a smug grin splitting my face as Stevie glides onto the stage. 'She's a star.'

And I'm not being biased. Stevie is wearing an incredible, emerald-green gown. It has streams of fabric billowing in different directions and a corset coated in stones, which glisten when the light catches them. She's wearing a white-blonde wig, which twists above her head, and heels so thin and pointy that it makes my insides squirm.

Mom definitely didn't used to own heels like *that*.

As the music starts, Stevie starts to flip and twist her body. The audience goes wild, and as I get to my feet and pull Remy up to join me, I notice someone standing on the other side of the bar and my heart stops.

I don't believe it. I was right.

It's Annie.

Chapter Thirty-Seven

Annie

For goodness' sake, why am I crying *again*?

I dab the heel of my hand against my eyes, but they well up again almost immediately. I can't help it. I'm so full of emotion that it's literally spilling out of my eyes.

Stevie Trixx came on stage about thirty seconds ago, and I can't stop staring at her. She's amazing, there's no doubt about that. She's split-leaping and jumping across the stage, dancing and spinning and making the crowd go wild. But it's not just that: she's wearing the outfit I made for her . . . and she looks incredible.

It fits her so much better than I could have imagined. It cinches her waist perfectly and billows out around her like cascades of water. The monkey on the back of the cape sparks every time the light catches it, like it's winking at the audience. Stevie was beside himself when I gave it to him. I guess, to him, I was just a random girl in a sewing shop that Jade vouched for. He was so desperate, I think he would have taken anyone's arm off who had a functioning sewing machine. I'd asked him if I could play around with the design a bit, promising to keep it to the Wicked Witch of the West. And well, I don't think he was expecting what I gave him. He was gobsmacked. So much so that he insisted on giving me, Penny and Tanya tickets to see his show that same night, saying I had to see him wear it in person. It's the first time I've ever seen a client actually wear the costume rather than just getting a static photo. I could see the way it fitted her body properly, how it moved, how it caught the light, how it bent with her curves.

I take a sip of my prosecco and laugh as Tanya screams, throwing her arm in the air.

'God, she is so amazing,' Penny shouts in my ear. 'And she looks *insane*. I can't believe you made that.'

'I didn't make all of it,' I yell back. 'I just tweaked it.'

Penny nudges me in the ribs. 'Annie, that costume has you written all over it.'

I laugh. She's right. I was so emotional yesterday when I was making it that I let myself go a bit wild with it. Normally, when I'm working on a commission I'll pull it back a bit, make sure that it isn't *too* 'me', in case it's too much for the customer. But I didn't care with this one. I only panicked when I was waiting for Stevie, back at the fabric shop, in case I'd ruined his dress and, therefore, his career and – in my anxious, dramatic state of mind – his life. But it was the opposite: Stevie said it was the best dress he'd ever had.

It's a miracle I didn't burst into tears right in front of him.

I finish my prosecco as Tanya hands us both another glass. We decided that I'd take a few days to really think about Pam's offer and not make any rash decisions. So, with that in mind, I decided that I really didn't want to talk about it.

Instead, I would just like to pretend that none of these big, scary life choices were happening to me, and actually, Penny, Tanya and I were staying in our flat and renewing the lease for another ten years.

I pull out my phone and take a picture of Stevie to send to Mum and Dad. God, they'll *love* this. If they lived nearer then I would have got them tickets. Although I—

'Annie?'

I almost drop my glass in shock as there, standing metres away from me, is Nate.

A whole tsunami of emotions crashes over me. Love, excitement, fear, hurt, anger, humiliation. I'm so paralysed by all the feelings coursing through me that I freeze to the spot.

Penny eyes me and then turns to Nate. 'Hey,' she says. 'I'm Penny.'

'Nate.'

'Oh hi . . . *Nate?*' Penny gasps, immediately hitting Tanya. 'This is *Nate*!'

Tanya spins on the spot and eyeballs Nate, but his eyes are fixed on mine. 'Not *the* Nate?' She glares at me for confirmation and then turns back to him. 'Well! I have a few things I would like to say to *you*!'

'What are you doing here?' I say, cutting across Tanya quickly before she starts verbally undressing him. 'Did you follow me?'

Nate laughs, but instead of the easy, fun laugh that I'd got used to, this one is sarcastic. 'Follow you?' he repeats. 'How would I have done that? You blocked me on everything. It's like I don't exist to you.'

'Well . . . I just, I didn't want to speak to you again.' I lift my chin. 'I don't like being one of many girls. It's not the type of person I am. I thought you knew that.'

'What?' Nate looks like I'm speaking another language.

'I know about the other girls!' I cry, losing my cool as I yell over the music. 'I saw the bra and the clothes in the flat and that message saying to call Jane. You lied to me! You told me there wasn't anyone else! And it made me realise that we aren't right for each other. I'm not like that.'

He stares at me, his jaw slack. '*That's* why you left?' he cries incredulously.

'Of course that's why I left!' I explode. 'What did you expect me to do? You're just one of those guys! Like, when did she even leave? Was it the night before I saw you?'

He drags his hand through his hair. 'Jane is someone I went on one date with weeks ago – that note was just Stevie winding me up – and that bra . . . That bra has *nothing* to do with me.'

'Oh please!' I cry, almost laughing myself now. 'Why else would it be there? You told me you lived with your brother, who's gay!'

'I *do* live with my brother!'

'Well then—'

'That's my brother!' He launches an arm towards the stage, where Stevie Trixx is currently doing a lip sync to Britney Spears' 'Toxic'. 'My brother is a drag queen!'

My jaw drops as every word I know falls out of my brain and I try to make sense of what Nate has just said.

That his brother . . . his brother is a drag queen . . . so the bra . . .

Oh my God.

'You know what? Forget it.'

I go to speak but Nate has stormed out of the club.

But I'm not letting him go. Not this time.

I push my way through the fire exit. It swings open and thwacks the outside wall with a bang and I fall through it. As soon as I step outside, icy, winter air wraps around my body and snatches my breath away, but I don't care. Nate is sitting on a wooden bench, right in the corner of the smoking area, fairy lights glittering around him. I can hear traffic roaring past on the road outside, and the distant sirens. But out here it's just us, and as I stare at him, trying to work out what to say, it feels deathly silent.

'Do you want a cigarette?'

He catches me off guard. 'You don't smoke, do you?'

Nate shakes his head. 'No. I don't have any cigarettes either . . . we're just . . . well,' he gestures around, 'in a smoking area.'

We drop into a silence which seems to stretch across eternity. It's unbearable.

'Nate,' I say, walking towards him.

'Please,' he says, staring down at his phone. 'It's fine. I just want to be alone.'

My heart thuds. He sounds so different to the Nate I was with at the weekend. His voice has lost its spark, its sense of fun and excitement. It sounds flatter now. He sounds tired.

It was easy not to miss him when I was angry at him,

Falling For You

when I was convinced that he had fed me a string of lies. But now that I know he hadn't . . . fuck, I feel like I might die if I don't speak to him, if I don't make this right.

'I'm sorry,' I say, wrapping my arms around my body as the chill nips at my skin. 'But, like, you can see why I thought . . .' I trail off, hoping he might say it's all fine and he can see where I'm coming from and we can go back to how we were before, laughing with each other. So comfortable around each other. But he doesn't, he just stays tapping on his phone. It's like I'm not here at all.

'Nate . . .' I say gently, desperate for him just to look at me, 'Nate . . . I . . .'

'Yes,' he says, his voice flat. 'I can see why you'd see a bra and women's clothes and that stupid note and assume I'd been with another woman.'

Relief ripples through me. 'Exactly! So—'

'But why didn't you stay and ask?' His eyes flick up to mine and I flinch. They're not just angry, they're hurt.

'I was in the shower,' he says. 'I would have been out in five minutes. Like, do you not know me at all? We'd just spent all that time together – how could you think of me like that? I thought the world of you. I thought you felt the same way I did.'

The last bit tumbles out of his mouth and I feel a lump form in my throat.

'I'm sorry . . .'

'And you didn't even give me a chance to explain!' he cries. 'You just left and blocked me. You acted as if I didn't exist – how could you do that?' He eyes me, and when I don't respond he shakes his head. 'It's fine. I just guess I didn't know you as well as I thought I did.'

'I'm sorry . . .' I say again, my voice weak. 'I just thought . . . I've had guys do this to me before, I just thought . . .'

'You thought I was like everyone else?'

It's like he's got hold of my heart and is slowly pulling it out of my body, ready to crush it between his fingers.

I nod, tears brimming at the corners of my eyes. Because now I see him again, it's like the clouds in my mind have all parted. Because of course he isn't like everyone else. This is Nate. The guy who somehow makes me feel whole, even though we didn't even know each other a few weeks ago.

I open my mouth to speak but he gets there first.

'It's fine,' he says coldly. 'I'm going back to New York on Monday anyway.'

My stomach drops. 'Monday?' I repeat.

'Yup. I've just booked a flight.' He looks up at me, daring me to question him or to ask him to stay.

But . . . I can't.

'Right,' I say. 'And . . . are you coming back?'

He shakes his head. 'Nah. This isn't the place for me. I need to go back home. I better go back in.' He gets to his feet. 'Good luck with everything, Annie. I'm sorry for getting so angry,' he adds, and for a second I see a glimmer of the fun, caring Nate I spent the weekend with. 'Thanks for making my time here fun, I really did love it the most when I was with you.'

He goes to walk past me and I grab his arm. 'Wait!' I cry, my heart beating outside of my chest. 'Is that it? You can't just leave! I know I screwed up, but don't you want to fight for us?'

He looks down at me, his green eyes shining. I can see the idea playing in his mind; all he has to do is reach out and grab it.

But he looks away.

'I'm sorry, Annie,' he says. 'I just don't want to fight any more.'

He moves past me and walks inside, the fire door slamming behind him and making me jump. And suddenly, standing alone in the smoking area, the icy air feels as if it's freezing me from the inside. Cold dread fills my body and I let the wind whip around me, rattling my bones.

He's gone, and this time it's for good.

And if I hadn't run off in the first place . . . would he have stayed?

Chapter Thirty-Eight

Nate

'I've got a bone to pick with you.'

My eyes ache as I look up at Stevie, who has marched into the living room with his eyebrows raised, pointing his passport at me.

'What?' I ask, my throat dry and scratchy.

'I saw you,' Stevie says accusingly. 'You left halfway through my show! You've been in London for six weeks and this is the first time you come and see me, and then you leave halfway through!'

I drop my head into my hands.

I left as soon as I walked away from Annie. I just couldn't take it any more. The music was too loud, the scent of alcohol too strong, the lights were too bright, the laughter and screams were too . . . I don't even know. I just had to leave. I sent Remy a message and jumped in a cab. As soon as I got home, I lay on the sofa for hours, staring at the ceiling. My head was spinning from the mixture of spirits and adrenaline swirling around my body, a million different thoughts erupting.

I never thought I'd see her again. I'd written her off, I'd let her go.

Falling For You

Well, of course I hadn't actually let her go. Life would be much easier if you could let someone go just like that, someone who broke your heart, when hours before you were planning your life with them, thanking your lucky stars that you'd finally found the person you'd spent your whole life searching for. But I'd accepted the reality check. Life isn't a movie. Life is hard, and shitty, and sad.

Round and round the thoughts went until I finally fell asleep, waking up a few hours later with a stiff neck from Stevie's lumpy sofa as he came back. I crawled straight into bed, too tired to brush my teeth or even drink some water. Now, I feel as though something has died in my mouth. Although, I have made it back onto the sofa.

'I know,' I say, my voice muffled between my cupped hands. 'I'm sorry. Everything got a bit dramatic. You were so great, though.'

Stevie gives me an expectant look and then tuts. 'I've got breakfast plans,' he says. 'Do you want to come?'

I shake my head. 'I booked us flights for tomorrow, did you see?'

He nods, wrapping a large scarf around his neck. 'I've already started packing.'

I hold my hand up to him as a goodbye and he slams the door. It sends a shudder through my weak, pathetic body.

Why did I do shots? I flop back down onto the sofa and shut my eyes.

I didn't mean to get angry last night. It's not who I am, and I never would have thought I could be so angry with

Annie. The brightest person I've ever met. But as soon as I saw her, it all poured out of me. I couldn't see her and not be filled with a boiling rage. How could you leave so easily? Did you not feel the same way as I did? How could you do that to me?

But as soon as I said it I knew there was no point. I'd learnt my lesson. We weren't meant to be. I just needed to go back home.

I must have fallen asleep, because next thing I know I'm being pulled out of a dream where I'm about to do a penalty shoot-out for Chelsea, when my phone vibrates next to me. I lurch awake, a damp patch of drool pooled into the sofa. I scrabble around for my phone and see Mom is video-calling me.

God, how long was I asleep for?

I force myself to sit up and take the call, expecting to see her warm, smiley face that might, for a moment, make my hangover and inescapable existential dread disappear. But she looks furious.

'Mom?' I say, alarmed by her expression. 'Are you okay?'

'No!' Mom says at once, making me jump with her abrupt tone. 'What's this about you coming home?'

I raise myself up on my elbow and lean my throbbing head against my hand.

'I've booked flights for tomorrow,' I say. 'For me and Stevie.'

'And?'

I pause.

'And what?' I say.

'And you're coming back to live in New York, like your dad has just told me?' Her face is scrunched up in annoyance.

'Linda,' I hear Dad's voice somewhere in the background, 'he wants to come back home.'

I sigh. 'Yeah. I thought you'd be pleased,' I add, sounding like a petulant child.

'Well, I'm not!'

'Thanks.'

'You've been there five minutes, why are you coming home?'

How about, because the further away I go, the worse you seem to get? Because I'm terrified that I'm running away from you to live out my dreams like the selfish asshole that I am? Because I'm heartbroken and sad and, yeah, life here isn't like the movies we spent years watching, because guess what? Life isn't a movie.

But I don't say any of that. She wouldn't understand, and I could never bring myself to tell Mom that one of the reasons I want to come home is because of her. It would be too cruel.

'Because I want to,' I say eventually. 'I've got to go. I'll send Dad over our flight details. See you soon.' I hang up before I give her the chance to reply and throw my phone onto the floor. And then I fall back to sleep.

I wake up a few hours later from a loud banging on the flat door. My first thought is how the hell did Stevie ever survive without me if he can't remember his goddam keys. My head is still throbbing as I haul myself off the sofa, and

I vow to chug a gallon of water as soon as I let Stevie in. I tug the door open, rubbing my head, and am about to immediately turn back and throw myself back on the sofa when I take in the small, glamorous woman stood in front of me.

'Aunt Tell?' I manage. 'What are you . . .'

'Can I come in?' She walks past me before I have a chance to answer and I wince at the state of the flat. There are old beer cans and plates stacked up on the coffee table, and a stench of sweat and stale alcohol that I only notice as Aunt Tell walks in.

'Sorry,' I say quickly, rushing to open a window, 'I wasn't expecting anyone.'

'Remy said you'd be in,' she says, perching dubiously on the sofa. 'I thought I'd pop by.'

'Would you like a coffee?'

'He said that you were going back to New York.'

I'll take that as a no. I lean against the windowsill. 'I want to be with Mom.'

She purses her lips, looking around the room. The back of my eyes starts to throb as we sink back into silence.

'Look,' I say. 'Now isn't a great time. I—'

'I spoke to your mom.'

She keeps her eyes fixed on her handbag, which she's been idly fiddling with since she arrived.

'Oh?'

'We spoke on the phone,' Aunt Tell continues. 'It was nice. She's exactly as she's always been.'

I shift my body weight. 'You caught her on a good day.'

'We had a good laugh together.'

'Good.'

We fall back into silence. Why is she here?

'It's been quite lonely here, all these years,' she says, and to my alarm her voice has jumped up an octave. 'With all my family on the other side of the world. You guys are all that I have.'

I can't help it; my eyebrows rise sceptically. 'But you . . . you never speak to us.'

'I used to!' she says, her dark eyes snapping defensively. 'I rang your mom every week before everything . . . happened. I loved having you pop in and see me the other week, and come down to see my show. I told everyone in the company that my nephew was visiting. God knows, Stevie doesn't visit me any more.'

'You can't expect people to make an effort with you if you don't make an effort with them,' I say coldly.

She flinches at this and wrings her hands.

'No,' she says. 'I suppose you're right.' Her eyes downcast, she begins to twist a ring on her index finger. 'I'm ashamed to say, Nathaniel, that it took your visit to make me call your mom again. It was quite a hard look in the mirror, what you said to me.' I open my mouth to argue but she holds up a hand. 'I needed it. I listened to what you said, and I spoke with Remy. He's a good man, isn't he?' I nod, and she smiles sadly. 'What I'm trying to say is . . . I'm going to come home. Once my show is finished. Not for good, I love it here. But I want to be there for your mom. For Linda.'

Relief washes over me and I'm so exhausted that I feel like I could collapse. 'Really?'

She nods. 'Really.'

'That'll make her so happy,' I say.

Aunt Tell gives me a small smile. 'It'll make me happy too.'

Chapter Thirty-Nine

Annie

I take a deep breath and look at myself in the mirror as the lift skims up to the third floor.

I'm wearing a white woollen jumper and grey fitted trousers with smart, shiny shoes. The only glimmer of colour is the scarf in my hair, wrapped around my ponytail. I'm wearing my most professional, corporate outfit. Everything was bought in a high-street shop; nothing was made by me. It matches my expression: cold, serious.

After Nate left me in the smoking area, I should have gone back inside. Part of me wondered whether I should have chased after him. If I'd chased after him after the first time we met, all those weeks ago at the Halloween masquerade ball, would any of this have happened? But I couldn't. I heard him loud and clear. He'd lost the sparkle behind his eyes and the grin that pulled at the corners of his mouth. He looked exhausted. He'd made his decision, just like I'd made my decision a week before.

I sank into the corner where he'd been sitting, under the heated lamp, and just stared, my mind buzzing. Tears fell from my eyes of their own accord, like my body was grieving him without my mind clicking into place. I don't know how long I sat there for, but eventually Tanya and Penny came tumbling out. I don't know how drunk they were, but as soon as they saw me they snapped into protective-best-friend mode and bundled me up, insisting that we all go home. I didn't even get to speak to Stevie Trixx after her show and tell her how great she looked.

The next morning I woke up feeling like I'd stepped into a new chapter of my life. A week ago, my life was full of colour. I was riding high on excitement and that lovely, giddy feeling of 'what if'? What if I did take my business more seriously and create costumes and outfits full-time? What if I did spend my days sewing, designing and creating pieces I really loved? What if Nate was as great as I thought he was? What if I'd found the one? What if this was going to be my life now, forever?

Stupid. It's laughable now, all of it. I'm thirty-two and I was dancing around acting like a teenager. So, when I woke up yesterday morning, everything felt a bit clearer. Colder, but clearer.

I was going to accept the CEO job. Mum could take over the business, and I could make the odd costume if I had the time or if she needed help. But I was going to take control of my life and do this job. I'd get myself a flat and stand on my own two feet. It was the right thing to do. Just like letting Nate walk away was the right thing to do. Both made me feel like I was about to die, but that didn't matter. Nobody cares about your dreams when you're an adult; it's just taken me far longer than everyone else to realise it.

Falling For You

I smooth my hair down as the lift pings open. For the second time in the past week, I'm surprised to see Pam isn't hunched over her laptop, staring at it like she's being hypnotised. I look around, before I hear her laughter coming from the kitchen.

'Pam?' I call, following the sound of her voice.

As I walk into the kitchen, I see Pam and Rodney, their arms around each other as they sway back and forth to the radio. They're both laughing as Rodney holds out his arm and spins Pam round like a ballroom dancer, tipping her back and making her squeal. Rodney lifts her back up and spots me, suddenly looking incredibly embarrassed.

'I'm so sorry, Annie,' he says, his body immediately snapping back to the stiff, upright posture that I'm used to seeing. 'We didn't realise you were here.'

Pam flicks her hair back into place, her cheeks pink. She looks at her reflection in the toaster and turns to face me.

'I dragged Rodney into work with me today,' she says.

'I have a meeting at eleven in Moorgate,' Rodney explains. 'So I thought I could pop by.'

'That song was played at our wedding,' Pam says, gesturing to the radio as the final bars of 'Be My Baby' fade into a Lady Gaga song.

Rodney looks down at Pam and they catch eyes, their faces glowing as they beam at each other. It makes my heart ache.

'How long have you been married?' I ask.

'Thirty-seven years!' they chorus.

'And this is the first time he's come into work with me!' Pam says.

Rodney pulls a face. 'That's not true. I'm your accountant.'

'You were my *husband* first.'

She nestles into his chest and I feel myself grow warm. God, thirty-seven years together and they're still dancing with each other in the kitchen. How have they done it?

'Anyway!' Pam claps her hands and takes her foamy coffee out from under the machine. 'It's a Monday and we are at work, so let's get to it.'

She gives Rodney a crisp clap on the shoulder and he nods, suddenly back to looking like Rodney, our accountant, rather than Rodney, Pam's husband.

'Where's everyone else?' he says, picking up his briefcase. 'You have seven employees on your books.'

The corners of his mouth are turning up in amusement, but Pam waves a hand at him dismissively. 'It's always just me and Annie for the first hour or so,' she says, dropping into her wheely chair with such force that it starts to spin round. She grabs the corner of her desk and pulls herself towards her laptop, immediately adopting her natural position: hunched over, craned over the keyboard, chest and elbows bent forward, like the laptop is her only source of oxygen.

'It's really exciting about your plans to go travelling,' I say to Rodney. His whole face lights up.

'I can't believe we're actually going,' he beams. 'It's something we've spoken about for years, but I always thought it was just a pipe dream, you know?'

My chest aches. 'Yeah,' I say quietly. 'I know the feeling.'

'Right,' Rodney says, taking his cue from Pam picking up the phone. He doffs an imaginary hat at me and gives Pam a peck on the cheek. But she's in work mode now, her eyes squarely fixed on her screen. She does give a non-committal pout in his direction but doesn't dare break her staring contest with her inbox. Rodney steps into the lift and I sit down. As soon as I see him disappear behind the lift doors my heart rate picks up.

'So,' Pam says when she looks up from her screen. 'Why are you staring at me? Everything all right?'

'I'd like to take up your offer and be CEO,' I say. And although I'd practised saying this in my head my entire journey here and had every intention of sounding cool, calm and professional, it comes out more like: I'dliketotakeupyouroff erandbeceo.

Thankfully, Pam and I have worked together long enough. She's seen me in every state: nervous, excitable, stressed, anxious.

She turns to face me, spinning round and leaning back into her office chair. 'Really?'

I nod, trying to ignore the anxiety that's bubbling under my skin.

This is the right decision. This is the right decision.

'Yes,' I say, 'I love this job, and I think I'm quite good at it—'

'You're very good at it.'

'And I think it would be a good decision for me.'

Pam takes me in for a moment, before pulling out a packet of cigarettes from her breast pocket and sticking one in her mouth. She turns the packet towards me and I shake my head, before noticing that she's flicked open a lighter.

'Pam!' I cry. 'The fire alarms!'

She waves an arm at me, the glittering flame licking the end of the cigarette. 'I turned them off,' she mumbles, pausing to take a long drag. 'It's raining.'

I open my mouth to reply and decide against it. She's lit up now – what can I do about it?

'You look different today.'

I look down at myself. 'Ah,' I say. 'Yes. I did a wardrobe clear-out at the weekend.'

She raises her eyebrows. 'Why's that?'

'I'm going to be moving soon,' I say lamely. 'I probably won't get a wardrobe as big as mine, so I thought it would be a good time to sort everything out.'

I actually felt a bit disgusted at the sight of my bright, optimistic clothes when I woke up yesterday morning. It felt like they were all laughing at me, sniggering at how I'd fallen for their whimsical charm all these years and skipped through life thinking that everything would just fall into place. My stupid notebook was open on my desk. Half the page was filled with delicate strokes and details on Stevie's outfit, the other side with scribbles of how I could make my business work if I did it full-time.

I threw it all in the bin.

'Did you sell them?'

I frown. 'Sell what?'

'Your clothes.' She takes a long drag and releases the smoke into the air in a slow, steady stream.

'Oh,' I say. 'No. I just gave them to charity. Or I'm going to. I haven't got round to it yet.'

She knits her brow. 'Why aren't you selling them?' She

says it deadpan, like I've just tried to tell her that the sky isn't blue.

'Nobody would want my stuff,' I laugh.

'People buy your clothes all the time.'

'Yeah, but,' I shrug, feeling my face burn, 'that's like the odd thing.'

She looks at me for a moment, narrowing her eyes. 'Well,' she says eventually. 'I guess we need to celebrate, then!' She pushes herself to her feet and makes her way back to the kitchen.

'What are you doing?' I call after her.

'Champagne!' she shouts back at me. 'I'm sure we have some somewhere.'

'It's not even nine in the morning!' I laugh.

I hear her tut and I roll my eyes, trying to shake the uneasiness that's filling my body. I open my laptop as my phone vibrates and a message from an unknown number pops onto my screen.

Hi, Annie! My name is Max, Stevie gave me your number, we work in the clubs together (I'm a queen!). He said you made his costume, I'd love to work with you. Are you free this week for a coffee and chat?

I look down at the message, my skin feeling too small for my body. Normally, a message like this would fire me up. I'd be straight on the phone, and then spend hours all week designing and creating the perfect costume. But now, I just feel numb. If anything, I feel as though I could burst into tears.

'Oh,' Pam calls, breaking me out of my thoughts. 'I

suppose I'll ask Rodney to get some paperwork drawn up.' She pokes her head around the door to the kitchen. 'If you're sure about this, Annie?'

I tuck my phone away, switching it to silent.

'I'm sure.'

'I don't like this,' Penny says, her eyes narrowed at me, 'I don't like this at all.'

I laugh, folding up another jumper and placing it in a box.

Pam gave me some time off before starting my new job, and it's the week before the three of us leave our perfect little flat. So, instead of sitting around feeling sorry for myself and panicking about where I was going to live, I decided to go home and spend a week with my parents. I could give the clothes I made to Mum (after speaking to Pam, I couldn't bring myself to drop them at a charity shop, never to see them again), and spend some time looking at flats online and working out my finances with Dad. Because that's what dads are for, right?

But it does mean that I had to tell Tanya and Penny that I was moving out a week early. Which, needless to say, did not go down well.

'Well, I don't like it either,' I say, trying to sound pragmatic. 'But it just makes sense. If it were up to me then I'd stay in this flat with you both until we were eighty.'

'Me too.'

I hit Penny with a pillow as she sticks her bottom lip out at me. 'Shut up,' I say. 'You're excited to live with Mike, and I'm excited for you! He's great.'

'He won't be able to talk to me about my periods.'

'He will if he's a real man.'

'Right!' Tanya says, marching into my room with her label maker in one hand and a roll of packing tape in the other. 'How can I help?'

'What are you doing?' Penny turns to her accusingly.

Tanya blinks back. 'What?'

'You're *helping* her!' Penny says incredulously. 'You're helping her move out a week early. We should be locking her in her room and stealing her purse so she can't leave.'

I place a stack of books in a box. Obviously, I'm not planning on taking all my things with me on the train down to the Cotswolds. Paddington is bad enough as it is. But I'm trying to pack everything up, so when Mum and Dad come up with me at the weekend we can move out in some form of order. I owe it to them after they turned up to move me out of university in third year and found me asleep, unpacked, hungover, with absolutely no idea what they were doing there.

I just thank the lord there wasn't anybody I had to stuff out of a bathroom window.

'It's just a label maker,' Tanya says in a small voice. 'Oh!' she adds, spotting a Marian Keyes book. 'Can I have this? Have you read it?'

'Sure.' I hand it to her.

'You'll have to finish it by Friday,' Penny says stroppily.

'Or you can post it back to me,' I say.

Tanya's face scrunches up with worry, and I laugh. 'Tanya, I'm joking, you can keep it.'

'What is all this?' she says, looking around at my boxes.

I've been super organised and labelled them 'keep', 'sell', 'bin'. She is eyeing my 'sell' box suspiciously.

'If you want anything in there, take it,' I say. 'Now is your last chance.'

'You can't sell this!' Penny cries in outrage, as she pulls out a particularly garish jumper I knitted last year. It's made out of pink, glittery wool with a black cat sat on an orange pumpkin on the front.

'Why not?'

'Annie, you love this jumper!' Penny says, waving it in my face. 'Why would you sell it? What's going on? I'm worried about you.' She turns to Tanya. 'We need an intervention.'

Tanya nods. 'I'll get the biscuits.'

'What, no!' I say, grabbing Tanya's arm. 'Nothing is going on, I'm *fine*. I'm just trying to . . . you know, get my life in order.'

'By selling your favourite clothes and taking a corporate job and giving up your dreams?' Penny shoots back.

'You sound like Nate,' I mutter under my breath, turning back to my piles of books. I keep my back firmly to them both, even though I can feel them exchanging worried glances. We haven't spoken about Nate since Saturday night. Even then, I only told them the headlines of what happened. He wasn't seeing other girls, I fucked up, it's over.

'Have you heard from him?' Tanya says gently.

'Nope,' I say. 'And I won't. He's gone. But I've decided it's a good thing,' I hear myself add, apparently making that decision as soon as I voice it.

'Why?' Penny sinks back onto my bed.

'Well, like . . . was he ever real?' I shrug.

Tanya and Penny glance at each other.

'We . . . we did meet him, Annie,' Tanya says nervously.

I roll my eyes. 'No, I mean, he was too perfect! All the romance and chance meetings, the perfect dates and great, easy conversation and the instant connection . . . that's not real, is it? Nobody has a relationship like that in real life.'

I'm saying it like it's a fact, but I can see the doubt on their faces.

'Annie,' Tanya says eventually. 'You deserve all of those things.'

'And you will have them,' Penny adds, her voice stern.

I wave them both off. 'He was a fantasy, the whole thing was a fantasy. And it's fine.' I force myself to smile brightly at them both. 'Really, everything is great.' I keep my smile for as long as I can, until it starts to burn at my cheeks. 'Oh, fuck it,' I say, letting my smile drop. 'Tanya. Get the biscuits. I need it.'

Tanya immediately springs forward and darts out of the room into the kitchen. Penny reaches out and grabs my hand.

'You're the best person I know, Annie. You do know that, right?'

I smile, my throat starting to ache. 'You won't say that when I live in yours and Mike's spare room for the rest of my life.'

'We don't have a spare room,' she says earnestly. 'But you can live under the stairs for as long as you like.'

And as I look back at Penny with her serious green eyes, I know she means it.

Chapter Forty

Nate

I drum my fingers on the side of the plastic chair, eyeing Stevie as he saunters over to me, holding two Costa coffee cups, expertly dodging the swarms of people rushing for their flights.

'Here you are,' he says. 'I got us a scone to share, too. Have you even had one of these since you've been here?'

I wrinkle my nose as he pulls open the brown paper bag and I see a squat, white circular baked good.

'Nope,' I say. 'Never heard of it.'

He starts sawing it in two with his plastic knife. 'God. You're going back to New York and you've barely done anything British. Did you have fish and chips?'

'Nope.'

'Pie and mash?'

I shake my head.

'A roast dinner?'

I snap my fingers. 'That I have had.'

'Where?'

'At the pub with Remy.'

Falling For You

Stevie seems to accept this. He pulls out his phone and my eyes flit back up to the announcement board.

Our flight is in four hours. Stevie insisted on us getting here early so he could 'comfortably' make his way through the airport. He said he wanted a coffee and a giraffe in peace, which I later found out was a fast-food restaurant.

'Ah,' Stevie says, leaning back into his seat and flicking his sunglasses onto his face, 'I'm looking forward to a holiday.'

'You do remember what New York is like this time of year, don't you?' I raise an eyebrow at him.

Stevie ignores me. 'Do you think Mom will recreate a thanksgiving dinner for us?'

I shrug. 'Probably.'

'And I'd like to go to Target. Oh, and Pottery Barn!'

I give him a look. 'Target?'

'You miss these things when you're away for a long time,' he says. I turn my phone in my hands.

'How are you feeling?' I ask.

'Tired,' Stevie says at once. 'But hopefully I'll perk up after this.' He holds up his coffee and takes a sip.

'No,' I press on. 'How are you feeling about going home?'

I keep looking at Stevie, waiting for him to push me aside or pull out his phone in a defensive huff, but he doesn't. Since our chat last week, he finally seems willing to talk to me. It's a miracle really.

'I feel . . . okay,' he says. 'I've actually been doing some research.'

He unzips his carry-on bag and waves a bunch of Post-it notes in my face.

'What are they for?'

'To help!' he says happily. 'I read a great blog about a woman with dementia and how she decided that it wasn't going to define her. She was just going to live with it. And that's how I think Mom feels about it.'

I nod, taking a sip of my coffee. 'I agree.'

'She had loads of tips on there, and one of them was sticking Post-it notes with reminders of appointments, tasks, that sort of thing. I thought it could be something we do together this week.'

'That's a great idea.' I put my hand on his shoulder and give it a shake.

He shrugs me off, embarrassed. 'I just want to be helpful.'

'I get that.'

We slip back into silence, staring at the throng of people zipping through the airport. They weave in and out, manically looking over their shoulders to check they haven't lost anyone from their party as their wheeled suitcases drag loudly across the marble floors.

'So, why are you going back?'

I break from my stare, his question catching me off guard.

'Is it because of Annie?'

I frown, shaking my head. 'Of course not,' I say, a bit more tartly than I'd meant to. 'I didn't even know her six weeks ago.'

'Why, then?'

I sink further into my seat, hoping that Stevie will catch

on that I don't want to get into it all. Unfortunately, he does the opposite.

'Look, we've got another four hours before our flight. You might as well tell me the truth,' he says, his voice all light and superior. It makes my toes curl.

'Why do you care?'

'Because you're my brother.'

I huff, snatching the paper bag from Stevie and taking a bite of scone. It sticks to the roof of my mouth like a claggy chunk of bread and Stevie looks at me in horror.

'You're supposed to have jam and cream on it, you lunatic.'

I force myself to swallow the congealed ball of stodge and take another sip of my coffee to try and wash it down.

'I'm going back because I don't like it here,' I say, coughing slightly as the scone sticks to my windpipe.

'Right . . .' Stevie says slowly. 'And why's that? Because it isn't all sunshine and roses like the films make it out to be?'

'Yes, actually.'

'That can't be the reason you're going back to New York,' Stevie scoffs. 'That's the stupidest thing I've ever heard. What are you, six years old?'

I glare at him. 'It's not just that.'

'Well, what is it, then?'

I roll my eyes, debating whether to do what I always do, stuff this part down further inside me and pretend it doesn't exist. But I'm so tired of fighting with myself, I don't know if I have the energy.

'Ever since I got here, I feel like I'm being punished,' I say eventually. Stevie turns to face me, but he doesn't say anything. 'Back home was really rough, looking after Mom,' I continue. 'I'd just moved out when she started to be . . . well, when she started acting different. I tried to go with the flow, but then it got worse, Stevie. You know you said she didn't recognise you? She used to do that to me, only once or twice, but enough to make you feel like the worst person in the world. And the thing is, she always had an excuse for it after. She'd say that she hadn't slept well, or it was the lighting. A lot of it was easy to explain away. Like, we all lose our keys or forget our pin numbers. But when it started getting really bad, well, that's when I gave up more of my time to be with her and to help Dad. I only came here because Mom overheard me telling Dad about it, when I had the idea that Aunt Tell might make things better for her. Mom was desperate for me to go, and she was so excited that I let myself get wrapped up in her idea of it all. How I'd move here, live with you, find this amazing, exciting life, fall in love . . . just do all the things everyone around me seemed to be doing while I was stuck at my parents' house, following Mom around, ready to catch her and piece her back together. I felt so bad about coming here, man. And then when I arrived and everything started being shit, it just felt like one big punishment for being selfish in the first place. Then I met Annie and everything was great, like, it was so amazing, and I finally thought that *this* is what I'd come to London for. But that fucked up too. You know, she asked if I'd fight for us on Saturday, and I just left. It felt like the final nail in the coffin. I needed to grow up and come home, take care of Mom, do what I needed to do.'

'I think Dad does a pretty good job of taking care of Mom,' Stevie says in a small voice.

'Well, what about Dad, then?' I cry, finding it hard not to explode. 'Who is taking care of him?'

'Nate . . .' Stevie says. 'You know it's not your job to take care of everyone, right? I mean, you do a good job of it. But you need to take care of yourself, too.'

I shake my head, running my hand roughly through my hair. We both look forward, the clock flicking over to seven thirty.

'Annie's so talented,' Stevie says eventually. 'You know she made my costume for Saturday? I only asked her to mend it, but she transformed it.'

'Yeah,' I sigh, 'she's really talented. I think she's going to do it as a business, so you should use her again.'

Stevie pulls out his phone. 'Nah. She said my costume was the last she was making. My friend asked if she'd do a commission for him and she said no.'

'What?' My eyes snap up from my coffee. 'She's giving it up? She can't do that!'

Stevie looks at me. 'And why's that?'

'Because she's incredible!' I cry, throwing my arms in the air. 'I mean . . . she just can't do that.'

To my annoyance, I notice Stevie start to laugh.

'What?' I snap hotly. He holds his hands up defensively.

'It's just all so mad to me!' he says. 'I mean, fuck, you're a better person than I am, but all *the drama*. You think you're cursed because you've had a few bad weeks in London?'

'Fuck off.'

'And you do know that you're proper into Annie, don't you? And she asked you to stay and fight for her but you're here, sat with me, waiting to go back home so you can, what? Live in our parents' spare bedroom for the rest of your life?' I shoot him daggers but he's still grinning at me. 'You're the one always harping on about the universe and luck and all that bullshit. Are you really going to leave it like this?'

'Well, what do you expect me to do?' I demand.

'I don't know.' Stevie shrugs nonchalantly. 'Tell her how you feel. Call her, at least.'

'She's blocked my number.'

'Ooohh . . . romance.' I glare at him and he laughs again. 'Go find her, then!' he says, exasperated. 'Who cares if she tells you to go to hell or it all fucks up? You can't leave without properly telling her how you feel. Otherwise, what is the point in all of this?'

I open and close my mouth, emotions flying around my body like wild birds.

'I have her number.' He holds up his phone. I go to grab it but he snatches it away. 'But I think you should go and find her instead. We both know you want to. It's far more romantic.'

'I can't . . . how would I even find her?'

Stevie sighs. 'Well . . . she's going to her parents tonight.'

I gape at him. 'How do you know that?'

'She told me,' he shrugs. 'I asked her about payment and she said she'd message me when she was back from visiting her parents.'

I stand up clumsily. 'Do you . . . do you really think I should?'

Stevie nods, smirking at me. 'Go and tell her how you feel? Yes. Go on.' He waves a hand at me. 'Go live out your best Hugh Grant fantasy. I know you've been desperate to since the moment you got to England.'

'But, our flight . . .' I say, spinning around to look at the announcement board. Stevie looks down at his phone.

'She was only going this evening . . . you might be able to catch her at the station.'

'Paddington!' I gabble. 'The train goes from Paddington.'

'Go get her then, Nate,' Stevie grins at me.

He gets to his feet and we clap hands together.

'And Nate?'

'What?'

'You deserve the world. Don't fuck this up.'

Chapter Forty-One

Annie

Right now, sitting on this bench, I'm actually really proud of myself. There are four reasons why.

1. I haven't cried in the past hour. Depressingly, this is a big deal.
2. I've managed to fit everything into my suitcase, even though I ended up packing after half a bottle of wine.
3. I haven't had a McDonald's. Even though I really, really want one.
4. I haven't thought about Nate in thirty minutes. Well, apart from now. Bollocks.

I stare longingly at the McDonald's, sitting squarely opposite me. The golden arches are luring me in, the queue of people who are nicer to themselves than I am snaking around the corner of the station.

The next time I'll see Tanya and Penny will be moving day, which I'm trying not to think about too much. We'll still speak and see each other all the time, and lots of friends don't live together and are still as close as ever. It will all be fine. Better than fine! Everything will be great.

I take a deep breath as the tears threaten again.

I've been trying really hard not to think about Nate. I've tried every tactic that's worked in the past. I've tried hating him, making up reasons that he's somehow a huge arsehole and that I'm better off without him. I've tried convincing myself that he's actually really ugly and I've never fancied him in the first place. I've tried telling myself that it's a *good thing* and I'm much better single anyway. I've even tried gaslighting myself into thinking that it wasn't as good as I think it was and I imagined the whole thing.

But here's the problem. Every time I force myself to think these thoughts, it's like something in my body is screaming at me that it's fake. The same part that glowed the first time that we kissed, just behind my chest. It has this fierce, unwavering conviction that will not let Nate go. I'm scared it never will.

I get to my feet as I see my platform finally announced.

I messaged Mum and Dad to tell them that it was over with Nate, and that I didn't want to talk about it. What I need is to go home and clear my head. I'll find a great new place to live in and make some plans for the next year with my new, exciting job. Maybe I'll book some trips.

I've had messages from four different people since Stevie's show, all asking if they can work with me to make their costumes.

I walk towards the barrier and put my ticket in the

machine. It sucks it through and I push my suitcase forwards.

I will get to the stage where I don't see Nate everywhere I go. I will get over him. I will.

Chapter Forty-Two

Nate

I jab my bank card against the ticket barrier but it stays shut. I slam it down again, and again.

I can see her, she's halfway across the platform. I tried shouting her name, but it was carried by the bustle of people streaming past me. My heart lurches as I look up and see the train pull into the station.

I'm so close. I can't let her go now.

'Excuse me.' I grab a man wearing a station uniform. 'Please help me. My card isn't working.'

He looks down at my card dubiously.

'That's because you need a ticket to get through that barrier,' he says in a bored voice. 'Do you have a ticket?'

I blink at him mindlessly. 'No, I have a . . . this, I have a . . . this!' I wave my bank card at him. 'How much is a ticket?' I blurt.

'Where are you going?'

'Nowhere. Wherever that train is going.' I hurl an arm in the direction of the platform, trying to spot Annie.

I can still see her. The doors to the train haven't opened yet.

'Depends where you're getting off. Tickets to Worcester cost forty pounds.'

'Fine,' I gabble, 'I'll buy one.'

'The ticket machine is over there.' He holds up a non-committal arm towards the other end of the station and I feel my stomach drop.

'What?' I manage. 'Can I not just buy one off you now? I really need to get on that train, I can't miss it.'

It's taking everything in me not to grab hold of his lapels and beg.

'I need to go and tell that woman how I feel about her!' I cry, hoping the romantic appeal might tug on his heartstrings. Instead, he just rolls his eyes at me.

'Ticket machine is over there,' he says again, and before I can think of anything else to say, he turns his back on me and is swallowed into the crowd.

I hear a whistle blowing and stare at the ticket machine. A line of people, at least seven deep, is standing patiently behind it. There is no way I'll make it. And then I'll miss her. I'll miss her for good.

Before I can think about it, I race towards the ticket barrier. I slam my hands against the edges of the barrier and launch myself over the top. In the background, I can hear people shout in alarm but it's too late, I'm racing through the crowds. People have started to slowly move into the train carriages now and I bang on the windows, scouring each one for her face.

'Annie?' I yell. 'Annie?'

But it's no use; each window I get to I can't see her. And

Falling For You

then the doors shut with a final slam and before I can even breathe, the train pulls away. My heart leaves with it.

She's gone.

I can't believe after all that I've—

'Nate?'

I whip round, and there she is. She's wearing a purple beanie, her dark hair is curly around her face and her eyes are wide. She's looking at me as if she's seen a ghost. My heart races as I stare at her, my chest rising and falling heavily.

She's there, she's standing right in front of me. I did it. I made it. She's here.

But now, as I look at her, my mind is blank. I'm frozen to the spot. I don't know how long we're staring at each other for, but it's enough for the train to leave the station.

Eventually, I speak.

'Stevie told me you're quitting your business.'

Her face falls. 'Yeah.'

'I . . . I don't think you should do that.'

She scoffs at me, 'Nate, I just missed my train and you're here to give me career advice?'

'You're really talented,' I stumble, feeling my face burn.

Oh God, what am I saying? This isn't why I came here! Why didn't I think about what I was going to say?

'Thanks,' she says coolly, and I realise with a jolt that I've been silent again.

I need to say something or she's going to leave for good. 'I'm sorry for how I spoke to you on Saturday.'

She places her suitcase onto the floor and I fight the urge to carry it for her.

'It's fine,' she says. 'I'm sorry I ran out on you and assumed the worst. I should have known better . . .'

We drift into silence again, and just when I think I'm about to start chatting about the weather in some desperate attempt to say *something* to her, Annie explodes.

'Fuck, Nate! Why are you here?' she cries. 'Why can't you just let me forget you?'

My heart thuds. 'Is that what you want? To forget me?'

She stares back at me, and I notice her eyes glisten. She turns her back on me, throwing her arm in the air.

'No!' she cries, turning around again. 'Of course that isn't what I want. But I don't have a choice, do I? You're going back to New York.' I hold my breath. 'Aren't you?' she adds, when I don't respond.

I give a small nod.

'It's just not meant to be, is it? The universe doesn't want us together.' She gives a small laugh. 'Just go, Nate. I don't know what you're doing here.'

I close my mouth, a cold stone dropping through my body as I suddenly start to question what I'm doing here too.

'Sure,' I say eventually. 'I just . . . I just don't think you should quit your business. You're the most talented person I've ever met. Really, you're great.'

I turn on the spot and begin to walk away, when her voice calls after me.

'I really was falling for you, you know.'

Her voice is scratchy and desperate, like it's forced itself out of her mouth of its own accord.

'What?' I look back to face her. Exasperation is spreading across her face.

'You asked me if I felt the same as you did,' she says. 'I do. And I know you're going back to New York, which probably is a good thing as it was all too perfect anyway, but just so you know, I really, really like you. More than I think I've ever liked anyone, which is mad since I didn't even know you a few weeks ago, and fuck! Every sign from the sodding universe seems to be destined to keep us apart or together or fucking apart again, but this is just how I feel and I'm sorry but I—'

But her words are lost, because by this point I've walked up to her. I've placed my hands firmly on her face and I've kissed her. I've kissed her with everything in my body, and she's kissing me back, our arms wrapped around each other like we're never going to let each other go.

And that's a promise I make to myself right there.

Annie: I will never let you go.

Chapter Forty-Three

SIX MONTHS LATER

Annie

I look around my bright, airy apartment in West Norwood. Second floor, new-build looking out over a stream. White, neutral walls (I'll be changing *that* pronto) and glistening, slick kitchen cupboards and drawers.

'What do you think?' I smile.

'I hate it.'

I roll my eyes, laughing, as Penny stomps out of the bedroom.

'Where the hell am I supposed to sleep?' she demands. 'And Tanya? We can't all fit in here!'

'Well, that's because neither of you are living here . . .' I say, plucking three mugs from the top cupboard.

'How dare you!' Penny huffs.

'I love it!' Tanya squeals, throwing herself onto the sofa. 'Honestly, Annie, it's so gorgeous. I can't believe you live in a place like this. Why did you live in our shitty little flat for so long when you could be living here?'

'Well,' I shrug, 'I didn't know I could be living here. And obviously,' I add quickly, catching Penny's outraged expression, 'I loved living with both of you so I never thought about moving out.'

Penny peers at me for a moment before nodding in acceptance and pulling the milk out of the fridge.

So, when did we last catch up?

Oh yes . . . Nate.

I thought I was hallucinating when he came barrelling down the train platform, banging on every window and screaming my name. I thought I was so upset at us splitting up that I had started picturing him everywhere like an absolute madwoman. But I wasn't, he was actually there.

And guess what? He went back to New York with Stevie. We kissed for what felt like hours, I unblocked his number and he promised he'd call me once he landed. We spoke almost the entire week. I met his parents on FaceTime, I had endless conversations with Stevie about costumes and Nate and I just . . . Well, we just chatted about everything. While he was gone, I told my parents everything, including about how I'd made the outfit for Stevie and he'd since given my number out to several of his drag friends and I was being bombarded with requests to make their outfits too. Dad tried to be very supportive about me taking the corporate job and giving up my business making costumes . . . Mum, not so much. She was absolutely outraged. She could not understand why I was walking away from it all, just as it was starting to take off. When I said about not making enough money to survive in London, she waved me off and said that

I'd find my way. Which felt absolutely terrifying at the time. But here we are.

Pam was actually quite relieved that I turned down the job. She said that after I'd accepted, she went home to Rodney and they talked about my 'horrible, grey, anti-Annie outfit' and they both knew it wasn't right. Apparently, Rodney already knew someone who was happy to step into Pam's shoes.

As soon as I accepted the jobs from Stevie's friends, others came rolling in. Before I knew it, I had enough work to last me for months. And enough money too. I moved back in with Mum and Dad to get on my feet . . . and now I'm here.

Living on my own, doing the job I love more than anything in the world.

'Urgh, that's not tea, is it?'

I beam. And Nate's here too. He's still living with Stevie, but he's here all the time.

Penny thwacks him playfully on the arm. 'You cannot be a proper Brit and not like tea, Nate.'

He loops a heavy arm around me and I snuggle into his chest.

Well, if I thought the universe couldn't make up its mind as to whether it wanted us together or apart . . . it certainly made up its mind by the time Nate came home. Thankfully, it seems to like us together. Which is good for me, as that's my general opinion too. He stayed in New York with his mum over Christmas, and sent me pictures of his Aunt Tell sitting with them round their family dinner table. But then he came back, to give life in London another go. To give us another go.

It's all worked out, and even if the universe had any other ideas, I know we'd find each other again.

Because now I just know.

Nate: I will never let you go.

Acknowledgements

I loved every second of writing this book, and that's mainly due to the fantastic team of publishing and writing gurus I've been lucky enough to have around me.

Firstly, I have to thank my incredible agent, Sarah Hornsley, who has believed in me right from the beginning and seems to have this incredible knack of getting the best out of me. I couldn't do any of this without you!

Thank you to Katie Loughnane, my first editor. Our time together was short but it was so much fun working with you. I hope I've done you proud!

An infinite thanks to my fantastic editors at Penguin, Susannah Hamilton and Charlotte Osment. Your vision for the book and editorial steer made this story one hundred times better and I'm super grateful for all of your insights, ideas and patience while I wrangled these characters into a story! I've loved working with you.

Thank you to my copy-editor, Sarah Bance, and proofreader, Sarah-Jane Forder. I think you're both geniuses and without you I'm sure this book would be a continuity nightmare.

Thank you to Rose Waddilove for answering my constant questions and being so supportive, and Rosie Grant for all of your marketing wizardry!

I wrote the second half of this book in one of my favourite places, Anstey Harris's writing retreat: Write South West Scotland. It's essentially an entire week of workshops, yoga, food and writing alongside fellow writers and I absolutely love it. This time I was lucky to spend the week with six incredible women who were the best champions and inspiration as I ran away with this book. So, thank you to Laura, Nicola, Vicky, Karen, Phyllis and, of course, Anstey. I can't recommend her retreats enough. They're the ultimate gift for yourself.

Thank you to Nicola Gill, who was kind enough to chat to me and to read an early edition of *Falling For You* and help me navigate certain parts. Nicola is a beautiful, beautiful person and also a fantastic writer. *Swimming for Beginners* is one of my favourite reads – so go read it!

It takes a village to write a book, and that village is mainly inhabited by fellow writers who are ready to cheerlead, check in and talk you out of hiding under the bed and changing your name so you don't have to look at your book any more because it feels so awful. I'm really lucky to have fantastic authors around me, but particular thanks have to go to my Love and Chocolate ladies, who are filled with wisdom and – more times than not – chocolate.

Thank you to my wonderful, wonderful friends who always gee me up when imposter syndrome takes force and are ready with my drink of choice, a cup of tea. I love you all.

Thank you to my soon-to-be in-laws. I've really won the in-law lottery with all of you!

Thank you to my family for always championing me: my

gorgeous nephews for bringing me so much joy, my brothers and sister for all of your support, my grandad for the chats that wake up my mind, and my mum and dad for being the best cheerleaders I could ask for. There is a little piece of all of you in everything I write.

This one feels really surreal to write, but a special thank-you has to go to my daughter – who has been with me almost the entire journey of working on this book. I've never been more inspired and excited to write since being pregnant with you. By the time this book comes out you'll be here, but right now you're in the final stages of cooking. I can't wait to meet you.

And finally, my biggest thanks go to my fiancé, Chris. I could write the soppiest spiel here – but I'll save you all from that. In short, thank you for always being there, for helping me when I'm at my lowest, constantly celebrating me and showing me what love really is. I never could have written anything as joyous and giddy about falling in love if I hadn't fallen so madly in love with you.

Also, thank you for helping me with any of the football references. Reader – any mistakes in that department are well and truly my own. Chris did his best, but something strange happens when he starts to explain football to me where I can't hear him that well and start to daydream about what to have for lunch instead? A condition I must look into.

One more before I go – thank you to you, the reader. I hope the book made you smile, and if it left you craving a pumpkin-spiced latte then go get one. And a muffin! You deserve it!

Actually – I'm going to go get one too!

On a station platform, with nothing to read,
and a four-hour train journey stretching ahead of him...

That's where the story began for Penguin founder Allen Lane.
With only 'shabby reprints of shoddy novels' on offer,
he resolved to make better books for readers everywhere.

By the time his train pulled into London, the idea was formed.
He would bring the best writing, in stylish and affordable
formats, to everyone. His books would be sold in bookstores,
stationers and tobacconists, for no more than the price
of a ten-pack of cigarettes.

And on every book would be a Penguin, a bird with a certain
'dignified flippancy', and a friendly invitation to anyone who
wished to spend their time reading.

In 1935, the first ten Penguin paperbacks were published.
Just a year later, three million Penguins had made their
way onto our shelves.

Reading was changed forever.

—

A lot has changed since 1935, including Penguin, but in the
most important ways we're still the same. We still believe that
books and reading are for everyone. And we still believe that
whether you're seeking an afternoon's escape, a vigorous debate
or a soothing bedtime story, all possibilities open with a book.

Whoever you are, whatever you're looking for,
you can find it with Penguin.